true blue

David Baldacci is the author of fifteen consecutive *New York Times* bestsellers. With his books published in over 40 languages in more than 80 countries, and with nearly 70 million copies in print, he is one of the world's favourite storytellers. David Baldacci is also the co-founder, along with his wife, of the Wish You Well Foundation, a non-profit organization dedicated to supporting literacy efforts across America. Still a resident of his native Virginia, he invites you to visit him at www.DavidBaldacci.com, and his foundation at www.WishYouWellFoundation.org, and to look into its programme to spread books across America at www.FeedingBodyandMind.com.

David Baldacci

true blue

MACMILLAN

First published 2009 by Grand Central Publishing, USA

This edition published 2009 by Macmillan
an imprint of Pan Macmillan, a division of Macmillan Publishers Limited
Pan Macmillan, 20 New Wharf Road, London N1 9RR
Basingstoke and Oxford
Associated companies throughout the world
www.macmillan.com

ISBN: 978-1-4472-1722-0

1 3 5 7 9 8 6 4 2

A CIP catalogue record for this book is available
from the British Library.

Printed and bound by CPI Group (UK) Ltd, Croydon, CR0 4YY

To Scott & Natasha and Veronica & Mike,
part of my family and four of the coolest people I know

true blue

CHAPTER

1

JAMIE MELDON rubbed his eyes vigorously, but when he stared back at the computer screen it was still no good. He glanced at his watch; nearly two in the morning. He was toast. At age fifty he couldn't pull these all-nighters consistently anymore. He slipped on his jacket and pushed back his thinning hair where it had drifted down to his forehead.

As he packed his briefcase he thought about the voice from out of the past. He shouldn't have, but he'd called; they'd talked. Then they'd met. He didn't want that part of his life dredged up again. Yet he would have to do something. He'd been in private practice for nearly fifteen years, but now represented Uncle Sam. He would sleep on it. That always helped.

A decade ago he'd been a hotshot and highly paid criminal defense attorney in New York, legally hand-holding some of the sleaziest of Manhattan's underworld. It had been an exhilarating time in his career, and also represented his lowest point. He'd lost control of his life, been unfaithful to his wife, and become someone he'd grown to loathe.

When his wife had been told that she had perhaps six months to live, something had finally clicked in Meldon's brain. He'd resurrected his marriage and helped his spouse beat a death sentence. He'd moved the family south, and for the last ten years, instead of defending criminals, he was sending them to prison. Everything about that felt right, even if his financial circumstances weren't nearly as rosy.

He left the building and headed home. Even at two a.m. there was life in the nation's capital, but once he got off the highway and rode through the surface streets toward his neighborhood it grew quiet and he grew more drowsy. The blue grille lights flashing off his rearview mirror jolted him to alertness. They were in a straightaway not a half mile from his house, but one bordered on both sides by trees. He pulled off the road and waited. His hand slid to his wallet where his official credentials were contained. He was worried that he'd dozed off or been driving erratically because he was so tired.

He saw the men coming toward the car. Not uniforms, but suits, dark ones that made their starched white shirts stand out under the three-quarter moon. Each man was about six feet tall with an athletic build, clean-shaven face, and short hair, at least that he could make out under the moonlight. His right hand gripped his cell phone and he punched in 911 and kept his thumb poised over the call key. He rolled the window down and was about to hold up his official creds when one of the other men beat him to it.

"FBI, Mr. Meldon. I'm Special Agent Hope, my partner Special Agent Reiger."

Meldon stared at the ID card and then watched as the man flicked his hand and the familiar FBI shield appeared on the next slot in the leather holder. "I don't understand, what's this about, Agent Hope?"

"E-mails and phone calls, sir."

"With whom?"

"We need you to come with us."

"What? Where?"

"WFO."

"The Washington Field Office? Why?"

"Questioning," Hope replied.

"Questioning? About what?"

"We were just told to make the pickup, Mr. Meldon. The assistant director is waiting to talk to you."

"Can't it wait until tomorrow? I'm a United States attorney."

Hope looked put off. "We are fully aware of your background. We *are* the FBI."

"Of course, but I still—"

"You can call the AD if you want, sir, but our orders were to bring you in ASAP."

Meldon sighed. "That's all right. Can I follow you in my car?"

"Yep, but my partner here has to ride with you."

"Why?"

"Having a highly trained agent riding shotgun for you is never a bad thing, Mr. Meldon."

"Fine." Meldon slipped his phone back in his pocket and unlocked the passenger door. Agent Reiger climbed in next to him while Hope walked back to his car. Meldon pulled in behind the other car and they started on their route back to D.C.

"I wish you guys could have come to my office. I just came from town."

Reiger kept his gaze on the other car. "Can I ask why you're out this late, sir?"

"As I mentioned, I was at my office, working."

"Sunday night, this late?"

"It's not a nine-to-five job. Your partner mentioned phone calls and e-mails. Was he inferring ones that I made or received?"

"Maybe neither."

"What?" Meldon snapped.

"The Bureau's intel division gets chatter and scuttlebutt all the time from the dirtbag world. It might be that someone you prosecuted wants payback. And we understand that when you were in private practice in New York you did not leave on the best of terms with some of your, uh, *clientele*. It could be coming from that sector."

"But that was a decade ago."

"The mob has a long memory."

Meldon suddenly looked fearful. "I want protection for my family if there's some nut out there gunning for me."

"We already have a Bucar with two agents stationed outside your house."

They crossed over the Potomac and into D.C. proper, and a few minutes later neared the WFO. The lead car hung a left down an alley. Meldon pulled in behind it.

"Why this way?"

"They just opened a new underground garage for us to use with a hardened tunnel right into WFO. Quicker this way and under Bureau eyes 24/7. These days who the hell knows who's watching? Al-Qaeda to the next Timothy McVeigh."

Meldon looked at him nervously. "Got it."

Those were the last words Jamie Meldon would ever speak.

The massive electric shock paralyzed him even as a large foot stomped down on the car's brake. If Meldon had been able to look over he would've seen that Reiger was wearing gloves. And those gloves were curled around a small black box with twin prongs sticking out. Reiger climbed out of the car as a twitching Meldon slumped over.

The other car had stopped up ahead and Hope ran back to the second car. Together they lifted Meldon out and leaned him face first against a large Dumpster. Reiger pulled out his pistol with a suppressor on the muzzle. He stepped forward, placed the barrel against the back of Meldon's head, and fired one round, ending the man's life.

Together they heaved the body into the Dumpster. Reiger climbed into the dead attorney's car. He followed his partner's ride out of the alley, turned left, and then headed north while Meldon's corpse finished sinking into the garbage.

Reiger pushed a speed dial button on his phone. It was answered after one ring. Reiger said, "Done." Then he clicked off and slipped the phone back in his pocket.

The man on the other end of the phone did likewise.

Jarvis Burns, his heavy briefcase pressing against his bad leg, struggled to catch up to the rest of the party as they headed across the tarmac, up the metal steps, and into the waiting aircraft.

Another man with white hair and a heavily lined face turned back to look at him. He was Sam Donnelly, the Director of National Intelligence, which essentially made him America's top spy.

"Everything okay, Jarv?"

"Perfect, Director," said Burns.

Ten minutes later Air Force One rose into the clear night air on its way back to Andrews Air Force Base in Maryland.

2

"Sɪxᴛʏ-ᴇɪɢʜᴛ . . . sixty-nine . . . seventy."

Mace Perry's chest touched the floor and then she rose up for the last rep of push-ups. Both of her taut triceps trembled with this max effort. She stretched out, greedily sucking in air as sweat looped down her forehead, then flipped over and started her stomach crunches. One hundred. Two hundred. She lost count. And next came leg lifts; her six-pack ridges were screaming at her after five minutes and still she kept going, driving through the pain.

Pull-ups were next. She could do seven when she got here. Now she lifted her chin over the bar twenty-three times, the muscles in her shoulders and arms bunching into narrow cords. With one final shout of endorphin-fueled fury, Mace stood and started running around the large room, once, twice, ten times, twenty times. With each lap, the lady increased her speed until her tank shirt and shorts were soaked through to her skin. It felt good and it also sucked because the bars were still on the windows. She couldn't outrun them, not for three more days anyway.

She picked up an old basketball, bounced it between her legs a few times, and then drove to the hoop, which was a netless basket hung on a makeshift backboard bolted to one wall. She sank the first shot, a layup, and then paced off fifteen feet to the left, turned, and sank a jumper. She moved around the floor, set up, and nailed a third shot, and then a fourth. For twenty minutes she hit jump shot after jump shot, focusing on her mechanics, trying to forget where she was right now. She even imagined the roar of the crowd as Mace Perry scored the winning basket, just as she had done in the high school state championship game her senior year.

Later, a deep voice growled, "Trying out for the Olympics, Perry?"

"Trying for something," said Mace as she dropped the ball, turned, and stared at the large uniformed woman facing her, billy club in hand. "Maybe sanity."

"Well, *try* and get your ass back to your cell. Your buff time's up."

"Okay," said Mace automatically. "I'm going right now."

"Medium security don't mean *no* security. You hear me!"

"I hear you," said Mace.

"You ain't here much longer, but your ass is still *my* turf. Got that?"

"Got it!" Mace jogged down the hall that was enclosed by stacked cement blocks painted gunmetal gray, just in case the residents here weren't depressed enough. The corridor ended at a solid metal door with a square cutout at the top as a viewpoint. The guard on the other side pushed a button on a control panel and the steel portal clicked open. Mace passed through. Cement blocks, tubular steel, hard doors with tiny windows out of which angry faces peered. Clicks to go. Clicks to get back in. Welcome to incarceration for her and her fellow three million Americans who enjoyed the luxury of government housing and three squares for free. All you needed to do was break the law.

When she saw who the guard was she muttered one word. "Shit."

He was an older guy, fifties, with pale, sickly skin, a beer belly, no hair, creaky knees, and a smoker's caustically cracked lungs. He'd obviously switched posts with the other guard who'd been stationed here when Mace had come through for her workout, and Mace knew why. He'd developed an eye for her, and she spent much of her time ducking him. He'd caught her a few times and not one of the encounters had been pleasant.

"You got four minutes to shower before chow, Perry!" he snapped. He moved his bulk into the narrow passageway she had to navigate through.

"Done it faster," she said as she tried and failed to dart past him.

He spun her around and leaned his heft against her while she braced herself with her palms against the wall. He shoved his fat size twelve boots under the flimsy soles of her size sixes; now Mace was on her tiptoes with her back arched. She felt the brush and then grip of his meaty hand on her butt as he pulled her to him, doggie-style. He'd managed to position them both in the one blind spot of the overhead security camera.

"Little patdown time," he said. "You ladies hide shit everywhere, don't you?"

"Do we?"

"I know your tricks."

"Like you said, I only got four minutes."

"I hate your kind," he breathed into her ear.

Camels and Juicy Fruit are quite a combo. He slid a hand across her chest, squeezing hard enough to make her eyes water.

"I hate your kind," he said again.

"Yeah, I can really tell," she said.

"Shut up!"

One of his fingers probed up and down the cleft of her butt through her shorts.

"There's no weapon in there, I swear."

"I said shut up!"

"I just want to go take a shower." *Now, more than ever.*

"I bet you do," he said in his gravelly rumble. "I just bet you do." One hand riding on her right hip, the other on her butt, he shoved his boots farther under her heels. It was like she was tottering on four-inch stilettos now. What she wouldn't have given for a stiletto, just not the shoe kind.

She closed her eyes and tried to think of anything other than what he was doing to her. His pleasures were relatively simple: cop a feel or rub his hard-on against a chick when he got the chance. In the outside world this sort of conduct would've earned him a minimum of twenty years on the other side of these bars. Yet inside here it was classic he-said, she-said, and no one would believe her without some DNA trace. That's why Beer Belly only pantomimed it through the clothes. And throwing a punch at the bastard would earn her another year.

When he was done he said, "You think you're something, don't you? You're Inmate 245, that's who you are. Cell Block B. That's who you are. Nothing more."

"That's who I am," said Mace as she straightened her clothes and prayed for an early diagnosis of lung cancer for Beer Belly. What she really wanted was to pull a gun and lay his brains—on the off chance he had any—against the gray walls.

In the showers she scrubbed hard and rinsed fast, something you just innately did in here. She'd already experienced her initiation in here after only two days. She'd busted the woman's face. The fact that she'd avoided solitary or time tacked on had not endeared Mace to her fellow inmates. They simply tagged her as a privileged bitch, and that was about as bad as it could get in a place where your cell rep defined every right you had or didn't have. Nearly two years later she was still standing, but she wasn't exactly sure how.

She hustled on, every minute now precious, as she counted down her time to freedom, with both anticipation and dread, because on this side of the wall nothing was guaranteed except misery.

CHAPTER

3

A FEW MINUTES LATER a wet-haired Mace walked through the chow line and received her basic food groups so crapped and fatted up that in any other place—except possibly high school cafeterias and airline coach class—they would be deemed inedible. She swallowed enough of the garbage to keep from passing out from hunger and rose from her seat to throw the rest away. As she passed by one table a drumstick of a calf shot out and she fell over it, her tray clattering away, the goop on it painting the floor a nice greenish brown. Up and down the perimeter line, guards tensed. The inmate who'd done the tripping, a prisoner named Juanita, glanced down as Mace slowly got to her feet.

"You a clumsy bitch," said Juanita. She looked at her crew who sat all around the queen bee Juanita had become in here. "Ain't she a clumsy bitch?"

Every member of Juanita's crew agreed Mace was the clumsiest bitch ever born.

Juanita carried two-hundred-and-fifty-plus pounds on a wide six-foot frame, with each hip the size and shape of a long-haul truck's mud flap. Mace was five-six, about one-fifteen. On the surface Juanita was soft, mushy; Mace was as hard as the steel doors that kept all the bad girls inside this place. Yet Juanita could still crush her. She'd landed here after a sweetheart plea deal for murder in the second in which her tools had included a tire iron, a Bic lighter, and lots of accelerant.

It was said that she liked this place much better than she ever had her world on the outside. In here Juanita was queen bee. Out *there* she was just another GED-less fat chick to punch the hell out of, courier drugs and guns through, or make babies with before the man abandoned her. Outside prison Mace had known a thousand Juanitas. She was doomed from the moment she'd tumbled from the womb.

That might have explained why Juanita had done enough crazy stuff inside here, including two aggravated assaults and a weapons and drugs bust, to tack twelve more years onto her original sentence. At that rate the woman would be here until they hauled her carcass out and slipped it into a potter's field somewhere. Her fat and bones would soon fertilize the earth and no one would either care or remember her.

However, that left the living woman with nothing to lose, and that's precisely what made her so dangerous, because it carved normal societal inhibitors right out of her brain pattern. That one factor turned mush to titanium. No matter how many reps or laps Mace did, she could never match what Juanita had. Mace still had compassion, still had remorse. Juanita no longer had either, if she ever did.

Mace held the fork ready. Her gaze drifted for a moment to Juanita's wide hand planted flat on the table, orange nail polish muted against her skin that was obscured only by a tattoo of what looked to be a spider. An obvious target, the hand.

Not tonight. I already two-stepped with Beer Belly. I'm not dancing with you too.

Mace kept walking and slid her tray and utensils into the dirty bin.

Only as she was leaving did she glance over at Juanita, to find the woman still watching her. Keeping her gaze dead on Mace, Juanita whispered something to one of her crew, a gangly lily white named Rose. Rose was in here for nearly decapitating her husband's sexy plaything in a bar restroom using the gutting knife hubby kept for his fish catches. Mace had heard that the husband hadn't come to Rose's trial, but only because he was so upset she'd ruined his best blade. It was definitely more the stuff of Jerry Springer retro than Oprah couch chatter.

Mace watched as Rose nodded and grinned, showing the nineteen teeth she had remaining in her gaping mouth. It was hard to believe she was perhaps once a little girl playing dress-up, sitting on her father's knee, forming her cursive letters, cheering at a high school football game, dreaming about something other than one hundred and eighty months in a cage playing second fiddle to a bloated queen bee with the mental makeup of Jeffrey Dahmer.

Rose had visited Mace on the second day she'd been here and told her that Juanita was the messiah and what the messiah wanted, she got. When the cell door opened and the messiah appeared, she would like it. Those were the rules. That was just the way it was in Juanita Land. Mace had declined Juanita's offer several times. And before things had truly gotten out of hand, Juanita had suddenly backed off. Mace thought she knew why but wasn't sure. Yet it had led to two years of fighting for her life every day, using her wits, her street smarts, and her newly found muscle.

Mace trudged to Cell Block B and the doors slammed into place behind all of them at precisely seven p.m. So much for another exciting Sunday night. She sat on the steel bed with a mattress so thin laid over it that Mace could almost see right through the damn thing. Over the two years she'd slept on it her body had absorbed every buckle and bend in the old metal. She had three more days to go. Well, now really only two, if she made it through the night.

Juanita knew when Mace was getting out. That's why she'd tripped her, tried to bait her. She didn't want Mace to leave. So Mace sat in her cell, crouched into a hard, tight wedge in the corner. Her fists were clenched and there was something shiny and sharp in each one of them that she kept hidden in a place not even the guards could find. The darkness came and then strengthened into the time of night when you figured nothing much good was going to happen because the evil that was coming scared all the good away. And then she waited some more. Because she knew, at some point, her cell door would open as the guards on the night shift looked the other way in consideration for drugs or sex, or both.

And the messiah would appear with one goal in mind: to never again let Mace experience the light of a free day. For two years she'd been building herself up for this moment. Her buffed body waited with anticipation as adrenaline pumped with each exhalation of breath.

Three minutes later the cell door slid open, and there she was.

Only it wasn't Juanita.

This visitor was tall too, over six feet with the one-inch polished boots she wore. And the uniform was not like that of the guards. She wore it well, not a baggy part or dirt stain to be seen. The hair was blond and smelled good in a way that no hair in here ever could.

The visitor took a step forward, and though it was dark, there was enough light coming from somewhere out there that Mace could see the four stars on each shoulder. There were eleven ranks in the District of Columbia Metropolitan Police Department, and those four stars represented the highest one of them all.

Mace looked up, her hands still clenched, as the woman looked down.

"Hey, sis," said the D.C. chief of police. "What say we get you the hell out of here?"

CHAPTER

4

Roy Kingman pump-faked once and then darted a bounce pass between his defender's legs and into the paint, where a giant with rockets in his legs named Joachim stuffed it home, the top of his head almost above the rim.

"That's twenty-one and I'm done," said Roy, the sweat trickling down his face.

The ten young men collected their things and shuffled off to the showers. It was six-thirty in the morning and Roy had already gotten in three games of five-on-five full-court at his sports club in northwest D.C. It had been eight years since he'd suited up for the University of Virginia Cavaliers as their starting point guard. At "only" six-two without rockets in his legs, Roy had still led his team to an ACC championship his senior year through hard work, smart court sense, good fundamentals, and a bit of luck. That luck had run out in the quarters of the NCAA when they'd slammed headfirst into perennial power Kansas.

The Jayhawks' point guard had been a blur of cat quickness and numbing agility, and, at only six feet tall, could easily dunk. He'd poured in twelve threes, mostly with Roy's hand in his face, dished off ten assists, and harassed the Cavs' normally solid point man into more turnovers than baskets. It was not exactly how Roy wanted to remember his four-year collegiate career. Yet now, of course, that was the only way he could recall it.

He showered, dressed in a white polo shirt, gray slacks, and a blue sports jacket, his standard work wear, threw his bag in the trunk of his silver Audi, and headed to work. It was still only a little past seven, but his job demanded a long, full day.

At seven-thirty he pulled into the parking garage of his office building in Georgetown located on the waterfront, snagged his briefcase off the front seat, chirped his Audi locks shut, and rode the elevator car to the lobby. He said hello to Ned the thirty-something heavyset guard, who was cramming a sausage biscuit into his mouth while leisurely turning the pages of the latest *Muscle Mag*. Roy knew that if Ned had to get up from his chair and simply shuffle fast after a bad guy, he not only would never catch him but someone also would have to perform mouth-to-mouth on old Ned.

As long as it's not me.

He stepped on the office elevator and punched the button for the sixth floor after swiping his key card through the slot. Less than a minute later he reached his office suite. Since Shilling & Murdoch didn't open until eight-thirty, he also had to use his key card to release the lock on the law firm's glass doors.

Shilling & Murdoch had forty-eight lawyers in D.C., twenty in London, and two in the Dubai office. Roy had been to all three places. He'd flown to the Middle East in the private plane of some sheik who had business dealings with one of Shilling's clients. It had been an Airbus A380, the world's largest commercial airliner, capable of carrying about six hundred ordinary people or twenty extraordinarily fortunate ones in ultimate luxury. Roy's suite had a bed, a couch, a desk, a computer, two hundred TV channels, unlimited movies on demand, and a minibar. It also came with a personal attendant, in his case a young Jordanian woman so physically perfect that Roy spent much of the flight time pressing his call button just so he could look at her.

He walked down the hall to his office. The law firm's space was nice, but far from ostentatious, and downright slum-dogging it compared to the ride on the A380. All Roy needed was a desk, a chair, a computer, and a phone. The only upgrade in his office was a basketball hoop on the back of the door that he would shoot a little rubber ball into while yakking on the phone or thinking.

In return for ten- or eleven-hour days and the occasional weekend work he was paid $220,000 per annum as a base with an expected bonus/profit share on top of that of another $60,000, plus gold-plated health care and a month of paid vacation with which to frolic to his heart's content. Raises averaged about ten percent a year, so next cycle he would ratchet to over three hundred grand. Not bad for an ex-jock only five years out of law school and with only twenty-four months at this firm.

He was a deal guy now, so he never set foot in a courtroom. Best of all, he didn't have to write down a single billable hour because all clients of the firm were on comprehensive retainers unless something extraordinary happened, which never had since Roy had worked here. He'd spent three years as a solo practitioner in private practice. He'd wanted to get on with the public defender's office in D.C., but that was one of the premier indigent representation outfits in the country and the competition for a slot was intense. So Roy had become a Criminal Justice Act, or CJA, attorney. That sounded important, but it only meant he was on a court-approved list of certified lawyers who were willing basically to take the crumbs the public defender's office didn't want.

Roy had had his one-room legal shop a few blocks over from D.C. Superior Court in office space that he'd shared with six other attorneys. In fact, they'd also shared one secretary, a part-time paralegal, one copier/fax, and thousands of gallons of bad coffee. Since most of Roy's clients had been guilty he'd spent much of his time negotiating plea deals with U.S. attorneys, or DAs, as they were called, since in the nation's capital they prosecuted all crimes. The only time the DAs wanted to go to trial was to get their in-court hours up or to arbitrarily kick some ass, because the evidence was usually so clear that a guilty verdict was almost inevitable.

He'd dreamed of playing in the NBA until he'd finally accepted that there were a zillion guys better than he would ever be, and almost none of them would make the leap to professional hoops. That was the principal reason Roy had gone to law school; his ball skills weren't good enough for the pros and he couldn't consistently knock down the threes. He wondered occasionally how many other tall lawyers were walking around with the very same history.

After getting some work lined up for his secretary when she came in, he needed some coffee. It was right at eight o'clock as he walked down the hall to the kitchen and opened the refrigerator. The kitchen staff kept the coffee in there so it would stay fresher longer.

Roy didn't get the coffee.

Instead he caught the woman's body as it tumbled out of the fridge.

CHAPTER

5

THEY RODE in a black Town Car, an SUV loaded with security behind them. Mace glanced over at her older sister, Elizabeth, known as Beth to her friends and some of her professional colleagues. However, most people just called her Chief.

Mace turned and looked at the tail car. "Why the caravan?"

"No special reason."

"Why come tonight?"

Beth Perry looked at the uniformed driver in front of her. "Keith, turn some tunes on up there. I don't want you falling asleep. On these roads we'll end up driving off the side of a mountain."

"Right, Chief." Keith dutifully turned on the radio and Kim Carnes's jagged voice reached them in the backseat as she crooned "Bette Davis Eyes."

Beth turned to her sister. When she spoke her voice was low. "This way we avoid the press. And just so you know, I've had eyes and ears in that place from day one. I tried to run interference the best I could for you."

"So that's why the cow backed off."

"You mean Juanita?"

"I mean the cow."

She lowered her voice further. "I figured they'd planned on giving you a parting gift. That was the reason I showed up early."

It irritated Mace that the chief of police had to have the radio playing and whisper in her own car, but she understood why. Ears were everywhere. At her sister's level, it wasn't just about law enforcement; it was about politics.

"How'd you manage the release two days ahead of schedule?"

"Time reduced for good behavior. You'd earned yourself forty-eight whole hours of freedom."

"Over two years, it doesn't seem like that big an accomplishment."

"It's not, actually." She patted Mace on the arm and smiled. "Not that I would have expected it from you."

"Where do I go from here?"

"I thought you could crash at my place. I've got plenty of room. The divorce was final six months ago. Ted's long gone."

Her sister's eight-year marriage to Ted Blankenship had started to unravel before Mace had gone to prison. It had ended with no kids and a husband who hated his ex principally because she was smarter and more successful than he ever would be.

"I hope my being in prison didn't contribute to the downfall."

"What contributed is that my taste in men sucks. So I'm Beth Perry again."

"How's Mom?"

"Still married to Moneybags and the same pain in the ass as always."

"She never came to see me. Never wrote me a single letter."

"Just let it go, Mace. That's who she is and neither one of us is going to change the woman."

"What about my condo?"

Beth glanced out the window and Mace saw her frown in the reflection off the glass. "I kept it going as long as I could, but the divorce took a big slice out of my pocketbook. I ended up paying alimony to Ted. The papers had a field day with that even though the file was supposed to be sealed."

"I hate the press. And for the record I always hated Ted."

"Anyway, the bank foreclosed on your condo four months ago."

"Without telling me? They can do that?"

"You appointed me as your power of attorney before you went in. So they notified me."

"So *you* couldn't tell me?"

Beth glared at her. "And what exactly would you have done if I had?"

"It still would've been nice to know," Mace said grumpily.

"I'm sorry. It was a judgment call on my part. At least you didn't end up owing anything on it."

"Do I have anything left?"

"After we paid off the legal bills for your defense—"

"*We?*"

"That was the other reason I couldn't keep paying on the condo. The lawyers always get their money. And you would've done the same for me."

"Like you ever would've ended up in a pile of crap like this."

"Do you want the rest of the bad news?"

"Why not? We're on a roll."

"Your personal investment account got wiped out like everybody else's in the economic freefall. Your police pension was history the moment you were convicted. You have a grand total of one thousand two hundred and fifteen dollars in your checking account. I talked your creditors into knocking your debt down to about six grand and got them to defer payments until you got back on your feet."

Mace was silent for a long minute as the car rolled along winding roads on the way to the interstate that would eventually carry them into Virginia and then on to D.C. "In all your free time while you were running the tenth largest police force in the country and presiding over the security details for a presidential inauguration. Nobody could've done better. I know that. And if it had been me overseeing your finances, you'd probably be in a debtor's prison in China." Mace touched her sister's arm. "Thanks, Beth."

"I did manage to keep one thing for you."

"What's that?"

"You'll see when we get there."

CHAPTER

6

THE SUN was starting to come up when the Town Car turned down a quiet residential street that dead-ended in a cul-de-sac. A few seconds later they rolled to a stop in the driveway of a comfortable-looking two-story frame house with a wide front porch that sat at the very end of the road. The only giveaway that this was where the highest-ranking cop in D.C. lived was the security stationed outside and the portable barricades that had been moved out of the way when they'd turned onto the street.

"What the hell is this for, Beth?" Mace asked. "You never had a security detail at your house before. You usually don't even have a driver."

"Different world and the mayor insisted."

"Has there been a threat?"

"I get threats every day. Stalkers at HQ, here at home."

"I know, so what's changed?"

"Not for you to worry about."

The car slowed and Beth Perry rolled down her window and exchanged a few words with the officers on duty, and then she and Mace headed into the house. Mace dropped the duffel bag containing everything she'd brought to prison with her and looked around. "You're not going to tell me the truth about all the new security?"

"There's nothing to tell. I don't particularly like it, but like I said, the mayor insisted."

"But why did he—"

"Drop it, Mace!"

The sisters did a staredown and Mace finally backed off.

"So where's Blind Man?"

As if on cue, an old fifty-pound mutt with gray, black, and tan markings came into the room. As it sniffed the air, it gave a yelp and bounded toward Mace. She knelt and scratched Blind Man behind the ears and then gave the dog a lingering hug, pushing her nose into its smooth fur as Blind Man happily licked her ear.

"I think I missed this guy almost as much as I missed you."

"He's been pining for you."

"Hey, Blind Man, you missed me, man, you missed me?"

"I still can't believe they were going to put him down just because he can't see. That dog's nose is so keen it's better than having two pairs of twenty-twenties."

Mace rose but continued to stroke Blind Man's head. "You always have been one to bring in strays with special cases. The deaf cat, and three-legged Bill the boxer."

"Everybody and everything deserves a chance."

"Including little sisters?"

"You've lost weight, but otherwise you look to be in great shape."

"Worked out every day. Only thing that kept me going."

Beth looked at her strangely. It took Mace a few moments to interpret. "I'm clean, Beth. I was clean when I went in and I didn't touch anything while I was in there, although let me tell you there were more drugs in that place than at Pfizer's world headquarters. I exchanged meth for endorphins. I'll take a pee test if you want."

"I don't, but your probation officer will as a post-release condition."

Mace took a deep breath. She'd forgotten that she was now officially on probation for a full year because of some complicating factors in her sentencing. If she screwed up they could send her right back for a lot longer than twenty-four months.

"I know the guy. He's okay. Plays fair. Your first meeting is next week."

"I thought it would be sooner than that."

"It usually is, but I told him you'd be staying with me."

Mace stared fixedly at her sister. "Any news on who set me up?"

"Let's talk about it later. But I've got some ideas."

There was something in her voice that made Mace decide not to argue. "I'm starving, but can I grab a shower first? Two minutes a day of cold drizzle over two years gets to you."

"Towels, soap, and shampoo are all set upstairs. I've got the rest of your clothes in the guest bedroom."

Thirty minutes later the two sisters sat down in the large, airy kitchen to scrambled eggs, coffee, bacon, and toast that Beth had prepared. The chief had changed into jeans and a sweatshirt with "FBI Academy" stenciled on the front. Her hair was pulled back in a ponytail and she was barefoot. Mace had on a white long-sleeved shirt and a pair of corduroy pants she'd last worn over two years ago. Snug before, they now rode low on her narrow hips.

"You're going to need new things," said her sister. "What are you now, about one-fifteen?

"A little less." She ran a thumb inside the waist of the saggy pants. "I didn't know I was such a porker before."

"Yeah, a real porker. You could sprint circles around most of the force even back then. No donut runs for Mace Perry."

As sunlight spilled through the windows, Beth watched as Mace took her time with each bite and drank the coffee in careful sips. Mace caught her sister eyeing her and put her fork and cup down.

"Pathetic, I know," Mace said.

Beth leaned across and wrapped long fingers around her sister's forearm. "I can't tell you how good it is to have you back safe. What a relief it is—"

Beth's voice faltered and Mace saw the tall woman's eyes suddenly tear up; the same eyes that had stared down the worst the city had to offer. Like Mace, she'd started as a beat cop in the toughest neighborhoods of D.C. that no tourist would ever have ventured into unless he was tired of living.

The chief hurried over to the counter and poured another cup of coffee, gazing out the window into the small backyard while she regained her composure. Mace returned to her meal. In between bites she asked, "So what was it you kept for me?"

Relieved by this change in subject, Beth said, "Follow me and I'll show you."

She opened the door to the garage and nudged the light on with her elbow. It was a two-bay arrangement. In one parking slot sat Beth's black Jeep Cherokee. The vehicle sitting in the other space caused a grin to spill over Mace's face.

A Ducati Sport 1000 S motorcycle painted cherry red. It was the only thing Mace had ever splurged on. And still she'd gotten it dirt cheap and secondhand from a portly cop who'd bought it after going through a midlife crisis only to realize he was terrified to ride the damn thing.

She stepped down to the garage floor, ran her hand along the upside-down high-performance Marzocchi front forks forged from glorious brushed aluminum. Then her fingers slipped over the Sachs shocks that had softened journeys over some rough terrain when she'd used her private ride to chase down some bad guys off-road. The bike had a removable tailpiece cover to give it a sporty, aerodynamic look, but if you popped it off, it revealed a seat and became a two-person ride. However, Mace liked to ride solo. It had a six-speed gearbox, Marelli electronic fuel injection, L-twin cylinders, and its engine generated nearly a hundred horses at eight thousand rpms. She'd kept the bike far longer than any man she ever had, because she loved this machine far more than any guy she'd ever dated.

"How'd my creditors miss this?"

"I assigned it over to myself, so there was nothing to miss. I did it in lieu of payment for administering your affairs." She held out the key. "Your license still valid?"

"Even if it wasn't, you couldn't keep me off it."

"Nice thing to tell the chief of police sworn to uphold and protect."

"Just *uphold* that thought, I'll be back."

Mace slipped the helmet on.

"Wait a sec."

She looked over in time to see Beth toss her a black leather jacket she'd bought for her when she'd gotten the bike. Mace slipped it on.

Her shoulders had widened enough to where it was a tight fit, but it still felt wonderful, because those shoulders and the rest of the body attached to it were now free.

Mace engaged the engine.

From behind the door to the kitchen there came the sounds of claws scratching and then Blind Man started to howl.

"He's always hated you on that thing," Beth yelled over the roar of the bike's engine.

"But God, it sounds so good," Mace shouted back.

Beth had already hit the control for the garage door. Good thing, because a few seconds later the Ducati roared out of the bay and into the crisp morning air, leaving its signature mark in burned-off tread on the cement.

Before the security detail could even react and move the barriers, Mace had already whipped around the staggered portable walls, angling the Ducati almost parallel to the ground. The machine responded flawlessly, like she and it had already fused into one organism. Then she was gone in a long exhale of Italian-engineered exhaust.

The security detail scratched its collective heads and turned to look back at the chief. She raised her cup of coffee in mock salute to their dedicated vigilance and returned to the house. She kept the garage door open, however. Four years ago she'd lost one garage door to her little sister's overeager entry. She did not plan on repeating that mistake.

CHAPTER

7

MACE KNEW that D.C. was the sort of town where on one block you were as safe as you would be in the middle of a small town in southern Kansas on Sunday afternoon in front of the local Methodist church. Yet one block over, you better have Kevlar covering every square inch of your body because chances were very good that someone was going to get shot. That was where Mace wanted to be. Her brain was wired to run toward the gunfire instead of away from it. Just like her sister.

She'd been working another assignment when a slot had opened with the Narcotics and Special Investigations Division. She'd applied. Her arrest record was stellar, her late-to-work and tardies nonexistent. She'd impressed the brass board and gotten the position. She'd worked 4D Mobile Force Vice, though it was now called Focused Mission Unit, which to her didn't sound nearly as cool.

She'd started doing jump-outs as a plainclothes, which basically meant you cruised looking for dealers and when you saw them you jumped out and arrested as many as you could. In certain areas of D.C. you couldn't miss them. She could hang as many as she wanted. The only thing holding her back was how much paperwork she wanted to do and how much court OT she could stomach.

She'd cut her teeth on street-level dealers hand-selling rocks and making two grand a day. They were small fish to be sure, but they also shot people. Then there were the scratch-offs. They were either checking a rock of crack in their palm or doing a lottery card, it was virtually the same hand motion. And lots of lottery tickets were sold where Mace worked. Yet she'd gotten so good that she could tell by the motion of the index finger at twenty feet whether it was a rock or merely Lotto. Later, she'd gone undercover in the drug and homicidal hell of the Sixth and Seventh districts. That's when all the trouble really began. That's why two years of her life had vanished.

Mace flew through block after block enjoying her first free day in nearly twenty-four months. Her dark hair whipped out from under the racing helmet as she quickly moved from the fortress of solitude around her sister's house, to fairly decent and safe D.C., then to a neighborhood whose turf battle had not yet been fully decided between cops and bandits, and finally onto ground where the thin blue line had failed to establish even a beachhead.

This was the Sixth District, or Six D in the MPD's carved-up fiefdom. If Mace had a hundred bucks for every time she'd seen a PCP zombie running naked screaming through the streets here at midnight, she wouldn't have been so ticked about losing her police pension. In certain sections of Six D there were shuttered houses, trashed buildings, and cannibalized cars on blocks. At night on virtually every corner here something bad was going down and gunfire was as ubiquitous as mosquitoes. All of the honest hardworking citizens— and that constituted most of the folks who lived here—just stayed inside and kept their heads down.

Even in daylight people moved around on the streets with furtive looks. It was as though they just knew stingers launched from nickel-plated Glocks with drilled-off serial numbers or else hollow-points exploding out of virgin pistols looking for first kills could be heading their way. Even the air here seemed to stink, and the sunlight felt degraded by a cover of hopelessness as thick as the carbon emissions eroding what was left of the ozone.

She slowed the Ducati and watched several of the people walking by on the street. The homicide rate in D.C. was nowhere near what it used to be in the late 1980s and early 1990s when young drug kingpins wearing brutish crowns formed from the tendrils of the crack cocaine era enjoyed their reign of terror. Back then a body violently dropped on average *over* once a day, every single day of the year, including the Sabbath. Yet currently nearly two hundred mostly young African American males every year required a medical examiner's certification as to their cause of death, so it wasn't exactly violence-free either. The men around here craved respect, and they seemed to believe they only would get it in increments of nine-millimeter ordnance. And maybe they were right.

She stopped the bike, lifted off her helmet, and shook free the static from her hair. Normally coming here on a fat-cat motorcycle at any time of the day or night was not smart, particularly if you were white and weaponless, as Mace was. Yet no one bothered her, no one even approached her. Maybe they figured a woman not of color coming here alone on a Ducati was obviously psychotic and thus apt to blow up herself like some suicide bomber.

"Hey, Mace! That you?"

She twisted around on her seat to look behind her.

The gent coming toward her was short and stick-thin with a shaved head. He had a pair of two-hundred-dollar LeBron James sneakers on his feet minus the shoelaces.

"Eddie?"

He approached and looked over the bike.

"Nice, nice shit. Heard you were in."

"I got out."

"When?"

"About five seconds ago."

"Just a deuce, right, so you just be an inmate." He grinned at this insult.

"Just two years, that's right. Not a con. Just a lowly inmate."

"My little brother's already done ten, and he's only twenty-five. No family court crap for little bro. Hard time," he added proudly.

"How many people did he kill?"

"Two. But them assholes both had it coming."

"I bet. Well, two years was plenty long enough for me."

He patted the Ducati's gas tank and grinned, showing teeth so white and perfect that she assumed he'd gotten a nice deal on some veneers, probably bartering some prescription pills for them. Being seen talking to even a former police officer was not smart around here. However, Eddie was just a bottom-level huckabuck, a street thug. Not too bright and not connected at all, and the most illegal thing he'd ever done was to retail bags of processed weed, a few C-rocks, and handfuls of stolen OxyContin pills on the street. The real players here knew that, and they also knew that Eddie had no information about their operations that he could possibly sell to the cops. Still, Mace was surprised he was alive. The dumb and the weak around here were usually eradicated extremely efficiently. So maybe he was wound tighter than she thought. Which could make him useful to her.

"Neighborhood all the same?"

"Some things don't change, Mace. People pop and drop. You know that."

"I know someone screwed me."

His grin faded. "Don't know nothing 'bout that."

"Yeah, but maybe you know somebody who does know."

"You out now, girl. Ain't no good looking in the rearview mirror. There might be something you ain't want to see. Besides, your sister already had her boys come down through here with a fine-tooth comb. Hell, they were just down here last week."

"They were? Doing what?"

"Asking questions, doing their CSI thing. See that's the cool thing having a police chief in the family. Cold case don't never go cold. But I bet she gets some shit for it anyway. Not everybody loves the top blue, Mace."

"Like what shit?"

"How the hell I know? I just on the street getting by."

"Her guys talk to you?"

He nodded. "And I told 'em the truth. I ain't know nothing 'bout nothing." He patted the Ducati's gas tank again. "Hey, can I take it for a ride?"

She removed his hand from the Ducati. "There's an old saying, Eddie, to go forward, you have to go back."

"Whoever said that ain't from 'round here."

She eyed his windbreaker, the way his left elbow was clenched tight to his side, and how he leaned ever so slightly that way because of the weight of what was in his pocket. "You know, bro, if you want to carry a gun and not have the cops know, you're gonna have to learn to walk a straighter line and loosen up your arm."

Eddie glanced down at his left pocket and then looked up, grinning. "Got to protect yourself 'round here, Mace."

"You find out anything, you let me know."

"Uh-huh," Eddie said, his veneers no longer visible.

Mace drove through the neighborhood, drawing more stares from folks sitting on their tiny porches or clustered on the street corners or peering out windows. A lot of peering went on around here, usually to see what the sirens were coming for.

She was not making this circuit just to celebrate her release. She wanted to let certain powers-that-be know that Mace Perry had not only survived prison but also was back on her old turf even if she no longer had a badge, gun, and the might of the MPD gang backing her.

But what Eddie had told her was troubling. Beth had apparently continued to investigate the case long after Mace had gone to prison, devoting scarce police resources to the matter. Mace knew several people who would use that if they could to attack Beth. Her sister had already done enough for her.

She finally turned around and rode back to the house. One of the cops on protection duty waved her down as she approached the barricade. She braked to a stop and lifted her visor.

"Yeah?" she said to the man, a young cop with a buzz cut. She could easily tell that he was an egg, meaning a rookie.

Sit on them until they hatch.

She remembered her T.O., or training officer. He was a vet, a "slow walker" who wanted to pull his shift as easy as possible and go home in one piece. Like many cops back then, he didn't like women in his patrol car, and his rules were simple: Don't touch the radio, don't ask to drive, and don't complain when they went to what cops referred to as the hoodle. It was a gathering place, usually a parking lot, where the police cruisers would cluster and the cops would chill out, sleep, listen to music, or do paperwork. The most important rule of her T.O., however, had been to just shut the hell up.

She'd endured that ride for one month before getting "checked out" by a sergeant and certified to roll on her own. And from that day forward Mace's call signal had been 10–99, meaning police officer in service *alone*.

"I understand you're the chief's sister."

"Right," she said, not desiring to volunteer anything more than that.

"You were in prison?"

"Right again. You got another personal question or will two do it for you?"

He stepped back. "Look, I was just wondering."

"Right, just wondering. So why's a young stud like you pulling barricade action? You oughta be running and gunning and locking up and getting some court OT so you can buy a new TV or a nice piece of jewelry for your lady."

"I hear you. Hey, put in a good word for me with the chief."

"She doesn't need any help from me on that. You like being a cop?"

"Until something better comes along."

Mace felt her gut tighten. She would have given anything to be a blue again.

He twirled his hat and grinned at her, probably thinking up some stupid pickup line.

Her teeth clenched, Mace said, "Piece of advice, don't ever take your hat off while on protective duty."

The hat stopped spinning as he stared at her. "Why's that?"

"Same reason you don't take it off when you're on a suspect's turf. Just one more thing to get in the way of you drawing your gun if something hairy goes down. *Egg.*"

She double-clutched, popped a wheelie, barely avoiding his foot as he jumped back, and roared on into the garage.

8

HER SISTER was waiting for her in the kitchen, fully dressed in a fresh uniform. A stack of documents was on the table in front of her.

"Homework?" said Mace.

"Daily Folder, Homicide Report, news clips, briefing for internal ops meeting. The usual."

"You wear the four stars so well," said Mace as Blind Man sniffed around her ankles and she scratched his ears.

"How was the ride?"

"Not as enlightening as I'd hoped."

"I *hoped* you'd disappoint me and not go back to Six D."

"Sorry not to disappoint you." Mace poured another cup of coffee and sat down at the table. "Saw Eddie Minor."

"Who?"

"Small-fry huckabuck," replied Mace. "He said your guys were down there asking questions about my case just last week."

Beth put down the folder she was holding. "Okay, so?"

"So you still working it?"

"I work all cases where justice hasn't prevailed."

"Eddie said you might be pissing off some high-ups over this."

"Come on. You're listening to a huckabuck's take on D.C. politics?"

"So it is political?"

"I've obviously forgotten that you tend to take every word literally."

"Is that what the heightened security's for?"

"What do you mean?"

"People gunning for you because you won't let the case go?"

"If there are some higher-ups in town who think I'm being a little overzealous in pursuing what happened to you, they sure as hell aren't going to order a hit on me. They have other avenues they can employ."

"So why the extra security?"

"The number of threats against me has gone up a little. Some of them are credible, so a few extra precautions were in order. I don't like it but I have to live with it."

"Where are the credible threats coming from?"

"Don't lose sleep over it. If I had a dollar for every death threat I've gotten over the years."

"It only takes one, Beth."

"I've got lots of folks watching my six."

"Well, you just got one more added to the group."

"No! You focus on you."

"Beth—"

"Focus on *you.*"

"Okay, so what exactly are my options?" she asked bluntly.

"You don't have many."

"That wasn't my question."

Beth sat back, double thumbing her BlackBerry with skill. "You have a felony conviction involving a firearm and you're now out on probation. You obviously can't be a cop anymore with that hanging over you."

"Someone kidnapped me, strung me out on multiple meth cocktails laced with who knows what, and forced me to participate in armed robberies while I was whacked out of my mind."

"I know that, you know that, but that's not what the court found."

"The jury and the judge got steamrolled by an overzealous U.S. attorney who had it in for me and you."

"That overzealous U.S. attorney now heads up the entire office."

The color slipped from Mace's face. "What!"

"A month ago Mona Danforth was named interim U.S. attorney for the District of Columbia by the AG."

"U.S. attorney! Dad's old office?"

"That's right," Beth said with disgust.

"The attorney general named her? I thought they had to be Senate confirmed after the president appointed them."

"The AG gets to appoint Mona for a hundred and twenty days. If the president doesn't name a permanent candidate and have that appointee confirmed by the Senate by then, the authority to appoint goes to the district court. The problem is, the AG, the president, and the district court folks all love Mona. So she's a lock for the job any way you cut it. I expect the president to formally name Mona any day now. And from what I understand the Senate confirmation is a gimme."

"I can't believe that woman is running the largest U.S. Attorney's Office in the country. She has the least morals of any prosecutor I've ever been around."

"She's still out there screaming that you got a sweetheart deal because of your connections. Meaning me, of course. And if we hadn't gotten the sentence knocked down on appeal she might have been crowing instead of screaming."

"*She* ought to be in prison. How many times has she looked the other way when evidence got doctored or else went missing when it didn't cut to her side? How many times has she sat and listened to people on the stand commit perjury by feeding back the lines *she* wrote for them?"

Beth slid her BlackBerry in her pocket. "Proof, little sister. Hearsay won't cut it. She's got everyone who matters to her climb up the ladder snookered."

Mace put her head in her hands and groaned. "This has got to be the parallel world where Superman is evil. How do I get off the ride?"

"You never get off the ride. You just learn to hold on a different way."

Mace looked at her sister through a gap in her fingers. "So, is the political pressure on you coming from Mona and her demented heavyweight supporters?"

"Mona has never been my biggest fan."

"I'll take that as a hell yes."

"And I can handle it."

"But it would be better if you backed off trying to find out who set me up."

"Better for whom? The bandits or Mona? Neither of whom I give a crap about. There is no law against the police investigating crimes. And if we get lucky and nail the bastards, you get your record expunged and also receive an official apology and reinstatement to the force."

"An apology from who, Mona?"

"Don't hold your breath."

"Okay, we were talking options?"

"You can't do anything that would require a security clearance, which in this town cuts out a lot of possibilities, and the overall job market sucks right now."

"If you're trying to pep up my spirits, please stop before I stab myself in the heart with a fork since I can no longer own a gun to use to kill myself."

"You wanted options. I'm giving them to you."

"I haven't heard an option. All I've heard is what I *can't* do."

Beth slid a paper across to her. "Well, here's maybe something you *can* do."

Mace looked down at what was written on the sheet.

"Dr. Abraham Altman? I remember him."

"And he remembers you. Not many college professors run afoul of one of the worst drug crews in Ward Nine."

"That's right. Nice guy, just doing some research into urban issues. The HF-12 crew didn't see it that way and came over to G-town to give him grief."

"And you stepped in and saved his ass."

"You've kept up with him?"

"I was a guest lecturer in criminal justice over at Georgetown when you were in West Virginia. He and I reconnected."

"So what does that mean for me?"

"He's looking for a research assistant."

Mace gaped at her sister. "Beth, I didn't even finish college. My 'graduate work' was sixteen weeks at the police academy, so I'm not exactly the poster girl for research assistants."

"He's doing urban research, specifically into impoverished and crime-ridden areas of D.C. I don't think there's anyone out there more qualified to help on that issue than you. And Altman's got a big federal research grant and can pay you well. He'll be home tonight. Around seven, if you can make it."

"So you arranged all this?"

"All I really did was make a suggestion to Altman. He was already your second biggest fan."

It took a moment for Mace to interpret this remark. "Meaning you're my biggest?"

Beth rose. "I've got to run. I've got testimony on the—"

Her cell phone buzzed. She answered, listened, and clicked off. "Change of plan."

"What is it?"

"Just got word that some big-shot lady lawyer dropped out of a fridge at her law firm. Board's been called," she added, referring to the ambulance. "Bandit apparently long gone."

Mace looked at her sister expectantly.

"What?" Beth asked.

"I don't have anything to do."

"So relax, go sleep on a real bed. There's some Rocky Road in the freezer. Go put some weight on those bones."

"I'm not tired. And I'm not hungry. For food, anyway."

"What, you want to go to the crime scene?"

"Thanks, Beth. I'll follow you on the bike."

"Hold on, I didn't say you could go."

"I just assumed."

"Never assume, Mace. If Dad taught us one thing, it's that."

"I won't get in the way. I swear. I . . . I just . . . miss it, Beth."

"Mace, I'm sorry. I don't think it would be a good idea—"

Mace cut her off. "Fine, forget it. You're right. I'll just go eat some Rocky Road and take a nap. And try not to die from excitement."

She started to walk off, her head down, her shoulders slumped.

"All right, you can come," Beth said grudgingly. "But keep your mouth shut. You're invisible. Okay?"

Mace didn't answer; she was sprinting to her bike.

"And stop whining," Beth called after her.

CHAPTER

9

Roy Kingman had hit thirty-one shots in a row on his behind-the-door basketball hoop. The police had swarmed the place minutes after he'd phoned 911. It still didn't seem possible that he'd gone to make coffee, opened the fridge, and caught Diane Tolliver's dead body before it hit the floor. He'd been asked lots of questions by lots of people, some in uniform and some not. As the other lawyers had arrived at work, word had quickly spread as to what had happened. Several partners and a few associates had stopped by to see him, offering supportive words and also expressions of sympathy, puzzlement, and fear. One fellow lawyer had even seemed a bit suspicious of him.

The cops wouldn't tell him anything. He didn't know how long Diane had been dead. He didn't even know what had killed the woman. There was no blood or wounds that he could see. Although he'd defended accused murderers when he'd been a CJA and had seen his share of autopsy photos, he wasn't exactly an expert on violent death.

He looked at his desk full of work to do and then glanced away. Not today. The clients could wait. He hadn't been Diane Tolliver's closest confidant, but he had worked with her and liked her. She'd taught him a lot. And somebody had killed her and stuffed her in a fridge next to a container of days-old potato salad.

He palmed the little rubber ball, cocked his arm back, and with a smooth motion released his thirty-second shot. It sailed straight and true right to the hoop. Only the door opened and the rubber ball hit Beth Perry in the head instead. She bent down to pick it up and tossed it back to him as he rose from his chair, his mouth agape as his gaze took in the four stars. Not that he needed that to know who she was. The D.C. police chief was in the media spotlight quite a bit.

People marched in behind her. The last one closed the door. The last one was Mace, doing her best to get lost in the crowd. Beth introduced herself and some of the folks with her. She'd already interviewed the first responders and looked at the body. Other than Roy there were no witnesses, at least that they had found so far. The paramedics had preliminarily pronounced Tolliver dead, and the ME was on the way to make that pronouncement official.

As two detectives took notes, the chief guided Roy through the events of the morning and what he knew about the dead woman. Her questions were crisp, her methodology spot-on. This was not by accident; she'd worked homicide for two years.

Roy finally said, "You always do the questioning, ma'am? I thought you'd have, you know, some bigger butts to kick around." He added hastily, "I meant that with all due respect."

In the back of the room Mace smiled at his comment. Beth did too.

Beth said, "I like to keep my hand in things. So you were a CJA?"

"That's right."

"You didn't like it there?"

"I like it here better."

"So no reason you know of that someone would want to harm Diane Tolliver?"

"None that I can think of. She wasn't married. She went out some, no serious dating, at least that she talked to me about."

"Would she talk about things like that with you?"

"Well, probably not," he admitted.

"Were you one of her nonserious dates?"

"No. It wasn't like that with us. She was, well, she was a lot older than me."

"Forty-seven."

"Right. I'm about to turn thirty."

"Okay. Go on."

"Her clients were mostly big companies, most of them overseas. She traveled. We both did. She never mentioned any problems."

"When you say you traveled, you mean together?"

"Sometimes, yeah."

"Where, for example?"

"We have an office in London and one in Dubai too."

"An office in Dubai?"

"Lot of money and development going on there. And they need lawyers."

"Did she usually work late?"

"Only occasionally. I do too sometimes."

"Did you ever work late together?"

"A few times."

"You were the first to arrive this morning? Around seven-thirty?"

"Yes, at least I didn't see anyone else."

"The office space has a security system?"

"Yep. We're each assigned cards, so that'll tell you exactly when she came in."

"And exactly when *you* came in too," the voice said.

Everyone turned to stare at Mace, who'd looked chagrined the second she'd finished speaking. Her sister frowned and turned back to Roy, who had his gaze dead on Mace. He squeezed the rubber ball tight in his hand.

"But you don't need the key card to *leave* the space after hours?" asked Beth.

"No, there's a door release button you push."

"And of course during business hours the security system is turned off?"

He said, "That's right."

"The garage elevator doesn't have a key card access?"

"That's right, but you need a key card to access the garage."

"If you're in a car."

"Yeah, it is a gap in security, I know."

"A real gap," she said, eyeing Roy closely.

He shifted uncomfortably. "Look, am I a suspect?"

"We're just collecting information."

His face flushed. "I called 911. I caught her damn body in my arms. I was just going to make coffee. And I had no reason to kill her."

"We're getting way ahead of ourselves, Mr. Kingman. So just calm down."

Roy took a breath. "Okay. Do you need anything else from me?"

"No, but I'm sure my detectives will have some follow-up. No travel plans to Dubai coming up, I hope?" She was not smiling when she asked this.

"I don't think so, no."

Beth rose from her chair. "Terrific. Let's keep it that way. We'll be in touch."

They all filed out. Mace held back while the others disappeared down the hall.

He eyed her. "Can I help you?"

"I don't know. Did you kill her?"

Roy stood, towering over her. "Are you a cop?"

"No, just tagging along for fun."

"You think murder is fun? Are you some kind of sick freak?"

"Well, if you put it that way I guess I am."

"I've got some work to do." He glanced at the door.

Instead of leaving Mace plucked the ball from his hand. In one motion, she turned and drained the shot, hitting nothing but net.

He said, "Nice mechanics."

"High school girls' basketball. We won the state title my senior year."

He appraised her. "Let me guess, you were the leave-it-all-on-the-court point guard who could score and also play some wicked D, including the occasional knocked-on-their-ass flagrant foul to cold-face the other teams?"

"I'm impressed."

"I'm not."

"What?"

"You just basically accused me of murder. So why don't you get the hell out of my office."

"All right, I'm going."

"Best news I've heard all day."

10

THE D.C. Metropolitan Police Department headquarters was located on Indiana Avenue, near the D.C. Superior Court building. It was named after Henry J. Daly, who'd been a homicide sergeant with twenty-eight distinguished years on the police force before an intruder had gunned him down in the building. It was a multistory structure with lots of people in uniform coming and going. And lots of people not in uniform hanging around either waiting for court time next door or else cooling their heels while friends or relatives had some quality face time with the cops inside HQ. The probation and parole offices, along with the Department of Motor Vehicles, were also located in the Daly Building. That pretty much guaranteed that no one going in or out of the place was particularly thrilled to be there.

The chief's office was in a secure area and one had to pass locked doors and lots of cubicles containing people who brought guns with them to work. The office was a corner suite; the door was a keyed entry. The room was large with nice moldings and two windows. A wall of shelves contained ceremonial mugs and hats, stuffed animals, and stacks of newspapers and official reports. The American flag was in front of one window. There was a small sitting area with an ornate chess set on a coffee table. A plasma screen on a hinged arm hung on one wall. There was also a large wooden desk that had seen a lot of wear and tear over the years. This included numerous coffee cup rings marring the surface and probably a few hundred angry fists slamming down on the wood.

Beth sat on the "chief" side and Mace on the other.

"I took a leap of faith letting you tag along," Beth said as she stared at the stacks of files and phone messages on her desk. "It apparently was a mistake on my part to believe that you might just remain quiet and unobtrusive. I'm not sure how I miscalculated considering it's only happened a few thousand times before."

"It just popped out. I'm sorry."

Beth pointed to the pile of phone messages. "Your little 'pop' has already gotten a lot of attention. The mayor, in fact, wants to know why a recently released convicted felon was even allowed near the crime scene, sister or not."

"I'm really sorry, Beth. I don't know why I did it."

"Just go see Altman tonight and become gainfully employed."

"Is he still at G-town? Because the address you gave me is in McLean."

"He's on sabbatical but the address is for his home."

"McLean? Fancy area. They must be paying professors better these days."

"Wait a minute, didn't you know?"

"Know what?"

"Altman is one of the wealthiest people in the Washington area."

"How'd he make his money?"

"He didn't."

Mace gave her sister a funny look. "What?"

"You used to be a pretty good detective. You'll figure it out." Beth pointed to the door. "Now go, I have to play police chief for a while."

Mace headed to the door but then turned back. "I am sorry about today, sis."

Beth smiled. "If that's all I had to worry about, it would be a very good day."

"What about Mona and the mayor?"

"The mayor's a good guy. I can deal rationally with him."

"And Mona?"

"Mona can go screw herself."

The secure door clicked open and Beth's assistant, Lieutenant Donna Pierce, looked in. "They're here for the meeting, Chief."

"Send them in."

The door opened wider and a man with white hair and dressed in a custom-tailored pinstripe suit walked in, followed by a fellow in a baggy gray suit who limped awkwardly, his fat briefcase in his right hand.

The white-haired gent put out his hand. "It's been too long, Beth."

"Crazy schedules all around, Sam."

"Hello, Chief," said Jarvis Burns, the man in the baggy suit.

"I don't think either of you ever met my sister, Mace."

"Mace, this is Sam Donnelly and Jarvis Burns."

Donnelly gave Mace a searching look. "I'm really surprised we've never run into each other before."

"I've been away for a while."

"I know. What happened to you was a case of prosecutorial overreach. That is my *personal* opinion," he hastily added. "Off the record."

"We know the president loves Mona," Beth said grudgingly.

"And I serve at his pleasure," added Donnelly.

When Mace looked at him inquiringly Beth explained, "Sam is the DNI, Director of National Intelligence."

"Yes, but Jarvis here does all the heavy lifting," amended Donnelly. "I just try to keep everyone playing nicely together."

"Then I'll let you and Beth get to it."

"Nice meeting you, Mace," said Donnelly while Burns opened his briefcase. But his gaze trailed her until the door shut.

"She just got out, didn't she?" said Donnelly as he seated himself at Beth's small conference table.

"That's right."

"Any plans?"

"Some things in the works."

"I hope things come together for her."

"They will."

CHAPTER

11

Two patrol cops, one senior and one junior, were admiring Mace's Ducati when she came out of HQ.

"Nice ride," said the older blue as Mace slid onto the seat.

"Yes, it is," she said.

"Ducati?" he said, looking at the name label.

"An Italian-engineered street machine that once you ride it, you dream about it."

The younger cop checked out her lean, buffed figure and pretty face and his mouth edged into a grin. "Wanta take me for a ride one night? Maybe we can share a dream."

"Get back to your shift and stop wasting time talking to ex-cons!" The voice came with such a bark that both cops and Mace jumped. When Mace saw who it was, her hand went reflexively to the spot where she would normally wear her sidearm.

The two cops faded away as the woman marched forward.

Mona Danforth had on her usual expensive two-piece Armani suit, and a bulky litigation briefcase large enough to carry the fates of several targets of the lady's professional ambition tapped against one shapely leg. To add insult to injury, Mona was tall and exceptionally lovely and not yet forty. The way her blond hair curved around her swan neck Mace had to grudgingly concede would turn most guys to mush. She had legs about as long as Mace's entire body. She'd graduated from Stanford Law School, where, of course, she'd been editor in chief of the law review. She was married to a sixty-five-year-old multimillionaire based in New York who provided all the financial resources she would ever need and wasn't around very much. She lived in a fabulous penthouse with wrap-around terraces near Penn Quarter that he'd bought for her. And her looks, money, and power position weren't even the primary reasons that Mace hated her guts, although they certainly didn't hurt.

Mace knew that being U.S. attorney for D.C. was just another stepping stone on the climb up for the woman. Mace had heard that Mona had her life all mapped out: a short stint as the U.S. attorney for D.C., then attorney general of the United States, next a court of appeals position, and then the prized plum, a lifetime appointment to the United States Supreme Court. When she was wasn't trying and winning cases by any means necessary, including bending the rules until they shattered from the torque, she was lining her pockets with all the political favors she would need to fulfill that ambition.

She had already been to the White House for dinner, not once but twice. Her hubby had been a big donor to the current president's election campaign. Beth Perry, who'd reached the top of her profession on hard work and guts and by playing by the rules, hadn't even been invited once. That still rankled her little sister.

Mona stopped and looked down at Mace, who sat astride her Ducati, her helmet dangling in one hand.

"My God," said Mona. "You look like shit. I figured you weren't nearly as tough as people made you out to be, and I guess I was right. And, hell, you were only in a kindergarten lockup for *two years*. Just think what a hag you'd be if you'd done the proper time in a max. A deuce for that was a joke. Thank goodness for you that big sister was around to hold your sweaty little hand."

Mace slipped on her helmet and fired up her bike. Then she lifted up the visor so she could eyeball the woman. "Hey, Mona, I've been gone for twenty-four months and the best you can do is *interim* U.S. attorney? You need to ratchet up the political humping, babycakes, before your looks *really* slide into your ass."

Mace popped the clutch and sped off. In the side mirror she saw Ms. Interim staring at her. That had been pretty stupid, Mace had to admit, but she had actually shown restraint. What she'd really wanted to do was find a wood-chipper, stuff Mona in it, and get right to work.

She had a chunk of time before she was to meet the rich Altman and she knew exactly how she wanted to spend her first day of freedom. She clicked the Ducati into high gear.

As she roared along down by the river, the seagulls dipped down to grab shiny trash off the muddy Potomac before tilting their wings and angling skyward. The monuments basked in the glow of a warming sun. Tourists wandered around, maps in hand; Secret Service agents hovered at 1600 Pennsylvania Avenue keeping the man safe. Over on Capitol Hill, senators, House reps, and armies of aides and golden-tongued lobbyists shuffled through their elaborate dance of running the country right into the dirt.

In many ways the town was sick, corrupt, maddening, frustrating, and patronizing. Still, Mace couldn't help but smile as the Ducati blew past an Old Town Trolley carrying a load of out-of-towners eyeballing with awe the shrines to Tom, Abe, and the mighty white obelisk to George.

That was because this was *her* town.

Mace Perry was back.

CHAPTER

12

Roy Kingman was sitting in the managing partner's office that was only a bit larger than his space, though it did have a water view. Chester Ackerman was a few inches shorter than Roy, and he carried the heft of a man who liked his food rich and often. He had a horseshoe of graying hair around his broad head and a large nose with a bump at the end. Roy guessed he was about fifty-five, though he suddenly wondered why he didn't know for sure.

Ackerman brought in far more business to the firm than anyone else. Roy had always found him sharp, tough, and big-voiced. Today, the man was none of those things. He sat across from Roy, his face sweaty, his hands trembling, and his voice low and croaky.

He wagged his head from side to side. "I can't believe this shit. I can't believe it happened. Here!"

"Just calm down, Chester."

"How the hell am I supposed to calm down? There was a murder three doors down from my office."

"And the police are investigating it, and they're probably already running down some solid leads."

Ackerman lifted his head and stared at him. "That's right, you used to work down there, right?"

"Down where?"

"With the cops."

"I was a defense attorney, so I was actually on the other side. But I know how the police work a crime scene. And this is high-dollar Georgetown, so they'll pull out all the stops. Hell, even the chief herself was down here asking me questions."

Ackerman blurted out, "Who do you think might've done it, Roy?" He looked ten seconds from stroking.

Roy said, "I have no idea who could've done it. I worked with Diane but I didn't really know her personally. You were fairly close to her, weren't you?"

"No, not really. I mean, she never really talked about her personal life with me."

"You talked to the police?" he asked.

Ackerman rose and looked out the window, his hands fingering the striped braces he favored. They had gone out of style sometime in the nineties, only the man apparently hadn't noticed or didn't care. "Yeah. They asked me some questions." He turned around to face Roy. "And I told 'em just what I'm telling you. I'm scared and I don't know a damn thing."

"It could just be random, you know."

"Random, what the hell are you talking about?"

"Guy follows Diane in, kills her, and exits. Maybe it was a simple robbery."

"But there's a guard in the front lobby."

"Ned's more of a joke. I can't tell you the number of times I've come in the building in the morning and he's nowhere to be found."

"What the hell do we pay building fees for?"

"If you want serious perimeter protection, hire a real security firm who'll send a trained person who carries a gun. The only thing Ned can do is whack an intruder with a frozen sausage biscuit."

Roy popped up from the chair. "Is there anyone we need to call?"

The other man looked at him with a confused expression. "Call?"

"Yeah, like her relatives?"

"Oh, I've got folks doing that. Her father's dead, but her mom lives in Florida, retired. Diane didn't have any kids. She has an ex-husband, but he lives in Hawaii."

"Did you just find that out?"

"What?"

"You said you didn't know much about Diane personally, but you know all that."

"I just found out!" Ackerman snapped.

Roy put up his hands in mock surrender. "Okay. That's cool."
He headed to the door. "Do you mind if I take the rest of the day
off? I don't have anything critical pending and what with everything
that's happened."

"No, sure, go on. Get some fresh air."

"Thanks."

"Roy, what was it like? Finding the body?"

Roy slowly turned around. "I hope you never have to find out."

13

Roy GRABBED his jacket, waved goodbye to his secretary, and took the stairs instead of the elevator. The police had already questioned Ned, who now sat in his swivel chair with a look of terror interrupted by momentary pangs of what Roy assumed was hunger.

"Hey, Ned. How're you doing?"

"Not too good, Mr. Kingman."

Roy leaned against the marble reception console. "Police give you the once-over?" He nodded. "And *were* you away from the front at any time this morning?"

Ned eyed him a little hostilely. "Am I supposed to talk to you about this stuff?"

"Not if you don't want to, no."

"Guess it doesn't matter. I don't know that much, really."

"So you saw Diane come in?"

"Not exactly."

"Well, either you saw her or you didn't."

"I heard her."

"*Heard* her? Where were you?"

"In the back microwaving my biscuit. It always gets cold before I get here."

"What time was that?"

"Around six. I'd just come on duty."

"But you were eating a biscuit when I came in an hour and a half later."

"I eat like five sausage biscuits every morning, but I try to space them out. I'm a big guy: I need constant fuel."

"Did she come up through the garage elevator or by the front doors?"

"I don't know. Like I said, I didn't see her."

"Okay, so what did she *say* when she came into the lobby?"

"She said, 'Hey, how you doing.' And I called back that I was doing fine. When I got back to the front, she'd already gone up in the elevator."

"You're sure it was her voice?"

"Yeah, I've heard her lots of times. She's usually with someone when she leaves the building, you know, for lunch or stuff, and she has a pretty husky voice for a lady."

"But Ned, not to raise the obvious point, if you were in the back and she couldn't see you, how do you know she was even talking to *you*? More likely she was saying hello to someone else coming in the building the same time as her."

Ned looked puzzled. "I hadn't thought of that."

Roy continued, "The person had to be coming through the front doors. If she'd ridden up with him in the elevator from the garage she would have already said hello. And there's only the one garage elevator, so it wouldn't have had time to go back down and come back up with another person before Diane would've headed up in one of the office elevators."

"You're getting way over my head now, Mr. Kingman."

"Did she routinely say hello to you when she came in?"

"Not exactly, no."

"Does that mean she did it once, twice, every other time? Never?"

"Uh, never."

"Did you hear another person's voice?"

"No, but like I said, I was using the microwave. It makes some noise. And then it makes a big 'ding' when it's done."

"Yeah, I know." Roy glanced up at the security cameras mounted in each corner of the lobby. "Did the police take the security tapes?"

"It's on a DVD. But no, they didn't."

"Why not?"

"Because the DVD loaded in the central board was full from a long time ago."

"But once it got full won't it just record over what's already been filmed?"

"The system here doesn't work that way. The disk gets full, it automatically shuts down until you put a new disk in."

"Well, don't people check it?"

Ned looked red-faced. "I did, I mean sometimes. But nobody ever told me how to really do it the right way, and I got to the point where I thought I might screw up, so I stopped checking it."

"Well, you got that right. You *did* screw up."

Ned said in a whining tone, "But I thought the cameras were just there for looks anyway, you know, to make people *think* they were under surveillance. I mean, *I'm* on duty for security purposes."

"In light of what happened this morning that's very reassuring," Roy said sarcastically. "Did you see anyone leaving between the time you heard Diane and when I came in?"

"There were only a few people who came in during that time. All regulars."

"Anybody from Shilling?"

"Not that I recognized, no."

Roy scrutinized Ned. "Did you maybe take another break?"

"No, I swear, I was here the whole time. Okay, I was reading, but I couldn't have missed someone passing by. The lobby's not that big."

That was true, thought Roy. And anyone coming up from the garage elevator would have to pass right in front of the security desk.

"So are you saying you saw nobody leave during that time?"

"That's right. Just people coming in. I mean, it was early, who'd be leaving?"

At least one person might have, thought Roy. *The killer.* "And you told the cops this?"

"Yeah, everything."

"Does your firm carry lots of insurance?"

"How the hell should I know?"

"Well, if I were you I'd find out, because your screwup affected a law firm big-time. And don't forget, they can sue you without even having to hire an attorney."

"Jesus, do you think they might come after me? I mean, they can't, right? I'm just the security guard. I don't have any money."

"The courthouse is open to anyone, Ned. And, hell, they might go after you just for the sheer fun of it."

Roy walked out into the sunshine. Whoever had killed Diane had probably gone up in the elevator with her. And maybe instead of leaving, that person had then stayed in the building somewhere. He or she might even be there now, working in another office.

Or in my office.

Diane had come in about ninety minutes before he had. Had she been killed immediately and the murderer long gone before Roy got to the office? Or had it happened minutes before he got there? Or had it happened while he was in his office and he hadn't heard a damn thing? He tried to remember how cold Diane's body had been. The fact was, if she'd been in the fridge two days or half an hour, she would still have felt pretty cold to him. Maybe the ME would have a better shot at answering that.

"You look like you're thinking way too hard."

Roy looked to his left where Mace Perry was perched on her Ducati staring at him.

14

"Wʜᴀᴛ ᴀʀᴇ ʏᴏᴜ doing back here?" Roy asked as he walked over.

"How do you know I ever left?"

"I can see the front entrance from my office. I've been staring out at it the last few hours." He eyed the Ducati. "I wouldn't have missed these wheels."

"Look, I know we got off on the wrong foot. And I came back to try it again."

Roy didn't look inclined to accept her offer, but he said, "I never got your name."

"It's Mace."

"Mace? That's a weapon, isn't it?"

"Yes, I am," she quipped.

"Come on, what's your name?"

"Really, my name is Mace."

He shrugged. "Okay."

Mace looked toward the building. "I saw you talking to the security guard. What did he say?"

Roy looked at Ned through the glass. "Not much. Ned's not exactly all that with it."

"Tolliver might've ridden up in the elevator with whoever killed her. Ned was probably somewhere taking a sugar-slurp break. Killer did the deed and then either walked out or to his office in the building. Maybe at your law firm."

"That's one theory."

"I'll give you another one. You were the one who went up in the elevator with Tolliver, and she used her key card, so that leaves no record of you. You killed her and stuffed her in the fridge. You snuck down the stairs and waited until the guard came back. Then you waltzed in the building from the garage elevator side like it was the first time, so he could time-stamp you in his head. You go up to the office, fuss around at your desk for a while, go to the kitchen, open the fridge, catch the poor lady—which would explain any trace of her being on your person and vice versa—and then you call the cops in a fake-freak voice."

Roy stared at her, his features darkening. "Is this how you try to make a fresh start? By accusing me again?"

"I'm not accusing you. But you're a lawyer. You know what's coming. You were on the scene alone with a dead woman. The cops will go down this very same trail with you at some point. So you better be prepared to answer. You can practice on me."

"Why, so you can go back to the cops, tell them, and they can run holes right through my explanations?"

"I told you, I'm not a cop. And if what you're saying is the truth it would be pretty tough to pin a murder rap on you."

"Okay, I'll play along. I accessed the parking garage with my card. That shows I got in around seven-thirty. Took the elevator up to my office, did some work. Went to make coffee and found Diane. I made the call to 911 at two minutes past eight. Records show she was at the office ninety minutes before I got there. I didn't even know she was there."

"That won't cut it. You could've parked your car down the street, walked into the garage, waited for her to arrive, ridden up in the elevator with her, killed her, left, driven your car to the garage, and the same scenario follows."

"Ned said he heard Diane saying hello to someone. That doesn't fit with your scenario."

"The testimony of morons is always heavily discounted by the blues and the courts. And the fact is, you could've come in when you said, at seven-thirty, gone up in the elevator, killed Tolliver, stuffed her in the fridge, and called the cops. Plenty of time."

"Okay, what's my motive?"

"I'm a purist chick when it comes to a criminal investigation, meaning I eyeball opportunity first. Motive usually comes later. But if it's there, the cops will find it."

"So what should I do? Grab the next flight to a country that has no extradition with the U.S.?"

"Nah, it'll probably be okay."

Roy looked startled. "Probably?"

"I've got a good nose for killers, and it's not twitching around you. So where'd you play basketball?"

"How do you know I did? Just because of the office door hoop?"

"It's partly your height, and the way you walk, and how you dissected my playing career earlier."

"And what's the other part?"

"I saw a set of Audi keys on your desk earlier. I checked the garage here. There was an Audi parked near the entrance, which would peg it as yours since you got here so early. In the backseat were a duffel bag, three basketballs, and four pairs of expensive B-ball shoes that pretty much only collegiate or professional players will put out for."

"University of Virginia Cavaliers."

"I actually already knew that since you also have the big cool orange sticker on your rear bumper."

"You know, you look like the police chief."

"She's a lot taller than me."

"I meant in the face, and the eyes. You both have green eyes, with some flecks of bronze." He looked at her more closely. "And a tiny bubble of magenta in the right one."

Mace studied her eyes in the Ducati's side mirror. Incredibly enough, for the first time, she did see bronze and the pop of magenta.

"I don't know any guys who even realize magenta is a color."

He pointed at her. "I knew I recognized you. You're her sister, Mace Perry. Should've remembered as soon as you said your name." He broke off. "But the newspapers said your name was originally Mason Perry." He looked at her funny. "Mason Perry, Perry Mason the TV lawyer? Is that a coincidence?"

"My father was a prosecutor, but he really wanted to be on the other side. So Mason Perry it was. But I go by Mace, not Mason. In fact, I had it legally changed."

"What does your father think of that?"

"I don't know. He was murdered when I was a kid."

"I'm sorry, Mace. Didn't know."

"No reason for you to."

"But weren't you in—"

"I just got out."

"Okay." He put his hands in his pockets and looked awkwardly around while Mace fiddled with the straps on her helmet.

"For what it's worth, I think you got a raw deal," he finally said.

"Thanks. For what it's worth, I think you're telling the truth."

"You know, the only reason I believe in reincarnation is because of Mona Danforth."

"What do you mean?" she said curiously.

"How else can you explain Joseph Stalin coming back as a girl?"

Mace grinned. "You had run-ins with her as a CJA?"

"I wasn't important enough to actually warrant the lady confronting me head-on. But her lieutenants ground my face into the legal dirt on more than one occasion. And the stories about her around PD are legendary."

"You up for lunch? We can take turns devising torture methods to use on Mona."

"Where do you want to go?"

"Ben's Chili Bowl. I've been dreaming about Benny's half-smokes for two years." She slid off the passenger seat cover. "Hop on."

"I don't have a helmet."

"Then don't hit your head if you fall off. Pretty sure my insurance lapsed."

The Ducati sped off a few seconds later.

CHAPTER

15

So you just got out and you're messing around with a homicide?"
They were sitting at the crowded counter in the legendary Ben's
Chili Bowl next to the Lincoln Theater on U Street. Roy bit into his
chili dog and licked the mustard off one finger.

"I'm not messing with anything. Just getting acclimated to the
outside world."

Mace slowly inserted her half-smoke in her mouth before chew-
ing it up and tonguing her lips. She slid a handful of chili-cheese
fries into a pool of ketchup and stuffed them all in her mouth.

The deeply contented look on her face made Roy grin. "You
want a cigarette?"

"Maybe."

"Prison food really does suck, doesn't it?"

"Yes, it does."

"I still can't figure who'd want to hurt Diane."

"Did you really know her all that well?"

"Worked with her for about two years."

"That doesn't mean you know her. Ever been to her home?"

"Twice. Once for an office party about three months ago and
another time before I joined the firm. She was in charge of associate
recruitment."

"Was it a tough pitch?"

"Not really. Lot more money than I'm worth."

"But you're on the billable hours treadmill."

"It's not like that."

"What do you mean?"

"Don't get me wrong, I work full days. But at Shilling we don't have to keep track of billable hours."

"I thought that's how lawyers made their money. Like in the Grisham novels."

Roy shook his head. "We work off retainers. Deep-pocketed, sophisticated clients prefer it that way. We know what the workload looks like and they know what their nut is and they pay it. The firm divvies up the spoils and rewards people for the work they do and the business they bring in. No surprises. And a lot more efficient than sucking clients dry."

"But what if something unusual came up off the retainer radar?"

"We write the agreements to take that into account. Then we get paid more."

"Litigation or deals?"

"Deals. Litigation we hand off to other firms, but retain oversight responsibility."

"So how much do you make?"

"That's private."

"Well, if it were public I wouldn't have to ask you."

"Like I said, more than I'm worth."

"My father said that the law was a noble profession."

"It can be, just not for everyone."

"Yeah, I didn't believe him either."

She finished the rest of her half-smoke in one bite.

Later, as they walked out, he said, "So what are you going to do now?"

"Tonight, I've actually got an appointment about a job."

"Doing what?"

"Research assistant."

"I don't see you in a lab wearing a white coat with eyeglasses on a chain."

"Not that kind. The professor is doing research on urban issues. Apparently in parts of the city I know, or at least knew pretty thoroughly."

"The crime-ridden ones?"

"Bingo."

"Who's the professor?"

"Abraham Altman."

"Bill Altman's dad?"

"Who's Bill Altman?"

"He worked at PD when I was a CJA. He's older than me, about forty-five. Good lawyer. He's one of the noble profession guys."

"I don't know if they're related."

"Abe's a professor at Georgetown and is out-the-butt wealthy."

"Then it is the same guy. My sister told me he was like billionaire rich, but hadn't worked for it."

"That's right. So you know him?"

"I helped him out once."

"But you didn't know he was rich?"

"That didn't factor into what I was helping him with. So how did he get his money?"

"Abe's parents lived in Omaha across the street from a young guy who was starting up his own investment firm. They put all their money with the man."

"Omaha? You don't mean?"

"Yep. The Oracle of Omaha, Warren Buffett. Apparently Abe's parents kept investing with him and the earnings compounded until they were one of the largest shareholders of Berkshire Hathaway. When they died decades later I think it totaled well over a billion dollars even after the tax bite. And it all went to Abe; he was an only child."

"And here I was wondering how a college professor could afford me."

"Just tell him you want six figures, full health, paid vacation, and a 401(k) with an employer match. He probably won't blink an eye."

"How about you tell him for me?"

"What?"

"You can be my negotiator."

"You want me to come with you to see Altman?"

"Yeah, I'll pick you up at six-thirty from your office."

"I wasn't going back to my office."

"Then I'll pick you up at your house."

"Condo. And do you always work this fast?"

"I have ever since I lost two years of my life."

16

THE D.C. Police Department finally had a first-rate facility to conduct forensic testing, the most important of which was the postmortem. Beth Perry, accompanied by two homicide detectives working the case, walked into the six-floor building located at the intersection of 4th and School streets in Ward Six. In addition to the OCME, or Office of Chief Medical Examiner, the building also housed offices for the Metropolitan Police Department and the Department of Health.

A few minutes later Beth stood next to the chief medical examiner. Lowell Cassell was a small, thin man with a short graying beard and wire-rimmed glasses. Except for the tattoo of a fish on the back of his hand, from his days in the Navy as a submariner, and a small scar from a knife wound on his right cheek suffered when on liberty in Japan while drunk in the Navy, he would've looked like a typical member of a college faculty.

The body of Diane Tolliver lay on a metal table in front of them. Beth and the detectives were here to get at least two answers: cause and time of death. The ME took off his glasses, wiped his eyes, and put the spectacles back on. "Fast-tracked the postmortem as you requested."

"Thanks, Doc. What do you have for me?"

"When I saw the bruising on the neck base I felt sure I'd find ligature marks on the neck or evidence of smothering, with homicidal asphyxia being the cause of death."

"But it wasn't?"

"No, the lady basically had her neck broken."

"Basically? Without full ligature marks?"

"Well, there's more. A lot more, actually. Pretty severe injury."

"Atlanto-occipital disarticulation and not simply a dislocation?"

Cassell smiled. "I forgot how well versed you are in forensic matters. Yes, a *disarticulation* clearly."

With one of the detectives' assistance he turned Tolliver's body on its side and pointed to the base of her neck. "Cranio-cervical junction injury." Cassell pressed his fingers against points along the base of the skull and the upper spine. "Brain stem and upper to mid-cervical spinal cord, above C4."

"Full disruption of the cardio-respiratory regulation centers. Immediately fatal."

"Are you angling for my job, Beth?" he said jokingly.

"No, Doc, do you want mine?"

"Good God no!"

"So someone crushed her neck. What else?"

"Hemorrhages in the soft tissues of the back of the neck and injuries to basilar blood vessels. She also had considerable facial bruising and a cut on her right chin, all pre-death. All fairly straightforward until we get to this."

He opened a laptop and pulled up some images of the inside of Diane Tolliver's head. "The X-rays showed separation of the atlas from the base of the skull. You can see the atlas in the foramen magnum—"

"But the spinal canal isn't visible. Okay, that's classic disarticulation."

"Yes, but the brain stem was also *transected*."

She glanced up sharply from the laptop screen. "Brain stem transection?"

"It's most often seen in car crashes where you have massive deceleration. A basilar skull fracture is what killed Dale Earnhardt at Daytona. Or when there's some sort of lengthy fall involved. The brain stem pops and death is instantaneous."

Beth pointed to Diane's body. "This lady was found wedged inside a refrigerator at her law firm about two hours after she walked in the door of her office. She wasn't driving in the Daytona 500 and she didn't fall off a building."

The ME again pointed to the base of the neck where there was considerable discoloration. "A blow right here did the trick. Her being placed in a refrigerator certainly did me no favors, but there are definite signs of bruising before death at this location."

"A blow? With what, Doc?"

"Now that's the strange part. I found no trace evidence, no hairs, fibers, plastics, metals, or anything else relating to the injured area."

"So what was used to kill her, then?"

"My guess is a blow from a foot."

"A foot?"

Cassell pointed to the abrasions on Tolliver's face. "It could have happened this way. She's held down on the floor, facedown with her chin pressed against the linoleum, which accounts for the cut and bruising there when the killing blow was struck. Then someone, a large, powerful man probably, stomps on the back of her neck with all his weight. Now, if a board or pipe or hammer or bat had been used, they might well have left a patterned injury mark on the skin. But as you can see, there was nothing like that here. However, a human foot is flexible and could well have left no discernible marks. Even a fist would have left some sort of pattern, knuckles or even the shape of a palm, for instance. Plus, of course, you can generate much more force with a leg stomp than an arm strike because you can deploy most of your weight in a downward motion."

"So a foot. But wouldn't a shoe have left a mark?"

"Possibly, although human skin is not as revealing as a nice wet patch of grass or dirt. I may be able to discern an image at the wound area provided you find me a shoe, a patterned sock, or a foot to compare it with."

"Okay, but when have you ever seen a brain stem transection from a weaponless assault?"

"Only once, but it was a nonhuman assault."

She looked at him curiously. "Nonhuman?"

"Years ago I was on vacation at Yellowstone National Park. There unfortunately was a fatality with a camper and I was recruited to perform the autopsy."

"What killed the person?"

"A grizzly bear. Probably the most dangerous predator on land." He smiled at Beth. "Other than man, of course, as we both know so well. Anyway, this unfortunate camper had surprised a full-grown male bear while it was scavenging a carcass."

"But there are no grizzlies in Georgetown, Doc."

"No, but there is at least one person with abnormal strength and skill. That bruise is in the exact spot necessary to transect the brain stem. I doubt the location of the blow was a coincidence."

"So was she already unconscious? Or was someone holding her down? If it was just one bandit you'd think she would have fought back and we'd have defensive trace under her fingers."

"Her cuticles were clean."

"Drugged?"

"Tox reports aren't back yet."

Beth studied the body. "Bandit could've had a gun, ordered Tolliver to lie facedown. Then he kills her. That would only take one assailant."

"Quite right."

"Okay, what else?"

"We took an inventory of her clothes. We found a couple of fibers that were not from her garments."

"Her attacker?"

"Possibly. There was also some soiling on her jacket that seemed odd."

"What kind of soiling?"

"Like grease or dirt, we're analyzing it now."

"Not residue from anything in the fridge that might have spilled on her."

"We inventoried that too. No, it didn't come from that source."

"It's the start of the day, she goes from parking garage to office, and she's got dirt on her clothes. Bandit leave-behind?"

"Probably." Cassell shook his head. "It's still confusing. I spent ten years at the Bronx ME's office."

Beth nodded in understanding. "I know, NYPD says perp, MPD says bandit. Can you give me a window on *when* she died?"

"Extremely problematic, Beth. She was found in a refrigerator set at thirty-eight degrees Fahrenheit and then her body was at room temp for several hours. When I arrived at the crime scene she was very cold to the touch. And then she was parked in one of our morgue freezer beds on arrival here. Now fully freed of those icy conditions, the body is decomposing quite on schedule. She's still in rigor, as you can see." He lifted one of the stiff arms. "But the initial refrigeration forestalled the normal post-death chemical process."

"Stomach contents?"

Cassell clicked some computer keys and then scanned the screen. "At most ME shops unless there's suspicion of a drug overdose or poisoning we don't typically do a detailed gastric content analysis. But I knew if I didn't run it, you'd just tell me to do it."

"Working relationships just get better with age, don't they?"

"She had no breakfast, but apparently she had some dinner last night. About six hundred cc's worth of gastric contents including partially digested red proteins."

"In other words, bits of steak?"

"Most probably, yes. Peas and corn and what looks to be red-skinned potatoes. Spinach too. The stomach and duodenal mucosal lining were a bright green."

"Broccoli will do that as well."

"But broccoli along with corn does not digest readily in the stomach. I would have found parts of it in the gastric content. The corn was there as noted, but no broccoli."

"Anything else?"

Cassell made a face. "This lady liked her garlic. The smell was overpowering."

"Remind me to buy you a pair of clothespins. So time of death? Any thoughts?"

He took off his glasses. "If you've got reliable witnesses on both ends substantiating a two-hour window of when she was killed, I can't do any better than that even with all my fancy equipment and tests."

"I'm not sure yet how *reliable* my witnesses are. What else?"

"When I said we did an inventory of her clothing I forgot to mention that one item was missing."

"Her panties."

"Of course I am assuming that the lady typically wore underwear."

"She was forty-seven years old, a partner in a law firm, lived in a million-dollar town house on the water in Alexandria, and was wearing a Chanel suit when she was *stomped*. I think we can safely assume she was the sort of woman who wears underwear. What did the sex assault workup find? Was she raped?"

"Bruising around her genitalia clearly evidenced a sexual assault."

"Please tell me what I want to hear, Doc."

"The fellow left a few pieces of himself behind."

Cassell led her over to a microscope. She examined the slide under magnification and her smile was immediate. "The holy grail of forensic detection."

"Sperm," Cassell added, with a note of triumph. "High up in the vaginal vault and some deposited on the cervix."

"You said the fellow left *pieces*?"

"Two pubic hairs with root balls that do not belong to the deceased."

"Let's hope we get a database hit. Anything else I should know?"

Cassell hesitated. "Not on the case, no, but I hear that Mace is out. Please tell her I said hello."

"I will."

"How is she?"

"You know Mace. Everything slides right off her back."

"Tell her that there is indeed a heaven and that Mona will never make it there."

Beth smiled. "Will do."

CHAPTER

17

GATES. Big gates. And a wall. A long, high wall.

The gates opened when Roy pushed a button on a squawk box out front and announced their arrival. They'd ridden over in Roy's Audi since he didn't want to chance serious head trauma on Mace's bike without a helmet.

"You'll have to get one if you want to ride with me, then," she'd told him.

"I'll think about that," he'd said back.

"The helmet?"

"No, whether I want to ride with you again."

They drove up the winding paved road. The property was set high up on what folks in the D.C. area would call a ridge, although people from places with real mountains would simply call it a slightly elevated mound of dirt.

Mace looked out the window. "I didn't know anyone in northern Virginia had this much land."

"Looks like a compound of sorts," said Roy. He pointed to a large structure whose roof must've been thirty feet high. "I wonder what's in there?"

As they rounded a bend the mansion came into view.

"Damn!" they both said together.

"It looks like one of the buildings on the Georgetown campus," said Roy.

"Only bigger," added Mace.

They pulled to a stop next to a full-size Bentley. Beside that was a two-door dusty and dented Honda, which created the impression of a dinghy next to a yacht. They got out and walked up to two massive wooden doors that would not have looked out of place at Buckingham Palace. Before Roy could ring the bell, one of the doors opened.

"Come in, come in," said the man.

Abraham Altman was of medium height, a few inches taller than Mace, with white hair to his shoulders and a clean-shaven face. He had on faded jeans and an untucked long-sleeved shirt open at the neck that revealed a few curls of gray chest hair. Open-toed sandals covered his long feet. His eyes were blue and active. He was in his seventies but seemed to have the energy of a far younger man.

Altman shook Mace's hand vigorously and then abandoned formality and gave her a hug, actually lifting her up on her tiptoes in his exuberance.

In a rush of words he said, "It's so wonderful to see you again, Mace. Your sister told me what happened. Of course I'd read about it in the papers. I was unfortunately in Asia during the whole debacle or rest assured I would have been a character witness for you. What an injustice. Thank God you came out unharmed."

He abruptly turned and held out his hand to Roy. "I'm Abraham Altman. Please call me Abe."

"Roy Kingman. I know your son Bill."

"Wonderful. That's his Bentley out there."

"He's here?" said Roy.

"No, he's out of the country with his family. He's leaving it here until he gets back."

"Who does the Honda belong to?" asked Mace.

"That's mine."

"So old Bill has a Bentley?" Roy said inquiringly. "Does he still work at the public defender's office?"

"No, he left there last year. He's doing other things now." Altman didn't seem inclined to elaborate. "Come into the library. Would you care for something to drink?"

Roy and Mace exchanged glances. Roy said, "Beer?"

"I was actually thinking of tea. It's late for afternoon tea, of course, but we'll call it evening tea. I admire many things of our English friends, and afternoon tea is one of them."

"Tea's good," said Roy, exchanging an amused glance with Mace as they headed into Abe Altman's humble thirty-thousand-square-foot abode.

CHAPTER

18

A SMALL MAN in a spotless gold tunic and brown slacks brought in a large tray with a pot of hot tea, cups and saucers, and some scones and muffins and set it down on a massive ottoman covered in a tasteful striped pattern that seemed inconsequential considering the massive scale of the room they were in. The ceilings were high, the walls paneled in leather, and the bookcases solid mahogany and filled with tomes that actually looked as though they'd been read. There was a metal globe at least six feet tall in one corner and a large and old-fashioned slanted writing desk near one of the windows. Another long, low table had dozens of books on it, most of them open and lying page down.

After the man departed Altman said, "That's Herbert. He's been with me for ages. He handles all domestic duties. I could not get along without Herbert."

Mace said, "We should all have a Herbert in our lives."

Altman poured the tea and handed out the food.

"Quite a place you have here," said Roy as he balanced a teacup and saucer on one thigh while biting into a blueberry scone.

"It's far too large of course for me now, but I have lots of grand-children and I like for them to have a place to come. And I do like my privacy."

"Beth said you had a job offer for me?"

Altman solemnly gazed at her. "Yes. And I have to say that I can never repay you for what you did for me. Never."

Mace looked down, embarrassed by his obvious adoration. "Okay."

Altman glanced at Roy. "This woman saved my life. Did you know that?"

"No, but I can certainly believe it."

"The HF-12 gang," Altman added. "Nasty buggers."

"HF-12?" said Roy.

"Heroin Forever, and there were a dozen in the crew," said Mace. "They were bad guys but not that creative with names. Half of them are locked up."

"The other six?" asked Roy.

"Dead."

"I came to see you several times," said Altman. "But they wouldn't let me in the prison."

"Why?"

"My reputation precedes me. That correctional facility in West Virginia has been the object of my wrath on several occasions."

"You should've talked to Beth. She could've gotten you in."

"I did not want to further add to the distress of your sister's situation." He glanced at Roy. "There's a U.S. attorney who has it in for Mace and her celebrated sister."

"Mona Danforth," said Roy.

"Precisely." Altman turned back to Mace. "There was even talk a year ago of Beth being replaced."

Mace put down her cup. "I didn't know that. She never said."

"Your sister internalizes things, sometimes too much." He gazed keenly at Mace. "And I believe you share that attribute. Fortunately the mayor wisely put a stop to all talk of firing Beth."

"So what is it exactly that you do, Professor?" asked Roy.

"Making the world, or at least the nation's capital, a safer place by attacking problems before the fact and not after."

Roy nodded. "Education, preventative, that sort of thing?"

"I mean giving people a *real* choice between good and evil, right and criminal. It's been my experience that when a real choice is offered, invariably almost everyone chooses the law-abiding path."

Mace said, "Which brings us to why I'm here."

"Yes. The project I'm conducting is based on a research grant I was awarded."

"Beth said it involved going into some of the worse-off areas in D.C."

"Yes. Areas you used to work in when you were with the police force."

"What are you looking for?"

"Hope."

"That's tough to find in those places."

"Which is precisely why I picked them."

"So what would my duties involve?"

"I want you to go and meet with certain people in those areas. I've worked with Social Services to identify ten of them. I want you to talk to them and explain my proposal. If they accept then we'll go from there."

"So Mace would make the initial contacts?" asked Roy.

"That's right." He glanced at Mace. "Is he your representative?"

"Something like that. So what's your proposal?" asked Mace.

"An internship, I like to call it. We will take the people out of their current environment, place them in a totally different environment, and immerse them in a rigorous education and social refocusing program. We will gauge their interests and ambitions and help them to fulfill those goals. We will expose them to opportunities they would otherwise never have."

"Sounds sort of like *My Fair Lady*," said Roy.

"With a critical difference," answered Abe. "The connection to their present world will not be severed. They will have full contact and indeed we will encourage that contact with their present life. The goal of the program is to foster and then spread hope. These folks will serve as ambassadors of hope, if you will."

"But no one can afford to do internships like that for everybody living in poverty," said Mace. "Not even you. So aren't you spreading *false* hope?"

Altman smiled. "What you say is true. No one person can afford to lift all the folks that need help and place them in a different world. But if for every person we help it inspires just one other person to break out of the cycle of disempowerment they're currently in, the benefits can be immeasurably positive. Then we have ten people outside the program who in turn can inspire others. What that also does is gain the attention of government. And government does have the financial wherewithal to help large numbers of people."

"Our government is pretty tapped out right now," noted Roy.

"But any government's greatest resource is its citizens. Most studies conclude that less than half the adult population in this country is achieving its potential. If you want to equate that to financial terms, we're speaking of trillions of lost dollars per year. Now, even the cynical folks in D.C. would sit up and take notice of numbers like that. And beyond the government you have the private sector that is constantly complaining that they can't get decent help to fill their job requirements. I have to tell you that some of the most creative and quick-thinking people of my acquaintance are sitting in jail right now. For some folks they see justice in that. For me, I see wasted opportunity. I can't make every criminal into a law-abiding citizen. But if I can make even twenty percent of them choose another path that would enable them to contribute to society instead of detracting from it, it would have an enormously beneficial impact."

"You're definitely an optimist, Abe," said Mace. "I agree that a lot of bandits are smart and savvy and could probably run circles around a lot of business types, but what you're talking about doing is a tall order."

"I've lived my entire life through rose-colored glasses of sorts. Sometimes I'm right and sometimes I'm wrong, but I keep trying because I believe it's worth it."

"But I've been out of the loop for a couple of years. I'm not sure how much help I'd be to you."

"I have no credibility with the people who live in those areas. I realize that. But you do. With you I really believe I can make a difference." Altman took off his glasses and cleaned them with a handkerchief. "So are you amenable to such an arrangement?"

"Well, I don't have—"

Roy cut in. "So what sort of pay are we talking here? And benefits?"

Altman's eyes twinkled. "Now I understand why your friend is here."

"I'm not really good with business stuff," explained Mace quickly.

"I completely understand. Well, your salary will be three thousand a week, plus full health care, transportation, a reasonable expense account, and room and board. The project will last about a year, I would assume. So that would be about a hundred sixty-five thousand dollars as a base salary. And if the project is successful there will be more work to do at similar compensatory levels."

Roy looked at Mace and she looked back at him.

"I think the salary is *adequate*," Roy finally said, while Mace nodded vigorously in agreement.

She said, "I already have transportation, but you said room and board?"

"Hours for this sort of venture will be irregular. Much better if you stayed here at the guesthouse. It's behind the gymnasium complex."

"Gymnasium complex?" asked Roy. "The big building on the left coming in?"

"Yes, it has a full-size basketball court, weightlifting and cardio room, sauna, whirlpool, thirty-meter indoor pool, and a full kitchen and relaxation room."

"A full-size indoor basketball court?" said Roy.

"Yes. I never played the game in school but it has always fascinated me and I love to watch it. Ever since moving to this area decades ago I've been a huge Maryland Terrapins fan. I almost never miss a home game, and have attended the last thirty-seven ACC tournaments." Altman studied Roy. "You look familiar to me now."

"I played point for UVA about eight years ago."

Altman clapped his hands together. "Roy Kingman, of course! You were the one who beat us in the ACC finals."

"Well, I had a lot of help from my teammates."

"Let me see, thirty-two points, fourteen assists, seven rebounds, and three steals. And with six-tenths of a second left you drove to the basket, made a reverse layup, drew the foul, calmly made the free throw, and we lost by one."

"Pretty awesome memory, Abe."

Altman turned to Mace. "So will you do it?"

"Yes."

"Excellent." He pulled a key from his pocket and tossed it to Mace. "The key to the guesthouse. Taped to it is the gate code. Do you have a cell phone?"

"Uh, no."

He opened a drawer, pulled out a cell phone, and handed it to her. "Now you do. Would you like to see where you'll be staying?"

They drove over in a golf cart. The guesthouse was set next to a small spring-fed pond. It was like a miniature of the main house and its level of comfort and the quality of the furnishings and amenities was beyond anything Mace had ever experienced.

Roy looked around at the large, open spaces. "How big is this place?"

"Oh, about six thousand square feet, I suppose. Bill and his family stayed here while their new home was being built."

Roy said, "My condo is twelve hundred square feet."

"My cell was eight by eight," said Mace.

As they rode back to the main house, Altman said, "It's funny, you know."

"What's that?" said Roy, who was sitting in the backseat of the four-person cart.

"Growing up in Omaha with him, I never thought Warren Buffett would ever amount to much."

"People said the same thing about me," Mace quipped.

19

WHAT YOU'RE DOING is a mistake."

Beth had changed from her uniform into sweats. She'd pumped some dumbbells and done a half hour on the elliptical set up in the lower level of her house. It was nearly midnight yet neither sister seemed sleepy as they sat across from each other in the living room. Blind Man was curled up by Mace's feet.

"I thought you *wanted* me to take the job."

"I'm talking about Roy Kingman. You shouldn't be hanging out with *him*."

"Why not?"

"We haven't cleared him as a suspect in the Tolliver murder, that's why. You're on probation. That means avoiding all contact with people of questionable character."

"But that's the reason I am hanging out with him. To keep tabs on him."

"You could be passing time with a killer."

"Wouldn't be the first time."

"You were undercover then."

"I'm sort of undercover now."

"You're not a cop anymore."

"Once a cop always a cop."

"That's not how it works. And I thought we had this discussion?"

"Maybe we did."

"I'm working the case, Mace. You start poking around then it might get all blown up. And that hurts you and me. You need to focus on moving forward with your life."

Mace sat back and said resignedly, "Okay, okay, I hear you."

"Good, I'll hold you to that. So when do you start with Altman?"

"Two days. And he wants me to move into the guesthouse on his property."

Beth looked surprised. "I thought you'd stay with me for a while."

"I can actually do both. Hang here and hang there when work requires it."

"Okay," Beth said, her disappointment clear.

"I'm not abandoning you."

"I know. It's just been two years without you. I need a big Mace Perry fix."

Mace gripped her sister's arm. "You'll get it. We have a lot of catching up to do."

"Before we get all blubbery, Mom called. She'd like to see you."

Mace punched a pillow she was holding. "That's actually the only thing that *could* make me cry. When?"

"How about tomorrow?"

"Will you come with me?"

"I've got a full schedule, sorry."

"Does she still live on the plantation with all the slaves?"

"The last time I checked she was paying her staff a living wage."

"And hubby?"

"Firmly under her thumb and usually not underfoot."

"How about instead of doing the visit I run naked through Trinidad in northeast with 'DEA' stenciled on my back?"

"Might be safer, actually. Oh, Lowell Cassell said hello. And he also said, 'You tell Mace that there is indeed a heaven and Mona Danforth will never make it there.'"

"I knew I loved him. So what did he find?" She added quickly, "I'm not poking around, just curious."

"Tolliver was raped."

"Sperm leave-behind?"

"Yes. He also found a couple of foreign pubic hairs and a bit of fiber. There were also soil stains on Tolliver's clothing."

Mace rose. "Well, I guess I should get some sleep if I'm going to survive Mom. You turning in?"

Beth had pulled out her BlackBerry and was answering e-mails. "Just two hundred and sixty-three to go."

"You still answer every e-mail in twenty-four hours?"

"It's part of the job."

"You still never turn it off, do you?"

Beth looked up. "Like you ever did?"

"I had some fun."

"I've had fun too."

"Yeah, your ex was a real barrel of laughs. I lost two years, sis, you lost eight."

"I'm not saying it was all Ted's fault. My career—"

"It wasn't like he didn't know that going in."

Beth stopped thumbing the BlackBerry. "Get some shuteye, you're going to need all your energy for Mom."

20

Mace was flying along the winding roads leading out to horse country where old money melded, often uneasily, with new. She was going to see her mother but was now lost. Backtracking, she became even more turned around. Finally she stopped her bike at the end of a dirt path surrounded by trees. As she was trying to get her bearings she heard something move to her right. When she looked that way her heartbeat spiked. She reached for her gun, but of course she didn't have one.

"How the hell did you get out?" she screamed.

Juanita the Cow was waddling toward her, Lily White Rose with the nineteen teeth right behind. Juanita carried a wide smile along with a Smith & Wesson .40, while Lily White had her gutting knife. Mace tried to start her bike, but the ignition wouldn't catch. The two women started to run toward her.

"Shit!" Mace jumped off the bike and sprinted to the woods, but her boot caught in a bump in the dirt and she fell sprawling. By the time she turned over the women were standing over her.

"No big-sis bitch to help you now, baby," cooed Juanita.

Rose said nothing. She just cocked her blade arm back, waiting for the word from the queen bee to plunge the serrated edge into Mace's jugular.

"Do it, Lily White. Then we got to get the hell outta here."

The blade flew down with a speed that Mace was not prepared for. It hit her square in the neck.

"No!"

Mace fell out of the bed. She felt warm blood spurt out of her nose as it smacked against the nightstand. She landed awkwardly on the carpeted floor and just lay there.

Blind Man, who'd been asleep on the floor next to where she'd fallen, licked her face and gave off little mournful noises in her ear.

"It's okay, Blind Man, I'm okay."

She finally rolled over, sat up, and backed her way into a corner. She squatted there in a defensive ball, her hands made into fists, her eyes looking out at the dark, her breath coming in waves of uneven heaves. Blind Man lay in front of her in the darkness, his thick reddish nose probably taking in each and every dimension of her scented fear.

An hour later she was still there, her spine digging into the drywall that her sister had painted a soothing blue especially for her return. Only she wasn't thinking of Juanita or the gut-chick Rose. Her images were of herself, strung out on meth, huddled in a corner, her body going through shit it had never suffered before.

She'd never seen any of them, none of the bandits who'd snatched her out of an alley where she had set up an observation post on a drug distribution center in Six D. After they'd injected her multiple times with stuff for three days running she didn't even know her own name. The next thing she vaguely remembered was climbing in and out of cars, holding a gun, going into stores and taking what didn't belong to any of them.

Once, shots had been fired. She recalled pulling the trigger on her weapon by instinct, only no round had come out of the barrel; turned out her weapon wasn't loaded and never had been. She was finally arrested holding an unloaded Sig and enough evidence to put her away for a long time while the rest of her "gang" conveniently had disappeared.

So the little sister of the D.C. police chief was busted for armed robbery while caked on meth. Some dubbed her the Patty Hearst of the twenty-first century. The arrest, the trial, the sentencing, the appeals galloped by in a blur. Mona had gone for the carotid, and the female legal threshing machine had come within one appeal of putting Mace away for twenty years at a max a thousand miles away from D.C. She'd argued forcefully that Mace had gone so deeply undercover that she had eventually succumbed to the dark side. Mace remembered sitting in the courtroom watching the vitriol-spewing DA pointing her finger at her and pounding the counsel table demanding that this "animal" be sent away for good. In her mind, Mace had killed the bitch over a hundred times. Yet when she finally had gotten the twenty-four-month sentence, just about everybody had turned on her and her sister.

When the van that had taken Mace in shackles arrived at the prison the news trucks were all lined up. It seemed the warden was reveling in the national spotlight, because he'd personally escorted Mace through the gauntlet of media and the hostile crowd. Trash was thrown at her along with insults of every conceivable degree of vulgarity. And still she'd shuffled along, her head as high as she could hold it, her eyes dead ahead, staring at the steel outer doors of her home for the next two years of her life. But even for tough Mace, the tears had started to gather in her eyes, and her lips had started trembling with the Orwellian strain of it all.

Then the crowd of onlookers had suddenly parted and a tall figure in full dress blues and four stars had marched out and started walking right next to Mace. The stunned look on the warden's face showed that this development was totally unexpected. The crowds stopped screaming. Nothing else was thrown at Mace. Not with Chief of Police Elizabeth Perry with her gun and her badge striding right next to her sister, her face a block of granite as she stared down the crowd, willing them from hostility to numbness. That image, that final image of her sister next to her before Mace entered the house of hell, was really the only thing that had kept her going over those two years.

It was with this last thought that Mace finally fell asleep right on the floor. Two hours before dawn, she woke with a start, staggered to the bathroom, washed the crusted blood off her face in the bathroom, and got back into bed. Exhausted, she slept for nearly three hours, until her sister gently shook her awake.

Mace sat up in bed, looked around the room with an unsteady gaze.

Beth handed her a cup of black coffee and sat next to her. "You okay?"

Mace drank some of the coffee and lay back against the head-board. "Yeah, I'm good."

"You look a little out of it. Bad dream?"

Mace tensed. "Why? Did you hear anything?"

"No, just thought it was probably normal. Your subconscious probably thinks there are still bars on the doors and windows."

"I'm fine. Thanks for the java."

"Anytime." Beth rose.

"Uh . . ."

Beth looked down at her. "Something on your mind?"

"I remember what a media circus it was when I went to prison. I was just wondering."

"Why there wasn't a media army camped outside on your return?"

"Yeah."

"The easy answer is you're old news. It's been two years. And every day there's some national or international crisis, big company collapsing, people getting blown up, or some psycho with auto-matic weapons and body armor gunning people down at the local mall. And since you've been away hundreds of newspapers have folded, existing ones have cut their staff in half, and the TV and ra-dio folks usually chase stuff far more bizarre than you to get the big ratings. But just in case, I sort of pulled a reverse strategy on the media grunts."

Mace sat up. "What do you mean?"

"I offered to make you available to them for a full interview. I guess they figured if it was that easy, why bother?"

"That's pretty slick, Beth. Busy day today?"

"Nope, didn't you hear? Last night all crime miraculously went away."

Mace showered and changed and checked her hair, face, and clothes in the mirror. Then she got mad at herself for even doing this. No matter what she looked like, her mother would find some-thing wrong with her appearance. And frankly, it would be easy pickings for the woman.

Minutes later she fired up the Ducati. Immediately, Blind Man started howling from behind the door. She smiled and revved the gas. Soon she was heading due west, left D.C. proper, and entered Virginia over Memorial Bridge. As she cut in and out of traffic, Mace started to think about the upcoming encounter with the woman who had given birth to her over three decades ago.

Part of her would take prison again over that.

21

MACE RACED DOWN the straightaway of Route 50, weaving in and out of the dregs of the morning rush hour. The one traffic light in Middleburg caught her and she geared down the Ducati, finally braking to a stop. The street parking here leaned to Range Rovers and Jag sedans with an occasional Smart car thrown in for green measure. The small downtown area was hip in an upscale rural way. And here one could, for millions of dollars, purchase a really swell place to live. Years ago Mace and Beth had visited their mother, seen the fancy estate, dined at a nice restaurant, done some window shopping, and then gone back to busting bandits in D.C. One visit for Mace was truly enough.

Though Beth Perry was only six years older than her sister, she had played far more of a nurturing role for Mace than their mother ever had. In fact, the first person Mace could ever remember holding her was Beth, who was already tall and rangy at age nine.

Though he'd died when Mace was only twelve, Benjamin Perry had left quite an impression on his younger daughter. Mace could vividly recall sitting in her father's small den doing her homework while her dad put together his legal arguments, oftentimes reading them to her and getting her input. She had wept harder than anyone at his funeral, the casket closed to hide the gunshot wounds to his face.

As she flew past lavish estates residing majestically on hundreds of acres, Mace knew that her mother had ascended to this level of wealth principally by design. She had methodically hunted and then snared a fellow who'd never worked a day in his life but was the only child of a man who had earned a fortune large enough to allow his offspring to live decadently for several generations. By then both daughters were grown and gone, for which Mace was enormously grateful. She was more coach fare and Target than private wings and Gucci.

Beth had gotten her height from her mother, who was several inches taller than her husband. Mace had always assumed that she inherited both her father's average stature and his pugnacity. Benjamin Perry's career as the U.S. attorney in D.C. had been tragically cut short, but during his tenure he'd prosecuted criminals through some of the most violent years in D.C. history, quickly becoming legendary for his scorched-earth pursuit of bandits. Yet he also had a reputation for always playing fair, and if exculpatory evidence came along, defense counsel always saw it. He had told Mace more than once that his greatest fear was not letting a guilty person go free, but sending an innocent one to prison. She had never forgotten those words, and that made the appointment of Mona Danforth to her father's old position even more difficult for her to accept.

Benjamin Perry's murder had never been solved. His daughters had taken various cracks at it over the years, with no success. Evidence was lost or tainted, witnesses' memories faded away, or they died. Cold cases were the toughest to solve. But now that she was out of prison Mace knew, at some point, she had to try again.

A few miles past Middleburg proper she slowed the bike and turned off onto a gravel path, which would become a paved cobblestone road about a half mile up. She drew a deep breath and pulled to a stop in front of the house. They called it by some Scottish name because hubby was Scottish and took great pride in his clan back home. While Mace and Beth were there previously he had even entered the room dressed in a kilt with a dagger in his sock and a bonnet on his head. That had been bad enough, but the poor fellow had caught his skirt on the sword handle of a large armored warrior standing against one wall, causing the skirt to lift up and reveal that the lord of the manor wore his kilt commando style. It was all Mace could do not to blow snot out of her nose from laughing. She thought she had carried it off fairly well. However, her mother had sternly informed her that her husband had not taken kindly to Mace rolling on the floor gasping for air while he was desperately trying to pull his skirt back down to cover his privates.

"Then tell Mr. Creepy to start wearing underwear," Mace had shot back in earshot of her stepfather. "I mean, it's not like he's got anything down there to brag about."

That had not gone over very well either.

As she rounded a bend the manor came into full view. It was smaller than Abe Altman's, but not by much. Mace walked up to the front door fully expecting a uniformed butler to answer her knock. But he didn't.

The thick portal flew open and there stood her mother, dressed in a long black designer skirt, calf-high boots, and a starched white embroidered tunic shirt over which a gold chain was hanging. Dana Perry still wore her whitish-blond hair long, though it was held back today in a French braid. She looked at least ten years younger than she was. Beth had her mother's facial structure, long and lovely, with a nose as straight and lean as the edge of an ax blade. The cheekbones still rode high and confident. Her mother cradled a comb-teased Yorkie in one slender arm.

Mace didn't expect a hug and didn't get one.

Her mother looked her up and down. "Prison seems to have agreed with you. You look to be lean as a piano wire."

"I would've preferred a gym membership, actually."

Her mother pointed a long finger at her. "Your father must be turning over in his grave. Always thinking of yourself and never anybody else. Look at what your sister's accomplished. You've got to finally get it straight, little girl, or you're going right down the crapper. Do you understand what I'm saying?"

"Do you actually want me to come in, or will your ripping me a new one on the front porch satisfy as a visit so I can get back to the real world?"

"You actually call that garbage pit of a city the real world?"

"I'm sure you've been tied up the last two years, so I can understand you not bothering to come see me."

"As though seeing you in prison would've been good for my mental health."

"Right, sorry, I forgot the first rule of Dana, it's all about *you*."

"Get in here, Mason."

She had lied to Roy Kingman. Her father hadn't named her Mason. Her *mother* had. And she'd done it for a particularly odious reason. Chafing under the relatively small salary her husband drew as a prosecutor, she'd wanted him to turn to the defense side, where with his skill and reputation he could have commanded an income ten times what he earned on the public side. Thus, Mason Perry—Perry Mason—was her mother's not-so-subtle constant reminder of what he would not give her.

"It's Mace. You'd think after all these years you might get that little point."

"I refuse to refer to you as a name of a weapon."

It was probably a good thing, Mace thought as she trudged past her mother, that she could no longer carry a gun.

CHAPTER

22

Roy Kingman had skipped basketball that morning. He passed by Ned, who looked far more attentive than usual and even had the tie on his uniform tightened all the way to his fleshy neck. Ned gave him a jaunty two-finger salute and a confident dip of the chin as though to let Roy know that not a single murderer had slipped past him today.

You go, bro.

Roy took the elevator up to Shilling & Murdoch. The police were still there and Diane's office and the kitchen were taped off while the cops and techs continued to do their thing. He had snatched conversations with several other lawyers. He had tried to play it cool with Mace, who'd obviously seen far more dead bodies than he had, but finding Diane like that had done a number on his head. He kept replaying that moment over and over until it felt like he couldn't breathe.

He walked by Chester Ackerman's office but the door was closed and the man's secretary, who sat across from her boss's office, told him the police were in there questioning the managing partner. Roy finally went to his office and closed the door. Settling behind his desk, he turned on his computer and started going through e-mails. The fifth one caught his eye. It was from Diane Tolliver. He glanced at the date sent. The previous Friday. The time stamp was a few minutes past ten. He hadn't checked his work e-mails over the weekend because there had been nothing pressing going on. He had intended to do so on Monday morning, but then Diane's body had tumbled out of the fridge. At the bottom of the e-mail were Diane's initials, "DLT."

The woman's message was terse and cryptic, even for the Twitter generation.

We need to focus in on A-

Why hadn't she finished the message? And why send it if it wasn't finished?

It could be nothing, he knew. How many flubs had he committed with his keystrokes? If it had been important Diane would have e-mailed again with the full message, or else called him. He checked his cell phone. No messages from her. He brought up his recent phone call list just in case she had called but left no message. Nothing.

A-?

It didn't ring any immediate bells for him. If it was referring to a client, it could be any number of them. He brought up the list on his screen and counted. Twenty-eight clients beginning with the letter *A*. And eleven of them were ones that he and Diane routinely worked on together. They repped several firms in the Middle East, so it was Al-this and Al-that. Another lawyer at the firm? There were nearly fifty here, with twenty-two more overseas. He knew all of the D.C. folks personally. Doing a quick count in his head, there were ten whose first or last names started with *A*. Alice, Adam, Abernathy, Aikens, Chester Ackerman.

The police, he knew, had already copied the computer files from Diane's office, so they already had what he had just found. Still, should he call them and tell them what he'd just discovered?

Maybe they wouldn't believe me.

For the first time Roy knew what his clients had felt like when he'd worked criminal defense. He left his office and took the elevator down, with the idea of simply going for a walk by the river to clear his head. On the fourth floor the doors opened and the sounds of power saws and hammers assailed him. He watched as an older man in slacks, short-sleeved white shirt, and a hard hat stepped on the elevator car.

The fourth floor had been gutted and was being built out for a new tenant. All the rest of the building's occupants were counting down the days until completion, because the rehabbing was a very messy and noisy affair.

"How's it coming?" he asked the man, who was holding a roll of construction drawings under one arm.

"Slower than we'd like. Too many problems."

"Guys not showing up to work? Inspectors slow on the approval?"

"That and things going missing."

"Missing? Like what?"

"Tools. Food. I thought this building was supposed to be secure."

"Well, the uniform at the front desk is basically useless."

"Heard about some lady lawyer getting killed here. Is it true?"

"Afraid so."

CHAPTER

23

Roy headed along the riverfront, stopping near one of the piers where a forty-foot cabin cruiser was docked. What would it be like, he wondered, to live on a boat and just keep going? Watch the sunset and grab a swim when he wanted? See the world? He'd seen his hometown, lived in D.C., Charlottesville. He'd visited lots of cities, but only to bounce basketballs on hardwood before heading on. He'd viewed the Atlantic and Pacific oceans at forty thousand feet. He'd seen Big Ben, and sand in the Middle East. That was about it.

He smelled him before he saw him.

He turned, his hand already reaching into his pocket.

"Hey, Captain."

"Roy." The man gave him a quick salute.

The Captain was in his late fifties and the same height as Roy. However, whereas Roy was lean, the Captain was built like a football lineman. He must've outweighed Roy by eighty pounds. It had once all been muscle, Roy was sure, but the streets had made a fatty transformation of the man's once impressive physique. His belly was so swollen now that the bottom three buttons on the jacket could no longer be used. And his body listed heavily to the left, probably as did his spine. Eating crap out of Dumpsters and sleeping on cement did that to you.

Roy called him the Captain because of the marks on his jacket. From what he'd learned of the man's history, the Captain had once been an Army Ranger and had distinguished himself in Vietnam. But after returning home things had not gone well. Alcohol and then drugs had ruined what should have been an honorable military career. Apparently the VA had tried to help him, but the Captain had eventually fallen through the cracks and into a life on the streets of the capital of the country he had once defended with his blood.

He'd been homeless for over a decade now. And each year his uniform grew more tattered and his skin more permanently stained by the elements, much in the same way that buildings became filthy. However, there was no one to come and give him a good power wash. Roy had first met him when he'd worked as a CJA. Before he'd settled on G-town, the Captain's foraging range was wider and his manner more aggressive. He'd had a couple of assault charges, mostly for harassing tourists or office dwellers for money or food. Roy had defended him once, gotten him probation, and then tried to get him help, but the VA was swamped with needy soldiers from current wars, and the Captain had never been good about follow-up.

It was sad, and yet all Roy could do was open his wallet, look into the darkened, grizzled face that housed a pair of dimming, vacuous eyes that indicated the owner was not all there, and say, "How about I get you some food?"

The Captain nodded, pushing a huge hand through his tangle of filthy gray and white hair. He wore tattered gloves that had once been white but were now even blacker than his face. As they trudged along together Roy looked down and noted that the Captain's shoes were really pieces of cardboard held together with twine. He had survived the previous winter and the heavy spring rains, and the night chills were gone now. Yet Roy wondered, as the Captain coughed up some phlegm and spit it out into the Potomac, if the older man could survive another year out here. As he gazed at the Captain's jacket and saw the Combat Bronze and other medals on his chest, including the designation for two Purple Hearts, he thought that a country's warriors deserved better than this.

The Captain dutifully waited outside the café, like an obedient dog, as Roy bought the food. He came back out, handed the bag over, and watched as the Captain settled down on the curb and ate it all right there, drinking down the coffee last. He wiped his mouth with the paper bag and rose.

"What size shoe do you take?" Roy asked.

The Captain looked down at his feet. "Big. I think."

"Me too. Come on."

They walked back to the office building and into the underground garage. From the backseat of his Audi, Roy pulled out a pair of nearly new basketball shoes. "Try these on." He tossed them to the Captain, who was quick-handed enough to snare them both.

He sat down on the cold floor of the garage and stripped off his cardboard and twine. When Roy saw the blackened, raw skin festered with lumps and green-colored cuts, he looked away.

"Good to go," the Captain said a minute later. Roy was sure they would have fit if the man had had to cut off his toes. "You sure, Roy? Bet these cost probably a million dollars, right?"

"Not quite and I've got plenty." He studied the Captain. If he gave him cash it would go for booze or some street drugs that the Captain didn't need in his system. He had driven him to shelters on three occasions, but the man had walked out of each one within a day or so. Roy was not going to take him to live at his condo. His neighbors would probably not approve, and there was no guarantee that the former military man would not suddenly go nuts and use Roy for a cutting board.

"Come around in a couple days and I'll have some more stuff for you, okay?"

"Yes, sir," the Captain said amiably, giving him another snappy salute.

Roy suddenly noticed something missing and wondered why he hadn't before. "Where's your cart?" Like some homeless people, the Captain kept everything he had in an old rusted shopping cart with two busted front wheels. You could hear him coming a mile away just from the screech of metal.

"Some pricks stole it!"

"Do you know who?"

"Damn Vietcong. I'll catch 'em. And then. Look." The Captain reached in his pocket and pulled out a large clasp knife. It looked military-issued.

"Don't do that, Captain. Let the police handle it."

The Captain just stared at him. Finally he waved a big hand at Roy. "Thanks for the shoes."

24

Unfortunately, her mother's husband, Timothy, *was* there. Fortunately, he wasn't wearing a kilt. To Mace, he looked like a person of leisure who desperately wanted to be perceived as a man of the land with a British twist. This translated into an outfit consisting of tweeds, an old-fashioned shotgun vest with holders for the shells, a cute pocket kerchief that exactly matched his checked shirt, and nearly knee-high brown leather riding boots, though there wasn't an equine in sight. When Mace saw him she felt her cheeks begin to quiver and had to look away quickly before the next sound that was heard from her was a snort.

An older woman in a maid's uniform brought coffee and little sandwiches out to the faux English conservatory they were sitting in. She looked as though she would rather be driving tenpenny nails through her skull with a hammer than playing maid for Timothy and Dana. The sandwiches weren't nearly as wonderful as the spread Abe Altman had offered. Still, Mace filled her belly and had her caffeine fix.

The little Yorkie, whose name Mace had been told was Angelina Fernandina, sat on a plump pillow in front of her own little gold tray of high-end vittles, happily nipping away with teeth the size and shape of splinters. Mace inclined her head at precious Angelina. "Do you dress her in clothes too?"

Dana answered, "Only when we travel. Our jet makes her cold."

"Poor thing," said Mace.

"So does Beth still have a menagerie of misfits?"

"Just me and Blind Man, but he's going strong. Probably be alive and well when you're planting old Angie there in the dirt."

Timothy sucked in a breath at this remark and gave Angelina a little pat with the *back* of his hand, which told Mace that he didn't actually like dogs, hair-teased or not.

"So, how's the rural aristocratic life treating you both?"

Timothy daintily patted his lips with a monogrammed napkin and glanced at Dana, apparently waiting for her to respond.

"Timothy has been elected to head up the local planning commission. It's an important position because you wouldn't believe what people want to do out here development-wise. It's a travesty."

You mean like putting up a twenty-thousand-square-foot Scottish castle smack in the middle of farmland and raising your working-class neighbors' property taxes tenfold? Mace thought. But she said, "Congratulations, Timothy. That's great."

His chest puffed out a bit as he swallowed the last bit of sandwich. When he spoke it was as though he were addressing an adoring audience of thousands. "I will endeavor to carry out my duties to the best of my abilities. I take the stewardship that has been granted to me very seriously."

God, you are the biggest prick. "I'm sure you do," Mace said pleasantly.

Dana said, "So what are your plans, *Mason?*"

Mace slowly put down her coffee cup. "I'd actually considered stripping on Internet webcams for food, but then a job offer came along."

"What sort of job offer?"

"An assistant to a college professor."

"Why would a college professor want *you* as an assistant?" scoffed her mother.

"He's blind, on a tight budget, and I'm apparently cheaper than a seeing-eye dog."

"Will you please be serious for once in your life, Mason!"

Okay, I tried playing patty-cakes and I don't like it. "What does it matter to you what I do? I'm sure we can agree that you're a few decades late on playing mommy."

"How dare you—"

Mace could feel her ears burning. She didn't want to go there. She really didn't. "Oh, I always dare. So just back off, lady."

"Then let me explain to you quite clearly why it *is* my business. If you can't support yourself, guess who you'll be running to with your hand out?"

Mace formed fists so tight all of her finger joints popped. She leaned into Dana until their noses were only separated by a bare inch. "I would gnaw off my hand before I came to you or Scotch Bonnet Boy over there for one freaking dime."

A scarlet-faced Timothy scrambled to his leather-booted feet. "I think I'll go do some yoga. I feel my balance is off."

Dana immediately put out her hand for him to take. "All right, dear. But remember, we have dinner tonight with the mayor and his wife at the French Hound."

The moment he'd fled the room, Dana whirled on her youngest daughter. "It's nearly impossible to believe, but I think prison has actually made you worse."

This barb was so weak that Mace simply ignored it and studied her mother in silence for a few moments. "So why are you still all so kissy-kissy to him? You've got the ring. You're legally locked to Lord Bonny Butt."

She said stiffly, "He's a Scottish earl, not a lord."

The truth suddenly hit Mace. "Bonny Butt's got a kick-ass pre-nup, doesn't he?"

"Shut up, Mason! This minute."

"So how does it work? You vest a few diamond bracelets, some cash, and a bushel of Triple A bonds for each year of matrimonial bliss?"

Her mother snapped, "I don't even know why I invited you here."

Mace rose. "Oh, that one is easy, actually. You just wanted me to see how fabulous your life is. Well, I'm duly impressed. I'm happy that you're so obviously happy."

"You're a terrible liar. You always were."

"I guess that's why I became a cop. I can just pull my badge and figure out who's trying to screw with me."

"But you can't be a *cop* anymore, can you?" This came out as a clear taunt.

"Not until I figure out who set me up."

Dana rolled her heavily made-up eyes. "Do you really think that's going to happen?"

"I don't think. I *know* it will."

"Well, if I were you, I'd work very hard for your little college professor. Because I see 'assistant' as being as good as it gets for you from here on."

"Thanks for the encouragement. I'll see myself out."

But her mother followed her as far as the front door. As Mace strapped on her helmet, Dana said, "Do you know how much trouble you've caused for your sister?"

"Yeah, actually I do."

"And of course you don't care at all, do you?"

"If I told you otherwise would you believe me?"

"You make me sick with your selfish ways."

"Well, I learned from the master, didn't I?"

"I spent the best years of my life with your father. We never had any money. Never went anywhere. Never did a damn thing. And we never would."

"Yeah, punishing the wicked and making the world a better place for all was just the pits, wasn't it?"

"You were only a child. You had no idea."

"Oh, I had more than an idea. Talk about me? *You'll* never have it nearly as good ever again. I don't care how many rich *Timothys* you marry."

"Oh, you think so?"

Mace lifted her visor. "Yeah, because Dad was the only man you ever really loved."

"Just please go away!"

Mace noticed the slight tremble in her mother's right hand. "Do you know how lucky you were to have a man that good so in love with you? Beth never had that privilege. And I sure as hell haven't."

She thought she saw her mother's eyes turn glassy before the door slammed shut.

Mace mangled the Ducati's gears in her sudden panic to get out of this place. Maybe her mother was right. Maybe she would never be a cop again. Maybe this was as good as it would ever get for her.

25

B<small>ETH READ THROUGH</small> the report on her computer screen three times. This was something her father had taught her. Read through once for general conceptualization and then a second time for the nitty-gritty details. And then read it a final time, at least an hour after the first reading, but do so out of order, which forced your mind and your eyes from their comfort zones.

Beth refocused. They had scrubbed Diane Tolliver's computer at work and at her home without revealing any surprises. The work computer had yielded a mass of legal documents and research items and correspondence on dozens of complicated deals. The woman's town house in Old Town Alexandria had yielded no clues or leads. They would work outward now, from her job and personal life. Murders were almost never random occurrences. Family, friends, acquaintances, rivals, spurned lovers—those were the categories from which the takers of human life were most often spawned.

She looked down at the one interesting item on Diane Tolliver's work computer. The e-mail she'd sent to Roy Kingman Friday night. The missive was cryptic and she was hoping that Kingman could explain it, but when interviewed by her detectives over the phone he claimed to have no idea what it meant or why it had been sent to him.

They also knew from the electronic records from the garage that Tolliver had left the office Friday night at two minutes before seven and returned at a little before ten, leaving again around ten-forty. The cleaning crew had come in at seven-thirty and left around nine-thirty. They had seen nothing unusual.

What did people do for a few hours on a Friday evening? They had dinner. The fact that she had driven showed it was too far to walk. They were accessing the woman's credit card records to see what restaurant she'd gone to. That would only work if she had paid the bill, of course, but it was a viable lead.

Need to focus in on A-

That was the message she'd sent to Kingman that he claimed not to understand. Was that the whole message or had it been cut off? She might have been interrupted. If so, by whom at that late hour? But she'd been alive on Monday morning. Beth frowned as she thought about her sister hanging around Kingman. Could he crack a brain stem? Yeah, he probably could.

There were other messages Diane had sent over the course of the weekend, all from home. Just routine ones to various friends, and she'd ordered some items for her home from two vendors. Her BMW 735 was in the parking garage in her normal space, and the gate record showed she'd accessed the garage at six a.m. on the dot. Her car had been searched without revealing anything of use.

Tolliver's purse had not been found, so robbery couldn't be ruled out. Yet she'd been raped; that might have been the primary motivation. And then killed to prevent her from fingering who'd done it. No one at Shilling & Murdoch had come into the office over the weekend, including Diane Tolliver.

From what Beth had learned, Tolliver usually got in around nine. So why had she come to the office so early on Monday? They were interviewing everyone who worked at the law firm to verify where they were on Monday morning. However, Beth was really counting on getting a database hit on the sperm.

They could find no one who'd talked to Diane over the weekend. One neighbor reported that he saw her drive off in a hurry on Sunday around nine in the morning but did not speak to her. She lived in an end-unit town house with a garage. She could come and go without interacting with anyone, as she apparently had the weekend before she'd been killed.

There were dirty dishes in the dishwasher and trash that indicated she had eaten in over the weekend. She had a cleaning service that came three times a week, but not over the weekend. Her home phone records showed no calls going out, and the only messages on her voice mail had been from solicitors. She, like many people, apparently used her cell phone to communicate most of the time.

They couldn't find her iPhone because it had presumably been in her purse. But they had requested the phone records from her carrier. She'd made many calls on her cell phone over the weekend. None of them had been to friends or coworkers, though. These were all normal things that one did during a weekend. Tolliver had not known, of course, that it would be the last weekend of her life.

The previous Friday, her last full day at the office, had been spent in meetings with various clients. Three of them were local and had been interviewed, but had told them nothing of interest. Tolliver had seemed perfectly normal to them. Two of her client meetings had been with men from overseas. Both men had flown out Friday night and were now in the Middle East. Neither was obviously her killer.

Her cell phone chirped.

"Hello?"

"You working late?" said Mace's voice.

"Had a community outreach event but it got canceled. What are you offering?"

"Dinner, on me. Pick a nice place. I mean really nice, where you actually have to wear shoes and everything."

"Did Altman give you an advance on your salary?"

"No, I just cleaned out my bank account."

"Mace, what about your creditors?"

"I'll start paying them off with my first paycheck. Let's just have a nice meal."

"Mom was that bad?"

"She's still alive and so am I, so how bad could it be?"

"Okay. How about eight-thirty? I'll call you with the place."

Mace clicked off and Beth went back to her notes.

Her office phone rang.

She picked it up and listened for two minutes.

There'd been another murder.

And this one had cut close to home. A U.S. attorney was dead. Mona Danforth wasn't the one killed. Beth managed to avoid tacking "unfortunately" onto the end of this thought. But they had just discovered Jamie Meldon's body in a Dumpster in northwest Washington.

26

On the drive over Beth spent the time thinking about the dead man. Jamie Meldon was one of Mona Danforth's top assistants and was as unlike his boss as it was possible to be. He was a fine, diligent lawyer who'd made enemies in the criminal world as all good prosecutors did. And one of those enemies might have murdered him. She obviously was not going to make dinner with Mace. But if there was one thing her sister would understand it was that in their line of work the job trumped everything else.

When she got to the crime scene she was not surprised to see the FBI there along with her people. Meldon was a U.S. attorney and thus his murder was a federal crime. What did shock her was seeing her police and forensics personnel packing their stuff up to leave.

"What's going on?" she asked the officer in charge.

"We've been told in no uncertain terms that this is a federal investigation and we are persona non grata."

"Like we've never worked a homicide with the Bureau. Where's the SAIC?" she asked, referring to the special agent in charge.

He pointed to a man in a suit near the Dumpster.

Beth marched over with two of her district homicide detectives in tow. "Can I ask what's going on?"

The man turned around to look at her. "Hello, Beth."

Beth recognized him as soon as she saw his face. "Steve? I didn't think the AD came out to homicides."

Steve Lanier, the assistant director of the FBI's Washington Field Office and a man Beth worked with closely, said, "Well, I can't say the same about you because I know you come to every one."

"Did you know Jamie Meldon?"

"No."

"So why are you here, then?"

He glanced over at a group of men in suits. "Do you know who they are?"

"No, should I?"

"They will be coming over here shortly and informing you that national security interests are at stake and the police will not be involved in this investigation."

"What does national security have to do with a prosecutor's murder?"

"Well, I don't suppose we'll ever find out."

"*We*? They might be able to pull the rug out from under us, but you're the FBI."

"In ordinary circumstances that would be true."

"So what's extraordinary about this?"

"All I can tell you is that it came straight from Pennsylvania."

"The White House?"

"And don't bother asking who they are. They won't tell you."

Beth looked puzzled. "CIA? Langley has no law enforcement jurisdiction. Hell, they can't even operate domestically."

"It may not be the CIA."

"Steve, are you saying you don't even know which agency they're from?"

"That's right."

"Then how the hell did they get access to a restricted crime scene?"

Lanier smiled glumly. "They showed their driver's licenses."

"Are you shitting me! Their driver's licenses?"

"The FBI director himself told me that they would be here, what their names were, and that they should have unfettered access to the crime scene, because they were taking over the investigation. So they didn't have to show me their creds."

"This is unbelievable."

"Yes it is."

"Chief Perry?" said one man in his forties and who was the apparent leader of this little group of unknowns.

"Yeah?" Beth said in a stern tone.

"Perhaps the assistant director here has filled you in on . . . things?"

"That you're trumping my jurisdiction based solely on your legal right to drive a motor vehicle? Yep, he mentioned it, but maybe you can run me through it with particulars, including your names and the agency you work for."

"That won't be happening," said the man pleasantly. "The mayor should be e-mailing you—"

Beth's BlackBerry started buzzing.

"Right about now," said the man, smiling.

Beth checked her device. The mayor was polite and diplomatic but the message was clear. Back off now.

"Can I expect copies of reports?" she asked.

"No."

"Can I see the body?"

"Same answer," said the fellow.

"Will you tell me when and if you find the killer?"

"We'll expect you and your people to be gone in the next two minutes."

The men turned and left.

Beth looked at Lanier. "Do you hate them as much as I do, Steve?"

Lanier said, "Oh, even more than you do. Trust me."

"Care to give me their names? I'm assuming you remember them from the driver's licenses."

"Sorry, Beth, I got my marching orders too."

She stalked back to her car. At least she'd be having dinner with her sister tonight after all.

CHAPTER

27

AT THE SOUND of the knock Roy looked up from a contract he was reviewing.

"Yeah?"

The door opened and a young man dressed in corduroy pants, striped shirt, and a cheap paisley tie stood there holding on to the front bar of a mail cart. It was old-fashioned, but even in the digital age sometimes lawyers still needed materials that were actually contained in books or written on real paper.

"Special delivery," the young man said.

"Just put it on the desk, Dave."

Dave came forward clutching the book. "Creepy."

"What's creepy?'

"Ms. Tolliver."

Roy shrugged. "I doubt whoever killed her is going to come back."

"Not what I meant."

Dave put the book down on the desk.

Roy leaned back in his chair. "Okay, don't keep me in suspense."

Dave tapped the book. "This is from Ms. Tolliver."

Roy snatched up the book. "When did she put it in the mail room?"

"Don't know."

"Why don't you know? I thought there were procedures."

"Most of the time folks call and we come and pick up the package. They have a delivery sheet filled out and we put it in the pipeline."

"So why don't you know when this book came in?"

"It was just in the mail room with the sheet filled out. She must've done it herself. I checked with Ms. Tolliver's secretary and she didn't know anything about it."

"But she was killed Monday morning. It's now Tuesday afternoon and I'm just getting this?"

"We didn't deliver the mail yesterday because the police were all over the place. Just getting to it now. I'm sorry."

Roy examined the cover of the book. It was on contract law, an out-of-date edition. Lawyers never sent old textbooks to each other. What would be the point?

"Did you see it in the mail room on Friday?"

"Don't think so."

"But you're not sure?"

"No. I'm not."

"Okay, but did you see it in the mail room on Monday morning?"

"Can't really say. It was so crazy around here. But it had to be there on Monday morning. I mean, she couldn't have done it after she was dead."

"If she was the one who put the book in the mail room, Dave. We have no way of telling if she physically did it or not."

"Oh, right." Dave looked at him nervously. "Am I in trouble?"

Roy sat back, his sudden flame of anger gone. "Probably not. Thanks, Dave. Sorry I got testy. I guess we're all a little stressed out."

After Dave closed the door, Roy looked at the mail slip clipped to the book. It was in Diane's neat handwriting that he'd seen on many documents. The mail form had a date and time-of-day box to show when it had gone into the system; however, Diane had not filled in this information. The form did have his name on it as the recipient, so the book *was* meant for him. There was no reason for her to send it to him. But she had. He flipped through some pages, but it was just an old book.

His phone rang. "Yeah?" His mouth formed a smile when he heard the voice.

Mace said, "You must've billed nearly a hundred hours so far today."

"I told you this is a humane law firm. We don't have to lie by the hour."

"You got time to talk?"

"Sure, when?"

"How about now?"

His door opened and Mace waved to him. Roy shook his head and put down his phone. "Are you always this weird?"

"You haven't begun to see my weird side."

"That is truly terrifying."

"I know. I get that a lot."

28

Mace closed the door behind her and sat across from him. "Thanks for repping me last night with old Abe."

"Just wait until you get my bill." He held up the book. "Diane Tolliver sent this to me in the office mail."

"Okay?"

"Like very recently. But she had no reason to. It's an old textbook."

"Put it down. Now!"

He quickly set the book on his desk.

"Who else has pawed it, other than you?" she said severely.

"At least one other, the mail room guy."

"Great."

"He didn't know any better."

"But *you* should have known better."

"Okay, maybe I should have. But I didn't. So now what?"

"You got a hanky?"

"No, but I do have some tissues."

He handed some over. Mace used one to open the book slowly.

"I glanced through a couple of pages, didn't see any cryptic writing. But we could pour lemon juice on it and see if the invisible ink is revealed."

"Or we could just do this." She held the book by the spine and swung it back and forth, the pages flapping open.

A small key fell out and landed on the desk.

"Don't!" Mace cautioned as Roy reached for it.

Using the tissue, she picked up the key by its ridged end.

Mace said, "Not a safety deposit box key, maybe a post office box."

"That narrows it down to a few hundred million. And we don't even know if this key came from her."

"She ever mention a post office box?"

Roy shook his head. "No."

Mace stared down at the key with such intensity that it seemed that she expected the bit of metal to suddenly confess all its secrets. "And you had no other communication from her?"

Roy started to say no, but then he stopped. He clicked some keys and turned the screen around for her to see. "She sent me an e-mail late on Friday night."

"Do the police know about this?"

"Yep, because they already questioned me about it today. I told them I didn't know what it meant."

Mace read the line. "You sure nothing rings a bell?"

"No, but it's awkwardly phrased. 'Focus in on'? Why not just say 'focus on'?"

"I don't know. You're the guy that gets paid by the word. Any viable candidates for 'A'?"

"Too many. But I didn't think you were on the police force anymore."

"There's no law that says a private citizen can't investigate a crime."

"But—"

"Getting back to the key and e-mail, any thoughts?"

"Well, you can't hold me to anything."

"Just tell me, Roy."

"Chester Ackerman. He's the managing partner of the firm. I spoke with him yesterday. He was really nervous, upset."

"One of his lawyers got stuck in the fridge, there's a lot to be upset about."

"I know, but, and this is just my gut, he seemed scared beyond what the situation would compel, if you know what I mean."

"Like he was scared for his own skin?"

"And I think he was lying about something too."

"What?"

"I don't know. Just something."

"What do you know about him?"

"He's from Chicago. Has a family. Brings in tons of business."

"Okay, so basically you're telling me you know nothing?"

"I've never had a reason to dig much deeper on the guy."

"So maybe now you do have a reason."

"You want me to spy on the managing partner?" he said incredulously.

"And anybody else who seems productive."

"For what is most likely a random killing?"

"Your partner got stuffed in a fridge. Who's to say it doesn't have something to do with this place?"

Roy picked up his rubber ball, and shot at the basket. And missed.

"Mechanics are off. Murder closeup sometimes does that." She perched on the edge of his desk and used the tissue to go through the book page by page. "No mob players on the old client list by chance?"

He shook his head. "We don't do criminal work here. Just deals."

"Business clients get into legal trouble all the time."

"Like I told you before, if it's litigation, we farm it out."

"To what firm?"

"Several, on an approved list."

"We're not making much progress here."

"No, we're not," Roy agreed.

"How much do you make?"

His eyes widened slightly. "Why do you keep asking me that?"

"Because you haven't given me an answer. Don't look all pissed. It's a legit question."

"Okay, more than Altman is paying you."

"How much more?"

"With bonus and profit-share and bennies, nearly double."

"An entry-level cop on MPD pulls less than fifty thou a year."

"I never said life was fair. But just so you know, as a CJA I never made close to fifty a year." He studied her. "So why did you want to know how much I make?"

"Your firm clearly has money, so that's a motive to kill."

"Okay. Maybe I can look into some stuff and get back to you. What are you doing tonight?"

"Dinner with big sis. But I'm free after that."

"What, you never sleep?"

"Not for the last two years."

She pocketed the key still wrapped in tissue.

Roy looked nervously at her. "I don't want a withholding evidence charge leveled against me."

"And I want to find out what the hell is going on around here. I'm like addicted to things that seem to make no sense."

"But you're not a cop anymore, Mace."

"So everybody keeps reminding me," she said, as she left his office.

29

Mace sat on her bike with material evidence from a homicide investigation ripping a black hole in her jacket pocket. She had just committed a felony in a city where her sister was the top enforcer of the law.

"You are an idiot," she muttered as the Ducati idled at a stoplight. "A moron. A reckless piece of crap that never knows when to say, 'No, don't do that!'" She'd promised her sister she would not do exactly what she was doing. Meddling in the case.

But something had happened to her in prison that not even Beth knew about. She'd read an old news article about an FBI agent who'd been convicted of witness tampering, aiding a mob boss, and helping to transport weapons across state lines. He had protested his innocence the entire time, claiming he'd been framed but to no avail. He was tried, convicted, and served his full sentence. On getting out he'd moved to another state, secretly gone undercover, and infiltrated a violent drug ring. He'd collected a mountain of evidence at great personal risk and turned it all over to the Bureau, who'd made the bust. He'd even gone on the stand to testify against the ringleaders. The media had picked up the story and run with it and the public outcry had been immense.

The thinking was, why would a guilty man have done something like that? He must've been innocent. There had been a clear miscarriage of justice. The public pressure filtered to the politicians on Capitol Hill, resulting in the Bureau going against its own rules and reinstating the agent despite his being a convicted felon. The man had gone on to head up an FBI office in the Midwest and his career had been full of accolades and achievements.

The agent's name was Frank Kelly and a desperate Mace had written to him from prison and explained her situation. Kelly had actually come to West Virginia to see her. He was a big, solid fellow with a no-nonsense attitude. He'd read up on her case and told her he believed her to be innocent. But while commiserating with her situation he'd been blunt. "You're never going to get your record clean. Too many obstacles and crap in the way. Even if you do find out some stuff, proving it to the level necessary will be pretty much impossible. There will always be people aligned against you, people who don't want to believe you. But what you can do is get back in the saddle when you get out. You go out on your dime and nerve, no cop shop backing you up, and lay your ass on the line like I did. Then you have a shot at being able to clean your record de facto, in the court of public opinion. There are no guarantees," Kelly had added. "And I have to tell you I got real lucky. But at least this way you can control your own destiny a little. You at least have a shot. Otherwise, you'll never be a cop again."

"That's all I ever asked for," Mace had told him. "A shot."

He'd shaken her hand and wished her luck.

That's all I want, a shot to be a true blue again.

There were those on the police force who believed that because she was Beth Perry's sister Mace received preferential treatment, when actually the reverse was true. Beth had gone out of her way not to show favoritism and had actually driven Mace harder than anyone else under her. Mace had earned every promotion, every commendation, and every scar, including those hidden and those in plain sight. She'd graduated from the Metropolitan Police Academy with some demerits but a far greater number of superlatives. Instructors who'd handed out these black marks also thought she was, hands down, the best police recruit to join the capital city's thin blue line since, well, since her sister had graduated at the top of her class years earlier.

In record time she'd gone from rookie beat cop to sergeant, and then made the leap to CID, or the Criminal Investigations Division where she'd been assigned to the Homicide and Sex Offenses Branch. She'd cut her teeth on stacks of gruesome murders, sex assaults, and cases so cold the files had turned blue along with the bodies. She'd made up procedures on her own, and while she'd sometimes been dressed down for doing so, many of these same methods were now part of the investigative techniques curriculum taught at the police academy.

During her career she'd made friends because she was loyal and had never rolled on any of them even if they deserved it. And she'd made enemies that she would keep until the day she or they croaked. But Mace had also made enemies who could be convinced that they owed her. That was why she was here.

Mace parked her Ducati in front of the shop with the fancy red awning over the top of which was the name of the establishment: Citizen Soldier, Ltd.

Cute.

She tugged open the door and walked in.

Shelves lined the walls and were filled with pretty much every conceivable personal defense item on the market. Behind barred wall cabinets were shotguns, rifles, and assault weapons just waiting for itchy trigger fingers to set them free. Inside belly-button-high locked display consoles were a wide variety of auto and semi-auto pistols and old-fashioned wheel guns.

"Hey, Binder," she called out to the man in the back near the cash register. "Still selling whack jobs SBRs built from reconfigured AR-15 pistols without getting ATF approval and paying the appropriate taxes?"

Binder wore cammie pants and a tight-fitting black muscle shirt that showed off his buffed pecs, delts, and biceps. Military boots were on his feet. They were worn down and looked like the real deal. That's because they were, she knew. He'd pulled years in the uniform of Uncle Sam but also had some stockade time and a dishonorable discharge because of a little drug dealing on the side that had nearly cost two fresh-from-boot-camp grunts their lives from injecting ill-cooked crystal meth. He wore his hair in a big throwback afro that reminded her of a young Michael Jackson. This was quite remarkable-looking since the man was white, had nearly pupil-size freckles all over his face, and his hair was flame red except where it was edged with gray at the roots.

"*Send in the clowns*," she sang under her breath.

Binder wheeled around. A Garrett handheld scanner was in one hammy fist and a tactical folding knife in the other.

"Wow, you look really happy to see me," she said.

"When the hell did you get out?" This came out more like a hurled piece of spit than a question formed with words.

"I didn't. I escaped. You want to turn me in for the reward?"

He put the tact knife on a shelf containing a pile of other blades, all with price tags attached. "I'm busy," he grunted. "I know you ain't a cop anymore more, so harassment time is over."

Instead of leaving, she dug into the pile of blades on the shelf and picked up a knife that had twin wooden handles. With a flick of her wrist she flipped free the six-inch razor-edged shaft. "Whoa, a channel-constructed handmade Filipino Balisong with an IK Bearing System. Very cool. But unfortunately their importation into the U.S. was banned in the eighties."

Binder didn't look impressed by this information. "Is that right?"

"And the Balisong can technically be considered a gravity or butterfly knife or a switchblade. They're illegal in D.C. and Maryland and you can't sell 'em in Virginia."

"Somebody forgot to send me the memo. I'll talk to my lawyer."

"Good, while you're doing that I'll call the Five D commander and let him run a second set of eyeballs over your inventory list. If you want to dress in drag I can recommend a very nice facility in West Virginia for the next few years." She eyed his bushy redtop. "And the really good news is you won't even have to get a haircut."

Binder leaned down into her face. "What the hell do you want, woman!"

"Some equipment. And I'll pay, just not full price because I'm poor and cheap."

She held up the Balisong and with a flick closed the blade. "And next time, Bin, hide the plainly illegal shit in the back. I mean, at least make the CID guys work for it. Otherwise they'll get rusty."

"What kind of equipment?"

"My wish list starts with a UV blue-light lamp, fluorescent dye, and contrasting spectacles. FYI, pulling out the cheap made-in-China crap will not make me happy. I got enough lead in my system from eating prison food."

"I've got a nice kit for three hundred plus tax," he mumbled.

"Great, I'll give you fifty for it."

His broad face swelled with anger, making his freckles look like giant amoebas. "That's a ripoff. You know what my damn rent is here?"

"You won't have any rent in prison. But I do know the Aryan Nation scuzzballs *are* partial to redheads."

Binder deflated as quickly as he'd inflated. "What else?" he said sullenly.

"Well, let's have a look-see at all the goodies," she said sweetly.

After she'd finished, she loaded her purchases in a large backpack she'd made Binder throw in for free. A belt with an extra feature loaded in the clasp that she'd purchased from him had already been slipped around her waist and tightened down. She'd paid and was heading to the door when he called out, "Twenty bucks says you're back in prison in six months."

She whipped around. "And I've got fifty that says any illegal shit left in this place gets confiscated in forty-eight hours by MPD's finest."

Binder slammed his fist against the counter. "I thought we had a deal!"

"I don't remember anything about a deal. I just mentioned *switchblades* and you gave me a really nice discount. I thought it was like a code word for preferred customers."

"You . . . are . . . a . . . *bitch*!"

"Took you all these years to figure that out, scumball?"

He eyed the backpack. "What the hell are you going to do with all that stuff?"

"I'm not sitting on the sidelines, Bin."

"What's that supposed to mean?"

"Two years in hell, and the blue ripped right out of my heart, that's what that means."

30

Roy closed the door softly behind him. Playing snoop while homicide detectives were still on the premises was not the smartest career move he'd ever made. Yet there was something about Mace Perry that just made him not want to disappoint the woman. Maybe it was the fact that she could probably kick his ass anytime she wanted.

Chester Ackerman's office looked as though the man never did a lick of work, and without billable hours to be counted up, there was no way to tell if he did or not. Still, he brought in more business than any partner in the firm and in the legal world that was the big stick. It was also principally why he was managing partner. As quickly and as efficiently as he could, Roy opened file and desk drawers, checked the pockets of the man's suit coat that hung on the back of the door, and tried but failed to access his computer records.

He heard footsteps coming and started to panic before those sounds eased away down the hall. He listened at the door and slipped out. He bypassed his office and headed to the mail room. He talked to Dave again, gained no useful information, and next questioned the other mail room guy, who was similarly clueless. He waited until both men headed out with items for delivery before searching through the mail room but finding nothing.

The space had one odd feature, a large dumbwaiter that had been built especially for the mailroom. Shilling & Murdoch also had office space on the fifth floor, and this motorized dumbwaiter ran directly into a storage room set up there for the firm's archives. It was more convenient to keep the materials on-site for ready access. And it was far more efficient to send heavy boxes down a straight shaft than cart them through the office and then down the elevators.

As he stood there a weird thought occurred to him.

He rode the elevator to the fourth floor. When the doors opened the sounds of nail drivers and power saws hit him right in the eardrums. He stepped off and was immediately met by a wiry guy with Popeye forearms covered in colorful tattoos and wearing a yellow hard hat.

"Can I help you, buddy?"

"I work at the law firm on the sixth floor."

"Congratulations, but you can't be here."

"I'm also on the building's oversight committee. We've been notified that there have been some thefts of property from your work site and I was asked by the committee chairman to come down to get further details. It has to do with our property and casualty insurance reporting requirements and also our D&O rider, you understand?"

It was as though the minute he'd passed the bar Roy's ability to bullshit on demand had clicked to a whole new level. Or maybe that was *why* he'd gone to law school in the first place.

It was painfully clear from the expression on Hard Hat's face that he hadn't comprehended one syllable Roy had uttered.

"So what does that mean?"

Roy said patiently, "It means I have to look around and report back and maybe your company will get some money from our overlap insurance coverage to help cover some of the losses."

The man tossed a hard hat to Roy. "Works for me, I'm just the carpenter. Only watch your step, dude. Lawyers fall down and get a boo-boo, I don't even want to think about what that would cost."

Roy slipped on the hat and started walking around the space. One of the passenger elevators had been fitted with pads so the construction crew could bring its materials in because the building didn't have a dedicated freight elevator.

Roy didn't know how many of the construction crew had been given key cards. He found the carpenter and asked this question. The guy was driving screws into a metal wall stud.

"Crew chief has one. He lets me in if I get here before the building opens. Most guys report at eight-thirty, so they can just walk right in."

"When does everyone leave?"

"Right at five-thirty. Work rules."

"No overtime? Weekends?"

"Not for me. I don't want it. I like my downtime. Have to ask the crew chief if anybody else works off the clock."

"Where is he?"

"Long lunch." The man put down his power screwdriver and tipped his hard hat back. "See, that's what I want to be when I grow up. A crew chief."

Roy continued to walk around the space. He heard a machine whirring and was surprised to see the building's day porter. He was standing in front of a microwave set up in a little cubby off the main work area where there was also a fridge.

"Hey, Dan, what are you doing here?"

Dan, a slender man with silver hair and a matching mustache, was dressed in a neat blue work uniform. "Missed lunch. Just warming up some soup, Roy."

"You come up here often?"

The microwave dinged and Dan took the bowl out and started spooning tomato soup into his mouth. "They're paying me a little on the side to keep the place tidy."

"Who? The crew chief?"

"Yep. Worked for him before on a job a couple years ago before I got this gig. He remembered me. Few extra dollars don't hurt. I mean, I get all my work done for the building first, Roy," he added quickly.

"I've got no problems with that. But I hear they've been having some problems?"

Dan nodded. "Stuff missing. Some wrenches and some food. I told the crew chief not to keep food up here, but the guys don't listen. They cram their munchies all over the place. And stuff in the fridge there."

"They ever think of hiring a security guard?"

"Too much money for this small a job. I come up here in the

evenings to clean up, but I'm always gone by seven. Never seen or heard anything."

"They work weekends?"

"No, client won't pay the overtime. Monday to Friday, according to my buddy."

"Any theories on who might be stealing?"

"Not a clue. But I doubt it's anybody from your place, unless you got some folks who'll risk their six-figure careers over a package of Oreos and cans of Pepsi."

Roy left the fourth floor and went back to his office. He had spent nearly an hour learning absolutely nothing. He hoped Mace was having better luck with the key.

CHAPTER

31

Performing this particular test at Beth's house was out of the question even for a risk-taker like Mace. So here she was in the ladies' room at a Subway restaurant.

She'd brought in her backpack, locked the door, put on latex gloves, sprinkled the dye on the key, put on her contrasting spectacles, and turned off the light. She powered up her handheld blue-light wand, and her fifty bucks paid to old Binder scored an immediate dividend.

"Friction ridges, come to Momma," she said softly. There *were* fingerprints on the key. She hit the surface with a magnification lens she had also pried from Binder's cold fingers. During her career Mace had looked at enough inked islands, dots, ending ridges, and other fingerprint ID points to be considered an expert. This print was good and clean with minutiae including a hook, a ridge crossing, and even a trifurcation. The other side of the key wasn't quite as good, but there was still plenty enough for a match.

Thumb and index she assumed, since those were the fingers one normally used to hold a key. She was thinking that the prints probably belonged to Diane Tolliver. How that advanced the investigation she wasn't sure, but at least it would show whether the dead woman had held it. She was surprised that the prints hadn't been wiped away by the key being pressed between the pages of the book, but sometimes the good guys got lucky.

Now she had one more favor to call in before she was done with this piece of evidence. Thirty minutes after visiting this last stop and getting some free service from yet another old "friend," she headed back to Roy's office after placing the key in a plastic baggie to protect the prints. She left the key with Roy and instructed him to turn it over to the police with the explanation of how he'd gotten it. As she was walking across the lobby to leave the building she noticed Ned staring at her. Mace changed direction and headed toward him.

"You're Ned, right?"

"That's right. I saw you and Roy Kingman ride off on your motorcycle yesterday."

"What an eagle eye you have. I bet you see everything that goes on around here."

His chest puffed up. "Not much that I miss. That's why I do what I do."

"Security, you mean?"

"That's right. Thinking about joining the police force, though. Kicking bad guys' asses. You know."

Mace ran her gaze over Ned's fat frame, perhaps a little too obviously because he hastily added, "Gotta drop a few pounds before I do, but it doesn't take me too long to get back in shape. I played ball in school."

"Really, what college?"

"I meant high school," Ned mumbled.

"Good for you."

"Hey, weren't you in here with the cops yesterday?"

"Yes, I was." Before he could ask whether she actually was a cop she said, "So do you have a theory on what happened?"

He nodded, leaned toward her, and said in a hushed tone, "Serial killer."

"Really? But wouldn't that involve more than one murder?"

"Hey, even Hannibal Lecter had to start somewhere."

"He was a fictional character. You know that, right?"

Ned nodded a little uncertainly. "Cool movie."

"So why a serial killer?"

"His M.O.," Ned said confidently.

"M.O.?"

"Modus operandi."

"Yeah, I know what the term means. I was referring to how you were using it in this situation."

"Stuffed his victims in a fridge, right? That's pretty original shit. I bet any day now we're gonna be reading about folks crammed in freezers, or meat lockers, or you know, like . . . um . . ."

"Other cold places?"

"Yeah."

"Maybe small people in under-the-counter fridges."

Ned laughed. "Like Popsicle Mini-Me's. Hey, maybe he'll call himself the Stone Cold Killer. Get it?"

"Yeah, that's real clever."

He leaned over the counter and assumed what he no doubt considered was an ultra-cool expression. "Hey, you ever go out for a drink?"

"Oh, lots of times. I'm one party girl."

"Well, maybe sometime we should do it together, party girl."

"Maybe we should."

He pointed a finger at her and pulled an imaginary trigger with his thumb and made a clicking sound with his mouth. At the same time he winked.

These were the moments when Mace so desperately missed her Glock 37 that chambered .45 G.A.P. "one-shot-and-you-drop" cartridges. The standard issue for MPD was the Glock 17 nine-millimeter, and undercover officers usually got the Glock 26 nine-millimeter, which regular officers routinely carried as their off-duty weapon of choice. Mace had dutifully carried the 17 as a cop, but her off-duty and undercover sidearm had been the 37, a gun she wasn't supposed to have. But she had never been that great at following rules, and the 37's superior .45 stopping power had saved her life on two occasions. Now, of course, she could carry no gun at all.

"Hey, Ned, piece of advice, when pointing even a pretend gun at someone, be prepared to duck or you might end up taking a double tap right here." She twice poked a spot dead center of his forehead.

He looked confused. "Huh?"

She merely winked and started to walk away.

"Hey, babe, I don't even know your name."

She turned back. "Mace."

"Mace?"

"Yeah, like the fire-hot spray in the eyes."

"You got my interest, babe."

"I knew I would."

CHAPTER

32

THE PLACE Beth had chosen for dinner was Café Milano, one of D.C.'s most chic restaurants, where folks loved to go see and be seen, in a Hollywood-esque sort of way. It had a wall of windows looking out onto a quiet street, although tonight there was a string of Carey cars and black government SUVs parked up and down its narrow confines.

The bar emptied out into the dining area so it was a little noisy, but Beth's high-ranking position garnered her a table in what was probably the quietest corner in the place. She had changed out of her uniform and was dressed in a knee-length skirt and a white blouse open at the neck, her blond hair splayed over her shoulders. Her work shoes had been replaced with black heels. The bulk of her security detail waited outside, although two armed plainclothes were at the bar enjoying multiple glasses of ginger ale.

Mace roared up in her Ducati, shook off her helmet, and slipped inside, dodging past a party of suited men and their rental dates, all of whom would have failed a breathalyzer test in any state in the country. Her cop's eyes watched them until they climbed into a white stretch Hummer driven by a sober driver in a black suit.

Mace scanned the room and saw her sister waving. She sat down and slid her bike helmet under the table. The tablecloth was white and starched, the aromas wafting from the kitchen pleasing, the crowd an interesting mix of young, middle-aged, and old, variously dressed in suits, jeans, sneakers, and spike heels.

"You clean up nice, sis," she said.

Beth smiled and gazed at Mace's clothes. Black slacks, low-cut gray clingy sweater, and high strap heels. "Did you do some shopping today?"

"Yep. Like you said, I've lost some weight."

"How were the stilettos on the Ducati's gear shifter?"

"No problem. I just skipped over the even ones."

The waiter came over and Beth ordered them two glasses of wine. After he left she said, "Since you're paying, and driving, let's go easy on the vino. And the list here can get pretty expensive."

"Sounds good. I guess you're not packing tonight."

"Not while drinking alcohol; that's still department policy."

"Is your off-duty carry still the .40 caliber or the Glock 26?"

"Twenty-six, same one I carry on duty."

"Must be nice."

"Nothing nice about having to carry a gun, Mace. It's a necessity in our line of work."

"In *your* line of work."

"Well, tonight, we're both out of bullets."

When the wine came they clinked glasses and Beth said, "Here's to many more decades of the Perry sisters hanging together."

Mace had regained her good humor. "Now that's something I can drink to."

Beth stared over her wineglass. "So your buddy Kingman found a key in a book that Tolliver sent him."

Mace munched on a hard olive roll and tried to look surprised. "Really? Key to what?"

"We don't know."

"Prints?"

"Yes."

"Tolliver's?"

"Yes again, how'd you know?"

"Assumed if she sent it, she had to touch it."

"Why did you go and see that sleazeball Binder today?"

Mace took a long slurp of wine before setting her glass down. "Are you having me followed, Beth?"

"I would not call it followed, no."

"Then what the hell would you call it?"

"I'm having you hovered."

"*Hovered*? Has the world changed so much in two years that I'm supposed to know what that means?"

"Beth!"

They both turned to see the mayor standing there, his entourage columned behind him. He was young and good-looking and had by most accounts done a good job for the city. Yet he was a cagey politician, meaning that the person he looked out for the most stared back at him in the mirror every morning.

"Hello, Mayor, you remember my sister?"

They shook hands. He leaned down and said in a low voice, "Good to see you. Let me know if I can be of any assistance. Right. Take care. Stay out of trouble."

This came out in such a blur of polished speech that Mace doubted the man had stopped for a breath or even heard what he'd actually said.

He stood straight. "Having a girls' night out, are we?"

"I guess we are," said Beth.

"Excellent. How we doing on the Tolliver case?"

"You getting calls?"

"I always get calls, I've just learned the ones to pay attention to."

"And these are such calls?"

"Just keep me in the loop."

"We're making progress. The minute I know more, so will you."

"Good, good."

"About that other case?"

"Right. Sorry about that. Above my pay grade." He turned and was gone as quickly as he'd appeared. His staff shuffled off behind their leader, each with a cell phone out, talking, no doubt, to suitably important people.

"That guy will be in office for life," said Mace.

"Long after I'm gone," replied Beth.

"So, getting back to *hover*."

Beth playfully crossed her eyes. "I thought this was a celebration."

"Fine, but I'm going to need another glass of wine. To celebrate being hovered."

"No, one is enough. And you're going to have plenty to eat and get some fresh air before you ride off on that bike."

"And here I was thinking Mom lived all the way out past Middleburg."

"Mace, please."

"I'm not going to embarrass you further."

"That's not what I meant. A DUI gets you sent back."

"Then let's order before I get totally wasted and you have to perform a field sobriety test right here on the table."

The food was excellent, the service attentive, the people coming up to greet the chief only a dozen or so in number and polite for the most part, except when they were either complaining or groveling.

"You're popular," remarked Mace. "Just think if you were in uniform."

"Maybe I'm too popular."

"What?"

"Don't look now, but here comes our favorite DA."

"Ah, hell, and I've only had one glass of wine and not a single controlled substance all day."

They both turned to watch Mona Danforth marching toward them.

33

The lady was wearing a dress that looked like it cost more than Mace's Ducati. The makeup and hair were perfect, the jewelry tasteful but heavyweight enough to still retain the "wow" factor. The only thing marring the package was the woman's expression. For a beautiful woman Mona Danforth could look very ugly.

"Hello, Mona," said Beth pleasantly.

Mona snagged another chair from an adjacent table, unmindful of whether anyone was actually using it or not, and sat down. "We need to talk."

The statement was directed at Beth, but Mace answered first. "Really, Moan, you've learned to actually do that? Congratulations."

Mona didn't even bother to look at her. "This doesn't concern you."

Mace started to shoot something back, but Beth nudged her leg under the table. "I'm assuming this has something to do with Jamie Meldon's death?"

"Why else would I be sitting here?"

"You know, Mona, we are on the same team here. Police, prosecutor? Do you sense a pattern?"

"I heard you got bumped from the case."

"Didn't even have time to step on any shell casings. Go talk to the mayor. You just missed him. Or the CIA, I'm sure Langley would love to fill you in."

Mace, not knowing what they were talking about, merely hunkered down and listened attentively as she would at any contest where one of the players has the potential to go home all bloody.

"One of my people was murdered in *your* jurisdiction. And you're not going to do anything about it?"

"I didn't say I wasn't going to do anything. But while we're on the subject, what exactly do you want me to do?"

Mona looked incredulous. "You're asking me how to do your job?"

"I know you've just been dying to tell me all these years. So here's your chance. Fire away." Beth sat back and looked expectant.

"This is unbelievable. I'm not a cop."

"But you are the interim chief of the largest federal prosecutor's office in the country outside of DOJ. So if you don't have a suggestion on how to do my job, let me give you some help on how to do *yours*."

"Excuse me?" snapped Mona.

"You're pissed that the case was snagged from MPD? In any event, since Jamie was technically a federal employee his murder falls under the jurisdiction of the FBI. Normally we would support that effort, but for some reason we got a muzzle thrown on us. So here's what you can do. Go talk to your high-up contacts at Justice and find out why we were pulled from the case. Do the same at the legal counsel's office at the Bureau. From there it's a short hop to the intelligence community. It was intimated to me that it was the CIA who yanked the cord, but I don't believe everything I'm told. Maybe it was DHS. You know folks over there. In fact a photo of you and the DHS director was in the Style section of the *Post* just last week. Your dress and cleavage were stunning and his drool was unmistakable. I'm sure his wife really enjoyed seeing that. And when you have everything in a nice box with a big red bow, you bring it all to me and I'll run with it. How's that sound?"

"It sounds like I'm wasting my time."

"Do you want to find out who killed Meldon?"

"Don't be condescending!"

"Then work your contacts. And I'll work mine and maybe we'll meet in the middle. But keep in mind that you may run into a wall at some point. Or you may tick somebody off. And your career might take a hit."

Mona stood. "I'm not listening to any more of this garbage."

Beth continued unperturbed. "Your career might take a hit," she repeated firmly. "But I know that in the interest of bringing Jamie's killer to justice you wouldn't have any compunction about professional sacrifice, right?"

"Don't make an enemy of me over this, Beth."

"By the way, how's Jamie's family doing?"

"What?"

"His wife and kids? I visited them earlier today, to express my condolences and to see if they needed anything. I'm assuming you did that too, wonderful, compassionate leader that you are."

With what could only be termed a snarl, Mona stalked off.

Mace leaned across the table and gave her sister a kiss on the forehead. "I bow before your powers of transforming mere words into machine-gun rounds."

"It didn't really get me anywhere."

"But it was so fun to watch. So what's this about a dead DA?"

Beth filled her in on Meldon's homicide.

"So you don't know anything other than his body was in a Dumpster?"

"A bit more than that. Like I said, I talked to his wife. He'd been working late Sunday night. She was surprised when he wasn't home on Monday morning, but not overly concerned since he slept at the office sometimes. When she didn't hear from him by late morning she called the police. His body was finally found this afternoon."

"And the CIA is involved?"

"Actually, that's not substantiated yet. I was actually told that the pushback directive came from the White House."

"The White House! But you didn't tell Cruella de Vil that."

She smiled. "No, I didn't."

Beth finished her second glass of wine. "Would you like another round?"

"And risk a DUI and being sent to the big house?" Mace said with mock terror.

"You can ride with me. I'll have them load your bike in a pickup truck and bring it to the house."

"You mind if I take a rain check on that offer?"

"Plans later?"

"Maybe."

"Would those plans be Roy Kingman?"

"And is that a problem?"

"I already stated my opinion on that subject."

"I know." Mace rose from the table. "I paid the bill. I did it when I went to the ladies' room."

"You really didn't have to do that, Mace." Beth paused and added, "But it was very sweet."

"Hey, we need to do this more often. But maybe we can aim for fast food next time. Easier on the wallet. Prices have really gone up over the last two years."

Mace turned to leave, but Beth reached over and placed an iron grip on her sister's arm, pulling Mace abruptly back into her seat. In a low voice that still managed to conjure images of razor wire, Beth said, "The next time you remove evidence from a crime scene, I will personally pistol-whip you before I arrest you for obstruction, are we clear on that?" There was not a trace of mirth in the woman's eyes. This was Chief Elizabeth Perry talking now, not sweet sister Beth.

Mace just gaped at her, unable to form a response.

"My techs found minute traces of fluorescent dye on the key. I heard old Binder was running a special on his blue-light print kit this week. I think I might pay him a personal visit tomorrow and shut him down."

"Beth—"

"You went over the line. After I told you not to. I told you to let me handle it. Maybe you don't think I'm good enough to get this done."

"It wasn't that."

Beth squeezed her sister's arm. "You get arrested for interfering in a police investigation, you're going back to prison for a lot longer than two years. And then there will be no way you'll ever be a cop again. I don't care if the president of the United States has your back. Is that what you want?"

"No, of course not. But—"

"Then quit screwing up!" Beth leaned away from her and let go of the arm. "Now get out of here." As soon as Mace stood, Beth added, "Oh, and tell Kingman I said hello."

Mace nearly ran out the door.

34

DRINKS ON the rooftop lounge of the Hotel Washington," said Mace as she and Roy sat at a table overlooking what was one of the nicest views of D.C.

"It's actually called the W Washington now," he said, as he freed three olives from a toothpick and dropped them one by one into his mouth and chewed slowly.

She pointed straight ahead. "Look, you can just make out the countersnipers on top of the White House." She looked at the street. "And there goes a cruiser on a call. Probably a lousy D&D at a bar."

"Could be a shooting."

"Gunshots get a minimum of two patrol units responding. We'd be hearing a lot more sirens. Probably burglar alarm D.C."

"Burglar alarm D.C.?"

"Burglar alarms go off, you respond, and you find out it's a malfunction. That's the principal action around here in 'safe' D.C. You want bullet banging or PCP zombie sprints, head to Sixth or Seventh district. They put on a great show there."

"You're a walking encyclopedia of local crime minutiae."

"That's *all* I am anymore," Mace said resignedly.

"Problems?"

"No, Roy, my life is five-star all the way."

"That didn't come out right."

"It never does with guys." She stood, leaned over the half-wall, and pointed to her left. "Right over there was the first bust I ever made on my own around here. I'd just been certified to ride alone.

Spotted a guy in a suit buying a bag of rock from a punk hucka-buck. Turns out he was a congressman high up on some anti-drug committee. What a shocker, right?"

As she turned back around, Roy quickly shifted his gaze away from her derriere. There was a tattoo of a cross partly visible where her sweater had ridden up, with the lower half of the cross well down on one butt cheek.

The tattoo artist must've had fun doing that one, thought Roy.

She sipped on her beer and munched some nuts. "So do you want to comment on my butt since you were staring at it for so long?"

Bumps of red appeared on each of Roy's cheeks. "Actually it left me pretty speechless."

"There was a prison guard who was really partial to it too."

He flicked a gaze at her. "Did he ever do anything to you?"

"Let's just say he kept his pants on and leave it at that."

"So you got a tattoo of a cross?"

"Don't all good Catholic girls have a cross on their backsides?"

"I don't know. I've never dated a Catholic girl. My loss, I guess."

"Yes, it is."

"You know, I thought about joining the police academy after college."

"Drive fast and shoot guns?"

He grinned. "How'd you know?"

"Way it is with most guys. There were forty-one recruits in my class. Sixteen-week course. Half washed out before the end. Ex-athletes with beer bellies couldn't even do a push-up. Academy was okay. Learned the phone book, spit and polish, a few training scenarios, but not much about actually being a cop."

"Phone book?"

"Policies and procedures, general orders. Paperwork basically. Plus physical training. Near the end they put me on a Christmas detail in Georgetown by myself with no gun and no orders."

"What'd you do?"

"Wandered around, wrote some parking tickets, and smoked some cigarettes."

"Law school was boring too."

"I started out on the north end of Georgia Avenue. They called it the Gold Coast, because it was relatively safe."

"And?"

"And I hated it. Didn't put on the shield and gun to be safe. I wanted to get into Crime Patrol. They hit the whole city, not some lousy five-block radius. They went after the good stuff."

"Not drug dealers then?"

"Lock up druggies you're just padding crime stats. CP went after the burglars, the armed robbers, the murderers, and the drug dealers turned exterminators. That was where the action was." She paused. "Now I'm on probation and working for a college professor. And I can't even dream about holding my Glock 37 again without heading back to lockup. Whoop-de-do."

"I know we don't know each other that well, but if you ever want to talk about things, Mace, I'm here."

"I'm more of a forward thinker." She stood. "Ladies' room," she said. "Be back in a minute."

After doing her business Mace came out of the stall, went to the sink, and splashed water on her face. As she stared in the mirror Beth's words came at her like hollow-points.

Quit screwing up. Trust me.

Mace didn't want to screw up. She *did* trust her sister. She sure as hell didn't want to go back to prison. Agent Kelly's words also came back to her, though.

She groaned. This was a total mental conflict. Her head felt ready to explode from the pressure.

At least you'll have a shot.

She splashed more water on her face and looked at herself in the mirror again.

"Scrub as hard as you want, the scum won't come off."

Mace whirled around to see Mona Danforth standing by the door.

35

Are you following me?" Mace snapped at D.C.'s chief prosecutor.

In response, Mona locked the door to the ladies' room.

"If you don't open that door I will use your head to crack it open."

"Threatening an officer of the court?"

"Engaging in unlawful detainment?" Mace shot back.

"Just thought I'd do you a little favor."

"Great. You can slit your wrists in the stall over there. I'll call the EMTs once you've fully bled out."

"I know all about Beth's little plan."

"Really? What little plan might that be?"

Mona snapped open her tiny purse, sauntered over to the mirror, and reapplied her makeup and lipstick while she spoke. Mace so wanted to stuff her in a toilet, blond hair first.

"Why, getting you reinstated, of course. You were set up, drugged up, forced to commit all those crimes, blah blah blah. Poor little Mace. The same crap the jury refused to believe." Mona closed her purse, turned and leaned her butt against the sink counter. "So Beth is sending her best detectives to work on the case in the hopes that some miracle will occur that will prove your innocence."

"I *am* innocent."

"Oh, please. Save it for someone who cares. But it won't work because I'm way ahead of her. In fact, I'm so far ahead of her that I don't mind telling you all about it. Then you can go running to Beth and tell her like you always do when you're in trouble."

Mace tried her best to keep her voice calm. "Tell her what exactly?"

Mona eyed her with clear contempt. "There are six people who would need to sign off on your reinstatement even if Beth finds some evidence of your innocence."

"And if she does I would assume these people would sign."

"It's not that simple. Slam-dunk evidence is never going to happen. If she finds an eyewitness I'll convince them the testimony was coerced by an overzealous police chief who will stop at nothing to see her beloved little sister exonerated. And anything else she brings to the table I'll show it was tainted or even fabricated for the exact same reason. And since I'm not a believer in letting the other side hit first, I've already spoken with all of the necessary signatories, including the dear mayor, who had me over for dinner last week, and laid the groundwork for the overwhelming validity of my argument."

"They'll never believe Beth would invent evidence. That's *your* M.O., not hers."

Mona flushed for an instant at this jab but then regained her composure. "They've come to understand, after much coaching by me, that the usually rock-solid Beth Perry is incapable of thinking clearly when it comes to *you*. She will do anything, even break the law, to help you, though you don't deserve it. I have to admit, Beth has some talent. You, on the other hand, are worthless."

"I'm done listening to this crap." Mace started to move past Mona. The attorney made the mistake of putting a hand on Mace's shoulder to stop her. The next second, Mona's arm was twisted behind her back and Mace had pulled the woman right out of her three-inch heels and pushed her face first against the tiled wall of the restroom, the DA's lipstick smearing it.

"Don't ever lay a hand on me again, Mona."

"Let go of me, you bitch," shrieked Mona as she struggled to free herself, but Mace was far stronger. With one more twist of the arm Mace let her go and headed to the door. A furious Mona straightened her dress and bent down to put her heels back on. "I can have you arrested for assault. You'd go back to prison, where you belong."

"Go ahead and try. Your word against mine. And then the public can get into the debate of why you followed me into the ladies' room and locked the door. Hell, *I* was the one in prison, Mona, don't tell me you're liking the girls now."

"Actually, I prefer to let things just play out. It'll be more fun."

Mace stopped with her hand on the doorknob. "What's that supposed to mean?"

"I can bag two Perrys for the price of one. Beth tries to get you reinstated. I show she crossed the line. She gets dumped from her job and you never wear the uniform again. It's the Christmas that keeps on giving."

Mace slammed the door behind her.

CHAPTER

36

When Mace returned to the table Roy obviously sensed something was wrong. "You okay?"

"Yeah, there was just something really disgusting in the ladies' room."

As she finished her Coke in one gulp Roy said, "The cops came and got the key."

"Yeah, I know. Messed up there."

"I did?"

"No, *I* did. I forgot how smart my sister is."

"She knew you'd taken the key?"

Mace nodded. "And if it happens again my butt will be right back in prison."

"Your sister is not going to arrest you."

"You don't know Beth then."

"Mace—"

"Drop it, Roy!"

"Okay." He fiddled with his drink. "I've been thinking about Abe Altman."

Mace said absently, "What about him? Want to renegotiate my deal?"

"I was thinking that there is no way he got a research grant that would pay an assistant six figures."

Now Mace looked curious. "I was wondering that too. What do you think?"

"That he's not taking a salary and he's giving those dollars to you. I mean, it's not like he needs the cash."

"Still nice of him, though," she pointed out.

"Well, it sounds like he wouldn't be here except for you."

"He was exaggerating."

"Why do I think that's bullshit?"

Mace shrugged. "Think what you want."

"I heard a snippet on the news that a DA was found murdered."

"Jamie Meldon. Did you know him?"

"No, you?"

She shook her head.

"I guess your sister has her hands full. That's a high-profile case."

"Actually, she's not working it."

"Why not? He was found in D.C."

"Above everybody's pay grades, apparently."

Mace sat there staring off, mulling Mona's words. She finally looked over at Roy. "Did you have time to do any snooping around your firm?"

"I did."

"And?"

"Ackerman's office was clean. In fact, I'm not sure the guy does anything."

"What do you reckon he makes for doing nothing?"

"Seven figures, easy."

"I hate lawyers."

"But he's a rainmaker. The biggest in the firm. He brings major deals in like clockwork. The worker bees like me get paid well. But the rainmakers get the gold."

"Good for him. What else?"

Roy brought her up to speed on the rest of what he learned, including his inspection of the fourth-floor construction site and his conversation with the construction supervisor and later discussion with the building's day porter.

Mace jumped to her feet. "Why the hell didn't you tell me that before?"

"Tell you what before? I just talked to the guy this afternoon."

"That was the day porter. You said you talked to the supervisor a lot earlier."

"Okay, so?"

Mace dropped some cash on the table for the drinks.

"Where are you going?"

"*We're* going to your office building. Right now."

He stood and grabbed his windbreaker. "My office? Why?"

"Not your office, your office *building*, and hopefully you'll get to see why."

"You want to follow me on your bike?"

"No, I need to hide in the floorboard of your car."

"What? Why?"

"Because I'm apparently being hovered!"

CHAPTER

37

THEY RODE up in the elevator to the front lobby from the garage.

"What exactly are we looking for here?" he asked as he followed Mace across the lobby to the office elevators.

"A case I worked about five years ago."

God, if it could only be. Nail the bastard. Get back on the force. To hell with Mona. And they couldn't touch Beth. It would be all me.

"What?"

"Just hang tight. I don't like questions while I'm on the hunt." She slipped her hand into her jacket pocket.

"Are you carrying a gun?"

"No, but a girl can protect herself, right?"

They got in the elevator. When Roy moved to hit the floor button for Shilling & Murdoch, Mace grabbed his arm.

"I said office *building*. We might do your office later."

"Do what in it?"

"You're a real funny guy, Roy."

She pushed the button for the third floor. Moments later they both peered out into the semi-darkened space.

"Now what?" Roy said in a confused voice. "Do we push all the floor buttons and then go running from the building laughing hysterically and look for a car to teepee?"

"Which way are the fire exit stairs?"

He led her down the hall past darkened offices and pointed to a door near the end of the corridor. Mace yanked it open with Roy right behind. She pointed to a door set into the wall by the fire exit door. She opened it. It was a broom closet.

"Are there more of these?"

"There's one on the first floor too."

"Boy, this place has great security," Mace said. "You arm the front doors, hire a security guard, albeit a loser one, and then secure the office elevators and the office suites and you don't secure the garage elevators? And then you have a perfect hiding place for some scumball right in the building?"

"The original building developer declared bankruptcy and the people who took it over finished construction on the cheap, and that didn't include secure garage elevators. No one wanted to pay for a retrofit."

"Well, I bet they will now. Okay, even if you come in through the garage you have to pass by the security desk to get to the fire exit stairs. You said the construction crew checks out at five-thirty and they don't work weekends. Ned comes on at six and exits at six. Exterior doors, office elevator, and your office suite all go secure at eight p.m. and go off at eight a.m. That leaves a huge window."

"Window for what?"

"Oh come on. Did you hit your head on the basketball rim one too many times?"

They continued up the stairs and the next door she opened was to the fourth floor. It revealed almost total darkness. Mace scooted forward and crouched down behind some building materials. Roy knelt next to her. "What are we looking for?" he whispered.

"Know it when I see it."

They crept forward with Mace in the lead. Roy noted that she moved like a cat, no noise, no unnecessary movement. He tried as best he could to mimic her. He did find that his hands were growing sweaty, and his pulse banged in his eardrums.

A minute later she stopped and pointed. Roy saw the dim wash of light coming from a far corner of the space where it wouldn't be directly seen from the windows.

Mace reached in her pocket and pulled something out. Roy couldn't see exactly what it was.

"Now what?" he murmured.

"You stay here. If somebody other than me comes flying past, trip them and then bash them on the head with like a two-by-four or something."

"Bash them on the head? That's a felony assault. And what if he has a gun?"

"Okay, sissy boy, let him kill you and then your survivors can file a civil suit against the bastard for wrongful death. I'll leave it up to you."

She headed on while he took cover behind a large toolbox on wheels. He looked around the floor and picked up a block of wood. His fingers gripped the chunk tightly and he mumbled a prayer that no one would come running by.

And I am not *a sissy boy.*

Two minutes went by. And then the silence ended.

He heard a yell, and then a sound like a long hiss. A scream and a heavy thud caused him to leap up and sprint forward. He tripped over a pile of ceiling panels, tumbled forward, landed on his back, slid a couple feet on the smooth concrete, and came to a stop next to a pair of strappy high heels.

Groaning and rubbing his head, he stared up. The light hit him in the eyes. He put up a hand to deflect the glare.

"What the hell are you doing down there, Roy?" asked Mace, who was holding a work light in a cage that she'd snagged off the floor.

"Coming to save you," he admitted sheepishly.

"Gee, that was sweet. I'll just take it as dumb luck that I didn't actually need you to save me, since we'd both be like dead if I had."

She helped him up.

"I heard a scream and a thud. What's going on?"

She pointed her light downward again. Roy's gaze followed the shaft of illumination. The Captain was lying on the concrete, his big body still shaking.

"What the hell did you do to him?"

"Zap knuckles."

"What?"

She held up a pair of black-coated brass knuckles. "Nearly a million-volt pop. He'll be okay. But right now his nickname is Twitchy."

He pointed to the knuckles. "Aren't those illegal?"

Mace copped an innocent look. "Why, Roy, I don't think so. But just in case they are, don't mention them to anyone."

"You know I am a lawyer and thus an officer of the court."

"But there is such a thing as attorney-client confidentiality."

"I'm not your lawyer."

She slipped a buck from her pocket, slapped it in his hand, and then jabbed him in the side with her elbow. "You are now."

"Why'd you zap the Captain?"

"Twitchy is the Captain? You know him?"

"Yeah, ex-vet who's now homeless."

She ran the light over the Captain's rags and filthy face. "I zapped him because he's a big guy, and I'm just a helpless girl."

"You're not helpless and I'm not even convinced you're a girl." He looked around. "So the Captain must've been the one stealing food and tools."

"Maybe more than that, Roy. Maybe a lot more than that."

"What do you mean?"

"How about killing female law partners?"

"The Captain? No, that's nuts. He wouldn't."

"How do you know him?"

"This is sort of his turf around here. I give him stuff. Money. Food."

"And shoes." Mace pointed her light at the Captain's feet. "I remember seeing those in your car."

"The poor guy was wearing cardboard for his shoes."

"So you only know him from the streets?"

Roy hesitated. "Well, not just from the streets."

"How else?"

"Does it matter?"

"It all matters, Roy."

"I defended him once."

"From what?"

"Assault charge. But that was three years ago."

"Yeah, and I can see that things have really looked up for him since then."

"I'm sure he came here just for food and to get off the streets. It's dangerous out there at night."

"Apparently it's dangerous in here too."

"He couldn't have killed Diane."

"Sure he could."

"How?"

"On Friday he snuck in through the garage after the hammer and nail crew left. A guy like him coming in the front door would have aroused too much attention. Old Ned was probably in the back hooked to a milkshake IV or else he waited until he was gone too. He times his movement across the lobby and hits the stairs. He hides out in that oh-so-convenient broom closet until your friend the day porter does his thing and leaves. Then, when things quiet down, he goes to the fourth floor, which he has direct access to from the fire stairs, and beds down for the night. On Monday he either pops awake when he hears the elevator coming up early in the morning or else he's already up because he knows he has to get back out before people start coming in. He hits the button over there to make the car stop on this floor. The doors open. Tolliver can't see him, but he can see her, a lone female trapped in a metal box, easy pickings. He grabs her and that's it."

"But if he knew Ned comes in at six why wouldn't he have already been gone?"

"You think it's all that difficult to slip past Ned?"

"Or maybe he doesn't have a watch."

She knelt down and lifted up the Captain's left sleeve, revealing a watch. She hit it with the light. "And it's got the right time."

"You said something about a case you worked?"

"Same M.O. Bandit hid in buildings where construction was going on. He'd hit the elevator button when he heard the car coming up or down late at night. If the doors opened and it was a chick all by herself, he'd pounce."

"Ever catch the guy?"

"Did better than that. I went in as bait. He tried to grab me and I shot him right in his most private of areas. The guy had butchered three women. So it was a real pleasure to put him out of commission permanently."

"Okay, but the Captain—"

"Look, the *Captain* maybe only plans to rob her, but things get carried away. I see two Purples and a Combat Bronze on his jacket. What branch was he in?"

"How'd you know it was a Bronze Star for combat?"

"Because of the Valor Device worn with the medal." She pointed to a small V on the Captain's chest above the Bronze Star. "That's only for combat heroism."

"I knew that because my brother is a Marine, but how do you know?"

"I've done my patriotic duty and dated guys from every uniformed branch. They liked to show me their medals. Plus my dad had one from Vietnam. So which branch?"

"Army Ranger."

"So he's both huge and strong and really skilled at killing people." She glanced down at the big man and then over at Roy. "The Captain have a real name?"

"Lou Dockery. I still don't believe he killed Diane."

"Spoken like a true defense attorney. But it's not up to you. In fact, you have to call the cops right now."

"Me?"

"Officially, I'm not here. My sister gave you a number to call. Dockery will be in la-la land for another twenty minutes or so. I suggest you make that call, right now."

Roy looked panicked. "What the hell do I tell her?"

"The truth, but leave the part about me out. Hang on a sec." She picked up a piece of wood and used a small knife to cut her hand, drawing a bit of blood that she smeared on the wood.

Roy looked stunned. "What the hell did you do that for?"

"Because I know my sister. And hang on to the chunk of wood."

"Why?"

"Again, because I know my sister. Now give me your key card."

"Why?"

"I want to have a look-see through old Shilling and Murdoch."

"You're not serious?"

She brandished her zap knuckles. "A million volts' worth of serious."

CHAPTER

38

AFTER LEAVING Café Milano, Beth had returned to her office to go over some files and respond to some e-mails. She was on her way home when she got the call from Roy. She ordered in the Mobiles and her caravan turned around in mid-street and galloped to G-town. Roy met them at the front doors and let them in.

"Nice uniform," said Roy as Beth walked in dressed in her Café Milano duds. "Hope I didn't interrupt anything fun."

Beth didn't bite. "Where the hell is Mace?"

Roy's smile disappeared. "I don't know."

Since Beth was wearing two-inch heels she was nearly eyeball to eyeball with the tall Roy. "You want to try that answer again?"

"We hooked up and then we parted company. And I came back here."

"Why?"

"I haven't gotten a lot of work done lately, for obvious reasons. Just trying to catch up. And I was going to make some phone calls."

"At this hour?"

"To Dubai. It's the next day there."

"Thanks for the geography lesson. Where is he?"

"Fourth floor."

He led them to the stairs.

"Why not the elevator?" asked Beth.

Because your little sister has my key card, thought Roy. But he said, "The elevators were acting a little funny when I came down. I don't want to get stuck in one."

They trooped up the steps, two armed plainclothes and a uniform in the lead. Other cruisers and unmarked cars were pulling up out front and a perimeter was being set.

"How did you go from working late to ending up on the construction floor in a confrontation?" Beth asked.

"Heard something."

"From the sixth floor!"

"I meant I heard something on the elevator ride up. Didn't think too much of it, but then I remembered the day porter telling me about stuff going missing from the construction site so I decided to check it out."

"You should've called the police right way. You're lucky you're not dead."

"I guess you're right."

They reached the fourth floor and the lawmen pulled their guns and lights and followed Roy's directions. They found the Captain still on the floor, only he wasn't twitching. He seemed to be asleep.

They gave the okay and Beth and Roy came forward.

She looked at the man on the floor.

"He's a big, tough-looking guy. Ex-military if the jacket and medals are real. How'd you subdue him?" She turned and looked at Roy intently.

Roy bent down and picked up the piece of wood that Mace had given to him. "I used this. You can see the blood on it."

"You whacked him with this? Did he attack you?"

"No, but I was afraid he might. It all happened so fast," he added.

Beth turned to her men. "Get Sleeping Beauty out of here." She glanced at Roy. "I think we can chance the elevator. I need your key card to access it."

Roy patted his pockets and checked his windbreaker. "Damn, I must've left it in my office. Now I can't get back in. I'm sorry, you'll have to use the stairs."

Several more uniforms had joined them and it took all of their combined strength to get the bulky Captain down to the lobby.

Beth said, "I want you to run through everything from the top."

"Okay, hey, you want to go get a drink while we do it?"

"No, Mr. Kingman, I don't want to go get a drink. I want the truth."

"I'm telling you the truth, Chief."

"From the top, then, and don't leave anything out, slick. I'm this close to busting your ass on obstruction, tampering, lying to the police, and for just being *stupid*."

Roy said wearily, "Are you sure you and your sister aren't twins?"

"Excuse me?"

"Never mind." He drew a resigned breath and started talking.

CHAPTER

39

MACE DUCKED through the yellow police tape blocking the kitchen and Tolliver's office and searched each place quickly and efficiently.

After finding nothing she had stared at the inside of the refrigerator for some time. Roy had told her that Diane Tolliver was nearly five-eight, about one-forty. Dead bodies were unwieldy things, she knew, having been around more than her fair share. Whoever killed her had to have really wedged the woman in, or else the body could have easily slumped against the door and pushed it open.

She went over the timeline again that her sister had told her and Roy had supplemented. Because Tolliver had had to use her key card that morning they had a pretty detailed understanding of her movements. The garage entry showed Tolliver had checked in at six. Ned had heard her voice in the lobby a minute or so later. She'd swiped her card in the elevator and entered the premises of Shilling & Murdoch ninety seconds after that. Roy had arrived at the office at seven-thirty and found her at a bit past eight. Mace didn't believe that Tolliver had been alive when Roy got to the office, so she was looking at about ninety minutes for the murder to have occurred and the lady to get stuffed in the icebox.

Tolliver had e-mailed Roy late Friday night. She also had sent him a book with a key in it, probably on the same day. An ex–Army Ranger had been hiding out on the fourth floor and right now was probably the prime suspect. Mace looked at her watch. Gazing out Roy's office window she'd seen the patrol cars pull up to the building. She figured Dockery was already under arrest, and they'd take a DNA sample from him. If it matched, he was done. Neat, tied together. And then Mace could tell Beth the truth of her figuring it out, nailing the guy, and possibly get her old job back.

So what was bothering her?

She trudged back to Roy's office so she could see when they brought Dockery out. Like Roy had said, he had a dead-on view of the front of the building.

She pulled something from her pocket. It was a copy of the key that Tolliver had left in the book for Roy. Mace had had a "friend" make the copy for her after she'd left Binder's goodie shop, with the warning that if he messed up the prints on the original key, she would Taser him until his brain started smoking. That actually would pale in comparison to what Beth would do to her if she found out about the key copy.

She thought of the e-mail Tolliver had sent Roy. *We need to focus in on A*. And the *A* was followed by a hyphen. A seemingly trivial detail, but she knew the seemingly unimportant usually became critical in a criminal investigation. She came by her investigative instincts honestly. Her father had been so good at observing and deducing things that the FBI had asked him to teach a course on fieldwork for them at the academy, a tradition that Beth had carried on.

Roy was right, though. It was awkwardly phrased.

We need to focus in on.

She looked down at the key in her hand. Why not just say, *We need to key on A-*?

"We need to key on A-," she said out loud, hoping something would click in her head. Just a coincidence? Key and key? Key on a key?

She sighed and looked out Roy's office window. Marked and unmarked cars were slung around the front with uniforms and plainclothes standing around, probably wondering when they could either go back on patrol or return to their hoodles and wait for their radios to bark.

No one was coming out of the building yet, so Mace sighed and lifted her gaze from the front entrance to the building across from where she was.

When she saw the neon, at first she couldn't believe it.

"Damn!"

She looked down at her key and back at the flashing sign. How in the hell had she missed it? It was purple! But then again she'd never looked out this window at night. But still. Some detective she was.

She snatched the phone from her pocket and fired off a text to Roy.

Come on, Roy, we need to talk like right now.

40

Roy snatched a peek at his phone after it started to vibrate in his pants pocket. This did not escape the attention of Beth, who was standing near him.

He looked up from the screen and found her gaze on him.

"Dubai calling?" she said coolly.

"No, just a bud in town."

"Bud's up late."

"We're both night owls."

"Good for you," she said, her tone of skepticism delivered like a cannon shot.

"Are we done here, Chief?"

"For now. But next time you hear strange sounds, call the police."

"You have my word."

"It's a good thing you don't do trial work anymore."

"Why's that?"

"Because your bullshitting skills aren't that good."

She turned and marched out of the building while Roy sprinted for the stairs.

Mace was waiting at the front doors to the law firm.

"What the hell is it?" he said as she grabbed his arm and pulled him into the suite. "Your sister was still with me when you sent the text."

"Come on."

They hustled to Roy's office.

Mace went to the window, Roy beside her. She pointed out. "Tell me what you see."

He scanned the darkness. "Buildings. The street. A pissed-off police chief."

"Think Viagra."

"What?"

"Purple!"

He saw the large purple neon sign over the door of a ground-floor shop in the building directly across from his. "A-1 Mailboxes! That's what the key's for?"

"That's right, genius. Focus in on? Try *key* on A-1. Right across the stupid courtyard."

"She must've figured it was outside my window and the e-mail she sent would be enough for me to figure it out." He looked chagrined. "I've been looking out this stupid window all day. But *you* figured it out."

"Don't feel too bad. If I hadn't looked out the window to see if my big sister was scaling the building like King Kong to grab my butt I never would've seen it."

"But now we can't do anything. The police have the key."

"Roy, Roy, I'm disappointed." She held up her key.

"You made a copy?"

"Of course I made a copy."

"Mace, that's evidence tampering. That's illegal."

"Now do you understand why I put you on retainer? So you can't squeal on me."

"I could lose my license over this!"

"Yeah, but you probably won't."

"Probably again? I don't like those odds."

"Fine, you can sit this one out. I'll check out the mailbox tomorrow."

"But you don't know which mailbox was hers."

"Roy, again, I'm very disappointed in you."

"You have a way to find that out?"

"There's always a way."

"Just so you know, your sister clearly didn't buy my cover story."

"Of course she didn't. Contrary to popular belief, one does not get to be police chief of a major city by being either stupid or gullible."

"Mace, what if she finds out you're investigating this thing on your own?"

"Well, there's always suicide."

"I'm being serious."

"Look, I know it's risky and stupid, but I've got my reasons."

"What are they?"

"Let's just say I had a revelation while taking a pee in the ladies' room. Now give me a ride back to the hotel. I need to pick up my bike."

"Okay, I need some shuteye too."

"I didn't say I was going to bed."

"What are you going to do?"

"Until we can check out the mailbox I need something else to occupy my mind. So I'm going to see some old friends."

"At this hour?"

"They do their best work in the dark."

He stared at her for a long moment. "You're not a cop anymore, Mace. You don't have the shield to back you up. These gangs are dangerous."

"As you should have realized by now, I can take care of myself."

"I'll go with you then."

"No. Me they'll tolerate. You, they'll kill, okay?"

"Don't do this. It's nuts."

"No, this is my world."

CHAPTER

41

MACE SLOWED her ride and then stopped. She'd changed in the hotel bathroom, trading in her Café Milano outfit and strappy heels for worn jeans, leather jacket, and her favorite pair of ass-stomping boots that an FBI Hostage Rescue Team assaulter with a crush on her had had made especially for her. She'd bolted through a series of main roads, back streets, and several alleys that she knew all too well. If anyone still had been tailing her, she was pretty sure that they no longer were. She waited three minutes and then reversed her route just to make certain. Nothing. She smiled.

Hoverees, one, Hoverers, zip.

Mace lifted her visor and did a quick recon. The part of D.C. she was in right now, within smelling distance of the Anacostia River, was not listed on any official map of the area for the simple reason that robbed, assaulted, or murdered out-of-towners were never good publicity for the tourism industry. Even with the new ballpark and attempts at gentrification in nearby areas, there were sections of turf here that even some of the blue tended to avoid if they could. After all, they wanted to go home to their families at the end of the day too.

Mace hit the throttle and moved on. She knew there were eyes everywhere, and she was also listening for the sounds of "whoop-whoop" or collective cries of "Five-O." This was the way the folks around here let it be known that blues were in town. The bandits' network even knew which fleet the MPD used for unmarked cars. Since the fleet purchases were large, the police force had to keep them for about three years. Before Mace had gone to prison, the array of unmarked cars had all been blue Chevy Luminas. Every night she'd heard the whoop-whoops as soon as she pulled down the street in her glow-blue ride. She'd gotten so ticked off she'd started renting cars with her own cash.

In one ear she had a bud connected to a police radio she wore on her belt. She was scanning calls to see where the action was. So far it was a quiet night, at least by D.C. standards. She figured she might find some useful intel at a hoodle.

Along the way she passed a bunch of hoopties, old junked cars lining the street. Many of them, she knew from experience, were probably stolen, used for a crime, and then dumped here. Yet enclosed spaces were popular around here for multiple reasons, so from habit, Mace peered in a few as she passed by. One was empty, one had a syringe shooter getting happy juice up his arm, and the last one was a fornication feature starring two girls and one very drunk guy who she knew would wake up in about an hour with his wallet gone.

Mace pulled slowly into a church parking lot and spotted a trio of cruisers parked side by side hood to trunk. This was a hoodle, the place where cops who'd made their rounds went until the dispatcher's squawk over the radio brought them back to fighting crime. She knew better than to zoom into this little circled wagon train. You didn't want to get drawn down on because you interrupted the rest of a stressed-out patrol officer. She stopped her bike well in front of one of the cruisers facing her, took off her helmet, and waved. Chances were good that she knew at least one of the blues in these rides, and her hunch was proven correct when one of the cop cars blinked its lights at her.

She slipped off her Ducati and walked over. The driver of the first cruiser slid down his window and the man leaned out his head.

He said, "Damn, Mace, heard you got your ass lifted out of West Virginia. Good to see you, girl."

Mace leaned down and rested her elbows on the ledge of the open window. "Hey, Tony, how's hoodle time?"

Tony was in his mid-forties with a thick neck, burly shoulders, and forearms the size of Mace's thighs, all the result of serious gym time. He'd been a good friend to Mace and had provided her with flawless backup on more than one occasion when she'd been with Major Narcotics. Next to him was a Panasonic Toughbook laptop that was about as important to a cop as a gun—although the most important piece of equipment any cop carried was his radio. That was his lifeline to call in help when needed.

Tony flashed a smile. "Quiet tonight. Not so quiet last night. Did the circuit, been here twenty minutes, listening to some tunes." He looked over at the young female cop next to him. "Francie, this is Mace Perry."

Francie, who had short strawberry red hair and braces and looked like she was about fifteen, smiled at Mace. Yet she had a blocky build with buffed shoulders that told you not to mess with her. Both officers wore gloves thick enough that a syringe couldn't penetrate easily. The last thing you wanted was to stick your hand under the front seat of a car you were doing a stop-and-search on and pull it back out with a needle sticking in it. Mace had known one beat cop who'd become HIV-infected that way.

"Hey, Francie, how long you been riding with this big old bear?"

"Six weeks."

"So he's your training officer?"

"Yep."

"You could do a lot worse."

Tony said, "Throwing arrests her way left and right. Getting in her courtroom OT. Being a real gentleman and teacher."

Mace smacked him playfully on the arm. "Hell, you just don't want to do the paperwork."

"Now don't go disillusioning the girl."

"Sometimes I still miss roll call."

Tony cracked a grin. "You're crazy, Mace. Same old, same old. Just doling out bodies and wheels and running around trying to find some damn car keys."

"Beats staring at a wall for two years."

Tony stopped smiling. "I bet it does, Mace, I bet it does."

"Same old same old bandits around here too?"

"Except the ones who're dead."

Mace glanced at the other cruisers. "Anybody I know?"

"Don't think so. They send folks all over the place now."

"So remind me how big your kids are?"

"One in college, two in high school and eating me out of house and home. Even when I pull my full twenty-five and get pensioned out, gonna have to get another job."

"Go into consulting. Doesn't matter what, it pays a lot better."

"So why don't you tell me what the hell you're doing out here at two a.m. on your fancy bike with no gun."

"How do you know I'm not packing?"

"Can you say probation violation?"

Mace grinned at Francie. "You see why he's such a good T.O. Nothing gets by this guy. He looks like a musclehead but the dude's got brains."

"Seriously, Mace, why here?"

"Nostalgia."

Tony laughed. "Go look in a photo album if you want that. Streets ain't never fair, especially around here." He turned serious. "You know that better than anybody."

"You're right, I do. Only they never found out who ripped me. That's not right."

"I know."

"So how many blues think I'm dirty?"

"Honestly?"

"Only way that matters to me."

Seventy-thirty on your side."

"I guess it could be worse."

"Hell yes it could be, considering who you share DNA with."

"Beth is a cop's cop. She came up right from the pavement, just like I did."

"But she's also a gal and you know some still don't like that."

"Well, hang in there, Tony, four more years."

"I'm counting, baby, every damn day."

She looked over at Francie. "And if Tony does pull his gun, just remember to duck. The son of a bitch never could shoot straight."

42

MACE RODE ON, venturing ever more deeply into an area that she, even with all her risk-perverse ways, shouldn't have gone near without a weapon and a two-cruiser backup. Yet she knew exactly where she was headed. She had to see it; she wasn't exactly sure why, only that she had to. It might have been what Mona had revealed in the bathroom. Mace could accept going down and maybe going back to prison, but what she could not accept was taking Beth with her.

She slowed her bike, very aware of silhouettes on the streets, pairs of eyes at curtained windows, heads eased against tinted car windows, all wondering what she was doing in this area at this hour. The human ecosystem here was both fragile and extraordinarily resilient, and also one that most citizens would never experience. Yet it had fascinated Mace for most of her life. The line between cop and bandit here, she knew, was both as thin and as thick as it could get. No layperson would understand what she meant by that, but any cop instantly would.

She looked up. It was straight ahead. Lodged in the middle of Six D like a glioblastoma among more ordinary tumors. It was an abandoned apartment building that had seen more drugs, death, and perversity than possibly any single building in the city. The cops had hit it time and again, but the bandits always returned, like an anthill after a blast of Diazinon granules. On the roof of this place she'd had her O.P., or observation post, set up, principally because no bandit would ever believe that a cop could infiltrate it. It had taken Mace a month of undercover work to wedge her way into this world, her camera and scopes hidden in her bulky clothing while she bought and sold drugs and fended off the sexual thrusts of an array of predators with her Glock 37 and a fast mouth. That was one of the good things about undercover work in that place. Not having a gun would have seemed suspicious, since everyone else was packing.

The roof had a dead-on view of a drug dropoff used by a trio of Latino brothers who had run one of the most violent gangs in D.C. Mace had been in Major Narcotics at the time, but she was looking for far more than just another drug bust. These guys were suspected in more than a dozen murders. Mace was taking pictures and members of her joint task force were tapping their cell phone conversations in hopes of taking the Lats down for life.

Nothing much had changed about the place. It was still a dump, still mostly abandoned, but no longer a beehive of criminal activity since Beth had placed a police satellite station on the first floor of the building. Two of the Lats had moved to the Houston area, or so she'd heard through the prison grapevine. The third brother had been found in Rock Creek Park, more skeleton than corpse. Word was his older brothers had found him skimming profits off their rock bag trade. Apparently, tough love started at home for those boys. Mace was convinced that the brothers had discovered her undercover surveillance either through the streets, dumb luck, or a mole at MPD and then exacted their revenge.

Why couldn't you have just put a round in my head? Quicker, less painful.

It occurred to Mace now, more vividly than it ever had during her two years in prison, that the bastards who set her up were probably going to get away with it. While lying on that metal bed she'd constructed all these elaborate plans about how she would follow up the most insignificant clue, spend every waking moment on the case, until she got them. And then she would march triumphant to the police station with her captured bandits and all would be right with the world.

Perched on her Ducati, she shook her head in bewilderment. *Did I really believe that?*

Thirty percent of the D.C. blues thought she was guilty. That represented twelve hundred cops. Thirty sounded a lot better than twelve hundred. Mace knew she shouldn't care, that it really didn't matter, but it did matter to her. She eyed the alley where she'd stepped out late at night after staring through a telephoto lens for hours and her life had changed forever. The soaked rag over her mouth that turned her brain to jelly. The strong arms pinning hers to her sides. The squeal of wheels, the fast ride to hell. The needle sticks, the nose snorts, the liquid poured down her throat. The retching, the sobbing, the moaning, the cursing. But mostly the sobbing. They'd broken her. It had taken a lot, but they'd won.

If I catch you, I will kill you. But it doesn't look like I will. And where exactly does that leave me? Hoping a homeless vet goes down for murder so I can say I caught him and get my stripes back?

And what about the key and the e-mail? How could Dockery have anything to do with that? There was obviously more there than what Mace had first thought.

Her mental pirouettes were interrupted when she heard the sound near her moments before she saw him. Her hand went to her pocket. The guy was black with a shaved head, only a few inches taller than she, but about ninety pounds heavier with none of it fat. Bandits, she knew, tended to work out religiously, just so they could outrun and outfight the cops if it came down to it. And it usually did at some point.

"Nice bike," he said. He wore a hoodie, jeans, and tongue-out burgundy-and-white basketball shoes.

Mace lifted her visor. "Yeah, I hear that a lot."

She knew he had a pistol in his right hoodie pocket, and the slight bulge in his pants bottom evidenced the throwaway strapped to the inside of his left ankle. Her hand tightened on the object in her own pocket.

"I bet you do. Probably don't hear this tho'." He pulled out a bulky semi-auto that Mace knew with a glance was an inaccurate knockoff piece of crap, but then you didn't have to be a Marine sniper to drop someone at a distance of two feet. "I want it."

"Can you afford the payments?"

He pointed the muzzle at her forehead. "'Less they making helmets with Kevlar, I think I can. And pull your hand outcha coat real damn slow or I'll kill you, bitch."

"It's just a phone."

"Show me."

She edged out her phone and held it up. "See, just a Nokia 357."

"You a funny bitch."

"You haven't heard the punch line."

"Yeah? What's that?"

The burst of pepper spray hit him in both pupils. He screamed, dropped his gun, and fell back on the sidewalk clawing at his eyes. She pocketed the pepper spray cannon that looked like a phone that she'd bought from Binder's personal defense shop. "I got the all-inclusive caller plan with self-defense add-on."

She snagged his pistol, dropped the mag, cleared the chamber of the lead round, and tossed the gun into a garbage can. His throwaway, an old .22 wheel gun, got the same treatment after she managed to tug up his pants leg and snag it from the ankle strap while he was gyrating uncontrollably. She got back on her bike and stared down at him still rolling and yelping on the pavement. "What's your name?"

"My eyes are burning out my head, bitch!"

"Then stop trying to rob people. Now what's your name?"

"I'll kill you, bitch. I'll kill you."

"Interesting, but not getting us anywhere. Name?"

"I ain't telling you my damn name."

"Tell me your name and I'll give you something to make the sting go away."

He stopped rolling, but his hands were still crammed against his eye sockets. "What!" he screamed.

"It's in my other pocket. Name?"

"Razor."

"Real name."

"Darren."

"Darren what?"

"I'm dying here!"

"Last name?"

"Shit, dammit. Kill you, muther!"

"Name?" she repeated calmly.

"Rogers! Okay! Rogers!"

"Okay, Darren Rogers." She pulled a small spray bottle from her other pocket. "Look at me."

"What?"

"Look at me, Darren, if you want the burn to go away."

He stopped writhing and sat up on his haunches, his fists still buried in his face.

"It doesn't work that way. Open your eyes and look at me."

He slowly pulled his hands away and managed to keep open his teary, inflamed eyes while his entire body shook with the effort. She sprayed both pupils with the liquid from the bottle. Within a few seconds, Darren sat back and took a deep breath. "What the hell is that shit?"

"Magic."

"Why'd you do me like that?"

"Call me overly sensitive, but it might have been the whole gun-robbery-kill-you-bitch thing."

"You even know where the hell you are? You from Iowa or something? Ain't no monuments 'round here, lady."

"Actually, I was born in D.C. and my office was right here for years."

Darren stood and started to rub his eyes, but she snapped, "You've got the pepper crap on your hands, Darren. Rub your eyes you go right back to screaming, and magic may not strike twice."

He let his hands swing at his side. "What'd you do with my guns?"

"In the can over there. Took the ammo out. By the way, the slider on your semi is for shit; jams every second shot. And your .22 throwaway is only good for a laugh."

"I paid two hundred bucks for that semi."

"Then you got ripped off. It's also about as accurate as a TEC-9 at a thousand yards, which translates to anything you hit with it is sheer luck."

"You know a lot 'bout guns?"

"In many ways, they were once my best friends."

"You a crazy bitch."

"There's that word again."

"What the hell you want to know my name for?"

"You live 'round here?"

"Why, you a cop?"

"No, just curious."

"Grew up couple blocks away," he said sullenly.

"What crew you with? Lots to choose from down here."

"Ain't got no crew."

"What, you failed the initiation?"

"Ain't got no crew," he repeated stubbornly.

"Okay, maybe there are a few freelance gun toters around here and maybe you're one of them."

"So what if I am?"

"So with crappy weapons and no crew how come you're still alive?"

"Why you think they call me Razor?"

"Let me take a wild guess and say because you're really sharp?"

"I get by."

He took a menacing step toward her, one hand shielding his face.

She held up the phone. "Don't even think about it, Darren. This button turns my little phone into a one-million-volt Taser and you into a Fry Daddy."

He dropped his hand and took a step back.

"You got family?" she asked.

"Can I get my crappy guns out the trash now?"

"After I'm gone. They don't call me Razor but I'm pretty sharp too."

"What you doing down here?" He looked around. "Like you say, lotta crews."

"They're too busy popping each other to worry about me. But thanks for the concern."

"I don't give a shit if you get your head blown off. Why should I?"

"Not a reason in the world. Go get your crappy guns, Razor, and enjoy what little time you've got left." She hit the gas and the Ducati roared off.

CHAPTER

43

MACE HEARD the car long before she saw it.

She checked her side mirror. Black sedan, tinted glass, big motor, and the rear passenger-side window easing down. Never a good scenario, especially in this part of D.C.

She hit the throttle and the Ducati leapt forward, but the sedan still muscled up closer. She saw the gun muzzle with a suppressor can through the slit of the open window. The shooter took aim through the scope on his sniper rifle while his partner handled the wheel with an expert touch. The crosshairs settled on Mace's helmet and the man's finger closed on the trigger. Sensing that the shooter had drawn his bead, Mace was about to jump the curb when there was a squeal of rubber. Another car flew between the sedan and Mace, and banged against the big car.

The man fired right at the instant the collision occurred and his shot got screwed. Instead of the round drilling a black hole in Mace's head, the driver's-side window of the car between Mace and the shooter exploded, with glass fragments propelled outward like tiny meteors.

Mace recognized the car that had saved her. "Roy!" she screamed.

The shooter cursed and fired again while his partner slammed the sedan into the smaller Audi. Roy ducked down as the second round zipped over his head and shattered the passenger window. He cut the wheel hard to the left and the Audi punched the sedan's front fender at just the right angle to send the bigger car into a counterclockwise spin. The shooter pulled his rifle back and closed the window while the driver tried to steer the car out of the spin.

Roy hit the gas and the Audi pulled next to Mace. Roy looked at her through the open window.

"I've got your back," he said gamely, glassy debris in his hair, his eyes wide with adrenaline and fear.

Mace lifted her visor and yelled, "Are you nuts!"

"Apparently, yeah," he said a little breathlessly.

"What the hell are you doing here?"

"Like I just said, watching your back."

"They could've killed you."

"But they didn't. Right?"

Mace checked their six.

The sedan had pulled out of the spin and was bearing down on both of them, its eight cylinders popping.

"Well, here they come again."

Roy looked behind him. "Oh, shit. Now what?"

Mace shouted, "Follow me, Roy."

CHAPTER

44

THE DUCATI hit ninety on a straight strip of road and then Mace decelerated and leaned into the turn at sixty. The battered Audi barely made the cut, its left rear taking out a line of trash cans on the curb, catapulting days-old garbage in all directions as Roy fought the wheel and finally righted the slide and fell in behind her ride.

Mace flicked her gaze in the mirror and saw the sedan take the turn while barely slowing. Her mind galloped as her observations roared into deductions. Pro driver. So probably pro shooter in the rear seat. She didn't want to find out how good he was. The third shot would not be all that charming for her or Roy.

Mace's knowledge of the area served her well. Whenever she saw the sedan edging up on Roy, she would rip down a side street, forcing the bigger car to fall back a bit. They did this dodge and dart for three more blocks while passing bandits doing business, but not a single blue working the streets that Mace could see.

Lazy asses!

She had no choice but to go for it. Up ahead was the church parking lot. She spied two cruisers still at the hoodle. She leaned into the turn, hit the lot, went fully airborne over a speed bump, and soared right at the twin rides of D.C.'s finest. She braked hard, almost laying the Ducati down, but the rear wheel tread fought the torque and held to the asphalt. The Audi torched the pavement with burned rubber as Roy smashed down on the brakes. Before Mace even got her helmet off or Roy leapt from his car, the cops were out, frozen in classic firing stances, gun muzzles aimed at Roy's and Mace's foreheads.

"Hands on your heads, fingers interlocked, and down on your knees. Now!" screamed one of them.

With slight panic Mace noticed that Tony and his rookie were not among this group. He must've gotten a call and left. She studied the four cops aligned against her. All men, all big, all looking pissed off. And she didn't know a single one. She glanced at Roy, who was taking a step forward, gallantly trying to put his body between her and them. She stopped his gallantry by driving her elbow in his side and pushing him behind her. She knew the look in the cops' eyes. She'd had it herself plenty of times. They were one second and one wrong move from unloading with double taps to the head and heart. Even shitty shooters couldn't miss at this distance, and she doubted any of them were bad shots.

"Hands on your head and fingers interlocked, Roy," she hissed. "And get on your knees. Now!"

They both dropped to the asphalt as the blues approached cautiously, firing lines and trigger fingers still set.

"Some guys in a car tried to kill us," barked Roy.

It was at this moment that Mace noticed the silence. No big sedan, no thumping V-8, no gun muzzle with a can pointed her way. Silence.

"What *guys*?" said one of the cops skeptically.

"In a big black sedan. It was chasing us."

The cop looked around. "I don't see a damned thing other than you two."

Another one pointed out, "All I ever saw were you and the chick on the bike coming at us hard."

"I was here about thirty minutes ago," said Mace. "I was talking to Tony Drake. He was parked here at the hoodle with an egg named Francie."

"You a cop?" asked one of them.

"Used to be. Tony can vouch for me."

The first cop shook his head. "We got here about ten minutes ago. And I don't know any Tony Drake. Or a Francie."

Roy started to get up. "Look, this is crazy."

"Stay down!" roared the second cop. His pistol was aimed right at Roy's skull.

"He's staying down," snapped Mace. "He's not going anywhere. No sudden moves. We're both cool. We've got no weapons."

"We'll see about that," said the first cop, as he holstered his gun and pulled cuffs from his belt. "You two look like you got stuff that would concern me. So you don't mind me searching you and your vehicles?"

Roy eyed the cuffs and said indignantly, "Where the hell are you coming from? We didn't do anything wrong."

"This is a stop, Roy, not a contact," said Mace. "We are definitely not free to go."

The other cop eyed Mace. "What, are you his lawyer?"

"Other way around, actually."

"You said you were a cop. Do I know you?"

Mace started to say something but then stopped. These guys might be part of the thirty percent who believed she was dirty.

"Don't think so."

The first cop was looking at the damage to the Audi. "You hit something, mister."

"How about that sedan and two big-ass rifle rounds?" snapped Roy.

"Right, the sedan," the cop said sarcastically. He nodded to his partner, who snapped the cuffs on Roy first, then Mace.

"Have either of you been drinking?" asked the first cop.

"For God's sakes!" yelled Roy. "They were trying to kill us. We came to you for help and all we're getting is hassled and cuffed."

"Shut up!" snapped Mace.

"In case you didn't figure it out, you're both under arrest," said the second cop.

"What's the damn charge?" exclaimed Roy.

"How about disturbing the peace, reckless endangerment, and assault on a police officer for starters? I thought you two were going to run right into us."

"That is bullshit! Look at my damn car. They shot out the windows. They were trying to kill us! Or at least her. What the hell did you want us to do? Now, can you take the damn cuffs off?" Roy pulled his arms free of the cop's hold.

"Okay, I just added resisting arrest. Anything else you'd care to tack on?"

Roy started to say something but Mace managed to jab him in the side. "It's bad enough. Don't make it worse."

The first cop said, "Lady's right. Now you both have the right to remain silent. You . . ."

As he performed the Miranda, Mace tuned out his words. Busted and not even out a week. Hadn't even had time to see her probation officer. She was completely and totally screwed.

I'm going back to prison.

45

I<small>T WAS</small> like déjà vu all over again. The barred door slid back and there she was, the stars all in alignment on her broad shoulders.

"It's really not what you think, Beth," Mace said quietly as she sat hunched over on a metal bench at the back of the cell.

Her sister sat down next to her. "So tell me what it is about. Please tell me what the hell you and Kingman were doing down there last night."

"We weren't together. I didn't even know he was there until his car flew in between me and the guys trying to shoot me."

"What guys?"

"Town Car. Tinted windows. Didn't the arresting officers fill you in?"

"I want to hear it from you. License plate?"

"No plates. At least on the front. I never saw the rear."

"Go on."

"They came flying at me. Rear passenger window came down a few inches. Saw the gun muzzle. A rifle barrel with a can attached."

"And they fired at you?"

"Twice. And they would've gotten me if it hadn't been for Roy."

"And then what?"

Mace explained how she had gone back to the hoodle for help. "But my buddy wasn't there, just two cruisers with blues I didn't know. They jumped to the wrong conclusion."

"Their report says they never saw another car."

"It obviously had already peeled off. But Roy's car hit it. You can take paint samples from his ride and see if you can get a match somewhere. And you'll find the rounds either in Roy's car or on the street somewhere."

"We found no slugs, either in his car or on the street, and I've had a dozen cadets from the academy walking the line for the last five hours."

"So you *do* believe me?"

"There's also a line of smashed trash cans that Kingman apparently ran into. You sure the damage didn't come from that?"

"Beth, I'm telling you the truth! There was a black sedan chasing us. Somebody fired a rifle from inside it. The rounds shattered the windows in Roy's car and almost hit him. You sure you didn't find anything?"

"No slugs, no casings."

"Any casings would've ejected in the sedan. They must've gone back and policed the slugs."

"That takes time, which makes it a big risk. Why would they do that?"

"I don't know."

"But who would want to kill you?"

"Do you have a few hours so I can give you a list?"

"Did you tell anyone you were going down there last night?"

"Just Roy. It was a spur-of-the-moment thing."

"Kingman said he met you for a drink after you left me and then he went back to work. And he just happened to find you in Six D later, right before someone tried to kill you?" Beth's frown hardened into a scowl. "Don't treat me like a chump, Mace. I don't deserve that."

Mace hesitated just a moment, but it was obviously enough for Beth. "Okay, when you're ready to actually tell me the truth, *maybe* I'll be waiting on the other side of the bars, okay?" She headed to the door.

"Wait!"

Beth turned back. "I'm waiting."

"I was with Roy at his office building last night while you were there."

"Wow! Never saw that one coming."

"Hey, you asked for the truth so don't rip me for giving it."

"Why were you there?"

"He told me about the construction site and things going missing and it made me think of the Liam Kazlowski case, you remember the elevator guy from five years ago?"

Beth nodded slowly. "I think of him sometimes sitting in his max security cell wondering where his balls went. You always did have excellent aim."

"So Roy and I went there to see if we could catch the guy."

"And calling your sister, the chief of police no less, never entered your mind?"

"For all I knew it was a wild-goose chase. I didn't want to call you out on a hunch. Not when you were dressed so pretty," she added lamely.

Beth's face was so tight, the balls of her cheeks so hard against the overlap of skin, that it looked like she had been shrink-wrapped. "I don't know whether to shoot you or drive you back to prison myself," she said in a low, barely-in-control voice.

"Beth—"

Beth lunged forward, forcing Mace to jerk back flush with the cement-block wall. Her voice came at Mace like the thrusts of a knife.

"Within hours of me letting you walk away from a tampering and obstruction charge and me telling you to stay the hell out of the case, you turn right around and stick your nose right in it. What the hell is the matter with you?" Beth was shouting now. "Will you please tell me how in the hell I'm supposed to get through to you?"

Beth's face was spotted with red anxiety flecks. Mace was pressing the back of her head so hard against the wall it felt like her scalp was being split open.

"It's the only shot I've got to get back on the force," Mace said in a calm voice that belied the emotion churning through her.

"What are you talking about? I told you I was working on it."

Mace hesitated but then decided to just get it out. "Mona's ahead of you."

Beth straightened up. "What?"

"Mona ambushed me in the ladies' room at a hotel where Roy

and I were having a drink. She knew your plan and she's already talked to all relevant parties with the result that even if you dig up people with signed confessions it won't matter. I'm never getting back on the force that way. I've never seen her happier."

Beth slowly sat on the bench next to Mace. "And that's why you—"

"Look, bottom line, it's not your battle, Beth. It never has been. It's mine. If anybody is going to do something, it has to be me. Mona was also hoping that you'd keep pushing on the case so she could nail you with some bullshit misuse-of-resource crap or building a bogus case to help me and then get you fired. I may go down, but I am not taking you with me. I'll go back to prison before I'd let that happen."

The two sisters sat there for a few moments in silence.

Beth finally said, "But if the guy you nailed last night is the killer?"

"Yeah, maybe I have a shot at reinstatement."

"You don't sound convinced."

"I'm not convinced about a lot of things. So has he spilled his guts yet?"

"He hasn't said a word except that he wants a lawyer."

"Really? He's not so stupid, then."

"I don't know if he is or not. He wants your drinking-buddy white knight as his shyster."

"Roy as his lawyer? Why?"

"Says he's the only one he'll talk to. Seems like they were good friends. Funny, Kingman never even mentioned to me that he knew him."

"Roy told me he helped the guy out some. Repped him once on an assault."

"So *you* whacked the guy in the head with a piece of wood, right?"

"He outweighed me by about two hundred pounds."

"It sure was a little piece of wood to knock out a guy that big."

"I built up quite an arm in prison," Mace said defiantly.

"Why'd you go down to Six D?"

"To see where it all went down."

"Where they grabbed you?"

"There was a huckabuck on the street named Razor. Heard of him?" Beth shook her head. "Well, he and I had a chat, then I rode on. About five minutes later, here comes the car with the rifleman. Then Roy showed up and the chase was on. That's all I know. I need you to believe me."

Beth sighed. "I do. A couple of my guys on CP rounds scrounged up two witnesses who saw the car bearing down on you and Kingman's Audi coming from out of nowhere."

"And the shots?"

"And the shots."

"If you knew that, why were you giving me the third degree, then?"

"Because I'm pissed at you and I wanted to make you sweat."

"Did your witnesses get a plate number?"

"There were apparently no plates on the rear of the car either."

"Okay. That's interesting."

"You see what happens when you lose my hover guys?"

Mace had a sudden thought. "So how did Roy follow me, then?"

"Why don't you ask him? It seems pretty convenient him showing up like that. If I were you I'd go a little slow with the man, not that you've ever listened to me when it comes to the male species."

"First time for everything," Mace said slowly.

"So they fired two rounds and left nothing behind. Not your typical street shooters, because those guys don't police their brass since nobody will squeal on them anyway."

"Does Roy know that this Captain dude wants him as his lawyer?"

"I told him."

"You've already talked to Roy?"

"I wanted to see how your stories matched up."

"Thanks a lot."

"Oh, and if someone is trying to kill you, I'd appreciate if you would confine your rides into the Valley of Death to daylight hours."

She turned back to the door.

"Is this going to screw up my probation?"

"You were never officially charged. Kingman's waiting down the hall." She thumbed the bars. "You're going to work this case, aren't you?"

"What would you do, Beth, if it were you?"

The chief left without answering.

CHAPTER

46

S o where're our rides?" asked Mace. She and Roy were standing out in front of the district police station while the sun rose
above them.

"Impoundment lot," he said, stretching his arms over his head.

"Are you kidding me?"

"That's what they told me inside."

Mace groaned. "Great. My Ducati's probably been chopped and
shopped all over the Northeast by now."

"I doubt your sister would let that happen. My Audi, on the
other hand, was pretty beat up. Should we cab it over there?"

It took a few minutes to run down a dilapidated taxi. The cabbie
seemed surprised to see them flagging him down.

"What's his problem?" asked Roy.

"Well, we don't look like we belong around here, do we, Roy?"

"Why, because we're white?"

"No, because we're not shoving a gun in his face and asking for
all his money."

When the cab pulled from the curb she turned to him. "Okay,
how did you show up last night? You followed me, right?"

"Not exactly, no."

"How not exactly?"

"I was waiting for you at the spot where the car came after you."

"I'm not liking where this is going."

"Hey, I'm not in cahoots with the guys in the black sedan."

"Oh, good, glad that's all cleared up. I think this is where you and I part company." She tapped on the cabbie's shoulder. "Hey, buddy you can let me—"

"Mace, will you hear me out! I almost got my head blown off last night."

She turned back to him. "Okay, I'm listening."

"You said you were going downtown. I knew what that meant, or at least I thought I did. To the place where you were kidnapped."

"How did you even know where that was?"

"I Googled you on my iPhone."

"What?"

"I Googled the stories. Two of them had the street location where it happened. I went there and waited, figured you'd show up at some point. You did. Then the car came at you and I, well, I . . ."

"Came to my rescue?"

"A little better than I did with the Captain, I guess."

"So you didn't see Razor, then?"

"Who?"

"Never mind. So why did you do it? I mean, you going there at that time of night in your fancy-pants Audi was pretty stupid."

"As stupid as a chick on a Ducati?"

"That's different."

"Anyway, they'd probably just assume I was looking to buy drugs or a hooker."

She folded her arms across her chest and her suspicious look faded. "I'd be in the morgue right now but for you. Thanks. I owe you."

"I also got us arrested with my big mouth."

"I ran to the hoodle, you were just following."

"You think it was somebody from your past shooting at you?"

"Don't see many street crews using suppressor cans and piloting Town Cars. Their usual method is a double tap to the head and then the sounds of running feet."

"Okay, what now?"

"I get my bike back, hopefully in one piece. And you get your Audi back in several hopefully repairable chunks."

"What about the key to the mailbox at A-1? You want me to check it out?"

"No, I'll check it out."

"What if we check it out together?"

"People are watching, you know. They see you with me, probably not good."

"Hell, I've spent more time with you over the last couple days than I've done with every girlfriend I've ever had."

"Really? Then no wonder things never worked out for you."

The cab dropped them at the impoundment lot. Beth had made arrangements so they weren't charged any fees. Mace's Ducati was parked right next to the small office building. A thick chain wrapped in plastic was wound around the front forks and the other end padlocked to a ten-foot-tall steel post. The bike was in pristine condition. It even looked like someone had washed it.

"Like I thought, your sister was looking out for you," said Roy.

Mace was staring at something. "But I don't think she has the same level of commitment to you." She pointed up ahead.

Across the lot Roy's Audi was parked next to a rear section of fence. The entire left side was crunched from the collision with the Town Car and the heavy trash cans. But someone had obviously come in the night to do some more damage. All its wheels were gone along with the passenger door. Someone had also keyed the entire body of the vehicle multiple times and slashed the convertible top. As they walked over and looked inside they could see that the steering wheel, gearshift, CD player, and built-in navigation system were also missing. The seats were ripped open and the foam torn out. Someone had dumped what looked to be antifreeze on the floorboards, where it had mixed with the glass fragments and two used condoms. The trunk had also been jimmied and the spare taken. All Roy's expensive basketball gear was also gone.

"I'm really sorry about your car," she said.

He sighed. "Hey, this is why people buy insurance policies. You hungry?"

"Starving."

He checked his watch. "I know this place. Eggs are good, the coffee hot."

"I guess you need a ride?"

"Guess so. But I don't have a helmet. And I'm not looking to getting busted again. Once a week is about my limit."

"Not a problem."

Mace walked back to the impoundment lot office and returned a few minutes later carrying a motorcycle helmet. A *police* motorcycle helmet.

"How'd you swing that?" he asked.

"You don't want to know."

She slipped her hand into a small black zippered pocket she'd had built years ago under the Ducati's seat and pulled out her pepper-spray cell phone and zap knuckles.

"Didn't really want the cops to find these on me." She put them in the pocket of her jacket. "Popped them in there while we were running from the bad guys."

"Good thinking," said Roy. "Because something tells me you might need them."

47

THE EGGS were good, the toast slathered in butter, the bacon crispy, and the coffee steamy. They ate their fill and then Mace and Roy sat back. He patted his stomach. "Gotta start playing ball again before I get a gut."

"So the Captain wants you to rep him?"

He took a sip of coffee and nodded. "I don't have any details yet."

Mace fingered her cup. "But you don't think he did it?"

"No, but I'll admit that my judgment is probably a little biased. I like the guy."

"Big teddy bear?"

"With a combat bronze and two Purple Hearts," he said sharply.

"I'm not making fun of him. It's shitty that a war hero is on the streets."

"But if he did kill Diane?"

"Then it's over, Roy, friend or not."

"At least he won't be living on the streets anymore."

"So you going to rep him?"

"I'm not sure. I work for Shilling & Murdoch. They don't do criminal defense work. *I* don't do criminal defense work anymore."

"There's always pro bono. Your firm can't have a problem with that."

"I thought you believed he was guilty?"

"Everybody deserves a good defense. Least I heard that some-where."

"I'll meet with him, go from there."

She pulled the key out. "Do you want me to let you know what I find?"

"Like I said, I'm going with you."

"You don't have to do this."

"I'll probably lose my license to practice before this is all over."

Mace looked confused. "But you still want to come with me? Why?"

"I have no rational basis for answering that question."

"Meaning you have an *irrational* basis?"

Roy put some cash down for the meal.

"So how are you going to find out which box was Diane's?"

"When I think of it you'll be the first to know. By the way, how much do I have left on my buck retainer?"

"After last night, ten cents. Use it wisely."

When Mace and Roy came out of the diner, Karl Reiger picked them up from his observation post tucked inside the mouth of an alley. Farther down the block Don Hope sat in a pale blue Chevy van, his glass on the same target. When Roy and Mace climbed on her bike and drove down the street, Hope eased the van forward and followed. Reiger backed down the alley, came out on the next street over, and ran a parallel course on their tail. They radioed back and forth on a secure communication line and switched out the surveillance every three blocks to knock down the odds of Mace picking up the tail.

Reiger settled back in his seat. It should have been over last night. And it would have been if the punk lawyer hadn't screwed his shot. That would not happen again. Reiger didn't like killing people, especially fellow Americans, but above all, he was going to survive this, even if no one else did.

48

THERE WAS ONLY one person working behind the counter at A-1 when Roy and Mace walked in. He was young with ear buds and lines dangling to an iPod hung on his belt. His head was swaying to the music as he sorted the mail on the counter. Mace led Roy over to the wall of mailboxes. A quick check showed that while they were numbered, none of the digits on the boxes matched the one Mace had written down from the original key.

"Plan B," she whispered to Roy.

Mace walked over to the guy at the counter. "Hey, dude, got a question."

The kid took one ear bud out but his head kept swinging. "Yeah?"

Mace held up the key. "My aunt fell down the stairs and broke her tailbone. That's the good news."

"That she broke her tailbone?" said the kid, perplexed.

"Yeah, because but for that she wouldn't have gone to the hospital and they wouldn't have checked her out and discovered she had like this weird form of leprosy she contracted in Africa or some crazy place. That stuff'll eat your skin right off. And it's like so contagious that if she like breathes on you, your eyeballs fall out. I've never seen anything like this crap. It's got some long-ass medical name."

"Damn, that sucks," said the kid, his head still swinging to the rhythm.

"Anyway, this is her key and she asked me to get her mail. Only she can't remember which box was hers."

"Oh."

"Yeah. So I can't get the mail. And she has some checks and medical bills she needs. It's a hassle but I'm the only relative she has."

"What's her name?"

"Diane Tolliver." Mace crossed her fingers, hoping that the kid had not read of the woman's murder.

He clicked some keys on the computer. "Yeah, she's got a box here."

"So what's the number?"

The kid took out the other bud from his ear and his expression hardened. "I'm not really supposed to give out that info. Mail regs or something. You know, like terrorist stuff."

"Damn, never thought of that." She looked at Roy. "Well, hell, you better go get Auntie and bring her in here then so she can show some ID." She turned back to the kid. "They couldn't keep her in that hospital anymore because they're not set up for contagious crap like that. So we're driving her to Johns Hopkins. We just got going and then she started screaming about her mail. Between you and me I think this stuff messes with your mind too. You know, like forgetting your mailbox number? I know it screws up your sex drive. Docs say it kills the libido like dead, especially in younger people. Anyway, she's out in the car with boils popping all over the place. And her face? It's like tar sliding off. Now, we got inoculated against this shit so we're good, but if I were you, I'd go hide out in the back or something. And anything she touches in here make sure you clean it up with like Clorox or something. The bacteria can live for like weeks on pretty much anything. An orderly at the hospital found that out the hard way." She looked at Roy again. "Go on and get her. Make it fast. I don't want to get caught in traffic going to Baltimore."

Roy turned to head out the door but the kid blurted out, "It's Box 716. Second to the left on the top row over there."

"You sure?" asked Mace. "I don't want you getting in trouble. And Auntie's right outside. She can walk but she falls a lot because of the boils bursting and her feet slipping in the juice. You ought to see the backseat of my car. It's beyond gross."

The wide-eyed kid took a step back. "No, it's cool. Go on ahead and open it up. Your auntie ain't got to come in here."

"Hey, thanks, man." Roy put out a hand for him to shake. The kid took another step back and picked up a large tub of mail. "Yeah, dude, you're welcome."

Roy and Mace headed to Box 716.

49

Beth was in the front seat of a patrol car heading to a meeting when she finished reading over the e-mail from Lowell Cassell. The medical examiner was comparing the DNA on the sperm left inside Diane Tolliver with the sample they'd taken from the residue of a cup of coffee they'd given to Lou Dockery. It was an old police trick. They had enough to hold Dockery until the test results were back. And even if this DNA sample was suppressed by defense counsel motion they could easily get a search warrant. It wasn't like Dockery could change his DNA in the interim. Beth had ordered the coffee cup tactic because she didn't want to waste time with him unless he was the guy who'd raped and murdered Diane Tolliver.

Her multitasking mind shifted gears for a moment. She was monitoring the radio calls in the Fifth District and did not like the paucity of responses from the scout cars to the dispatcher's calls. She picked up the radio.

"Cruiser One rolling in Five D. Cruiser One rolling Five D. Chief out."

Within seconds the chatter picked up and at least five scout cars were responding to each dispatch. Her driver glanced at her.

"Pays off working your way up from the pavement, Chief."

"You think?" she answered absently. Beth punched in the number. The ME answered on the second ring.

"How long?" she said.

Cassell said, "Beth, you asked me that not ten minutes ago. If it had been before the new lab opened, I'd say two to four weeks. We had to send it out back then."

"But not now. Now you have that fancy lab with all those fancy machines."

"We went back over the chain of custody on the sample found in the deceased and confirmed there was no tampering or alteration. We received the sample from Dockery." He paused and Beth could almost see his grin across the phone line. "You haven't used the coffee ploy in a while."

"I'm getting more impatient in my old age."

"It's not that easy pulling DNA off a sperm sample. The sperm heads are hard."

"As hard as the heads of the guys shooting them into women who don't want them to."

Cassell continued, "Then there is the amplification of the DNA and instrumentation. Next comes interpretation of the results. That's where mistakes are made. I don't want to blow up your case because of an error."

"You won't make a mistake, Doc, you're too good."

"Everyone's human. Normally, the protocols I just described take a full week."

"On TV the forensics team does it every episode in like ten minutes."

"Don't get me started on *that*."

"So give me the bottom line time-wise."

"I've put all other work aside and you'll have it by tomorrow. The next day tops."

"I'll take it tomorrow, thanks, Doc."

She clicked off and leaned back in her seat. A moment later they passed a corner that she instantly recognized. She'd been a rookie beat cop riding solo for only two weeks when a bandit had come tearing out of an alley with a TEC-9 and opened fire at a group of people in front of a shoe shop. To this day no one knew why.

Instantly, Beth had gotten her cruiser between the bandit and the crowd. Using her engine block as cover she'd pulled her sidearm and given him two taps in the head. She hadn't bothered with a torso shot because she'd spotted the edges of body armor poking out of his shirt. It wasn't until thirty seconds later, after she'd run over and confirmed the kill, that she discovered that the last TEC-9 round had killed a ten-year-old boy who'd been holding tight to a box containing his new pair of basketball shoes.

The other eight people in the crowd, including the boy's mother, had been saved by Beth's swift actions. The city hailed her as a hero. Yet she went home that night and cried until the sun rose. She was the only one who knew the truth. She had hesitated before firing. To this day she didn't really know why. Civilians could never understand what went through a cop's mind before they pulled the trigger.

Am I going to die today? Will I be sued? Will I lose my job? Can I get a clean shot off? Am I going to die today?

No more than two seconds went by before she'd ended the nightmare scenario. Yet it was enough time for the bandit to get off one last round. The killing round, as it turned out.

Her most vivid image was the box with the new shoes lying in a pool of ten-year-old blood. After calling in the ambulance she did everything she could to bring the little boy back. Tried to stanch the bleeding using her jacket. Breathed hard into his mouth. Pumped his small chest until her arms felt like they would fall off. But she knew he was dead. The eyes were flat, hard. The mother was screaming. Everything was happening in slow motion. Waiting for help to come; the paramedics pronouncing the boy dead; then the gauntlet of stars and bars, the captain, the district commander, and then, finally, the chief himself. It was the longest wait of her life, and all of it, from beginning to end, barely took ten minutes.

She still could feel the heavy, comforting hand of the chief on her trembling shoulder. He said all the right things and yet all Beth could see were those hard, flat eyes. Ten years old. Dead. Two seconds' hesitation. That's all it took. A deuce of seconds. A pair of eye blinks. That was apparently the difference between going home and playing hoops in your new shoes or heading to the morgue to get your chest cavity emptied.

One more crime stat for the books. And yet it wasn't just a stat. His name was Rodney Hawks. Beth had a photo of him from his fourth-grade class in her office on her shelf. She looked at it every day. It pushed her to work harder, try harder, to never leave anything to chance. To never again hesitate when her gun was cocked and locked on a target that required killing.

The shoe shop was no longer there. It was now a liquor store. But for her it would always be the place where she'd allowed Rodney Hawks to die. Where Beth Perry, who had never failed at anything, *had* failed. And a little boy had lost his life because of it.

Beth took a deep breath and pushed these images from her mind. She looked down at her notes and focused on the present situation. Had the homeless vet raped the power lawyer and then stomped on her neck hard enough to crack her brain stem? And then stuffed her in the fridge and gone about his business? The soiling on her clothes and the bits of fabric found at the crime scene also matched what was found on Dockery's clothing. But that didn't really matter. DNA was better than a print. And DNA from sperm was the gold card, particularly when it was found inside the woman. Taken together with the bruising in her genitals, there was no defense lawyer on earth who could spin that one into a positive.

She put the file down and picked up the phone and called her sister. There was no answer so she left a message letting Mace know that they would have the DNA results back soon. If it matched, Lou Dockery would spend the rest of his life in prison. Beth's mind turned to how Dockery's conviction might get Mace her old job back. Despite Mona putting obstacles in their way, if they could convince . . . Beth suddenly dropped this train of thought.

There was one loose end.

She flipped open the Tolliver file once more and looked at two evidentiary items.

A key. And an e-mail.

We need to focus in on A-

There was more here obviously than a homeless vet on a rampage. Yet the real question was, were they connected?

And then there was a shooter in a Town Car with tinted windows, no plates, and a can on the rifle muzzle aiming right at Mace. Was that from Mace's past or tied to this case?

A deuce of seconds. That's all it took.

She was not going to lose her sister again.

50

THERE WAS NOTHING in the mailbox. Nothing, that is, until Mace felt around the top of the inside of the box and her gloved hand closed around a piece of paper taped there. She unfolded it and read the brief contents.

"A name, Andre Watkins. And there's an address in Rosslyn. I guess for him." She looked up at Roy. "Ever heard of this guy?"

"No, and Diane never mentioned him."

"Did she go out a lot?"

"She liked to go to the Kennedy Center; she liked to eat out."

"Well, she probably didn't go alone."

Mace put the paper back inside the box and closed the door.

"Leaving it here?"

"So the police can follow it up if they figure it out."

"Or we could go and tell them about the letter right now."

"We could," Mace said slowly.

"But you want to solve this yourself?"

"It's a long story, Roy. Don't rag me about it. I'm not sure my answers will make any sense anyway."

Twenty minutes later, Mace had parked her bike in an underground garage and she and Roy were zipping to the tenth floor of the apartment building. A man answered the door on the second knock after looking at them through the peephole. This wasn't a guess, because Mace knew that he had. He was as tall as Roy, though about thirty years older, with a trim white beard to match his thinning hair. He was handsome and his skin was tanned a deep brown. He wore jeans that looked like they'd been ironed and a tuxedo shirt with the tail out. His bare feet were in a pair of black leather Bruno Magli shoes. He looked to Mace like the perfect image of the carefree and elegant aristocrat.

"Andre Watkins?" Mace said.

"Can I help you?"

"I sure hope so. Diane Tolliver?"

"What about her?"

"She's dead."

"I know that. Who are you? The police?"

"Not exactly."

"Then I have no reason to talk to you."

He started to close the door, but Mace jabbed her foot in the way. "She had a P.O. box that had a piece of paper with your name and address on it."

"I know nothing about that."

"Okay, we'll just turn it over to homicide and they can run with it. They'll be by to either talk to you today or arrest you. Or probably both."

"Wait a damn minute. I didn't do anything wrong."

"Well, you're sure acting like you did."

"You knocked on my door, two people I don't even know, and you start asking questions about a dead woman? What the hell did you expect me to do?"

"Okay, let's start over. This is Roy Kingman. He worked with Diane at Shilling & Murdoch. She sent him a clue. That clue turned out to be you. You could be in danger."

"And how do I know you're not the ones who killed Diane?"

"I have to tell you, if we'd wanted to kill you, you'd already be dead. One shot through the peephole." Watkins looked at her inquiringly. "I saw the door shift just a millimeter when you leaned against it to see who was there."

"I think I'm going to end this conversation right now."

"We can go to the Starbucks in the lobby and talk if you'll feel safer. All we want is some information."

Watkins looked over his shoulder into his apartment for a moment and then turned back. "No, that's all right, we can do it in here."

The interior of the residence didn't match the elegance of the man; it was sparsely furnished with what looked like rental pieces, and there was even a purple futon. They sat in the small living room that fronted a sliver of kitchen.

"So how did you know Diane?" Roy asked.

"When she wanted to go out, she'd call me."

"So you two were dating?"

"No, I'm an escort."

Mace and Roy exchanged a glance. "An escort?" said Roy.

"Yes. Diane liked to go out. But she didn't like to go alone. It's fun. And it pays well."

Mace ran her gaze over the cheap furniture. "Work dried up for you?"

"My two ex-wives seem in no hurry to get married again. That's actually why I got into the business. Escorting gives me all the fun of marriage without all the hassle."

"But you two got along?"

"I liked Diane very much. I was devastated when I heard she'd been killed."

"Who told you?"

"The anchorwoman on Channel Seven."

"So no one else knew you two were seeing each other?"

"I don't suppose Diane broadcast it around. She was attractive and smart. I knew she was divorced too. Maybe she'd had it with relationships. I know I have."

"So we're here because Diane left a clue that pointed to you."

"But she never told me anything important."

"Never about work or anything?" asked Roy.

"Well, I knew she was a lawyer at Shilling & Murdoch."

"She didn't talk about anyone she was afraid of? Phone calls or threatening messages she'd gotten? A man who was stalking her, nothing like that?" asked Mace.

"No. Our conversations usually were limited to the events we were attending."

"The police have a man in custody," Roy blurted out.

"What man?"

Mace scowled at Roy and spoke up. "I'm sorry, we can't fill in those details."

"So you have no theories for what happened to Diane?"

"No," Roy admitted. He handed Watkins a card. "If you think of anything, please give me a call."

Watkins fingered the card. "This man in custody? He killed Diane?"

"We'll know soon enough. But whatever Diane was trying to get at, it's a dead end," said Mace. "She must've been mistaken, and anyway the case is closed, at least it is for me. Thanks for your time."

Roy started to speak when they were outside, but Mace whispered, "Wait."

When they were back in the garage Roy turned on her and snapped, "You're just going to drop it? What the hell are you thinking?"

She looked up at him. "I'm thinking that the real Andre Watkins is probably already dead."

51

Hᴇʏ, Cᴀᴘᴛᴀɪɴ."

The big fellow looked up. "Hey, Roy. I messed up."

"Why don't we talk about it?"

"Okay, I ain't going nowhere."

Roy looked at the guard next to him. "I need to talk to my client. Alone, please."

The door clanged shut behind Roy as the officer left.

He sat next to the Captain, opened his briefcase, and pulled out a legal pad and a pen. "Why don't you tell me what happened."

"Like I said, I messed up. Took some food. I like the Twinkies. And some tools. Sold 'em. Dumb, huh, but they had lots of tools. Didn't think they'd mind."

Roy looked at him blankly. "Do you know why you were arrested?"

The Captain was staring off now. "Still cold at night. Warm in that building. Guess I shouldn't ate the Twinkies. They were pissed about that, right? And the tools. But it was just a couple of wrenches. Only got three bucks for 'em."

Roy leaned back in his chair. "Did they take anything from you?"

"Who?'

"The police."

"Like what?"

"Prints, bodily fluids?"

"They took my fingerprints." He chuckled. "Had to clean off my fingers so they could make 'em black again. And they gave me some coffee but then they came and took it before I was done. Ticked me off."

"Cheap trick to get your DNA."

"What?"

"But you told them you wanted a lawyer, right?"

"That's right. Ain't no dummy. Twinkie shit. Need a lawyer."

"Okay, maybe we have something to work with in case the DNA comes back bad. But then they'll either just get a search warrant or grand jury subpoena."

"Okay," the Captain said, though it was clear he had no idea what Roy was talking about.

"I checked with the police, they haven't formally charged you with trespass or anything else. But you *were* in the building unlawfully."

"I'm hungry. Got any food?"

"I'll ask the guard in a little bit."

"It's nice and warm in here."

"How long have you been staying in my building?"

"Ain't good with dates." He laughed. "I ain't got no social calendar, Roy."

"Okay, how did you get into the building? Not through the front doors?"

"Garage elevator. Snuck across the lobby. Picked the right time. Recon. I was a scout in 'Nam. I was damn good at recon."

"And the guard?"

"He ain't a good guard. He's almost as fat as me."

"Yeah, I know. Then up the fire exit stairs and onto the fourth floor?"

"Warm in there. And food. Got a fridge. And a toilet. Been a long time since I used a toilet, almost forgot how. I just took the Twinkies, Roy, and the tools. Swear to God."

"How did you know they were doing construction there?"

"Heard some guys talking about it on their lunch break."

"And the tools?"

"Just got three bucks for 'em. Some A-rab on the street. Bet the sonofabitch cheated me. I can give 'em the three bucks and call it square," he added hopefully.

"I don't think they'll go for that."

"'Cause of the damn Twinkies, right?"

"Tell me what happened on Monday, Captain, around six in the morning."

"Monday?" The Captain shook his head. "Monday?" he said again, his brow furrowed, his eyes vacant.

"The day before I gave you the shoes and bought you the food."

"Okay, yeah."

"You were in the building?"

"Oh yeah, always in the building."

"When did you leave?"

"I got me a watch." He held up his arm and slid back his coat sleeve to show it.

"The guard comes in at six."

"He ain't a good guard. He ain't hear nothing. He'd never made it in 'Nam." He added in a knowing tone, "He'd be dead."

"There's a security camera in the lobby." The Captain stared blankly at him. "You didn't know about that?"

The Captain shook his head. "Did it see me?"

"Apparently not. Getting back to Monday, did you see anyone at the building?" The Captain shook his head again. "What time did you leave?"

"Early."

"Show me on your watch."

The Captain hesitated and then pointed to the six.

"Okay, six o'clock. Can anyone vouch for that?" The man looked confused. "Did you see anyone who I can talk to that saw you leave at six, or who you might've talked to right after you left the building?"

"No, sir, ain't nobody like that," he said in a carefree tone.

"Where'd you go?"

"Down to the river. Sat on the wall and watched the sun come up. I like watching the sun come up. Ain't as cold that way."

Roy took a photo out of his pocket. "And you never saw this woman?" He showed him a picture of Diane Tolliver.

"Good-looking woman."

"Do you know her?" The Captain shook his head. "Did you see her on Monday?"

"Nope, but I seen her go in the building sometimes."

"But not on Monday morning?"

"No, sir."

"Did you hear the elevator? You must've been getting ready to leave by then."

"I didn't hear nothing." The Captain wiped his nose with his hand. "You think they got something to eat in this place? I'm real hungry."

"Okay, I'll see about it. So you're sure you didn't see anyone when you left?"

"Went out the garage."

"No cars coming in or out or parked there?"

"No, sir."

Roy took a long breath and nearly choked. In the close confines of the room, the Captain's "aroma" was overpowering.

"I just scoot out. I'm real good at scooting."

Roy put his pad and pen away and stood. "I'm sure you are. I'll go check on that food for you."

"Twinkies if they got 'em. And coffee."

After arranging for some food, Roy left and called Mace.

"How's it look?" she asked.

"An insanity defense is pretty appealing right now." His tone sharpened. "All right, I want to know about Watkins. You just dropped a bombshell and then—"

"Not over the phone, Roy. Let's meet later."

"Where are you?"

"Heading out to start my new job."

52

THANKS FOR MEETING with me on such short notice," Beth said.

She sat down across from the two men in a small conference room. Sam Donnelly, the nation's director of intelligence, was as elegantly dressed as ever. Jarvis Burns, his right-hand man, looked just the opposite. His suit looked like it had been pulled from the bottom of a trunk after a months-long journey. The DNI had offices in various places. Today, Beth was in downtown D.C. not far from police department headquarters, in a nondescript building that on the outside looked like nothing special. That was sort of the idea, she knew.

She'd been issued a radio frequency badge on arriving here. It had been encoded with her security clearance levels, which were very high. Still, they weren't high enough. Every room she'd entered, silent alarms had gone off, red lights installed on the ceiling had twirled, and computer screens automatically darkened because she was not cleared to see any of what was going on here.

"Always a pleasure, Beth." Donnelly fiddled with a ring on his finger while Jarvis rubbed his leg.

"Getting worse on you, Jarv?" she asked, eyeing the limb.

"I would not advise anyone getting shot and then stabbed with a bayonet wielded by an enormously skilled and suitably mad Vietcong infantryman. I was lucky enough to have killed him before he killed me. But at least he didn't have to endure this level of pain for the last three decades."

"Nothing they can do?"

"What they did on the battlefield back then sort of sealed my fate. Nerve and bone damage that were basically wrapped in Band-

Aids, ruptured blood vessels that were rerouted in crude ways." He slapped his thigh. "It is what it is and you didn't come here to hear me complain about it. What can we do for you?"

"There was a U.S. attorney found dead in D.C. His name was Jamie Meldon."

Donnelly nodded. "A real tragedy. We were briefed on it."

"Who by?" she said quickly.

Donnelly shook his head. "Sorry, Beth. I can't say specifically, but any such criminal act would come to the attention of the DNI through various channels."

"The crime scene was closed off to us and the FBI. We have no idea who took over the investigation. I've heard that the directive came from the White House?" She paused and looked at Donnelly expectantly.

"That's a neither confirm nor deny answer, Beth."

"Sam—"

He held up a hand. "All right, I can say that I have heard nothing that would connect this to the White House. And I think I would have."

"So who can it be? These guys basically walked off with Meldon's body based on waving around their driver's licenses. And the mayor told me in no uncertain terms to back off. Okay, sometimes that happens. But the FBI got called off too."

Donnelly glanced at Burns. "That *is* very unusual. Would you like me to look into this for you?"

"You're the first person I thought of to do it."

"We've always had a good working relationship," he said. "Your spirit of partnership with the federal side is much appreciated, I can tell you that."

"We have to keep the capital safe."

Burns's features darkened. "If terrorists can successfully attack this city, no American anywhere will feel safe. And the other side would have won."

"Preaching to the choir." She shook their hands. "I'll wait to hear from you."

Burns said, "By the way, how is your sister adjusting to life?"

"She's adjusting. But Mace always goes her own way."

After Beth left, Donnelly returned to his office. Jarvis Burns continued to sit at the table and rub his bad leg. He stopped long enough to type in a text on his BlackBerry and a minute later the door opened. The man with long white hair had changed from jeans and the tuxedo shirt that he'd worn while searching Andre Watkins's apartment into a suit and tie.

"Mace Perry?" said Burns. The man nodded. "And the lawyer?"

"Both there."

"She's probably confirmed that you're not Watkins."

"Should I have just killed them?" the man asked matter-of-factly.

Burns sat back and frowned. "Give me the briefing."

CHAPTER

53

MACE PUNCHED the code in the gate box and drove her Ducati through. Altman was waiting for her in the front courtyard. He was dressed as casually as before, but now his hair was tied back in a ponytail. In a backpack Mace carried some clothes and a few other essentials. He escorted her over to the guesthouse and waited while she put her things away before showing her how to operate the TV and stereo system and pointing out the computerized HVAC and alarm system controls. There was even a TV that rose up out of a beautifully carved cabinet at the foot of the California king-size bed in the master suite.

"Pretty snazzy place, Abe."

"My late wife, Marty, designed all this. She had such vision, such style. I can barely match my socks."

"I'm right there with you. So what now?"

"Let's go back to the main house and talk strategy."

Over cups of tea Altman outlined his plan in greater detail.

"I've been working with some wonderful folks at Social Services. They'll be expecting you and will lend you their full cooperation. They have background files on all the people of interest that I've already reviewed. As I told you before, I've selected ten people for the initial phase out of all the possibilities submitted thus far. It will be up to you to make the initial contact with them."

"Okay, what sorts of questions do you want me to ask?"

"Nothing too probing. I want you to set them at ease but at the same time let them know that you understand their situation and that we're not in any way prejudging choices they have made or not made. I'm not trying to take them out of their current world."

"But you are, aren't you?"

"I'm attempting to give them an opportunity to change their circumstances in *their* world for the better."

"That's sort of splitting words, isn't it?"

"Yes, it is. And if you question it, *they* certainly will. They will be very suspicious of my motives. The last thing I want is for them to think this is some sort of freak show. You have to convince them that this is a legitimate endeavor with the goal of making their lives better with the hope that they in turn will make the lives of others in similar circumstances better. There are many success stories out there, but the media almost never want to highlight them."

"Bad news gets better ratings."

"Yes, well, we need positive examples to be heard too."

"Most people I know down there are just looking to survive, Abe. I'm not sure how altruistic they'll be about helping others."

"You may be surprised. But you're right in certain respects, and that's fine, that's to be expected. It's only the initial contact. But it is still critical."

Mace's features clouded. "I'm just a little concerned, you know?"

Altman smiled. "That you have no real experience in this field and the hopes of a nation are riding on your ill-prepared shoulders?"

"Couldn't have said it better myself."

"The answer to that of course is that I know no one who's better prepared to do this than you, Mace. No one. If I did, I would've asked that person. I owe you much to be sure, but this project represents in many ways my life's work. I would not risk it all by choosing someone ill fitted for it. It's simply too important."

"Then I'll do my best for you. That's all I can promise."

"Now, I can have Herbert whip up some lunch. He does an amazing tuna salad."

"Thanks, but I'll take a pass. I'm going to grab a shower at the guesthouse. Then I'll hit some of these contacts."

"Excellent. I really appreciate this."

"Not any more than I do. My options were a little thin."

He put a hand on her shoulder. "Darkest before the dawn. A terrible cliché, I know. Yet so often true. And you may find you like the social sciences even more than police work."

"Actually, police work is basically social science only with a Glock and body armor."

"I think I see your point."

"It's all about respect, Abe. At MPD I was a member of the biggest gang out there. But because we were the biggest, we could never, ever afford to lose a battle."

Altman looked very interested. "How did you manage that?"

"By never going into a situation that I knew I couldn't win."

"I can see that."

"With a toot on my radio I could get help when I needed it faster than any other gang out there. I had to hold my own in a fight for three minutes, that was all. And if I had to thump somebody because they spit on me, I did, because once one blue lets disrespect slide by it endangers all the other blues on the street. Spit now, bullets in the back later. You either love me or hate me, but you will respect the uniform. But the same notion works for the bandits. Most of them are just trying to make a living and the blues are trying to catch them. Rolling Cheerios for a couple thousand a day versus tossing meat at Mickey D's for minimum."

"Cheerios?"

"OxyContin. They're just like you and me but they made different choices."

"And had limited opportunities."

"Right. Each side knows the rules. The bandits don't give a crap about getting their ass kicked or being arrested, or getting shot or being put in prison. Happens to them every day. But don't disrespect them. That is the one unforgivable."

"I think I just learned more in two minutes than I have in the last ten years."

"I'll see you, Professor. Keep the lights on for me." She turned back. "Oh, one more thing. My Ducati sticks out a little bit. Do you have a ride I can borrow?"

"Certainly. Do you want the Bentley or the Honda?"

"It's a close call, but I'll go with the Japanese."

54

MACE SHOWERED at the guesthouse and thoroughly washed her grimy hair. That was one bad thing about motorcycle helmets: your head sweats like hell in one. As she wrapped herself in a thick robe and strolled around the palatial house that was not even a third the size of the really palatial house next door, it occurred to her that it would be quite easy to get used to this sort of life if you were a normal person, which of course she wasn't. Yet she couldn't help but admire the quality of the furnishings and the high-level skill and attention to detail that had gone into the design and construction. Marty Altman must have been quite talented. It was easy to see from his comments about the lady that Abe had worshipped her.

What would it be like to have a guy worship me?

She dug through her backpack and pulled out a dog-eared notebook. In it she kept a list of contacts she'd used when she was on the police force. She found the name and made the call. It took several handoffs by other people, but she finally reached the lady.

"Charlotte, it's Mace."

"Mace Perry!"

"Come on, do you know any other Mace?"

"Are you still in that awful prison?"

"No, I'm done and out."

"Thank God for that."

"You still enjoying DMV?"

"Oh yeah," Charlotte said sarcastically. "I turned down all those movie offers from Hollywood so I could stay right here and deal with angry people all day long."

"So how would you like to deal with a happy one?"

"That's usually a precursor to you wanting a favor."

"I've got a name and address. And I'd love to get a photo of the guy."

"You're not back on the police force. I would've heard."

"No, but I'm trying."

"It's harder to help out these days, Mace. Electronic eyes every-where."

"How about an old-fashioned fax?"

"Now there's a novel idea."

"So you'll help me? Once more? For old times' sake?"

Mace heard a short sigh. "Give me the name. And your fax number."

Ten minutes later Mace was standing next to the fax machine in the small office on the second floor that Altman had shown her. Two minutes later the fax did its thing and the inked paper slid into the catch bin. Mace snatched it up. It was a copy of Andre Watkins's driver's license.

The real Andre Watkins had short, thick dark hair, wore glasses, and had no beard. His height was listed on the license and she saw that he was also several inches shorter than the guy they'd seen. So she'd been right. She wondered if the real Watkins was indeed an escort. It was such an out-of-the-mainstream occupation that Mace tended to think he probably was. That meant the imposter had dug into the man's background.

Heading back downstairs, she happened on a four-person Jacuzzi tub tucked in a private glass-enclosed space set off from a small den. Hesitating only for a moment, Mace raced to the kitchen, opened the wine chiller set into the wall there, uncorked a bottle of Cab, and poured out a glass. Then she hurried back to the Jacuzzi, figured out the buttons, heated it up, dropped her robe, and slid naked into the hot foamy water. A minute later she snagged her cell off the edge of the tub and phoned Roy.

"Where are you?" she asked.

"I'm at work. I do have a job, remember?"

"Okay, Mr. Grumpy. Guess what I'm doing."

"What?"

"Pampering myself."

"How. Taking target practice? Or zapping homeless people with those knuckle things for laughs?"

"I'm sitting in the buff in a Jacuzzi at Altman's guesthouse drinking a glass of red wine."

"I thought you were going to start your new job?"

"I met with Altman and went over stuff. I'm rewarding myself because I also managed to confirm through DMV that that was not the real Andre Watkins at the apartment today."

"So you were right."

"Yeah, but that leaves a lot of unanswered questions. When will you be done at work?"

"Four-thirty," he said. "I'm checking out early."

"I'll pick you up from work. I'll be in Altman's Honda."

"What happened to the Ducati?"

"Decided to give it a rest. Did you get a rental?"

"All they had available was a Mercury Marquis. It's as big as my condo."

"And your Audi?"

"Can you say totaled?"

"I'm sorry, Roy."

"So where are we going at four-thirty? And what do you need my help on?"

"I'll fill you in when I see you."

"Does it involve getting shot at?"

"Possibly."

"Okay, one request then."

"Tell me."

"The next time you call me while sitting naked in a Jacuzzi sipping wine, you can expect some company."

"Wow, Roy, you're so sexy when you go alpha on me."

55

Roy slid into the front seat of the Honda. "You look nice and refreshed."

"Beats the crap out of the prison showers."

"Got the photo of Watkins?"

She pulled it from her jacket and handed it over.

"He doesn't look like an escort."

"What is an escort supposed to look like?"

"I don't know. Sort of like a model."

"Maybe she went for brains and sensitivity over hunky looks."

"I'm assuming you do the same?"

She hit the gas but the old Honda merely puttered away.

"Just doesn't project the same image as the Ducati, does it?" noted Roy.

"It was either this or the Bentley."

"What tipped you that he wasn't the real Watkins?"

"He didn't want to go down to the Starbucks to talk even though that would have been the safest thing to do from his perspective. I think he was afraid someone from the building who knew the real Watkins might have overheard us and fingered him as an imposter."

"Or he just doesn't like coffee."

"And the guy didn't match the apartment. Three-hundred-dollar shoes, a Hickey Freeman shirt, and professional manicure do not compute with particleboard furniture. And the place had been tossed. Didn't you see the indentations in the carpet from where the hutch, the credenza, the TV cabinet, and the shelving system had been moved?"

"Uh, no, I guess I missed that."

"You notice he grilled us on what we knew and what we were guessing about? We weren't interrogating him so much as he was us."

"So who are they?"

"The only thing I know is they're good."

"What would they have been looking for?"

"Whatever Diane Tolliver left with Watkins."

"So *that's* why you told him you were hanging up the investigation."

She nodded. "It buys us some time. And for all I know that dude is mixed up with the guys who were trying to kill me last night. If they think we're harmless and raising the white flag, well, that's not a bad thing."

"So it looks like this might go a lot further than the Captain. They took his DNA, by the way."

"Let me guess. They used the fresh cup of coffee ploy?"

"How'd you know?"

"They'll check it against the sperm they found on Diane and that'll clear him."

"So it was a rape?"

"Apparently so."

"But, Mace, then it was probably just a random thing. Otherwise why would the bandit rape her?"

Mace gave him an exasperated look. "To make it *seem* like a random crime, Roy."

"But they left sperm behind?"

"And you can bet it won't match up to any database. Just like a weapon can be sterilized, so can sperm, no pun intended."

"Okay."

"If it is connected I'm wondering why the shooters came after me."

"You were at the crime scene."

"Along with a hundred other cops."

"Okay, you've been hanging out with me."

"So why not target *you*? You worked with her. You were down there in Six D all alone waiting for me. They could have easily popped you."

"That's nice to know."

"We need to get into her house."

"Diane's?"

"I struck out in her office. There has to be something at the house."

"I'm sure the police searched it."

"Then we need to search it again."

"Mace, if we get caught, you'll have violated your probation. Can't your sister help us?"

"No."

"Why not?"

"I've got my reasons."

"I'd like to hear them."

Mace sighed. "She's not exactly thrilled with me right now. So how do we get into Tolliver's house? Do you have a key?"

"No, why would I have a key to her house?"

"Well, we have some time to muddle that. Right now we're heading over to check out some stuff for Abe."

"Is that why you wanted me along?"

She glanced at him. "What, you mean for protection?"

"I'm not that stupid. I clearly failed the bodyguard test."

"Not when you put your car between me and the shooter. Those rounds could easily have hit you. That took real courage. But I thought you might enjoy hanging out with me. And bring you back to your old, wild CJA days."

"Long way from Georgetown."

"A lifetime, Roy. A lifetime."

56

THE PEOPLE at Social Services working with Abe Altman were both extremely helpful and laudatory of the wealthy professor.

"He's a man with vision," said the supervisor, Carmela, a young Hispanic woman with straight dark hair and dressed in a pleated skirt and blouse and flats. "He gets it."

"Well, I hope I *get* it too," said Mace.

They were sitting in the woman's office, a ten-by-ten square with a rusty window AC unit that didn't work. There were water stains on the ceiling and walls. The furniture looked like it had been rescued from the dump and the clunky computer on her desk was at least a decade old. The government purse had clearly not been opened very wide to outfit this place.

She said, "Mr. Altman mentioned that you used to be a cop."

"Don't hold that against me."

"I won't. My older brother drives a scout car right here in Seven D."

"Then he's got his hands full."

"You know this area?"

"Used to be my old stomping ground." Mace glanced down at the sheaf of papers in her hand. "So these are all the names?'

"Yes. We've made contact and they will be expecting you at whatever meeting times you give us. After you called to say you were on your way, I made contact with Alisha, the first on the list. She's expecting you in the next thirty minutes." She glanced at Roy. "You look like a lawyer."

"Mr. Kingman is assisting me in this project."

The woman gave him an appraising look. "You ever been down this way?"

"Was down in Six D just last night if that counts."

She looked surprised. "What for?"

"Looking for some excitement. And I found it."

"I bet. Well, the places you'll be going are a little rough."

"I assume that's why we're going to them," answered Mace. "We'll be okay."

"How rough?" Roy wanted to know.

"Even my brother doesn't like taking calls at some of the places on your list, unless he has a couple units as backup."

Roy glanced at Mace with a worried look. "Really?"

"Thanks, Carmela," said Mace, tugging on Roy's arm. "We'll be in touch."

They climbed back in the Honda. Mace read through the file and said, "Okay, Alisha Rogers here we come."

Roy had been reading over her shoulder. He said, "She's only sixteen and already the mother of a three-year-old?"

"Don't sound so stunned. We left the world of *Leave It to Beaver* a long time ago."

He read off Alisha's address. "Do you know where that is?"

"Yep. Middle of Cheerio Alley. How do you like your Cheerios, Roy?"

"Usually without OxyContin. How exactly are we supposed to go into places where the police don't want to go and come out reasonably healthy?"

"It's a little late to be asking that, isn't it?"

"Humor me."

"We're going to help people, not bust their ass. That'll count for something."

"That's it? We just tell them we're here to help people and the dangerous seas will part? This isn't a Disney flick."

"I never took you for a cynic."

"I'm not a cynic. I just want to go home alive tonight."

Mace's smile faded. "Never a bad goal to have."

57

ALISHA LIVED in an apartment house that more resembled a bombed-out building in the middle of Baghdad than a residence within an easy commute of the Capitol building. As they pulled into the trash-strewn parking lot where the skeletons of a dozen cars lurked, Roy looked around nervously. "Okay, I've definitely been in Georgetown too long, because we're still in the car and I'm already freaking out."

"There are more sides to life than the rich one, Roy. Sure, there's a lot of crime here, but most people who live in this area obey the law, work really hard, pay their taxes, and try to raise their families in peace."

"I know, you're right," he said sheepishly.

"But keep a sharp lookout because it only takes one bullet to ruin a perfectly good day."

"You could've stopped with raising families in peace."

As they headed to the building on foot they passed men and women huddled in tight pockets on low brick walls, sitting on dilapidated playground furniture, or else standing inside darkened crannies of the building's overhang. All these folks stared at the pair as they made their way to the entrance. Mace kept a brisk pace, though her gaze scanned out by grids, probing gingerly into the shadowy edges before pulling back. As Roy watched her it was like she was using antennae to sense potential threats.

"Okay, are we in imminent danger of dying?" he asked.

"You get that just by waking up every day."

"Thanks for being optimistic."

"Reefer, crack, H, Cheerios, meth, Oxy," recited Mace as they marched along.

"I can smell the pot, but the other stuff?"

Mace pointed to the ground where there were remnants of plastic baggies, elastic straps, snort straws, bits of paper, crushed prescription pill bottles, and even broken syringes. "It's all right there if you know what you're looking for. Which apartment does Alisha live in?"

"File said 320."

They walked inside and the smell of pot, urine, raw garbage, and feces hit them like a wrecking ball. In a low voice Mace said, "Don't even wrinkle your nose, Roy, we got eyes all around the clock face. No disrespect. Can't afford it."

They marched on while Roy's gut churned and his nose twitched.

"Elevator or stairs?" he said.

"I doubt the elevator works. And I don't like being locked in little places where I don't know who'll be waiting for me when the doors open."

"Taking the stairs will probably be dicey too."

"No probably about it. It *will* be dicey."

She opened the door to the stairs, pushing it all the way against the wall in case someone was lurking there. Her gaze moved up, to the next landing.

"Clear, let's hit it."

"What if somebody stops us?"

"Getting jumpy on me?"

"Actually it's been a real struggle keeping my underwear clean since we left the car."

"I know you're the lawyer, but if someone stops us let me do the talking."

"I have no problem with that."

"One thing, though, can you fight?"

"With words or fists?"

"Look around, this is not the Supreme Court."

"Yeah, I can. My Marine brother used to kick my ass on a regular basis until I grew six inches in one summer and started holding my own. Then he taught me the tricks of the trade."

"Marines are good at that. Might come in handy. Last time I was here I was wearing my badge and I barely got out alive."

"Thanks for telling me," muttered Roy.

They reached the third floor and found their way blocked by two enormous men in prison shuffle jeans with the waistbands down to the bottom of their butt cheeks and sporting short-sleeved shirts showing muscular arms so tattooed there was no bare skin left. When they tried to walk around them, the men moved with them, forming a wall that stretched right across the narrow hall. Mace took a step back, her hand sliding to her pocket even as she smiled.

"We're looking for Alisha Rogers. Do you know her?"

The men simply stared back without answering. One bumped shoulders with Roy, knocking him back against the wall.

Mace said, "Alisha knows we're coming. We're here to help her."

"She ain't need no help," said one of the men. He was bald with a neck so thick it seemed like a continuation of his bull-like trap muscles. From down the hall there came the sounds of screaming, the slamming of a door, and then what sounded like shots. An instant later, music started blaring from multiple sources and the screams and shots could no longer be heard.

"So you *do* know her?" Mace continued in a pleasant tone.

"What if I do?"

"There could be some money in it for her too."

"How much money?"

"Depends on how well our meeting goes. And no, we didn't bring the cash with us," added Mace as she spotted one of the guys' hands flit behind his back.

"Who you from?" asked Baldy.

"Social!" said a loud voice. They all turned to see a woman nearly as wide as she was tall marching up to them. She was dressed in a long jean dress stretched to its absolute maximum. A colorful scarf was wound around her head and her long toes poked out from the sandals she wore.

"You know them?" said Baldy.

The scarf lady clutched Mace's hand. "Damn right I do. Now get your sorry asses out the way right now! I am not messing with you today, Jerome, and I mean what I say."

The men moved quietly if grudgingly aside and scarf lady led Mace down the hall while Roy scurried after them, his gaze back on Jerome.

"Thanks," said Mace.

"Thanks doesn't come close to cutting it," Roy chimed in.

"Alisha told me Carmela called a little bit ago and she asked me to be on the lookout for you. But I was taking some laundry down and you got past me. Sorry about those jerks. Barks worse than their bite, but they still bite."

"Were those shots we heard a minute ago?" Roy wanted to know.

"Just a little disagreement probably. No blood no foul."

"What's your name?" Mace asked.

"Just call me Non."

58

Neither Mace nor Roy probably knew what to expect next. But what they certainly didn't expect was what they found in Alisha Rogers's apartment. The place was clean, smelled of Pine-Sol, and was amazingly tidy, particularly because in the hallway leading to her apartment they had passed twelve large bags of garbage stacked nearly to the ceiling. Maybe, Mace thought, that was the reason why Alisha used so much Pine-Sol.

The furniture was cheap, all probably secondhand, but arranged with some thought and even design. The small windows had what looked to be hand-sewn curtains. A few toys were stacked in one corner in an old cardboard crate that had "Deer Park" stamped on it. From what they could see, the place consisted of only two rooms, the one they were in and another, probably the bedroom, where the door was closed. The "kitchen" had a hot plate and an under-the-counter mini-fridge.

Non had a key to the apartment and had let them in.

"Alisha!" she called out. "Social's here."

There were footsteps in the other room, a door opened, and Alisha Rogers stepped out. A three-year-old boy was riding on her slim right hip. Her hair was long and pulled back and tied with a clip except for a tightly braided ponytail that poked out on the right side of her head. Her eyes were big, her face small, and her lips thin and cracked. At five-three she probably didn't weigh more than ninety pounds, while the little boy had to be almost half that.

Roy looked down at the file he was holding documenting Alisha's background. Roy had seen enough while at CJA that teenage mothers did not really surprise him, though he also knew that a child raising a child was never a good thing. Yet it was far better than leaving the little boy in a Dumpster. He had to admire Alisha Rogers for taking that responsibility when some others didn't.

Non said, "I'm gonna leave you folks to it. Alisha, you need anything I'll be down in the laundry room."

"Thanks, Non," Alisha said, her gaze on the floor as the boy stared at Mace and Roy openmouthed.

Mace stepped forward. "Alisha, I'm Mace and this is Roy. We met with Carmela this morning."

Gaze still on the floor, Alisha said, "Carmela's nice."

"And she was very excited about us meeting with you."

"That's a good-looking boy you have there," said Roy. "What's his name?"

"Tyler," she answered. She lifted one of her son's pudgy fists and did a small wave. When she let go, however, Tyler let his arm drop limply to his side and continued to stare at them, his mouth forming a big O.

"You want to sit down while we talk?" said Mace. "Tyler looks like a load."

While Roy and Mace sat on a small battered sofa with trash-bag-covered foam, Alisha put Tyler down on the floor and sat cross-legged next to him. She snagged a toy out of the Deer Park box and handed it to him.

"You play, Ty, Momma's got to talk to these people."

Tyler plopped down on the floor and obediently started playing with the spaceman action figure from *Toy Story* that was missing an arm and a leg.

Alisha looked up. "Carmela say you folks got something for me."

"To be part of a study," said Mace.

Alisha didn't look happy about this. "I thought it gonna be a job. A real job, you know, with child care and some health benefits."

"No, that's right. The study does have a money and training component."

"How 'bout school?"

"And an education component too. That's considered critical, in fact."

"Ain't got my GED. Dropped out to have Tyler. Went back but couldn't make it work."

"We can help with that. You still want to get your GED?" asked Mace.

"Got to if I want to get out of here. Here's just drugs or Mickey D's if I ain't got no school. Can't take care of Ty good." She reached out and stroked Tyler's wiry hair.

As Mace looked at the little boy's face it struck her that she recognized his features, but couldn't remember from where. "Let's go over the details and we'll see if it's something you're interested in."

"I'm interested in anything that'll get us outta here."

"You and Tyler, you mean."

"And my brother."

"Your brother?" Mace said questioningly. That had not been in the report.

"He just got back."

"From where?"

"Prison."

"Okay. How about Tyler's dad?"

She hesitated, her gaze darting to the floor.

Mace had seen that same maneuver a million times. The lady was about to lie.

"Dead probably. I don't know. He ain't here, that's all."

"How about your parents?" asked Roy.

"My daddy's dead. He sold heroin on the corner a block over from here. My momma left me with my grandma."

"Why did your mother leave you?" Roy asked.

"Had to. She in prison for killing my daddy."

"Oh," said Roy.

"Ain't like he didn't deserve it," she said defensively. "He beat her bad all the time."

"And your grandmother?" asked Mace.

Alisha's big eyes became watery. "Drive-by. She just walking down the street with her groceries and got caught between two damn crews. But she got to see Ty born. He got to see his great-grandma."

"That's pretty rare," said Roy. "Four generations."

"She was only forty-nine when she got killed. My momma was thirteen too when she had me."

Mace was about to ask another question when the door to the apartment opened. When Mace saw who it was she realized where she'd seen Tyler's facial features before.

"What the hell you doing here, bitch?" the man at the door screamed.

Darren Rogers, a.k.a. Razor, the guy Mace had pepper-sprayed, stood in the doorway. A moment later the "crappy" semi-auto pistol was pointed right at her face.

59

W<small>HAT THE HELL</small> *you* doing, Darren?" said Alisha as she jumped to her feet.

He pointed at Mace. "This the bitch what sprayed that shit in my eyes last night. I told you 'bout her."

"Well, in all fairness, I wouldn't have if you weren't pointing a gun at me."

Alisha stared at him. "Did you do that?"

"Hell no. The bitch just shot me with the shit while I was walking by. I never pulled no gun on her ass till right now."

Mace turned to Alisha. "He's also got a .22 caliber revolver in a left ankle holster. And his street name is Razor 'cause, as he told me, he's so sharp."

Alisha put her hands on her hips and scowled at Darren. "How she know all that if you just walking by and ain't pulled your damn gun?"

Darren's face screwed up in frustration. "How I supposed to know that?"

Mace turned to Alisha. "Is he your brother?"

"Hey, you talk to *me*," snapped Darren.

"Okay, are you her brother?"

"Yeah, so what?"

"What were you in prison for?"

"Who told you I was in prison?" Darren glanced darkly at his sister.

She said, "Darren, put that gun away before somebody gets hurt. Look at Ty, he's scared to death."

Unnoticed for the last couple of minutes, Tyler had crawled into a corner and tears were dribbling down his chubby cheeks. He was holding up his spaceman, apparently as a shield. Darren's hostile look instantly melted away. "Ah hell, Ty, I'm sorry, little man." He put the gun in his jacket pocket and hustled over to pick up the child. He held his cheek against Tyler's and talked softly to the little boy.

"He's not crying," said Roy curiously.

Alisha started to answer but Darren beat her to it. "He ain't crying, 'cause he can't talk. Can't make no sounds or nothing."

Mace looked at Alisha. "Have you had him checked out?"

Tears again filled Alisha's eyes. "It was 'cause I doing drugs. Ain't even know I was pregnant. Doctors say that messed up something in Ty's head."

"I'm sorry," said Mace.

Alisha rubbed her eyes. "My damn fault for getting pregnant."

"You got *raped*, Alisha," snapped Darren. "This ain't nothing you did."

"Raped? Did they catch who did it?" asked Roy.

Darren eyed his sister and then looked away in disgust.

"Alisha?" said Mace. "Did you report the rape?"

She shook her head.

"Why not?"

Darren spoke up. "'Cause the dude what raped her is named Psycho. He got the biggest crew around here. You go to the cops on him, you be dead. That's why!"

Mace sat back. "I know about Psycho. The guy's been running his drug and gun op for nearly ten years. That's a lifetime in that line of work. You've got to be real smart and even more dangerous to last that long."

"But the police can protect you," said Roy. He glanced at Mace. "Can't they?"

Darren laughed. "Oh yeah. Sure they can. See, last time the police protected somebody 'round here against Psycho they found his head in a trash bag floating in the Anacostia with a sock stuffed in the mouth. They ain't never found the rest of him. That's some damn fine protection, now ain't it?"

Darren put Tyler down on the floor. "So you tell me what the hell you doing here?"

"How about a chance to get out of here," said Mace.

"Outta here how?"

"I'm working on a project with a professor from Georgetown."

"Georgetown! What the hell that got to do with us?"

"I can explain it to you."

Darren looked like he was about to start shouting again, but then he sat down and motioned at her. "Go on then. Tell me."

Mace spent the next thirty minutes doing just that, filling in the basics first and then building on that. "The professor's theory is that to survive on the streets of virtually any large city requires exemplary intelligence, nerve, daring, risk-taking, and the ability to adapt on the fly. Most people require familial support, a bed, a roof, some food, and relief from danger to function properly."

Darren looked sullen. "Ain't that bad 'round here. Do what you got to do. We *got* a roof over our heads now. Food to eat. And she *got* family now. And ain't nobody coming in that door unless they go through me first."

"But it's not a normal life, Darren," pointed out Mace. "You can't reach your potential if you're always worried about becoming homeless or not having enough food to eat, or waiting for somebody to put a bullet in your head."

"I can take care of myself."

Mace turned to Alisha. "You were selected from the files at Social."

"Why me?"

"You've managed to support a special needs child while getting off drugs and after losing both parents. You currently hold down four part-time jobs while getting Tyler's basic health care needs taken care of out of sheer persistence and more than a dash of ingenuity. And you did all this while just having celebrated your sixteenth birthday. I'd say that was pretty special." Mace looked around the tiny apartment. "And you got this place using forged documents that showed you were eighteen and could legally sign a contract."

Alisha looked frightened. "I had to. After my grandma got killed folks came and took her apartment, kicked us out. After that we was living in a box in an alley off Bladensburg Road. Ain't no place for a child. And Darren was gone."

Darren took her hand. "But I'm back now, baby sister. I take care of you and Ty."

Mace looked over at Darren. She really didn't know what to do with him. "You can't take care of them by robbing people. You'll be right back in prison. Last night if I'd been a cop, you already would be."

Darren whirled on her. "You just get the hell out of here."

"When you go back to prison what happens to Alisha and Tyler? Psycho can come right through that door. Then what?"

Darren started to say something but then just stared at the floor.

Mace said, "So there it is, Alisha. That's the offer."

"You trust this professor dude?" said Darren suddenly.

"Yes I do. And he really cares."

"Why the hell he want to help folks like us?"

Choosing her words carefully, she said, "It's like he's building his own crew."

The angry look faded from Darren's face. "So he be the boss then?"

"Just until you can be your own boss," Mace replied.

Darren looked at his sister. "This shit sounds too good to be true. What next, some fat guy running in here waving a big-ass check with a bunch of balloons?"

Mace said, "Darren, just to be clear, we didn't know you were in the picture. I don't know if the offer extends to you or not."

Alisha stood. "I ain't gonna do nothing without Darren coming too."

"Hold on, hold on, girl," said Darren quickly. "We got to think this through."

Mace stood. Roy did too. She said, "You don't have to make up your mind now. It's your choice. We have other appointments to get to."

Darren eyed her warily. "So if Alisha says no, then he just gets somebody else?"

"That's the plan, yeah. There are ten to start with."

Alisha said quickly, "When do he got to know?"

"A week."

Alisha started to say something but Darren turned to Mace. "You tell your boss that Alisha's gonna do it."

"With you along, you mean? I'll have to check on that."

"No. He ain't got to worry about me. Just Alish and Ty."

"Darren!" cried Alisha. "You ain't know what you saying."

Darren turned to her. "I take care of myself. Always have."

"But you ain't got nobody. The jerks in this building be jumping you already."

"I said I can take care of myself."

"But Darren—"

He turned back to Mace. "You tell the man that Alisha be part of his crew. And Ty too. That's it, no more talking."

"Okay." Mace looked over at Tyler, who was watching all of this from the corner. For the first time in a long time, Mace actually felt a lump in her throat. "They have some great doctors at G-town. They can take a look at your son."

Alisha nodded. "Okay," she said in a low voice.

Mace turned back to Darren. "I thought I had you figured out. But I was wrong. And I'm almost never wrong about stuff like that."

"You listen up, anything bad happens to Alisha or Ty, you got me to deal with." He went into the bedroom and closed the door.

Roy and Mace left the apartment. They hadn't gone ten feet when Non ran up to them, looking scared.

"You two got to get outta here right now!"

"What's up, Non?" asked Mace. "Is Jerome on the warpath?"

"I wish it just be him. Psycho found out you were talking to Alisha. He's coming over here. I think he believes you're the Five-oh and Alisha told you stuff."

"Will he try to hurt her?" Mace said quickly.

"I don't know. But that man is bad news all around."

Mace grabbed Roy's arm. "Come on, this way."

She led him down the hall to a different set of stairs. They fled down them, passing pill poppers, syringe stickers, and one guy fornicating with his lady while smoking a joint.

"What about Alisha and Ty?" asked Roy worriedly.

"I'm trying to call Beth, only I can't get a damn signal in here."

They reached the ground floor, ripped open the door, raced down a short stretch of hall, and then ran outside. And stopped.

A dozen men stood there. One of them, the tallest, stepped forward. He had a big smile and his eyes had the look of a man who was used to telling people what to do.

Roy looked at Mace. "Please tell me that's not Psycho."

Mace didn't answer. She just kept her eyes right on the guy coming at them.

60

Psycho circled them once and then twice, nodding, smiling, and glancing at his men and then back at Mace and Roy. A little taller than Roy, he had on black jeans, a sparkling white T-shirt, and tennis shoes. Several gold chains were visible at the neckline of his tee. His hair was cut so short it was more like a membrane over his scalp. His forearms were veined, muscled, and heavily tattooed. Mace noted that his pupils were normal-sized and his forearms clear of needle marks. You didn't last in that business if you were a user, she well knew. Life and death were often separated by only a rational, nimble decision.

On the third pass he stopped and stood in front of them.

"How's Alisha?" Psycho asked in a surprisingly high-pitched voice.

"Doing okay."

"They say you with Social? Why don't I believe that?"

"We're not cops," said Mace.

"Hey, lady jumped right to it. Must be smart, so I know she's not the blue." His crew laughed. Psycho said, "Then let *me* play the 'blues' part, okay?" Not waiting for an answer, he stood straight and assumed a mock stern expression. "Now you two got anything on your person that might *concern* me?"

Several of his crew guffawed at this.

"Not unless you object to a set of keys and a couple cell phones," said Mace.

"Couple?"

"Yeah, one for business and one for pleasure."

Psycho flicked his hand and two of his men came forward and performed the frisk. One squeezed Mace's butt and he got an elbow driven into his gut for the trouble.

"Whoa, lady got some fire," said Psycho. "You step back in line there, Black," he said to the doubled-over man. "Before you get your ass thumped."

He eyeballed Mace. "So no guns, no badge, that still don't mean no cops. Could be undercover."

"Don't even undercover agents carry guns?" asked Roy. "Especially coming around here?"

Mace let a small groan escape as Psycho turned to Roy. "You got a problem with *around here*? What, you don't like *around here*, Mayonnaise Boy?"

Roy managed to swallow a sudden lump in his throat. "I never said that."

"Yeah, you ain't got to say it. I smell it." He glanced at Mace. "This your old lady?" He ran a tongue over his lips as he checked out Mace. "Fine-looking woman."

"It's a business relationship," said Roy, who instantly regretted having said it.

"A business relationship!" whooped Psycho. "A business relationship?" He turned to his men. "He got himself a business relationship with the chick."

They all laughed, and then Psycho spun around so fast it was a blur. "Then you ain't mind if I do this, then, business relationship dude?" He moved to squeeze one of Mace's breasts, but Roy grabbed his hand and pushed it away.

"Yeah I do mind."

The crew fell silent.

Psycho looked down at the hand Roy had grabbed and then back up, his grin intact. "You really want to go there, mayo?"

"Not really, no. And I won't so long as you keep your hands off her."

"So not you then?" Psycho's arm moved so fast Mace heard the impact before she even saw the swing of the fist. Roy staggered back, grabbing his face, and then fell down. The blood streamed down from his nose, and his eye was already swelling.

Mace quickly moved in front of him. "Look, we talked to Alisha about helping her and her son. That's all."

Psycho shoved her aside. " 'Scuse me, bitch, but I ain't done thumping me this asshole."

As Psycho advanced on Roy, Mace reached in her pocket for her Taser phone. But before she could snag it two of Psycho's men grabbed her and held her arms behind her back.

Psycho's foot snapped into Roy's gut, doubling him over.

Mace yelled, "We're leaving, okay? We're outta here right now."

Psycho turned back around. "*I* say when you outta here. And *how* you outta here. Walking or not. Breathing or not. Up to me. Me!"

He faced Roy and aimed a leisurely kick at his ribcage. The next moment Psycho had been spun around and was dumped on his knees. Roy's arms were angled through Psycho's arms and boxed around the other man's head, his blood dripping onto Psycho's scalp.

Roy said, "Seventy pounds of torque to the right and your spine snaps right in half. And there's not a damn thing you can do about it, you prick. And one of your guys pulls a gun, you turn into a corpse."

Psycho could only kneel there, his thick arms stuck uselessly out from his sides.

"They will kill your woman. All I got to do is say it."

"You're going to kill us both anyway. At least I'll have the pleasure of taking you along for the ride."

"What's this pounds of torque bullshit!"

One of Psycho's men stepped forward. "It's Marines. It's how they're trained to kill perimeter sentries. Shit's for real, boss," he added quietly.

Psycho looked up at his guy. "You in the Marines, Jaz?"

"Older brother was. He told me."

"You a Marine?" Psycho said to Roy.

"Would it matter?"

"You kill me, they kill you and the woman. Now if you don't kill me, *I'm* gonna kill you both. How 'bout that?"

Roy looked past where Psycho's men were standing. "How about another option?"

"What?"

"The really manly way to settle disputes."

"Knives? You ain't that dumb. I'll cut your mayo ass up."

"I said *really* manly."

"Meaning what?"

"Meaning basketball. One-on-one. There's a court and a ball right over there."

Mace turned her head to stare at the single netless hoop and the old ball resting next to the support pole.

"Basketball!" roared Psycho. "Just 'cause I'm black you think I play ball?"

Roy glanced down. "No. But you're wearing the same shoes that the UNC team wears on the court. And they're not just for show. They've got black scuffs all over the bottoms and the sides. That only comes from playing ball on the asphalt. In fact, I can tell from the scuff patterns that you're a drive-to-the-hoop and not a pull-up jumper kind of guy."

"So you know your basketball?"

"I'm a fan. Is it a deal?"

"Sure, man, no problem."

Roy tightened his grip on the man's neck. "Don't bullshit me."

"I ain't bullshitting you."

Mace said, "That's a good thing. Because if you say you'll do it and you don't, then you just lost the respect of your entire crew. They may not show it today, or tomorrow, but one day they will. Their boss, who wouldn't take a white boy on in hoops? Rather shoot his ass? Yeah, that's real easy. See, you already let him get the jump on you. And you may try to sound all cool and everything, but you're the one on your knees with another man making the decision whether you live or die. He could kill you right now. But he didn't. What he's offered you is respect. A way to settle this, man to man."

Psycho's superior manner slowly faded as he eyed his troops one by one. None of them would fully meet his gaze.

"So what's it gonna be?" said Mace.

"Play to eleven, a point a hoop and win by two," snarled Psycho. "Meaning *I* win by two. Now you let go of my neck so I can kick your ass."

Roy slowly released the man and Psycho stood, carefully wiping off the knees of his jeans. He looked Roy up and down. "Do you even know *how* to play ball?"

"A little."

"A little don't cut it, *around here*."

"We can flip a coin to see who gets the ball first."

"Oh, you can have it first. Be the only time you get the damn ball. Oh, and here's one more thing to keep in mind. You win, you both walk. I win, you're both dead."

61

Psycho stole the ball from Roy by burying a shoulder in his gut and knocking him down before dunking and scoring the first point. He walked back over to Roy, who was slowly getting to his feet. Psycho kicked him hard in the shin.

"That's one."

"That was also a foul," said Roy.

"Ain't no fouls on this court. Just man to man."

"Your ball."

Roy had played against every competition imaginable both on the college basketball court and on the streets. Most guys had one signature move, the best two, the very best three. He let Psycho drive past him and score, taking an elbow shot to the thigh.

That was one move, Roy thought to himself.

Psycho scored again, using a different move.

That was two moves.

He glanced over at Mace, who was staring at him anxiously. He gave her a quick wink and then went back on defense, setting his butt low, his feet and hands spread wide.

Psycho drove again and scored using his first move. Or he would have if Roy hadn't stuffed the ball so hard it knocked Psycho flat on his back on the asphalt.

"My ball," said Roy as he snagged it and dribbled it back and forth between his legs without even looking down.

As Psycho started to guard him, Roy backed up and banked a twenty-footer.

"That's one," said Roy.

A minute later a reverse dunk and then a twenty-foot fader by Roy tied it.

"Three-three."

Five minutes later, and despite Psycho fouling him brutally at every opportunity, Roy was up by six and his opponent was bent over clutching a stitch in his side while Roy wasn't even sweating.

With a perfectly executed crossover dribble that had Psycho frantically backpedaling and then falling on his ass, Roy drove past him and slammed the shot home.

"That's ten," announced Roy. "One more to go."

He took the ball and bounced it back and forth between his legs while he studied his staggered opponent. Psycho was humiliated, tired, and pissed. Roy could at least let the guy make it respectable.

Screw that.

He dribbled backward and stopped, set up, and nailed a twenty-five-footer. The ball didn't even touch the metal rim as it dropped through.

The ball bounced on the asphalt and came to a stop against the post.

"That's eleven. You lose. We walk." He headed over to Mace.

Psycho lunged forward and grabbed a gun from one of his men. Breathing hard, he pointed it at Roy's back.

Roy turned around. "Is there an issue?"

Wiping the sweat from his eyes Psycho said, "Where'd you learn to play ball like that?"

"On a court just like this."

"You lied to me. You said you knew how to play just a little."

"Everything's relative. You might not be as good as you think you are."

Psycho cocked the pistol's hammer back.

Mace pulled free from the two men holding her and moved between Roy and the gun. "Everybody here heard you set the rules. He wins, we walk. *Your* words."

Psycho eyed his crew and then looked back at Mace. The gun came down one inch at a time.

"Get your asses outta here. Now!"

"Just so we're clear, this is not a cop thing. We're with Social. We just came here to help Alisha get a better life, for her and her *son*. Don't make her a part of this, because she's not."

Psycho said nothing. He strode off. His crew followed quickly.

When they were alone Mace turned to Roy. "That was unbelievably kickass."

"Would it be really unmanly if I wet my pants right now?"

"I wouldn't think any less of you."

"So what about Alisha and Tyler? Do you think he'll leave them alone?"

"Call me stupid, but I don't trust anyone whose name is Psycho. I'm going to have Beth get her and the kid out of here."

"And her brother?"

"Yeah, I guess so."

"I suppose we can do some more interviews today," he said doubtfully.

"I think they can wait. Let's go back to Abe's."

"Is he home?"

Mace used her sleeve to wipe the blood off Roy's face. "I don't care if he is or not. I need to get my little hero cleaned up."

She took his hand and led him back to the Honda.

No one bothered them on the way out.

CHAPTER

62

MACE PUT the pack of ice over Roy's nose as he sat in the spa in Altman's guesthouse. "How's it feel?"

"Broken. But then so does my leg, my ankle, and my ribs."

"At least the swelling around your eye's gone down. You want to go to the hospital?"

"No, I'll be okay so long as I stop interacting with guys named Psycho."

"I was going to order out for Chinese, but when I called the main house to see if they had a take-out menu, Herbert seemed indignant. So he's preparing a Chinese dinner just for us."

"Very nice of Herbert. Where's Altman?"

"The Bentley's gone, so maybe he ran out to do something."

Roy sat up straighter, positioning the ice pack under his eye. "Did you get through to your sister?"

"She had Alisha and Tyler picked up and brought to Social Services."

"And her brother?"

"He wasn't there. That guy worries me."

"That he'll go after Psycho, you mean?"

"Yep. And that means he'll be dead."

She sat on the edge of the spa. "You know why I brought you along with me today?"

"For the comedic potential?"

"No, to keep an eye on you."

He took off the ice pack and swiveled around to look at her. "To protect *me*?"

"After those guys came after me I knew they'd run your license plate and find out who you were. I was worried. But the only thing I did was set you up in a death match with an asshole named Psycho. What a genius I am."

He gripped her hand. "Hey, you had no idea that was going to happen. And we did okay. Right?"

"You did great, not just okay."

"You must be rubbing off on me."

They stared at each other. She stroked his hair and he rubbed her arm.

"You up for getting wet, Mace?" he said quietly, his gaze melding into hers.

They heard a sound from downstairs. Mace jumped to her feet. "That must be Herbert. Do you want me to bring the food up here or do you want to eat outside overlooking the stunning gardens?"

He let go of her hand. "Stunning gardens sound good."

"Take your time, I'll keep the food warm."

As she fled down the stairs Roy slowly sank back into the water.

Beth had just come back to her office after attending a meeting in Four D when her phone rang. She picked it up. "Chief," she said.

"Please hold for Interim U.S. Attorney Mona Danforth," a woman's voice said in an overly formal manner.

Beth tapped her fingers on her desk as she waited for Mona to pick up. This was a stunt the lady pulled all the time. She'd probably been standing there watching her secretary make the call and then sauntered back to her office, just to make Beth wait.

Thirty seconds passed and Beth was just about to slam the phone down when the woman's voice came on the line. "Mona Danforth."

"Yeah, that part I got since *you* called *me*. What's up?"

"Something strange on the Meldon case."

"You have specifics?"

"The CIA is disavowing any knowledge of the matter."

"And you're surprised why?"

"Hey, you asked me to make some calls and get back to you."

Beth stared down at her desk as she tried to compartmentalize the one million things she still had to do today after already changing gears a dozen times. But mostly she was thinking of Mona's little plan to ruin both her and Mace. "Go ahead."

"I checked Jamie's caseload. He was not working on anything that would've caused anyone to kill him and throw him in a Dumpster."

"But he was a defense lawyer in NYC, right?"

"More specifically he was a mob lawyer. But the people he represented are either dead, in prison, or no longer in the business. The one guy who might've had a grudge against him is in Witness Protection. And U.S. Marshals don't ordinarily let their protectees run off to commit murders."

"So the CIA claims they're not behind the investigation into Jamie's murder. Let's say they're telling the truth for once. Who else could it be? I heard the order to stand down might've come from the White House. But then I talked to someone I trust who told me that probably wasn't true."

"Who'd you talk to?"

"Sorry, Mona, I start giving away my sources, I won't have any left."

"Fine!"

"Look, the mayor was the one to actually call me off, but when I asked him where the order had come from he clammed up."

"You think the Bureau is playing straight with us on this?"

"I know the director and his top guys, just like you do. They've usually played straight in the past. Why do you ask?"

"Because I got a message from a Fibbie asking to meet with me to go over the Meldon case."

"Why you?"

"I am the interim U.S. attorney, Beth. Jamie worked for me."

"But the last time I checked, a homicide committed in D.C. fell within my purview. I have to catch the damn bandits before you can prosecute them, Mona."

"Well, if you want to meet with him, feel free. I'm swamped as it is. And when I put it up as an option, he said he had no problem with that. In fact, I think he was planning on talking to you anyway."

Beth pulled a piece of scratch paper toward her. "Fine, what's his name."

"Special Agent Karl Reiger."

CHAPTER

63

THE SUN was setting as they finished their meal. Herbert had served the dinner in a Roman ruin–style pavilion next to an elaborate water garden with a pond, waterfall, and hundreds of thirsty flowers.

"I wonder if Herbert rents out for parties," said Roy, as he used chopsticks to push a last bit of spicy pork into his mouth.

"If you had a full-time gig here would you ever want to leave?" said Mace as she sipped on a glass of Chinese beer.

Roy glanced at her. "So about me asking you to join me in the hot tub—"

"What about it?" Mace cut in.

"Uh, nothing."

Her tone softened. "Look, it's just been awhile. The last few years did a number on me. Made it hard to have a normal relationship. Hell, if I ever could in my line of work."

"I understand that."

"But I like hanging with you. And you put a lot on the line for me. I won't forget that."

Mace leaned forward and made marks on a cloth napkin with her sticks. "Diane Tolliver's office."

"You want to go back to there? Why?"

"*Something* happened, Roy. Those guys came after me right after I was there."

"How would they have even known you were there? I was the only one up there with you and I didn't tell anybody."

"We also need to get into Diane's house."

"Won't the police have it taped off?"

"It's just tape."

"No, it's *just* a felony. More than one, actually. You could go back to prison."

Her face eased into a hard mask. "I'm already in prison, Roy, but I'm apparently the only one who can see the damn bars."

"What do you hope to find at her house?"

"She wanted us to talk to Andre Watkins. The bandits beat us to it. So we have to get that information from another angle."

"Come on, shouldn't we leave this to the police?"

"Some jerks tried to kill me. I'm not walking away from that."

"You have no idea if that's connected to what happened to Diane."

"My gut is telling me different. And I listen to my gut."

"It's never wrong?"

"Not on the important issues, no."

Roy eyed the immense gymnasium facility Altman had shown them across from the guesthouse.

"You up for a little B-ball?"

"What? You didn't have enough with Psycho?"

"I would assume it would be a little friendlier than that."

"Never assume. Remember how you described my play? I can hard-foul with the best of them. But I didn't bring my uniform."

"I bet a guy like Altman has all that stuff."

"What do you have in mind?"

"One-on-one?"

"I saw what you did to Psycho. You're out of my league."

"Come on, I'll take it easy on you."

"Gee, just what I wanted to hear." She paused. "How about a game of HORSE instead?"

"HORSE?"

"Yeah, you know the game, right."

"I think I played it once or twice."

"Well, in the interest of full disclosure, I spent the last two years of my life playing it every day. Still game?"

"No problem."

"Don't sound so confident. What are we playing for?"

"Playing for?"

"I'm not getting all hot and sweaty for nothing."

"You up for anything?"

"Not if the loser has to give the winner a full-body massage while naked, or some crap like that."

"No nakedness or bodily touching. I promise."

She looked at him warily.

"Come on, Mace, trust your gut."

"Okay, my gut says whatever you propose I accept."

"Okay. You win, we *both* keep investigating this thing without the cops. I win, we go to the cops and tell them everything and let them handle it."

Mace looked at him with a stony expression.

"You're not going to back off your gut, are you?" he said.

"I guess I expected a little more from you, Roy."

"I think you'll thank me at some point. You ready?"

Mace stood. "Better bring your A-game, Kingman."

64

I FEEL LIKE I'm back in college," said Roy as they gazed in awe at the facility Abe Altman had built with Warren Buffett–fueled riches.

"You were on a major college team. I only played girls' high school ball in a Catholic league, meaning we had no money. This is like hoops heaven to me."

Roy pointed to the rafters. "He even has a facsimile of the NCAA championship banners the men's and women's teams won at Maryland."

They spent a few minutes checking out the pool, full-size locker room with showers, sauna, steam room, and exercise room equipped with the latest machines. There was one room with workout clothing neatly laid out that looked like it had never been worn. Rows of athletic shoes lined one wall.

"This is like some sports fantasy," he said.

"Let's get down to business, because I'm really looking forward to kicking your ass," said Mace.

"Now who's overconfident?"

"You must really want out of this." Her tone was flat and hard.

"How about wanting to keep both of us alive? Doesn't that count for something?"

She bumped him with her shoulder. "If you want to call it living."

"What?"

"Being a chickenshit."

"So why'd you go along with the bet?"

"Like I said, because I really want to kick your ass."

They found a large room filled with all the athletic gear one could want, from baseball mitts to boxing gloves. There were at least fifty basketballs placed neatly on racks, many with college logos on them.

Mace pulled out one. "For old times' sake."

He looked down to see the familiar UVA Cavaliers logo painted on it.

They walked out to the court, where Roy did a mock cheer from the invisible crowd. She threw the ball hard at his gut. He easily caught it before impact. "So what was it like to play in front of thousands, Mr. Superstar?" she asked.

"Greatest time of my life."

"Glory days?"

"Being a lawyer pays the bills. It's not like I get out of bed every day thanking the Lord Almighty for the opportunity to make rich people even richer. It's not like what you used to do as a cop."

"Then get out of it. Go back to being a CJA, or join the public defender's office."

"Easier said than done."

"It's only hard if you make it."

"I'll keep that in mind. Ladies first." He bounced the ball to her.

"Shall we just dispense with the layup portion of the program?"

"Whatever you want."

She marched off fifteen feet at a hard right angle from the hoop. She set up and fired. Nothing but net.

Roy clapped. "I'm impressed. Not even warmed up."

"Oh, au contraire. I had the hot sauce on my noodles. And your loser bet made me even hotter. I'm like fire inside."

"Mace, I really think you'll thank me later for—"

"Just shoot!"

Roy took his place and swished it.

Twenty feet out at a forty-five degree angle Mace banked it in.

"About the limit of your range?" he asked.

"Guess you'll find out."

He made a swish.

Mace said, "Okay, that's H for you."

"What the hell are you talking about? I made the shot."

"I *banked* my shot, Roy. You swished it. You got an H." He stared at her openmouthed. "What?" she said. "You thought I banked it because I couldn't do it clean from twenty?"

She grabbed the ball from him, set up at twenty, and hit nothing but the bottom of the net.

"Okay, I've got an H," he said sullenly.

"Yes, you do."

After nearly an hour, over eighty shots and very few misses, each stood at H-O-R-S.

Mace set up her shot and banked in an arced twenty-five-footer.

"So just to be clear, do I need to bank or can I swish?" he asked.

"I'll take it easy on you, wimpy boy. You can choose."

Roy bounced the ball twice, took aim, and released. His shot missed not only the net but the rim as well.

Mace bent down, picked up the ball, and looked over, openmouthed.

"That's E," said Roy. "I lose. We keep working the case without the cops."

"So did you intend to lose on purpose all the time?"

"I guess that's something you'll never know. So what's our next move?"

"Are you sure about this?" She bounced the ball to him.

He bounced the ball back to her. "Don't ask me again. And don't get all mushy on me—not that that's likely to happen."

"Okay, Tolliver left the office on Friday around seven. The garage record told us that. And then she returned a little before ten."

"But she lived in the south end of Old Town. Why drive all the way out, turn around, and come back?"

"I called in a favor and found out that the cops pulled a credit card receipt. Diane ate at a place in Georgetown on Friday night called Simpsons. Do you know it?"

"Little hole-in-the-wall a block off M Street toward the river. I've been there. Good food. Was she alone?"

"No. The bill showed there were two meals served."

"Who was she with?"

"Don't know."

"Aren't the cops going to check with the people at the restaurant?"

"I don't know. They have the Captain in custody."

"But when the Captain turns out to be innocent?"

"Then we'll be ahead of the curve. But I've got to make one stop first."

"Where?"

"To see an old friend."

CHAPTER

65

Beth was piloting Cruiser One alone tonight, although she had a couple of uniforms in an unmarked car behind her as she sat in the deserted parking lot of a school. She was in uniform and still had her Glock 26 in its holster. Her policy was, when she wore the stars she carried the firepower too. Her radio hung from a clip on her shirt.

Most days the four stars on each shoulder felt like they weighed a ton apiece, and this day was no exception. This meeting tonight might add immeasurably to her professional pain. Yet she sat calmly and idly tapped a tune on her steering wheel as she listened to the police radio. By force of habit she was still monitoring the dispatches and responses from her officers. There'd been a shooting about six blocks from her location. Normally she would've gone to the scene. But tonight she was waiting. And not liking it.

She stopped tapping when the black sedan pulled into the parking lot. It just screamed FBI Bucar. She knew the shouts of "Five-oh" and "whoop-whoop" had started up the second the sedan had entered Five D. All Bucars looked the same, sounded the same, and even smelled the same. She knew that drugs, guns, gangs, and whores had silently pulled back into the shadows to let the Fibbies pass before they took up their illegal business once more. The sedan pulled to a stop next to her ride, hood to trunk. The driver's-side window slid down.

She saw the creds and badge first, the face second.

"Special Agent Karl Reiger." A second face appeared behind his. "My partner, Don Hope."

Beth said, "Your creds are Homeland Security. Danforth said you were Bureau."

"Misunderstanding. Happens sometimes. We actually were with the FBI up until a few years ago. Now we're assigned to a specialized division of DHS tasked to counterterrorism measures."

"Specialized division?"

"Yep. After 9/11 there're lots of them."

"Okay, let's talk."

"Our office or yours?"

Beth popped open her door, nodded to her men in the tail cruiser, and slipped into the backseat of the Town Car. Closing the door, she said, "Mona didn't really fill me in, so I'd appreciate a briefing."

Reiger and Hope turned sideways to look at her. Reiger said, "Up front, you have to know it's going to be limited."

"Not what I wanted to hear. When I get read into something I like all the pages."

"We've got orders just like everybody else."

"Specialized, you said?"

"Joint task force with a limited circle of need to know."

"That's just another name for 'you can't tell me.'"

"National security."

"That excuse I hate even more. The guys who pulled the crime scene plug on me, who where they?"

"Part of the task force."

"I've been doing this nearly twenty years. I have never seen someone waltz past the police tape simply by showing their damn driver's license."

"We don't like it any better than you."

"I doubt that. Did this all really come from the White House?"

"Who told you that?" Reiger said sharply.

"Sorry, can't read you in on that. I'm not sure you're cleared for it."

"Look, Chief, I know you're pissed. And I would be too, but national security —"

Beth cut him off. "I've played the national-security-trumps-everything game with the best of them. What I don't appreciate is being completely cut out of the loop on a homicide committed in my own backyard. I earned my badge and my creds, and I don't like getting blindsided by assholes with shields from DMV."

Reiger said, "We think Meldon was killed by domestic terrorists."

Beth leaned forward. "Domestic terrorists? What's the connection to him?"

"Case he was working. Remember the guy who tried to blow up the Air and Space Museum almost a year ago using four pounds of Semtex and a cell phone detonator?"

"Roman Naylor? How could I forget? It was one of my officers on K-9 duty that nailed the son of a bitch before he could kill a thousand kids from the Midwest who were there on a summer tour."

"Meldon was prosecuting the case. Naylor has groups of supporters in various states. United Sons of the American Patriot was one of them. They've been linked to three bombings of federal property in the last two years. We think that was just the warm-up act for something that will rival 9/11. A bunch of these homegrown whack jobs went underground after we and ATF came after them on a joint op. We suspect that three of Naylor's cronies were in D.C. last week to participate in a protest in front of the federal courthouse where he's being tried, and now they've disappeared."

"Wait a minute, Mona told me she'd reviewed Meldon's caseload and there was nothing he was working on that would account for his murder."

"And you trust Danforth?"

"Not really."

"Good, because that lady would lie to her grandmother on the woman's deathbed if she thought it would help her career. The fact is, we put Danforth on a short leash and *suggested* that she pass off the baton to you. She really didn't seem to mind. Lady doesn't like getting her nails dirty."

"Understood, but why did you suggest it?"

"Because we'd much rather deal with you than her."

"So you really think Naylor's cronies killed Meldon?"

"Doesn't take a big stretch."

"How did he die?'

Hope passed across a single sheet of paper. "This is a summary of the autopsy results. Contact gunshot wound to the back of the head, execution style. We got the slug. It was a .40-caliber round. But we'll never find a gun to match it to. His ride was found in western Maryland with only Meldon's prints on it. No trace at the crime scene. Neat and clean and the killers long gone."

"But if these guys were in D.C. how come I didn't get notice? How come Meldon didn't get protection?"

"We said *suspected*, not confirmed. And if it's the three we think it is, we didn't have anything to hold them on anyway except speculation and gut instincts, and the courts don't look too favorably on that. But we believe that they've been tasked to do the next Oklahoma City."

"If so, why risk it all by killing Meldon?"

"They were tight with Naylor. So it could simply be personal revenge. Now that the guy's dead the trial will be delayed."

"Any leads on these three?"

"Not yet. But we're running it down."

"And will I be in the loop when you do?"

"We can ask, Chief, that's all we can do."

"So by not really telling me anything, why did you call the meeting?"

"We told you our theory on who killed Meldon. And we gave you as much hard info as we could. Let me tell you, it was hell even getting that autopsy summary released."

"If you give me pictures of the three suspects, four thousand police officers can start looking for them."

"I highly doubt they hung around town after doing Meldon."

"Surprise, I also know police chiefs in other cities. And I even have some Feds I call friends."

"We have all that covered."

"So, again, why did you want to see me?"

"Professional courtesy," said Reiger. He paused. "And a high-up buddy of yours asked us to fill you in."

It didn't take Beth long to come up with the answer. "Sam Donnelly?"

"He's not the kind of guy who likes to take credit for stuff, but I won't deny it."

"I owe him."

"I'm sure he'll call in a favor from you one day. And I know this sounds unfair as hell, but if you get any leads we'd appreciate a heads-up."

Beth opened the door. "You'll get it."

"That easy?" said Reiger.

"Unlike you guys, I just want to catch the bandits. I don't really give a damn what agency gets the credit. Why don't you try to pass along that philosophy in your *specialized division*?"

A few seconds later Cruiser One was rolling with the tail car right behind.

As she drove out of sight Reiger looked at Hope, who said, "What do you think?"

"I think we did what we were told and now we report back."

"And the sister and the lawyer?"

"I'm not calling the plays on this thing, Don. I just execute them. But let me tell you, the further we go on this thing, the less I like it. I didn't sign on for this shit and I know you didn't either."

"They're paying us four times what we normally earn."

"Yeah, to kill our fellow Americans?"

"During the vetting Burns told us that we might have to go all the way. But it's to keep the country safe. Sometimes the enemies come from within. Hell, you know that."

"I still wanted to puke when I put that round in Meldon's head."

"Burns told us he was a traitor, showed us the proof. But if the truth came out, it would ruin years of intelligence work. He had to be taken out. This is black ops stuff, Karl, the old rules don't apply."

"Keep telling yourself that, you might start believing it."

Reiger steered the sedan out of the parking lot.

An unmarked car pulled slowly out of an alley opposite the lot and followed Reiger's sedan. The guy riding in the passenger seat said into the radio, "Mobile Two rolling and on their six."

Beth Perry's voice crackled into the car. "Where they go, you go. I don't care if it's hell and back. Chief out."

66

Remember me, Doc?"

Mace stood in the front lobby of the police forensic facility. Roy was waiting out in the car. Lowell Cassell, the chief medical examiner, smiled.

"I was both surprised and thrilled when they told me you were here."

"I see you're still in the habit of working late."

"Your sister has cut down considerably on the homicide rate, but unfortunately my backlog is still full."

They shook hands and then did a quick hug.

"It's so good to see you, Mace."

She smiled. "I missed you too, Doc."

Mace looked around. "They were just about to finish this place when I . . . went away."

Cassell nodded. "Yes. I hope Beth communicated my sentiments on that subject to you?"

"Loud and clear."

"So tell me, what can I do for you?"

"Well, I wanted to come by, see you, see this place."

"And?"

"I *was* wondering about a certain investigation."

"Diane Tolliver?"

"How'd you guess?"

"Let's discuss this in private."

A minute later they were seated in his office.

"Diane Tolliver?" Mace prompted.

"It's an ongoing investigation."

"That I know."

"Then you also know it's not something I can really talk about."

"Look, Doc, I know I'm not with the blues anymore."

"If it were up to me I'd show you the entire file, but it's not up to me."

"Beth told me some things already."

"She's the chief, I'm simply a worker bee."

"Anyway, hypothetically speaking, if I *were* working the case I'd like to see the autopsy report, list of trace found at the site, tox report, rape kit results, you know, the usual."

"*If* you were working the case."

Mace stood and paced. "Thing is, I can't work the case because I can't be a blue. At least with a felony conviction hanging over my head."

"That's right."

"Unless circumstances change."

He looked intrigued. "How would they change?"

"I prove I was innocent. Or else."

"Or else what?"

"I solve a case. A big case."

"I see. Wasn't there an FBI agent years ago who did something like that?"

"He actually came to visit me in prison."

"Then I can see your motivation."

"Doc, being a cop is all I know. Beth could be anything. She could be running some Fortune 100 company if she put her mind to it, or else be president of the United States. I'm a blue, that's all I can be."

"Don't short-change yourself, Mace."

"Let me rephrase that. It's all I've ever *wanted* to be."

"I can understand that. Especially considering what happened to your father."

"You knew him, didn't you?"

"I had that privilege. And it makes it doubly hard to accept that Mona Danforth is right this moment occupying his old office."

"When I was in prison all I thought about was getting out and seeing Beth. And then proving my innocence and getting back on the force. It seemed so possible in there."

"But now?"

"Not so possible," Mace said resignedly.

"But you have to try? Even if it means you might go back to prison?"

"I don't want to go back. God knows I don't. But living free outside the uniform?" She paused, searching for the right words. "It feels like I'm right back in the box with bars even though I'm free. I guess that's hard to understand."

"No, it's actually not."

"So I'm here asking for your help. Because I can't solve this case without some forensic information."

She sat down, her gaze squarely on him.

He stared back at her for a moment before rising. "I don't have the tox report or the DNA match results back yet."

"Okay."

He opened a file cabinet, took out some documents, and put them on his desk. "I need to use the restroom. Damn prostate. Be grateful you don't have one. I'll be back in a bit." Before he left, he lifted the cover on the tabletop copier on a credenza behind his desk. "Just replaced the toner and loaded in a full supply of paper."

He closed the door behind him. A second later Mace was copying as fast as she could.

67

"Y<small>OU LOOK HAPPY</small>," said Roy as Mace climbed in the car and he pulled off.

"I am. And you're right," she said. "This Marquis really is huge. You could fill it with water and use it for a pool."

He glanced at the papers she had in an expandable file. "What's that?"

"That is the result of a good friend taking a huge risk for me."

"What do you want to do now?"

"You drive us to your office and I'll read."

Twenty minutes later Roy pulled into the parking garage of his office building and Mace turned over the last page of the file she'd copied.

"And?" Roy asked.

"She was raped, but Beth already told me that. The DNA results from the sample taken from your buddy the Captain aren't back yet and neither is the tox report."

"How did she die?"

"Someone crushed her brain stem." She looked up. "Back of the neck. It would've taken a really strong person probably with some special skills to do that."

"Like a former Army Ranger who weighs about three hundred pounds?"

"You said it, I didn't."

"What else?"

"Trace and soiling on her clothes matched samples they took from the Captain."

"So that's why there's been no court appearance scheduled yet for him. They're waiting to see if they hit a home run on the DNA. Normally there's a presentment hearing within twenty-four hours of arrest."

"When they do charge him what are you going to plead?"

"Regardless of whether it's burglary or murder, we scream 'not guilty' and go from there. The prosecutor doesn't need any help from me." He glanced at the file. "Anything that doesn't point to the Captain?"

"Not really."

"But the DNA sample is going to come back as not a match. They can get the Captain on the burglary, but I'll take that over murder in the first."

"Who wouldn't?" Mace said.

"But Diane had dinner with someone on Friday night and it sure wasn't the Captain."

"Maybe it was this guy Watkins. The real Watkins, I mean."

"Hopefully, we'll find out."

They rode the elevator up to Shilling & Murdoch and Roy swiped his card across the contact pad, releasing the doors.

A minute later they were looking through the dead woman's space. Mace sat down at Diane's desk and stared into the large Apple computer screen. "Nice system."

"I'm surprised the cops didn't take her computer."

"They don't have to anymore. They just download everything to a flash drive. It would be nice to see what's on here." She glanced at him. "Any thoughts on that?"

"It's password-protected, but let me give it a shot."

Roy sat down, powered up the Mac, and stared at the password line that appeared.

"What do you use for your password?" Mace asked.

"AVU2778861."

"Okay, the letters I get. UVA spelled backwards. But what about the numbers?"

"Twenty-seven and seven was the record we finished with my senior year."

"And the eight-eight-six-one?"

"Eighty-eight to sixty-one was the score of my last game when we lost to Kansas in the NCAAs."

She gave him a sympathetic look. "Ever thought about just letting it go, Roy?"

"I've *thought* about it."

He refocused on the screen. "Okay, Diane, what would your password be?"

"She's not married, no children. Pets?" Roy shook his head. Mace glanced at the file she'd carried up with her. "Try her date of birth." She read it off to Roy and he hit the keys but the password box shook it off. They tried other combinations of the numbers. They tried her mother's maiden name that Roy just happened to know.

"It's going to lock us out with one more attempt," he said.

"We're not going to break it. Stupid idea." Mace stared at the top edge of the computer screen. "What's that thing?"

Roy looked where she was pointing. "A webcam. You can use it for videoconferencing and stuff."

Mace slowly moved out of the line of sight of the camera and motioned frantically to Roy to get up. But she said in a calm voice, "Well, that's all we can do here tonight. Might as well get going."

When Roy was out of the camera's view, Mace grabbed his arm and hissed in his ear, "Let's get the hell out of here."

She pulled him out the door and closed it behind them.

Roy snapped, "What's wrong?"

"That's why they came after me. They saw me searching Diane's office."

"Who saw you?"

"Whoever's on the other end of that camera. Come on, before they get here."

"Before *who* gets here?"

They both turned as they heard the sound at the same time. The front door to the offices of Shilling & Murdoch had just beeped open.

"Them!"

68

"THIS WAY." Roy grabbed Mace's hand and they raced down the hall away from the front doors. They reached the end of the corridor and turned left and the short hallway ended at a door. Roy threw it open and they were staring into a darkened room.

"What is this place?"

"The mail room."

"Great, Roy, now we can check out some cool travel magazines while we count down the last minutes of our freaking lives."

"I actually had another idea. Come on."

He led her to the back of the room where there was a small metal door flush with the wall and about four feet off the floor.

"The firm has some offices on the fifth floor and we also keep an archival space there." He smacked a red button next to the metal and the door slid up, revealing a three-by-three-foot space that barely looked big enough to hold one person.

"A dumbwaiter?" said Mace.

"This shaft feeds right into the storage space on the fifth."

They both turned when they heard the footsteps running down the hall.

"Get in, Mace."

"What about you?"

"There's not enough room for both of us."

She looked inside the space. "If you don't get in this box with me, the next box you will get in will be a coffin."

He boosted her in and then crawled in behind her. As the door to the mail room was kicked open, Roy reached out with a long arm and slapped the green send button. The metal door closed and a moment later the dumbwaiter lurched into action. The space was so tight that Mace's knees were touching her nose and the much taller Roy was curved around her body like a moat around a castle.

Mace squirmed. "Is that a flashlight in your pocket or are you just happy to see me?"

"It *is* a flashlight. I snagged it off a shelf before I jumped in."

The dumbwaiter stopped and the metal door slid open. Roy fell out and pulled Mace along with him. He clicked on the flashlight and a few moments later they were running down the hall.

"The elevators are no good. And they've probably got the stairs covered."

She said, "The stairs at the *bottom*, but not the others. Come on!"

As they raced along, Mace stopped for a moment, covered her hand with her shirtsleeve to eliminate the possibility of prints, reached out and pulled the fire alarm. As the loud clanging and swirling red lights chased them down the corridor she said, "There's a fire engine company not too far from here, but we still have a few minutes to survive on our own."

"So where do we go?"

"Fourth floor."

She led him to the fire stairs and they skipped down one flight. A moment later they were back in the place where Mace had subdued the Captain.

"Now we hide."

"Shouldn't we call the cops? I've got my cell."

She hesitated for an instant. "Yeah, do it."

Roy hit 911. "I've got no bars. What the hell!"

They sprinted to the back of the space.

"Quick, look around for a weapon," she said.

"They've probably got guns and you want to hold them off with what, a screwdriver?"

Mace scanned the floor and spotted it. A long length of chain. She snagged it and wrapped it around her arm. "We can use this."

"Wait a minute. When the fire truck gets here they'll find us and your sister will know you were here."

"I don't plan to be here when the fire trucks get here."

"But I thought—"

"If the bad guys don't come through that door in the next minute, then that means they were scared off by the alarm. Then you and I are going to get the hell out of here before the fire guys show."

"Not exactly the way I would've done it."

"Roy, I'm holding a ten-pound chain. Do not piss me off!"

Sixty seconds later they heard the sirens coming. Mace dropped the chain and they raced to the door and bolted down the stairs. They cleared the lobby and stepped into the elevator to the garage right as the firemen were coming in the front doors. They didn't bother with the Marquis parked in the garage, but fled out the exit and turned away from the building.

"Now what?" said a breathless Roy as they slowed to a fast walk.

She checked her watch. "You up for some coffee?"

"What? Some people were just trying to kill us and you want a stimulant?"

"Yeah, at Simpsons in Georgetown, where Tolliver ate on Friday."

"Oh, okay."

"Then after that we can break into Tolliver's house."

"Oh for the love of God."

69

LATER THAT NIGHT Don Hope and Karl Reiger walked down the long hallway. They were several stories underground and the walls were lined with materials that prevented any form of electronic surveillance. It was a good thing since there were few buildings in the country that housed more secrets than this one, and that included the CIA's command center in Virginia and the NSA headquarters in Maryland.

Both men looked anxious as they came to a stop in front of a metal door. There was a long hiss from hydraulic-powered equipment and the portal slid open. They stepped in and the door automatically closed behind them.

There were two chairs in front of the desk. They sat. Jarvis Burns was seated across from them. He perused his computer screen for another minute before turning to them. He slid off a pair of glasses and set them on the desktop. His hand ventured automatically to his right leg and started rubbing it. When Reiger started to speak, Burns held up his hand and shook his head. This was followed by a deep sigh. Reiger and Hope exchanged a nervous glance. Long sighs, apparently, were not a particularly good sign.

Burns said, "Interesting developments. Not pleased at all. Overly complicated now." Each short sentence came out like an MP5 set on two-shot bursts.

Hope said, "Permission to speak candidly?"

"Of course."

"The chief is covered. We fed her the info like you said and made it clear Director Donnelly was the source. As far as she's concerned it's domestic terrorists and she owes you. The sister and the lawyer are not really an issue, at least in my mind."

Burns sat back, made a temple with his fingers, and settled his gaze on the two men. "Your assessment based on what? Your failures?"

"We haven't failed."

"Really? 'Focus in on A-'? We had spyware on Tolliver's computer. You knew about that e-mail and left it there. You could have erased it from Kingman's computer before he even read it."

Reiger said, "We didn't do that because it sounded innocuous. We thought she'd just hit the send key by mistake. The message wasn't even finished."

"It was finished enough, because they figured out what it meant before you did. They got Watkins's name and went to his apartment just in time to catch one of my people searching it. He had to tap-dance pretty fast."

Reiger spoke up. "We didn't know she had a box there. She's never been to that mailbox place the whole time we've had her under surveillance."

"Well, either she went before you had her under the glass or she had someone else to do it for her."

"But your guy didn't have to answer the damn door at Watkins's apartment," Hope pointed out.

"Trust me, if he hadn't, Mace Perry would've broken in. And the police know about Watkins, too, of course. We could have removed the message after Perry and her friend found it, but then we would've risked her telling her sister and the paper being gone from the box would only have aroused the chief's suspicions. The damage, in any case, was already done. But on the bright side, they have the old soldier in custody and he will no doubt be charged with murder very soon."

"So maybe our work is done, then."

"No, your work is not done. But we cannot afford any more screwups."

Hope placed one large, muscular hand on the desktop. "We've been reactionary from almost the get-go. That's not how successful ops are done, black or otherwise. That's not why you brought us on board."

"You are only technically assigned to DHS, which does not engage in black ops. You and Reiger are actually sterilized weapons, cocked and locked at all times. And we brought you on board to do a job, whatever job you were told to do. There is nothing nice or neat about our line of work. It is invariably messy, dirty, and ever-changing. You do deals with one devil because he's slightly better than the next devil. If it were otherwise we wouldn't need you. But we do need you to clean up *your* mess."

"Look, they found nothing in the office, and the spyware surveillance established through Tolliver's computer has already been severed. I don't see what the problem is."

"Then let me show you." Burns clicked a button on his keyboard and spun the screen around to reveal a photo of Mace Perry. "*This* is the problem."

Reiger threw up his hands in frustration. "Come on, she's not even a cop anymore. She's on probation. Her options are limited. She's operating completely outside her sister's authority. I see her as a total non-issue."

"Really? Have you by chance read Perry's psych evaluation?"

"Her psych evaluation?" Reiger said curiously.

Burns rose from behind his desk and limped toward them. "The psych evaluation they did on the woman when she wanted to move to undercover. It's very interesting reading. She never gives up, Reiger. She never walks away. Her father was the U.S. attorney for D.C. I actually knew the man. He was murdered when she was twelve. She has never gotten over that. It burns in her belly with the potential explosive power of a mountain of C-4. She would rather die than be told she was wrong."

"If you're going to worry about someone, I think it should be the police chief. She's a block of granite with a very big brain."

Burns perched on the edge of his desk. "I've known Beth Perry for years. She *is* a formidable adversary. But she tends to operate within strict parameters. However, her sister does not and never will. Quite frankly, Mace Perry scares the crap out of me. And if she is allowed to screw this entire thing up, then none of us are safe." He eyed each man with studied deliberation. "None of us. What we are doing here is right and good for the country but not something the public would approve of once they became aware of it."

Hope said, "But she can't even legally carry a weapon."

Burns smacked his palm against the top of the desk. "Which begs the question of why it is so hard for us to eliminate her. Tonight at the law firm was a golden opportunity missed. I sent in a hand-picked team to get it done while you were occupied with Beth Perry, and it turned out like the Keystone Cops."

"But if she goes down you know her sister will move heaven and earth to find out who did it," Reiger pointed out.

Burns nodded. "It's clear the two sisters would each die for the other."

"See, that's my point."

"But I only need *one* of them to die. And we will help Beth Perry conclude quite clearly that it was the result of one of the many enemies her sister accumulated when she was a cop. A bullet to the head is a damn bullet to the head."

"This is stupid whack-a-mole," barked Reiger. "We pop one person but he or she talked to another person. Then we do that person, but turns out they sent a damn letter to someone else and we have to go after them. Where the hell does it stop, Burns?"

"Hopefully, with the intelligence sources and safety of this country still intact," Burns said as his gaze bore into Reiger. "And watch your tone. Or did you forget the concept of chain of command?"

Reiger let his own stare burn into the man for another moment and then he looked away.

Hope sat back in his chair. "Fine. Then let's do it the right way. We stop chasing her. We lead her down the path right to the target zone. Then we do it. Clean and quick."

"To add some urgency to your mission, we all feel the layers of the onion being peeled away."

"Resources?"

"You have preauthorization for the max push. You don't have to pull the trigger. We have others who will do it. People who will fit the right description, if you get my drift."

Reiger said, "We need to see these new orders in writing, with the proper chain of signatures before we do anything."

Burns didn't look pleased by this. "The elimination order was a standing one. You know that."

Don Hope spoke up. "But it's not guys with turbans we're killing here. It's Americans. It's different. We've already killed three of them and we want new orders."

"Where is it written that Americans can't be terrorists?" asked Burns pointedly. "Are you telling me that Timothy McVeigh wasn't a terrorist? I don't give a damn if he's wearing a turban or looks like my son. I don't give a shit if he's from Iraq or Indiana. If his goal is to harm Americans it's my job to stop him. And I will do so with every means at my disposal."

"All I'm saying is after this is over Karl and I need the get-out-of-jail-free piece of paper. So if you want it done, we need docs for each one with their names spelled out. We're not taking the fall for this. No Abu Ghraib low-level-grunts-run-amuck bullshit. Top down. We all go down. That's just how it's going to be or your sterilized weapons remain in the holster. That's just how it's going to be," he said again firmly.

"You are being compensated at four times your original salaries. You both will be wealthy by the time this is over."

"The paper or it doesn't get done. Period!"

Burns pursed his lips. "All right. You'll have it as soon as possible by secure courier." He returned to his computer screen.

Reiger eyed Hope and then cleared his throat.

Burns looked up, obviously irritated. "Something else?"

"How many people in *this* building know about the op?"

"Counting you, me, and your partner there?"

"Yeah."

"Three."

The tail car on Hope and Reiger had radioed in the results of their surveillance. Beth Perry was there within ten minutes. She slid out of her car and into the backseat of theirs. She was dressed not in stars and bars but in jeans and her FBI Academy hoodie. She trained her binoculars on the building.

"You're absolutely sure they went in there?"

"Chief, it's pretty damn hard to miss."

What she was looking at through her optics was the biggest office building in the world, with a footprint like no other, five-sided, in fact. She slumped back.

What the hell is the connection to the Pentagon?

70

Y EAH, I remember Ms. Tolliver. Used to come in here all the time."

Mace and Roy were seated at a table at Simpsons. The man speaking to them was a waiter. They'd made inquiries, and by luck this same fellow had waited on Diane Tolliver on Friday night.

"She wasn't alone, right?" asked Mace.

"No, a guy was with her. Damn shame what happened to her."

"Can you describe the guy?" asked Roy.

The waiter turned to him. "You think he had something to do with her death?"

"Haven't ruled out anything yet."

"Are you with the cops?"

"Private eyes," said Mace. "Hired by her family. Have the cops been by yet?"

The man nodded. "Yep."

"So you were going to describe this guy?" prompted Mace.

"White guy. Around fifty, salt-and-pepper hair, cut short and thinning. Not as tall as you," he said, indicating Roy. "About five-ten. Dressed in a suit."

"Glasses? Beard?"

"No."

Mace showed him Watkins's DMV photo.

He shook his head. "Wasn't that guy."

"You didn't get a name?" she asked.

"No, Ms. Tolliver paid the bill."

"See him with her before?"

"Nope."

"How were their appetites?"

"Real good. Ms. Tolliver had the filet mignon, mashed potatoes, and a side of veggies. Coffee but no dessert. The guy had the salmon with a salad and a cup of clam chowder beforehand."

"Wine, cocktails?"

"She had a glass of the house merlot. He had two glasses of chardonnay."

"Good memory."

"Not really. When the police came, I went back and looked at the ticket."

"You remember the times Tolliver and the guy came in and left?" asked Roy.

"In about seven-thirty, left over two hours later. I remember looking at the clock when they sat down because my cousin said he was going to stop by around quarter till and have a drink at the bar, and I knew it was getting close to that time."

"And you're pretty sure on when they left?"

"It was Friday night, but we've only got fifteen tables and traffic was slow. In fact, there were only two other tables occupied, so I did notice. And the bill has a time and date stamp when it comes out of the computer. They didn't hang out after she paid the bill. Bussed their table myself."

"Did either of them appear nervous or anything?" asked Mace.

"Well, they didn't come in together. She was here first and then he came in. They sat at that table over there." He pointed to an eating space in a small niche. "Pretty private because of the wall there."

"Did they leave together?" Roy asked.

"No. She went first, then he did. And he was kind of looking down the whole time, like he didn't want anyone to get a good look at him."

They asked him a few more questions, and Roy left his business card in case the waiter remembered anything else. As they walked along outside Mace pulled the reports she'd gotten from the ME from her pocket and glanced through them.

"What?" asked Roy.

"I don't know. Nothing, I guess."

"So it wasn't Watkins she had dinner with. There's another guy out there."

"Seems to be. And they obviously didn't want folks to see them together. Out-of-the-way place, secluded table, came and left separately."

"We left my car at the garage. What now? We can't walk to Alexandria."

"We can cab it to Altman's house, grab my bike, and then go from there."

"Do you think whoever's after us knows you're staying at Altman's?"

"It's possible."

"But what if they go after Altman for some reason? You know, leverage against you somehow?"

"Herbert told me there are three full-time security guards who live on the premises. I guess after the run-in with the HF-12 drug crew, Abe decided some of his own muscle wasn't a bad thing. One's a former Navy SEAL, another used to be a sniper with the FBI's Hostage Rescue Team, and the other one is former Secret Service with five years in Iraq under his belt in counterterrorism."

"Damn. I never noticed those guys when I was there."

"That's sort of the point, Roy."

The cab dropped them at Altman's. She took a few minutes at the guesthouse to slip some items into her knapsack. As they walked outside to where her bike was parked Roy said, "What's in the goodie bag?"

"Stuff."

"Stuff for breaking and entering?"

"Get on."

Roy barely made it on the Ducati before Mace punched the clutch with her boot and the back wheel gripped the asphalt for a single moment before its energy was released and they shot down the road. The automatic gates parted and Mace worked the clutch to top gear. Minutes later they blew down the windy, tree-bracketed GW Parkway, whipping past cars so fast Roy could barely see the drivers.

He finally yelled into her ear, "Why so damn fast?"

"I have a fetish for speed."

"You ever crash this thing?"

"Not yet," she screamed back over the whine of the Ducati's engine.

Roy clutched her waist with both hands and muttered a brief but heartfelt prayer.

CHAPTER

71

W<small>HY AM</small> I not surprised that you can pick a deadbolt?" Roy was staring over Mace's shoulder while she worked on the lock. They were at the fence-enclosed basement entrance to Diane Tolliver's waterfront luxury town home at Fords Landing. It was an upscale community a little south of the main strip in historic Old Town Alexandria.

Mace had her pick and tension tool inserted in the lock and was manipulating both instruments with ease. "Amazing what you learn in prison," she said.

"You didn't learn that in prison," he said in a scoffing tone.

"How do you know that?"

"Trust me, I just know."

"Are you insinuating that I bent the rules while I was a cop?"

"No."

"Good."

"I mean, I'm not insinuating it, I'm stating it as a fact."

"Go to hell, Roy."

"Wait a minute, how do you know the security system's not on?"

"I already snuck a peek through the glass sidelights on the front door. Green glow coming from the security touchpad means security off. Cops probably had the alarm company shut it down when they came to bag and tag. They almost always forget to tell them to turn it back on."

There was an audible click and Mace turned her tension tool like a key. "And we're in." They closed the door behind them and Mace clicked on a small flashlight with an adjustable beam. She widened the focus and looked around.

"This is a rec room with a full bar over there," Roy said as he pointed up ahead and to the right. "And there's a media room through that door over there."

"Nice."

"If the cops already bagged and tagged, what can we hope to find?"

"Stuff they missed."

They went room by room. One space had been outfitted as a home office. There was a large desk, wooden file cabinets, and built-in bookshelves but no computer.

"I think she had a laptop in here," said Roy. "The cops might've taken it instead of using the flash drive you talked about."

Mace was eyeing a pile of documents she'd pulled from a file cabinet. "Do all lawyers at Shilling bring this much work home?"

Roy ran the light over the papers. "Looks to be some docs from a private stock acquisition we did last month. We repped an oil exploration company in the U.A.E. that was buying a preferred minority interest in a Canadian shale oil field. It was done through a specialized broker in London and there were several other piggyback purchasers with packaged financing securitized over a number of debt platforms in about ten countries that had also had some sovereign fund participation and a buy-sell playing-chicken option."

"I have no idea what you said, but I think it just made me horny."

"If I'd only known that's all it took."

"So how much are we talking dollar-wise?"

"A little over a billion dollars. Paid in cash."

"A billion in cash!"

"That's how Diane could afford this place. She probably paid for *it* in cash."

Mace's brow creased.

"What are you thinking now?"

"I'm thinking I should have gone to law school," she growled.

While Roy went over Tolliver's office, Mace methodically covered the bedroom, guest rooms, bathrooms, and the garage. She finally arrived in the kitchen, which had a small brick fireplace with a wooden mantel and extended into the well-appointed dining area that had as its centerpiece a ten-foot-long table constructed from reclaimed wood. There were views of the Potomac through several large windows.

Mace checked the cupboards, the refrigerator, the stove, and the dishwasher. She opened jars and cookbooks, and dug into flowerpots in case Tolliver had bought one of those mini security boxes that look like something mundane. She examined piece by piece the trash that had obviously *not* been bagged, tagged, and taken by the cops. Roy joined her while she was seated in a chair still going through the garbage.

"Find any banana peels with secret writing?"

"No, but I did find a meat wrapper, veggie peelings, and a moldy piece of bread. Along with an empty bottle of red wine."

"So that was Diane's last meal."

"We'll all have one someday."

Mace rinsed off her hands in the sink. "Anything suspicious in her files?"

"Not really."

Mace started walking up and down the room, hitting the walls, floor, and ceiling with her light. "See all the shiny surfaces?"

"Fingerprint powder."

"That's right."

She reached the wall at the far end of the room, turned, and started back. When her light flicked to the ceiling she stopped. "Roy, grab a chair for me."

He brought it to her and she stood on it on her tiptoes, shining the light around the smoke detector mounted on the ceiling. She handed him the light. "Get up here and tell me what you see."

He stood on the chair. "Scratches on the paint and what looks to be dirt smudges."

"Somebody moved the smoke detector."

"Well, you'd do that to change the battery."

"How about this?"

Roy stepped off the chair and angled the light to where Mace was pointing at the carpet. He got down on his knees for a better look. "Paint flakes?"

"You'd think they would've been vacuumed up. Unless it happened after she was dead. Let me see that detector."

Roy got back on the chair, unhooked the wires, and handed it to her.

She turned it over. "Smoke detectors are popular items to substitute with surveillance pin cameras."

"Surveillance? Of Diane?"

"They tapped her computer, why not her home?"

"So why didn't the police find it?"

"They probably removed it before the cops searched the place. I think you need to go to your office tomorrow and do some real digging."

"You really believe it's tied to Shilling?" he said skeptically.

"Billion-dollar contracts? Companies in the Middle East? Uh, yeah."

"It's actually pretty boring stuff. Just business."

"One man's business is another man's apocalypse."

"What the hell does that mean?"

"Just humor me and check around. Come on, I'll drop you off at your condo."

Outside, they climbed on the Ducati. Before Mace started the engine, she turned and looked at him. "So why did you tank the HORSE game?"

"Why do you think?" Roy said quietly.

Mace found she couldn't meet his gaze. She slowly turned back around, engaged the engine, and they sped off.

"H<small>EY</small>, Ned."

Roy walked through the lobby on the way to the office elevators. He'd had pretty much a sleepless night listening for any sound of killers coming for him. He'd taken the bus to work and planned to drive the Marquis home. Ned was behind the marble desk looking excited.

"Roy, did you hear about the fire here last night?"

Roy tried his best to seem surprised. "There was a fire? Where?"

"Well, actually there wasn't a fire. Somebody pulled the fire alarm. That's a crime!"

"Yeah, I know. Who would've done that?" he said impassively.

"The fire department guys were pissed. I heard they traced it to the alarm pull on the fifth floor. I guess they'll run the key card access records to see who was here last night."

At this comment Roy's ass clenched like a boxer's fist. He'd used his key card to get in the building with Mace. That would be on the database. If no one else was in the building last night, how was he going to explain that? What was the penalty for falsely pulling a fire alarm?

This day could not get any worse, he thought.

He was wrong about that.

"Roy?"

He looked up as he entered the firm's lobby. Chester Ackerman was staring at him.

"Yeah, Chester?"

"What the hell happened to your face?"

Roy touched his still swollen eye and bruised cheek. "Ran into a door."

"I need to talk to you. *Now.*" Ackerman turned and marched off.

Roy eyed Jill, the young receptionist, who'd been watching the two men closely. "Any idea what's going on, Jill?"

"You're in trouble, Roy."

"That one I'd figured out. Any idea why?"

"You'll find out soon enough."

Roy dropped off his briefcase in his office and headed to Ackerman's. He closed the door behind him and sat down across from the man.

"You're looking less stressed out, Chester," Roy began amiably.

"I have no idea how that's possible," Ackerman shot back. "Because I feel like my damn head is going to explode."

Roy crossed his legs and tried to look mildly curious. "So what's up?" *Please, God, don't let it be about the damn fire alarm.*

"What the hell is this I hear about you representing the man the police have arrested for Diane's murder? Please tell me that is complete and total horseshit."

"Hold on, I can explain that—"

Ackerman rose, looking even more agitated. "So it's true?"

"I met with the guy. He wants me to rep him. I haven't—"

"You *know* Diane's killer? You actually know the bastard?"

"Wait a minute, it hasn't been proved that he is Diane's killer, Chester."

"Oh for God's sakes. He was in the building that morning. No, he was *trespassing*. And I understand some of the evidence the police found ties him to the murder."

"Who told you that?"

"What I want to know is how you could possibly think of defending this person?"

"I guess it's that whole innocent-until-proven-guilty thing they taught us in law school."

"Don't give me that crap. And besides, you work for this firm. We do not do criminal defense work. You cannot accept an assignment like that without the firm's approval, specifically my approval as managing partner." Ackerman added in a snarl, "And you don't have a chance in hell of getting it."

"I only met with the guy once, okay? I defended him on an assault charge when I was with CJA. But I don't think the guy did it, Chester."

"I don't give a damn what you think. You are not representing him. Period."

Roy stood. "I'm not really liking your whole tone here."

"Trust me, you'll like it a lot less if you go down that road."

"I can quit."

"Yes, you can. But why in the hell would you? Give up the golden egg for some homicidal homeless freak?"

Roy felt his face growing hot. "He's *not* a freak. He's a veteran. He fought and bled for this country. He's still got North Vietnamese shrapnel a few millimeters from his spine."

"Right, right. And he killed Diane. So make your choice."

Roy turned to the door. "I'll let you know."

"Kingman!"

"I *said* I'll let you know."

Roy slammed the door behind him.

Mace had barely slept at all. This time, though, it wasn't night-mares about Juanita and the throat-slicing Rose coming for her. It was the recurring image of her father in his coffin. She'd just turned twelve, Beth was eighteen and getting ready to head off to college at Georgetown on full scholarship. The day of the funeral the casket had been closed because of the disfiguring nature of Benjamin Perry's fatal wounds.

Yet Mace had seen her father that final day. She'd snuck away. Her mother was mush, collapsing on any shoulder she could find, while Beth was handling everything that their mom should have been dealing with. They had gotten to the church early, before the coffin had been brought into the chapel.

It was just Mace and the coffin in a small room next to where the memorial service would be held. She remembered every smell, every sound, and every breath she'd drawn in the few minutes she stood there, staring at the big wooden box with the metal handles on the sides containing her dad. To this day she wasn't sure why she'd done it, but she'd gathered her courage, walked up to the cas-ket, held her breath, and pushed the top open.

As soon as she saw him, she wished someone had stopped her. She stared at the body lying there for a few terrible seconds.

That face.

Or what was left of it.

Then she'd turned and run from the room, leaving the top still up. That wasn't her father. Her father didn't look like that.

Mace rushed to the bathroom, and ran cold water over her head and splashed some on her face. She looked at herself in the darkened reflection of the mirror. She could never shake the feeling that she had let him down somehow. If she had just reacted in a different way, seen or heard something, she believed that her father would still be alive. If she only had done something! Anything!

My fault. Age twelve. My fault.

Beth had found her hiding in a closet at the church after closing the casket. She too had seen her father dead. And neither sister had ever talked about it since. Beth had held Mace for what seemed like forever that day, letting her cry, letting her shake, but telling her that everything was going to be okay. That the body in the coffin was just a body, their dad had already gone on to a much better place. And he would watch over them forever. She'd promised. And Mace had believed her. Her sister would never lie to her.

Beth being next to her was the only reason she had made it through the service. It certainly hadn't been her mother, who'd blubbered through the whole event, including when the soldier had handed her the U.S. flag in recognition of her father's service in Vietnam. When the honor guard had started shooting their rifle salute everyone covered their ears. Everyone except the two Perry sisters. Mace remembered quite vividly what she had been thinking when those rifles fired a total of twenty-one rounds.

I wanted a gun. I wanted a gun to kill whoever had killed my dad.

And though she'd never asked, Mace felt certain that Beth had been thinking the very same thing.

Her mother had refused the shell casings offered by the honor guard. Beth had taken them and given eleven to Mace and kept ten for herself. Mace knew that Beth kept her bag of casings in her desk drawer at her office. Once when she'd been with the force and met with her sister to go over some work, she'd seen a pensive Beth open the drawer, take out the casings, and hold them tightly in her hand, as though channeling her father's wisdom.

Mace drank some water from her cupped hand, walked back into her bedroom, opened her knapsack, and pulled out her bag of eleven shell casings. Beth had of course kept them for her when she went to prison. She held them against her chest, the tears staining her cheeks as she desperately tried to absorb some wisdom of her own from the best man she'd ever known. But nothing came.

The aftermath of her father's murder and her mother's withdrawal from the lives of her daughters had made Mace increasingly vulnerable. It was a feeling she hated. She'd become a cop, in part, to allow the weight of the badge and the threat of her gun to override that vulnerability. She desperately wanted to belong to something. And the MPD served that desire.

Did she also want to follow her sister? Even show she might be better than her in certain respects? Mace couldn't, in all honesty, deny that.

A half hour later she changed into her workout clothes and did some stretching and push-ups. The blood rush to her muscles was very welcome, after the weary night and the early morning soul searching.

The sun was well up now and the air outside was warm, which was good because Mace couldn't seem to get rid of the chills. She stepped outside and started her run. The estate was big, with a well-marked trail that wound in and out of trees and head-high bushes. She'd been running for half an hour when she stopped, turned, and her hand flashed to her waist. To pull the gun that wasn't there.

"You *are* good," said the voice. "Lucky for me you're not packing."

The man stepped clear of the tree line. He was a shade below six feet and wore an Army green muscle shirt that showed off his ripped physique and jeans that were very tight around his bulging thighs. Lace-up combat boots were on his feet. A pistol rode in a clip holster on his belt; an extra mag for the weapon sat in a compartment next to the gun. His hair was shaved military short, his face tanned and weathered.

"I've been standing there for ten minutes waiting for you to come by. I didn't move a muscle. Heartbeat's at fifty-two and mellow, so you didn't hear that. Never made a sound. What gave me away?"

Mace walked over to him and lightly smacked him on the face. "Either cut down on the Old Spice or stay upwind of me."

He laughed and put out his hand. "Rick Cassidy."

"You're the former SEAL?"

He cocked his head and gave her a lopsided smile. "Okay, how do you figure? I'm wearing Army green."

"Most SEALS I know like to wear the Army green because they know they look better in it than the trench boys do. Your face has seen a lot of sun, salt, and ocean wind. You've also got on standard-issue Navy-class stomp boots. And a SEAL I dated said you guys swore by the H&K P9S that's riding in your belt holster." As he stared down at his gun she added, "Its silhouette and grip are pretty distinctive."

"You live up to your rep, Ms. Perry, I'll give you that."

"Already got a dossier on me? And the name's Mace."

"Everyone who comes here gets the same intel treatment. Mace."

"I've got no problem with that. How did you end up here?'

"Mr. Altman is a great guy. He made me a great offer." Cassidy paused. "And he helped take care of my little sister. Leukemia. My parents had no health insurance."

"Did she make it?"

"Graduating from college this year."

"That's very cool, Rick."

"Mr. Altman wants to see you up at the main house when you get a chance. I smelled croissants baking in the kitchen. Herbert's on a roll. And the coffee is always fresh. I understand there's a seat waiting for you. No rush. Whenever."

"Thanks, Rick. Any idea what he wants me for?"

"Something about a mom and her kid and a dude named Psycho. Ring any bells?"

"More than one, actually."

"Keep running hard, Mace."

"One more thing, Rick."

"Yeah?"

"This stuff I'm doing for Abe, it might lead to some unsavory characters taking a special interest in me. They might follow me back here. Just a heads-up."

"Forewarned is always a good thing, Mace. Thanks."

She turned to start up her run again. When she looked back, Cassidy had disappeared back into the trees. For a number of reasons, that gave her a great sense of comfort. She ran back to the guesthouse, sat in the hot tub for a while, showered, changed, and killed some more time as images of her dead father finally faded away. Then she trudged over to the main house. To talk about moms, babies, and bandits named Psycho.

74

The phone buzzed on Beth Perry's desk.

"Chief."

"Got a letter here for you," said her aide.

"Who from, Donna?"

"Mona Danforth."

"Bring it in."

Donna Pierce punched in the numbers on Beth's secure office door, brought the letter in, handed it to her, and then turned to leave.

"Who delivered it?" Beth asked.

"It wasn't Ms. Danforth, of course," Pierce said, barely hiding a smile. "Hard for her to walk all this way in those four-inch heels. Some wimpy guy in a suit who nearly ran out of here when I asked him if he wanted to speak to you directly."

"Thanks."

After Pierce left, Beth slit open the envelope and unfolded the heavy bond paper. The contents of the letter were short and the rise in Beth's blood pressure was swift. She clicked some keys on her computer and read down several screen pages. After that she called the courthouse to check on something. Then she hit her speaker-phone. "Pierce, get the wicked witch on the line for me. Now!"

Beth heard her aide struggle to suppress a laugh. "Yes, Chief, right away."

Pierce came back on a minute later. "Her assistant says she's not available for your call."

"Put it through."

Beth picked up the phone. "Chief Perry."

"Yes, I'm sorry, Chief, but Ms. Danforth is—"

"Standing right over your shoulder."

"No, she has court—"

"I just checked with the docket clerk. She's not in court." Beth shouted into the phone, "Mona, if you won't talk to me, then I'll just take this letter you sent me up to Capitol Hill and see what the folks on the Judiciary Committee will make of you abdicating your role as protector of the people. The ensuing sound you'll be hearing is your fading chances of being the AG, much less getting a seat on the Supreme Court."

Beth waited, envisioning Mona walking to her office, slamming the door, and—

Mona's voice barked out, "Listen, Perry, I don't appreciate you talking like that in front of my people!"

"You can either address me as Beth or Chief. You use surnames for underlings. I am *not* your underling."

"What do you want?"

"I read your letter."

"Well? I thought it was pretty self-explanatory."

"Yeah, you caved. In record time. And I want to know why."

"I don't have to explain my actions to you."

"You wrote me a CYA letter that basically says you've washed your hands of Jamie Meldon's murder investigation. What, did somebody threaten that you wouldn't get the USA nod if you didn't go quietly into the night? So much for him being one of *your* people."

"If you were smart you'd back off too, *Chief.*"

"It has nothing to do with self-preservation, Mona. It has to do with right and wrong. And something called integrity."

"Oh please. I don't need you to read me an ethics lesson."

"So what are you going to tell Meldon's wife and kids? 'Sorry, my career's too important. Just get over Jamie's murder and move on'?"

"I'm running the largest U.S. Attorney's Office in the country. I don't have time to run down every little—"

"This isn't little, Mona. Homicide is as big as it gets. Someone is out there who took Jamie's life."

"Then you tackle it if you care so much."

"A little tough to do when I was barred from the crime scene."

"Can't help you there."

"So that's your last word on it?"

"You bet it is!"

"Okay, here's mine. I *will* tackle this. And if I find the least bit of evidence that you or anyone in your office impeded our investigation, I will personally see to it that your Armani-covered *ass* lands right in prison."

Beth slammed down the phone, sat back, and took a deep breath. Her BlackBerry had been buzzing nonstop during her entire conversation. She checked it. Ninety-three e-mails all marked urgent. She had six meetings stacked back-to-back, the first of which was scheduled to begin in twenty minutes. Then she had two hours patrolling in Cruiser One and a roll call in the Second District, followed by her headlining two community events that evening. She also had to oversee the posting of nearly two hundred intersection cops because the president wanted to go to lunch at his favorite dive in Arlington, the Secret Service had informed her at six-thirty this morning.

A murder in Ward Nine last night had interrupted what little sleep she usually got. She'd finally made it to her couch at four a.m., catnapped for two hours, and was in the office at seven. Typical day in the neighborhood. And then there was the information she'd just received thirty minutes ago that had to do with Roy Kingman and her sister. Her phone buzzed again.

"Chief."

It was Pierce. "Guys in Social Services want to know what you want to do with Alisha Rogers and her son. They don't have room for them past this morning. Records show she has her own place so they say their hands are tied unless you really insist."

And if I do insist, someone will leak it to the press and tomorrow's breaking story will be about the police chief abusing her authority to get personal favors unavailable to other needy citizens—

"Donna, reschedule my first three meetings until this afternoon. Just cram them in somehow. I've got somewhere I have to go. Tell Social they can release Alisha and her son into my personal custody."

Beth pulled out her cell phone and punched in a number. "It's Beth. We need to deal with this. Now."

"I know," answered Abe Altman. "I know."

75

MACE HAD JUST finished breakfast and was pouring a second cup of coffee when Altman came into the eating area right off the kitchen.

"Hope you slept well," he said.

"Not bad. Met Rick Cassidy on my run this morning."

"A wonderful young man. He was planning on leaving the Navy to be closer to his sister, so I thought a job here would fit into that. She goes to George Washington and has accepted a full-time position with the World Bank in D.C."

"That was really nice what you did for her."

"When a poor man gives something, that is a sacrifice indeed. When a rich man gives something, it hardly rises to the same level."

"Well, I know some rich people who never give anything."

Altman was dressed in his usual manner, jeans and a long-sleeved shirt. He poured a cup of tea from a pot on the sideboard, bit into a biscuit, and sat down next to her.

"Herbert is a genius in the kitchen," he said. "I have two master's degrees and a Ph.D. and I can't even crack an egg properly."

"I know, I'm a klutz in the kitchen too. I had two croissants and a plate of eggs and had to stop myself from going back for more."

Altman took a sip of tea, set the cup down, and said, "Psycho?"

Mace wiped her mouth. "Look, it was no big deal."

"It was a very big deal. I heard from Carmela, who talked to Non at the apartment building. Non watched the entire confrontation from her window. You and Roy could have been killed. I feel terrible. Terrible, Mace. I had these people vetted with great depth but I had no idea of this man's involvement with Alisha."

"That's probably because everyone's scared of the guy. But we got out okay, and we also removed Alisha and Tyler from the situation. Beth helped me with that."

"I know."

"So you talked to her?"

"Yes. If anything had happened to you, I would never have forgiven myself."

She put a hand on his arm. "Abe, I'm assuming you recruited me for this job because I know my way around those places. That also included knowing how to survive there. My big mistake was taking Roy with me. That was stupid on my part. That won't happen again."

"I don't believe there should be a next time."

"What do you mean?"

"I can't justify sending you into dangerous places, Mace. I can't risk that. No study is worth that."

"Well, I think this study is. Look at Alisha. She's a good kid. She just needs a chance. And Tyler, we can't leave him in that place. He needs some special help. And there are thousands just like them in this town."

"It's too risky."

"I'm willing to take that risk. You offered me the job and I accepted. Now let me do my thing. Abe, you knew these areas were potentially dangerous. What's the big deal now?"

"It all looked good on paper. But paper is not real life. All my calculations aren't worth anything, it seems, when you have people like this Psycho around."

"I can take care of that."

"I thought when they learned you were trying to help folks in those situations, that it would protect you."

"And it will. But for those few who think otherwise, I'll deal with it. I don't think you'll win this one, Abe."

They both looked up to see Beth standing by the door holding pudgy Tyler Rogers. Behind her was Alisha clutching a small bag.

Mace rose. "Alisha? Are you and Tyler okay?"

The young mother came forward, her eyes wide as she took in

the interior of the mansion. "We're fine. Chief Perry took real good care of us."

Mace looked at her sister. "I really appreciated the assist, Beth. I didn't know who else to call when Psycho showed up."

"He's not a guy you mess around with. Although from what I heard you pretty much held your own." She paused. "Did Kingman really play him in one-on-one basketball?"

"And kicked his butt," said Alisha with ill-concealed delight. "I was watching with Non at the window. Kicked his butt," she repeated, tacking on a big smile.

"Where's Darren?" Mace asked.

"Who's that?" asked Beth sharply.

"My brother. He didn't come with us. Don't know where he is."

"So what are you all doing here?" said Mace.

Altman rose and came forward. "Beth and I spoke this morning and Alisha and Tyler are coming to stay with us. I was hoping that they could be in the west wing of the guesthouse if it's not an inconvenience to you."

Mace blurted out, "Inconvenience? That place is so big I'd need a map to find them."

"We staying here?" said Alisha looking around. "I don't have no money for a place like this."

"There is no charge," said Altman, taking her arm lightly after receiving a high sign from Beth. "And I'd be honored to take you and your son to your new quarters and help you get settled in."

Beth handed off Tyler to Alisha and the three left together. Beth turned to her sister and eyed her empty coffee cup. "You might need another jolt of caffeine, because we need to talk. Now."

76

I HAD my police scanner on last night. Heard about the homicide in Nine. Knew you'd be there. You look beat."

Beth took off her hat and sat down. "You look spent, too. Can't be the accommodations. Having nightmares again?"

"I *don't* have nightmares anymore."

"You sure about that?"

"You held me when I was twelve, Beth. You don't need to hold me anymore." Mace handed her a full cup of black coffee and sat down with her own. Beth took a swallow and spent a moment admiring the room.

"I can see why you split from me to come here."

"I've actually found the concierge service to be pretty average."

"I guess I can leave it to you to find trouble even as a research assistant."

"It's a gift."

"So you're going back in?"

"See no reason not to. So what do we need to talk about?"

Beth hunched forward. "Andre Watkins?"

Mace barely reacted, but it was enough.

Beth said, "I thought so. A-1? Since we're the police we had to resort to a search warrant, but the kid there said a woman and a tall man had come in previously with some story about a diseased aunt."

"You been by Watkins's place?"

"It's empty."

"It wasn't empty when we got there."

Mace told her about the man who'd been there pretending to be Watkins, including his description and her suspicions that the apartment had been searched.

"Nice to have known that before."

"And it wasn't Watkins having dinner with Tolliver on Friday night."

"I know. The description was pretty general. We have a BOLO out on Watkins," Beth added, referring to a "be on the lookout" order.

"The imposter said he was an escort. *Was* Watkins an escort?"

"Yes, worked for an agency in town. No one's seen him since Friday."

"Maybe Tolliver sensed that something bad was going to happen to her and she wanted some cover."

"So presumably they got on to him, either eliminated him or he took off running scared and they sent some goon to roll his place looking for answers."

"And he was doing just that when we knocked."

"Pretty ballsy of the guy to open the door to you."

Mace shrugged. "He peeped us, could tell we weren't the cops, or maybe recognized us and decided to play actor and pump us for info. Unfortunately, we were pretty accommodating." Mace eyed Beth. "Anything else?"

"Just a couple more questions. What were you and Kingman doing at the law firm last night? And which one of you pulled the fire alarm?"

Mace looked blankly at her.

Beth tapped the tabletop. "His key card access was the only one last night."

"That can't be right. The other guys—"

Beth snapped, "What other guys?"

"We had some visitors last night. I pulled the alarm so we could get away. I assumed they used Diane Tolliver's key card to get in."

"They didn't. And again, what guys?"

"I don't know for sure. Maybe the same ones who took a shot at me."

"How did they know you were in the building?"

Mace explained about the webcam on Tolliver's computer.

"We'll check it out." Beth leaned forward. "Remember when you asked me what I would do in your position? Would I risk everything to work the case and get back on the force?"

"You didn't answer me."

"No, because I didn't have a ready answer. But now I've had time to think."

"And?"

"And nothing is worth going back to that hellhole."

"That's you. But you're not me."

"Why are you really doing this?"

"We already covered this, okay? Mona torpedoed your plan, so proving my innocence won't work. And I told you I was going to work the case. If I go down, so be it."

"If you do, the odds are very good that you will go back to prison and you won't walk out alive this time. Where did you even get the idea to solve a case and use that as a way back on?"

"I had a lot of time to think over the last two years."

"Would it have anything to do with a visit you got from an FBI agent who resurrected his career after being convicted of a felony?"

"If you knew, why bother asking me?" she said angrily.

"What did Special Agent Frank Kelly tell you?"

"I'm surprised you didn't already track him down and ask him."

"I did. He said it was between you and him."

"And it is, Beth. Between him and me."

"I didn't think we kept secrets from each other."

"You're the police chief. I am not going to put you in a compromising situation."

"What happened to Kelly was a one-in-a-million shot."

"I'll take those odds."

"This is ridiculous."

"No, Beth, what's ridiculous is me spending over a decade laying it all on the line to protect people, only to have it all crater when someone framed me for shit I don't even remember. I lost two years of my life in prison where every day seemed like it would be my last one. Now I'm out but can't do the one thing that I was born to do. What, did you think I was just going to forget it? Say, 'Oh, well, shit happens'?"

The two women stared at each other, neither one seemingly willing to give in.

Beth's phone buzzed. She didn't move to answer it.

Mace said, "Better grab it. The law waits for no one, not even two pissed-off sisters."

Beth finally broke off eye contact and snatched up her phone. "Chief." She listened and then clicked off. "That was Lowell Cassell."

"I already know. Dockery's DNA didn't match."

"No, it was a perfect match. It was, without a doubt, his sperm inside Diane Tolliver."

77

Roy sat at his desk vigorously squeezing his miniature basketball in his right hand. His anxiety was justified. His secretary Janice had popped in to tell him that the entire firm had been sent an e-mail from Chester Ackerman about his connection with Diane's alleged murderer. She'd gone on to say that right now Roy was about as popular with his coworkers as Osama bin Laden would be.

He'd tried to defend himself. "Janice, will you hear me out. I—"

The slamming door had cut him off.

He clicked on his computer and started checking his e-mails. Work still had to be done and he and Diane had been in the middle of shepherding several large acquisitions through to closure. Ackerman had not yet assigned anyone to take over Diane's work permanently, so Roy was carrying the laboring oar on the legal end. He didn't mind that, but he missed being able to kick ideas around with her, or go to her when something didn't make sense. He wished he could go to her right now, because he was perplexed.

Your death makes no sense to me, Diane. Can't you tell me what happened? Who killed you?

That line of thought was clearly not going to get him anywhere. He returned some calls, opened some files, pulled up some half-finished contracts on his computer, and pored over laborious notes he'd taken at a recent client meeting. He worked for a couple more hours and then checked his e-mails again. There were lots of new ones, some from clients, some from friends, and a few from coworkers telling him to basically get his head out of his butt over defending Diane's killer.

For some reason, he scrolled far down the list and checked one old e-mail.

It was the last one he would ever get from Diane Tolliver.

We need to focus in on A-

Okay, they'd gotten that piece and run it down for naught. Roy's gaze next ran over the initials at the bottom of the e-mail.

DLT.

It was her initials, for Diane Louise Tolliver. He'd seen her full name on several diplomas she had hanging in her office. As he thought about it, her initials being there made sense, but it also didn't make sense. Roy quickly checked a dozen other e-mails that Diane had sent him over the last few months. None of them had her initials at the bottom. She invariably signed her e-mails, when she bothered to do so at all, by simply typing "Diane."

DLT?

For some reason those initials seemed familiar apart from Tolliver's name. Was there another reason she had put those letters in the e-mail? A backup in case the A-1 reference yielded nothing? Thinking back to the highly organized and intelligent lawyer that Diane had been, Roy had to admit that the woman's employing a second clue hidden in the same e-mail was entirely plausible.

But why direct all these clues at him? He worked with her, sure, but they weren't really close friends. Then again, maybe she didn't have any close friends. The woman used a paid escort, after all, when she wanted to go out. But why not go to the police? If she had learned of some criminal activity or even suspected something illegal was going on, why not just go to the cops? As far as Roy knew, Diane had never done any criminal work, but she was still a lawyer. She knew her way around the legal system better than most.

But I was a criminal defense attorney. Was that why she was sending me the clues?

A sudden fear gripped him. He stared at the tiny webcam mounted at the top of his computer monitor. What if they were watching him right now? But then his fears receded. Mace had been in here on the night she'd found out about the A-1 clue. They'd talked about her discovery here. If someone had been watching and listening, they would've gotten to the mailbox before Roy and Mace had.

Still.

He slid open his desk drawer, pulled out a Post-it note, and hastily stuck it over the webcam, pulling his fingers quickly back as though the damn thing might bite him.

His cell phone rang.

"Kingman."

It was Mace. Her few words hit Roy harder than Psycho had.

"I'll meet you there in twenty minutes," he said. He grabbed his jacket and sprinted out of the office. The Captain most definitely needed a lawyer now.

He'd just been formally charged with first-degree murder.

78

"Gᴏᴛ sᴏᴍᴇ damn good news today, Roy."

Roy and Mace were sitting across from the Captain. He'd showered and his wet hair was now slicked back, his revealed widow's peak solid gray. With part of the street grime gone, Roy could actually see some pink skin on the man's face. The Captain was also now wearing a prison jumpsuit. A shackle belt was around his large waist, though his hands and legs were free for the time being.

Roy could see that the Captain had once been a very handsome fellow. His features were sharply defined, there were remnants of a square jaw, and a pair of green eyes was now visible with the shaggy hair out of his face. The only time he got cleaned up was to be charged with murder. The irony was not lost on Roy.

He and Mace exchanged glances. He said, "What's that, Captain?"

"They found my cart."

"Who, the police?"

The Captain nodded. "They came and told me. Seemed happy about it."

"I'm sure. Look, Captain, do you understand what's going on here?"

The Captain sighed heavily. "Damn Twinkies. Always the damn Twinkies."

Mace said, "They don't shackle Twinkie thieves, Captain."

He looked at her with benign curiosity. "Do I know you, hon?"

"We met once. It was a pretty electrifying moment for you."

"Okay, hon. If you say so."

Roy hunched forward. "The photo of the woman I showed you

yesterday? They're charging you with raping and killing her in her office."

Strangely enough, the Captain laughed. "I know. They told me that. The cops just kidding, Roy."

"So you didn't do it?"

"No, sir. They got me on the Twinkies, though. And the tools, don't forget the tools, Roy. I took 'em. For the money." He glanced at Mace and added woefully, "Three dollars, hon. Guy in a turban ripped me off."

"Right, the tools, you told me," said Roy wearily.

"So you my lawyer?"

Mace looked expectantly at Roy. "*Are* you his lawyer?'

Roy hesitated, but only for a moment. "Yeah, I am."

"Then I got money to pay you," said the Captain.

"Okay, fine."

"I got two hundred dollars. Cops took it, but they said they'd give it back."

"Where'd you get two hundred bucks?" asked Mace quickly.

The Captain looked embarrassed. He said in a faltering tone, "I can't say. No, wouldn't be right, hon. Not in front of you."

Roy stood and paced. "Do you know what DNA is?"

The Captain squinted. "I think so, yeah," he said unconvincingly.

"Well, they found your DNA on the dead woman."

The Captain's face brightened. "Are they going to give it back?" He shot a glance at Mace. "It's mine, right? So I'll get my cart, my money, and my DNA. And I won't never take no more Twinkies, swear to God."

Roy let out a small groan and leaned against the wall. Mace walked over to him and whispered, "Has he always been this out of it?"

In a low voice he said, "He can carry on a basic conversation, gets simple concepts okay, but the abstract stuff is way beyond him. When I repped him on the assault three years ago, he was starting to show some early signs of dementia. He got a suspended sentence mainly because the prosecutor was a Vietnam vet too. But that was a simple assault. He's not going to get cut any slack for murder in the first. The problem is, he can carry on a conversation and he understands some things, so no one is going to buy that he didn't know what he was doing."

"I guess the moral is, if you're going to go nuts, go all the way."

"And they have his sperm in Diane's body. And he's admitted to being in the building at the time in question. How the hell do I defend that?"

"You can't. We just have to find the truth. It's the only way."

"Yeah, well, what if the truth is he did rape and kill Diane? What then?"

"I don't know. But my gut is howling that this whole thing stinks."

"Well, when you can get a jury to listen to your gut, let me know." Roy turned back to the Captain and pulled out a legal pad and pen from his briefcase. "Captain, I need you to focus for me. We need to go through some timelines. Can you do that?"

The man looked worried. "I don't know. They took my watch, Roy. I ain't no good with time without my watch."

"It's okay, you can use mine." He slipped it off and handed it to his client.

Mace said, "While you go over the case with him I'm going to have a chat with my sister."

79

WHEN MACE ARRIVED at Beth's office her sister was hastily shoving files in a briefcase. "Got two minutes, Mace. Late for a bunch of meetings."

"I'll walk with you. Thanks for your help with Alisha and Tyler, by the way."

"I'm assuming you're here for some more help." When Mace didn't say anything, Beth added, "They called me when you two showed up to see Dockery. So is Kingman going to rep him?"

"Looks to be the case. Dockery said you found his cart?"

"That's right. And would Kingman like to know what we found in it?"

"You have to tell him that anyway, Beth."

"He'll get all the proper evidentiary disclosures from the prosecutor's office. Well, at least I assume he will."

"What do you mean you assume he will?"

Beth gave her a knowing look. "Take a guess on who's trying the case?"

"Oh hell, not Mona? She's got an office full of homicide hounds to do that kind of work."

"Did you really think she was going to pass up a case like this? Fine upstanding female law partner in G-town struck down by a homeless nutcase and then stuck in a fridge? She'll get tons of ink on this. She's probably getting her hair and nails done as we speak. She won't do the heavy lifting, but rest assured she will be the voice of the U.S. Attorney's Office at all press conferences and other media opportunities. She'll probably do the closing argument too. If the case gets that far."

"Why wouldn't it?"

"Ever heard of a plea bargain? Although Mona won't plead this out unless your guy takes the max. She's not going to pass up her chance to get on Larry King for anything less than that."

"So what did they find in the cart?"

"Tolliver's missing panties and her purse. Credit cards and cell phone and office key card were inside but there was no cash."

Mace's mind flashed to what the Captain had said.

I got two hundred dollars.

"Two hundred dollars found on Dockery," said Beth, seemingly reading her sister's mind. "It does not look good, Mace."

"I still don't think the guy did it. I mean, look at all the other stuff going on here. The key Diane sent Roy. This Andre Watkins character. The guy rolling his apartment. The people after me. How do they all tie into Tolliver being murdered?"

"Did you ever stop to think that they don't? I agree that there is something strange going on with Tolliver and the stuff with you. But her being killed by Dockery might have been a simple crime of opportunity that has no connection to the other things."

"I just knew you were going to say that."

"Why?"

'Because it's so . . . freaking logical!"

"My apologies for being so freaking logical."

"But look, Dockery said the police found his cart, so it was missing. Anybody could've planted that stuff in there. And the other trace found at the crime scene too."

"Let's not forget the sperm in the woman's vagina. Does Kingman want to make the argument that was planted too?"

"Believe me, I get the point."

"How is his firm going to feel about Kingman defending the guy accused of murdering one of its partners?"

"Probably not too good."

"So why is Kingman doing it?"

Mace gave her an exasperated look. "Why don't you ever just call him Roy?"

"I only call my *friends* by their first names, with the exception of Mona. And I only do that because I found out she hates her name."

"He's doing it because he believes Dockery is innocent. Same as me."

As they walked down the hall, Beth said, "Did you ever wonder how a guy like Dockery is able to sneak into the building like that and no one ever sees him? Sounds to me like he had some inside help."

"What are you saying?"

"Maybe your lawyer friend is repping Dockery because he has a guilty conscience? He helps the guy get in the building, Dockery ends up going berserk and killing Tolliver, and Kingman comes in to help clean up the mess."

"So you think Roy actually believes Dockery is guilty?"

"Most people accused of a crime *are* guilty, Mace, you know that."

"Well, you know something, big sister?"

"What?"

"*I* wasn't guilty."

80

"Can I smoke in here?" asked the Captain.

"No, nonsmoking building," said Roy as he wrote some notes down.

"Hey, is it time to eat?"

"Soon."

"I'm hungry."

"I know. Okay, so you got in on Friday a little after six. Hid in the closet by the stairs on the main floor. Then around eight you went up to the fourth floor and settled in for the weekend. What time did you leave on Monday morning?"

"Can't remember."

"You have to try, Lou."

The Captain seemed confused by the use of his real name. Roy noted this and said, "Lawyer-client thing, I need to start using your real name."

"But I tell you what, those damn Twinkies were stale anyway. What's the fuss?"

Roy ran a hand through his hair and wondered why it wasn't falling out with all the stress he was under. "The fuss is they're not charging you with stealing Twinkies, they're charging you with *murder*." He pointed his pen at the Captain. "If you get no other concept down, Lou, please get that one."

"I didn't kill nobody. I would've remembered something like *that*."

"Please don't make that sort of statement to anyone ever again.

And the evidence says otherwise, namely that you did rape and kill her."

"Why I got you. Two hundred bucks. You send me a bill."

I will, to whatever prison you'll be spending the rest of your life in.

"Them cheapskates anyway."

"Who?"

"Twinkie people. Only time I heard church bells."

Roy put his pen down and stared helplessly at the man opposite him. It seemed like the Captain was finally really losing all touch with reality. "Church bells?"

"Yep. Why'd they have to lock up that refrigerator anyway?"

"Lock what refrigerator?"

"The one where I was staying. They didn't lock up the toilet. Or the Twinkies. And they ain't never had much in there anyway so why lock it up?"

"Lock it up how?"

The Captain made a circling motion with his hands. "Big old chain."

Roy had a momentary vision of Mace holding a "big old chain" as a weapon on the fourth floor the previous night when unknown people were coming after them.

"Did they wrap it around the fridge to keep it closed?"

"Why else? Big old padlock. Tried to pick it with my knife. No way, no how. Bet they had Pepsi in there. I like Pepsi better'n Coke."

"Was the chain on there when you got to the fourth floor?"

The Captain thought about this. "Don't know. I think I went to sleep. But it was on there when I woke up."

"Well, that makes sense, Lou, if they thought someone was stealing the food from inside it. They'd lock it up after hours."

"Oh, right. Didn't think of that. You smart, Roy. Glad you're my lawyer."

"Okay, what about the church bells?"

"Yeah, nothing to eat. Ain't staying there. So's I left to look for some food."

"Church bells? You mean you left on Sunday?"

"You sure I can't get me a smoke?"

"I'm sure. You were talking church bells?"

With a vacuous expression the Captain said, "Don't they still have church on Sunday or did they pick another day?"

"No, it's still on Sunday." Roy thought quickly. There were several churches whose bells could be heard at his building. He'd experienced their pealing himself when he'd worked weekends. "So you didn't actually stay in the building all weekend. You left on Sunday?"

"Well, yeah, didn't I already tell you that?"

"No, you didn't!" Roy snapped. "Before you said you left on Monday morning." He drew a calming breath and reminded himself that while his client was nearly sixty, his mental ability was closer to that of a young child. He said in a regular tone, "We've been going through the timeline for an hour now and you never mentioned that, Lou."

The Captain held up Roy's watch. "'Cause this ain't my watch, Roy. I can't tell no good time with yours."

Under different circumstances Roy might've laughed. "Okay, but once you left, did you come back?"

"No, sir. For what? No food is no food. I got me some grub."

"Did you buy it or find it?"

"I got two hundred dollars. I bought it."

"Where?"

"Little grocery store. Man I fought in 'Nam against, he runs it. Only he likes me now. Ain't never once run me off like some other folks."

Roy had a sudden inspiration. "The little shop next to the Starbucks on Wisconsin?" He'd bought some food for lunch there on occasion and had met the owner.

"Yeah, that's right. Starbucks? Sure could use me a cup of java about now."

"And this happened on Sunday when exactly?"

"They have bananas and apples right outside the door like when I was a kid. Bought me some. He likes me now, but back in 'Nam we were trying to kill each other. I sure remember him all right. He shot me and I shot him. Name's Yum-Yum or something."

Roy knew that the Captain hadn't fought against Yum-Yum, whose name was actually Kim Sung. He'd emigrated not from Vietnam but from South Korea into the United States and was only in his early forties. But it didn't matter anyway. Even if the man could place the Captain outside the building on Sunday he could still have sneaked back in to the fourth floor later and attacked Diane on Monday morning. Yet at least it was something. "Did you still hear the church bells when you bought the bananas?'

"Oh yeah."

"Sun was high up in the sky?"

"Yep."

"Okay, how about Sunday night and Monday morning?"

The Captain gave him an alarmed look. "What about 'em? They happened, right?"

Roy took a moment to press against the throbbing pain he had in his left temple. "Yes, they happened. Right on schedule. But, see, if we can find some people who saw you on Sunday night and Monday morning then we can tell the police that you didn't kill . . . that you didn't steal any more Twinkies on Sunday or Monday."

A light finally seemed to dawn in the Captain's emerald eyes. "Oh, right. That's the truth, I didn't. No more damn Twinkies. They were stale anyway. And stale Twinks? Not even Pepsi can make that taste good."

"Okay, I'll check with Kim, I mean with Yum-Yum, and get his statement. So was there anyone else who you saw?"

"Nope. Just went down by the river and got inside the runoff pipe. Slept there."

"And you saw no one? How about somebody in a boat? Early morning rower? Run into anyone when you climbed out of the pipe?"

"I'd have to do me some thinking on that, Roy. And I'm tired."

The Captain put his head down on the table and within a minute he was asleep.

Roy watched him while thinking it would be so easy to just get up and leave. Go back to his cushy job making his big bucks in fancy Georgetown. He didn't need this hassle, taking all the hits for defending some homicidal homeless lost cause. It was like Acker-man had said. Give up the golden egg for *this*?

But he didn't get up. He just continued to stare down at a man who'd pretty much sacrificed his life so Americans could keep on being fat and happy. He said in a tired but clear voice, "I'm going to do my best for you, Captain. And even if we don't win, we'll both go down fighting."

The Captain grunted and then sat up. He looked around grog-gily. "Is hon gone?"

"Hon? Oh yeah, she's still gone."

"Two hundred dollars, Roy."

"Captain, you don't have to pay me. I'm doing this pro bono, I mean I'm doing this on my dime."

"How I got it." The Captain looked embarrassed. "Peed in a cup."

"Excuse me?"

The Captain gazed at the tabletop and said in a hushed voice, "Peed in a cup."

Roy sat forward, still looking confused. "Someone paid you two hundred dollars to pee in a cup?"

"Not pee, the other thing." Now Roy could really see pink in the man's cheeks because he was blushing.

"The other thing?"

"They gave me a magazine to look at. Couldn't say this in front of hon."

"A magazine?"

"Girlie magazine. Not pee. You know. The other thing."

"You mean?"

The Captain eyeballed Roy with a knowing look. "Two hundred dollars to look at a girlie magazine."

Roy leaned forward and gripped the Captain's arm. "Where did you do this?"

"G-town. Not too far."

"Was it a fertility clinic, a sperm bank?"

The Captain just looked at him with a blank expression.

"Forget that, can you remember *when* you did it?"

"It was daylight."

"Okay, can you remember exactly where this place was?"

"Uh . . . It was white."

"Can you describe the person who asked you to, uh, pee in the cup?"

"Some guy."

"Never mind, I'll find it!" Roy banged his briefcase closed and raced out of the room.

CHAPTER

81

MACE LEFT the mansion and walked over to the guesthouse. Alisha and Tyler were sitting at the dining room table eating a meal that Herbert had prepared. Mace sat down next to Tyler, who alternated between carefully forking mashed potatoes into his mouth and taking large gulps of milk.

"I know, the food here is pretty terrific," said Mace, as she watched the little boy.

"Do you live here?" Alisha asked her.

"For now. You all settled in?"

Alisha nodded. "I can't believe it. I mean just yesterday I was in my little apartment and then at Social. And now. It's like a dream. It's like a movie." She gazed around the expansive room in wonder. She looked over at her son. "I think Ty likes it here too."

"Wait'll I show you the gym. It's got an indoor basketball court."

Ty's eyes widened.

"You hear that, Ty?" said his mother. "A basketball court."

"He likes basketball?"

"Oh, yeah. Don't get a chance to play much. But he likes watching. He was watching from the window when your friend kicked Psycho's butt. Shoulda seen Ty clapping and jumping."

Mace said, "I can show you some cool moves if you want, Ty."

The little boy took another mouthful of food and looked at his mother.

"That'd be good, right, Ty?"

He nodded quickly.

Afterwards they walked over to the gym. Mace got a ball and

took Ty onto the court while Alisha watched. Mace bounced the ball between her legs, turned, and shot. The ball swished through the hoop, barely grazing the net.

Ty's face lit up and he looked over at his mother. Alisha clapped and Ty clapped too, his little arms pumping away. Mace took his hand and they moved closer to the basket. "Hang on one sec, Ty." She hustled over to a switch on the wall that raised and lowered the basket. She cranked it down to about five feet high and rejoined Ty. She instructed him how to hold the ball and then helped him with the first few shots. Three missed, but the fourth one found the bottom of the net.

Ty opened his mouth, and though no sound came out it was clear that he was shouting for joy. Mace showed him to how to bank a shot in. Every time he made a basket he would open his mouth, raise his arms in triumph, and then look at his mother. A few minutes later Alisha and Mace chased Ty all over the court as he bounced the ball and played keep-away. Thirty minutes later the two women sat down on a section of pullout bleachers while Ty kept bouncing the ball and hustling around the court.

"Okay, I'm officially worn out," said Mace as she watched the little boy run.

"He wears me out too. That little apartment ain't big enough to keep him tired. But it better than some alley."

"You should feel good you got out of that, Alisha. Real good."

"That man, Mr. Altman, he say we can stay here long as we want to. And he say he got some folks to look at Ty."

"He's a very kind man. If anyone can help Ty, he can."

Alisha looked around the immense building. "But we can't be staying here too long. I need to get me a real job. Take care of Ty good. Get going on my own."

"That will all come, Alisha. It's all part of the program. Mr. Altman will explain it in more detail."

"Yeah, that what he said. He wants me to get my GED and then he talking maybe college."

"That's great."

She looked worried. "I don't know. Folks in college they real smart. And the way I talk and all."

"The way you talk is fine. And I wonder how many of them could have survived what you did. You can do this. You're smart too."

Alisha smiled. "Sound like my granny. Be anything you want to be."

"You can."

Alisha stretched out her hand and placed it over the top of Mace's. "Thank you."

"Have you talked to Darren?"

"Unh-uh. Thought he call me, but he ain't."

"And he knows what Psycho did to you?"

"I know I shouldn't told him. He in prison when it happened."

"What was he in for?"

"Carjacking and stuff. Stupid. He got in with some real bad dudes. But he's smart. He done real good in school. He got a job to help me and our granny. But then she got sick and ain't had no health insurance. He had to make more money."

"So drug dealing? Carjacking?"

Alisha nodded. "He got arrested on my birthday. Just turned twelve and he bought me a dress and we were having ice cream in the food court over at the train station. And the blues bust in and then he gone. Didn't really see him again till he got outta prison. They sent him all the way to Ohio. Ain't no way I can get there with Ty."

"You think he might try to go after Psycho?"

Alisha's lips trembled. "I pray to God he ain't do something that dumb. Psycho kill him."

"We'll do everything we can to make sure that won't happen." Mace looked over at Ty as the little boy lined up a shot and made it. "I think Ty needs an uncle in his life. And from what I saw at your apartment Darren is really good with him."

"Oh, he loves Ty and Ty loves him. Funny because they ain't been around each other all that long. But it like they know each other a long time, you know what I mean?"

Mace nodded and then her attention turned to the door of the gym as it shot open.

"Darren!" Alisha cried out and jumped to her feet.

Ty stopped bouncing his ball and looked around at his uncle.

Right behind Darren was Rick Cassidy, his arm on Darren's shoulder.

"You know this guy?" said Cassidy.

"We do," said Mace. "What's going on?"

"Caught him climbing the south wall," said Cassidy.

As she drew closer Mace could see that Cassidy had placed a gun against the small of Darren's back.

"It ain't like I gonna just walk up to the door of a place like this and knock," said Darren sullenly.

"You should've given it a try," said Mace in a scolding tone. "We would have let you in."

"Yeah, right."

"Rick, you can lose the gun," said Mace quietly as she saw Ty running toward them.

"Okay, but I confiscated two pistols from him."

"Keep 'em for now."

"You sure, Mace?"

"I'm sure."

Rick holstered his gun and patted Darren on the shoulder. "You were actually pretty stealthy coming over the wall and you sure can run. Might make a good Navy SEAL."

"Yeah? Well, I don't see that in my career future, okay?"

"Never know." Cassidy turned and left.

Alisha put her arms around her brother while Ty gripped his legs.

"Okay, okay, don't knock me over, little guy," Darren said in a mock angry tone. He reached down and lifted Ty up.

"I was worried 'bout you," said Alisha. "Tried calling, but you never answered."

"Got tied up doing stuff."

"How'd you know she was here?" asked Mace.

Darren smiled. "That lady at Social, Carmela? Think she likes me. And the Razor got him some moves." He glanced at the door. "Was that dude really a SEAL?"

"Yep. You're lucky he took it easy on you."

"When he grabbed my arm I couldn't break his grip. Man, it was like steel."

"Welcome to the world of special forces."

He looked around. "Damn, what is this place anyway?"

Ty jumped down, picked up his ball, and bounced it back to Darren. Darren caught it, did a couple of dribbles between his legs, and passed it back. Ty bounced the ball down the court and made a layup.

Darren shot his sister a glance. "Who taught him how to do that?"

Alisha pointed at Mace. "She did."

"Hey, Razor, why don't you go play with your nephew for a while," said Mace. "And keep all thoughts of Psycho from your head."

"Ain't nothing gonna do that, woman. Playing with Ty or not."

"See, that's the very reason you should. Ty and Alisha need you, Darren. Not in prison. And not dead. You let me worry about Psycho."

"What you gonna do about Psycho? You can't do shit about him."

"All I'm asking is that you let me try. That's all."

"Please, Darren," said Alisha. "Please." She gripped his arm tightly.

Darren looked back and forth between the two women. Then he pulled free from Alisha. "Gotta go teach my little man some street moves."

He jogged down the court to join Ty.

Mace's phone rang. It was Roy. His message was brief, blunt, and yet stunning.

"Alisha, I've got to go out for a while. Just chill and I'll be back, okay?"

"Okay. Sure."

Mace ran to her Ducati.

CHAPTER

82

Potomac Cryobank, LLP. You sure this is the place?" Mace asked Roy as she looked up at the sign over the door.

They were standing outside of a white brick building just off M Street in Georgetown. They'd driven over on her Ducati. The place was less than a ten-minute walk from Shilling & Murdoch.

"It's not like there are fertility clinics and sperm banks on every corner. Based on what the Captain told me, this is it. It's the only one within walking distance. And it's white."

They went inside and spent five minutes getting nowhere with the receptionist. Finally, a thin woman dressed in white pants, a blue smock, and rubber-soled shoes came out, steered them to a room off the foyer, and seated them at a small table.

"So what exactly is this about?" she asked sternly.

Roy explained as much of the situation as he could.

"That's ridiculous," said the woman.

"Why?" asked Roy.

"This person claims he just walked in off the street and was paid two hundred dollars for a semen donation?"

"That's right. Why is that ridiculous?"

"You don't know much about sperm banks, do you, Mr. Kingman?"

"No, actually, I've never had the need to come to one before. I've been pretty happy with my own product."

"That's why we're here," said Mace. "To become educated."

The woman excused herself and returned a minute later with a large stack of papers that she plopped in front of Mace and Roy.

"Let me give you the run-through of what it takes to become a semen donor," she said, with the irritating air of a person who knows lots of things others don't. She indicated the pages. "These are the forms one must fill out to even be considered as a donor. They're all available online from our website as well." She held up one form. "This is the initial donor app, which as you can see is lengthy and requires extensive medical, physical, and educational backgrounds and other pertinent information. If they pass that stage—and many do not—they are sent a second application covering three genera-tions of family medical history." She picked up another set of pages. "I'm referring to this one. After that comes a specimen screening. This involves a personal interview conducted on these premises and a semen evaluation. They are asked to produce three to four speci-mens over a two-week period. Those specimens are evaluated for quality and testing of freezing survivability."

"Freezing survivability?" said Mace.

"I'll get to that. Potential donors must be screened for infectious diseases of course, like HIV, syphilis, gonorrhea, hepatitis B and C, and also genetic diseases, as well as blood typing, rhesus factor, and so on. And they must undergo a general physical exam either by their own physician or ours. We expect a six-month commitment from our accepted donors and they must produce one donation per week over that period."

"And they're paid?" said Roy.

"Of course. People do not go through this out of the goodness of their hearts. Our compensation rates range from one to four hun-dred dollars per acceptable specimen. Precise individual compensa-tion depends on semen quality and the donor's commitment to the program."

"How is it collected?" asked Roy.

"Almost all on-site. Usually via masturbation into leakproof containers. Semen can also be removed surgically, but we don't do that here."

"Almost all, you said?" noted Mace.

"We sometimes do off-site collections in an emergency, but only if the collection is done at a hospital, clinic, or, in very rare cases, the person's home. With that method we provide donors with special condoms for collection purposes. And the specimen must be transported to us within one to two hours without being exposed to extreme temperatures. Otherwise it's not acceptable. But in the seven years I've been here we've only had two cases of off-site collection. We like to control all phases, you see."

"And if it's off-site, then you have no way of knowing if it's actually the person's sperm or not," pointed out Roy.

"That's right. We can of course do a DNA analysis to ensure it was from our donor. And it will still be subjected to the same rigorous checks, so, for example, no infectious diseases get through."

"And the freezing?" prompted Mace.

"The sperm has to be stored under specific and exacting conditions to fully preserve it. We have a cryo-storage room here with cryogenic vats. We use liquid nitrogen among other protocols to maintain the specimens."

"Can we see the room?" asked Mace.

"No. It's an environmentally controlled space and you need special equipment to work in there. I can tell you that each vat holds over seventy thousand semen specimens."

"How do you differ from a fertility clinic?" Mace wanted to know.

"Fertility clinics don't typically store sperm. They get it from us. We match their client's request as to race, height, physical appearance, for example, and provide them the sperm which they will then use for artificial insemination purposes."

"Is there any way to determine if the sperm found at the crime scene I described came from your clinic?" Roy asked.

"I can assure you it didn't," she said flatly.

"Just humor me. Please. A man's freedom is at stake."

She sighed heavily. "From our specific clinic? No, I don't believe so. But you can easily determine if it was a donation to a sperm bank like ours."

"How?" Mace asked quickly.

"As soon as the specimen is provided you have to inject buffers as a preservative into the semen. If done promptly and then frozen, semen can really be stored indefinitely. However, the maximum allowable time by current law is ten years unless the donor was under the age of forty-five when the specimen was given. And even then the sperm can only be used by the donor and his partner, and not given to anyone else."

"Ten years, wow," said Mace. "Long time to keep the little fellows swimming around."

"Without a preservative and proper storage the sperm contained in the semen will have diminished motility after two or three days and the sample will be no good to us after, say, five days. And our clients would not be very happy with that, would they?"

"So, shooting blanks, in other words?" said Mace.

The nurse sniffed. "Crudely put, but accurate. When we send semen out to our clients the specimens are cryopreserved in screw-top vials. The vials come inside a refrigerated tank or dry shipper since it is actually a metal vacuum bottle refrigerated with liquid nitrogen. The semen is sent with detailed instructions on thawing and utilization."

Sort of takes all the romance out of it, thought Mace.

"So to answer your question directly, we use a TEST yolk buffer solution as a preservative. Many other sperm banks do the same."

"Yolk? As in egg?" said Mace with a trace of disgust.

"Not exactly, no, and it's a perfectly accepted method of preservation."

Roy said, "So if it's not a semen donation?"

"Then there will be no preservative. And I can assure you that there won't be with the person you described. He would never have gotten past the initial round of medical forms. And if he's a Vietnam veteran as you mentioned he would've been disqualified right away."

"You disqualify Vietnam vets?" said Roy sharply.

"No, of course not, it's based on *age*. We, along with most sperm banks, don't accept specimens from anyone over the age of forty. Indeed, most of our donors are under the age of thirty, many of them college students."

"Looking for beer money," commented Mace.

"I wouldn't know about that."

"Are you open every day?" asked Mace.

"We're closed on Wednesdays and Sundays."

"So the building is empty then?"

The woman looked at her and said in a contemptuous tone, "That would usually be the case when we're *closed*. Now if you'll excuse me, I have to get back to work."

"Lots of eggs to crack today?" said Mace.

The woman led them out without saying another word.

When they were outside Roy said, "Wow, I really dig your interrogation technique. First, piss the person off, and then see what she won't tell us."

"That woman was not going to knowingly help us from the get-go, but she did tell us at least one thing of importance other than the yolk thing."

"What?"

"That they're closed on Wednesdays and Sundays. Now we need to get the sperm sample they found in Tolliver checked out. Lowell Cassell can do it."

"And if there's no yolk?"

"Then maybe the Captain is lying."

"I don't think he's mentally capable of coming up with something like this."

"I don't think so either, but nothing would surprise me anymore. If it does come back without the preservative, the Captain is probably going down for this."

"But what if he came here and they took sperm from him but didn't inject the preservative in it?"

"And why would they do that, Roy? Because they were planning to kill Diane Tolliver and blame it on the Captain? You think the petite sperm expert back there crushed your partner's brain stem and then injected her with sperm taken under false pretenses?"

"No, but maybe one of the doctors? The Captain said a white building. And he said some guy helped him. He obviously came here."

Mace considered this. "We'll have to get a roster of who works here and check out any viable suspects."

"In the meantime can you call Cassell to run the test?"

"No, but I'll phone my sister. I'll do it tomorrow morning."

"Why not now?"

"Because I have to work up the nerve, that's why!"

"Why not just bypass her?"

"How? I can't exactly order the ME to run the damn test."

Roy's phone buzzed.

"Hello?"

"Mr. Kingman? It's Gary, the waiter from Simpsons."

"Oh, right. Gary from Simpsons," he said so Mace would know. Roy hit the speakerphone button and held the phone up.

"Did you remember something else, Gary?"

"Well, it wasn't what I remembered. It's what I just saw."

"What you just saw? I don't understand."

"The guy Ms. Tolliver was having dinner with? I just saw him."

"What? Where? We're close to the restaurant. Is that where you saw him? We can be there in a few minutes. Can you stall him?"

"No, I'm not at work. I'm at my apartment near Adams Morgan. I meant I just saw his photo in the newspaper."

"Saw him in the newspaper."

"Yeah. He's dead."

"What? Who was he?"

"That attorney guy they found in a Dumpster? Jamie Meldon? He was the guy with Ms. Tolliver Friday night."

CHAPTER

83

H ELLO, Beth."

Beth looked up to see Sam Donnelly and Jarvis Burns coming toward her. It was the next morning and they were in an auditorium at the FBI's Washington Field Office where Beth was to give out some awards to local teenagers enrolled in the Bureau's Junior Agent Program.

"Sam, Jarvis, I didn't expect to see you two here."

Burns's eyes crinkled. "Why not? Some of these young people will be the intelligence operatives of the future."

Donnelly added, "And one can never start too early looking for talent and molding personalities."

"By the way, I spoke with your guys. I appreciate the effort you made."

"Well, they're not technically *my guys*," Donnelly said quickly. "But I value your professional friendship highly. Indeed, Beth, if you hadn't pursued a career in law enforcement you would've made a hell of an intelligence agent."

"High praise coming from you. So Reiger and Hope don't report to you?"

Donnelly and Burns exchanged a quick glance. Donnelly said, "Not even the same intelligence platform. Quite frankly, I made a few phone calls, did the Potomac two-step, and ended up with that pair. They seem quite capable. And their superiors obviously gave the okay to brief you."

"Well, it wasn't much of a briefing. National security tagline basically."

"That, unfortunately, is often the case. You know how these things work. No one wants to read anybody else into anything. The old cold war adage still applies as much today: Don't trust anyone."

"Do Reiger and Hope have any military connections?"

Burns shot her a penetrating stare. "Not that we know of. Why do you ask?"

"Just an observation. They had DHS creds but told me they'd once worked at the Bureau. And I checked into their backgrounds and quickly found that my security clearances weren't high enough to even have a peek into where they really came from."

Donnelly said, "With DHS, the FBI, and sixteen intelligence agencies floating around, it's nearly impossible keeping any of it straight. I know the goal when creating the Director of National Intelligence position was to orchestrate better oversight and coordination among all these unwieldy alliances, but—and you didn't hear this from me—it is a herculean task. Some might say impossible."

"I'm sure. I just have one city and four thousand cops to keep track of. You have the entire world."

"Don't sell yourself short. That one city is the nation's capital. And one of your constituents just happens to be the president."

"Who went for a pizza run yesterday, which cost me two hundred officers off the street for the motorcade deployment."

"The world's most powerful man can do what he wants when he wants." Burns drew closer. "As an aside, I heard you made an arrest in the murder of that female lawyer in Georgetown. Congratulations. The director actually mentioned it at our morning briefing."

Donnelly said, "That's right, Beth. Good work."

"Well, let's hope the case sticks."

"A homeless vet I understand?" said Burns.

"Louis Dockery. A homeless vet with a chest full of medals, including a pair of Purple Hearts and a Combat Bronze."

Burns wagged his head, his silvery hair tipping onto his broad forehead. "So very sad. I can certainly relate to the Purple Heart, I have a pair of those myself."

Donnelly said, "I have one of my own. But unfortunately the two ongoing wars are adding enormously to both the military and the VA's burdens. There's simply not enough funding to cover all the problems."

Beth said, "Well, Washington better rework its priorities. I can't think of a more important goal than taking care of the people who've defended this country with their blood."

Burns patted his bad leg. "When I got out I sought psychiatric counseling, although there was a certain stigma attached to that. Hopefully it's less so now."

"Well, you turned out all right, so there's hope."

"Some would argue with that."

"That there's hope?"

Burns smiled. "No. That I turned out all right."

Donnelly pointed to the teenagers set to receive their awards. "Now, go give them a great pep talk, Chief. In ten years they'll be the first line of defense for this country."

"Preventing attacks instead of responding to them, you mean?"

"Much better to crush the enemy before he can act instead of pulling the bodies of his victims out of the rubble. We save lives, Beth, you and I. We just do it a little differently in my part of the spectrum. But the goals are the same. Always remember that."

The men walked off and a moment later Beth's phone buzzed. She looked at the caller and her brow wrinkled. She almost didn't answer.

"Mace, I'm right in the middle of something. Can this wait? What?" She listened intently for sixty seconds. "I'll take care of it." She clicked off, glanced at the FBI agent emceeing the program, and held up one finger. He nodded.

She rushed to a corner of the auditorium and made a call.

Lowell Cassell seemed surprised. "All right, Beth, if you say so. It's easy enough to check for that. But if it's true that certainly will complicate things."

"Yes, it will."

"How did you come by this theory?"

"Take one guess."

"Your sister is keeping busy."

Beth clicked off and rushed up to the stage to personally greet the teenagers and then settled at the lectern to begin her remarks.

From a far corner, Donnelly and Burns, who'd been watching her intently while she'd been on the calls, turned and left the room.

CHAPTER

84

"THIS WAS a nice surprise." Karl Reiger's wife, Wendy, kissed him on the cheek as her husband flipped another burger on the grill.

"Kids had the day off so I thought what the hell. Nice, sunny day, summer around the corner."

"Well, I'm glad you did. You've been working such long hours lately, sweetie."

Reiger looked at his wife. She was in her mid-thirties, four years younger than him. She still possessed the classic beauty she had when they'd met in college. She wore jean shorts, a white sleeveless blouse, and a Washington Nationals ball cap over her shoulder-length light brown hair.

"Yeah, work is a real bitch right now."

"Oh look, Don and Sally are here."

Reiger glanced over at the driveway of his two-story brick house in Centreville, Virginia. Lots of federal agents lived out this way because everything inside the Beltway was far too expensive if your job was to merely risk your life in serving your country. Don Hope, his wife, and three kids were climbing out of a Dodge mini-van, hauling platters of food along with a baseball and several gloves. Hope's two sons put down the food on a wooden picnic table set up in the backyard and joined Reiger's two boys in throwing the ball around. The Hopes' daughter, a ten-year-old, went into the house with Tammy Reiger, who'd just turned eleven. Sally gave Reiger a hug and then she and Wendy busied themselves getting the meal ready.

Don Hope shut the doors of the van, grabbed two beers from a cooler he'd brought, popped the tops, walked over to Reiger at the grill, and handed him one.

Reiger took a long pull of the drink, finishing half of it.

"Cookout?" said Hope. "Little surprised to get the call."

"Why not? Normalcy. It's been a while."

"Guess you're right about that. No orders yet?"

"Why I'm flipping burgers instead of the other thing."

"You think Burns is setting us up to take the fall?"

"Every op I've gone into I'm prepared to be killed by the guys on the other side and screwed by the guys signing my paychecks."

"Hell of a way to make a living, Karl."

"I thought I'd be career military. See the world, good pension when you pull your time. Even do some good."

"Me too. Then—"

"We were too good at what we did, Don. That's why they came calling. They don't pick the dregs, they go for the cream."

"Feeling more like soured milk now."

Reiger slid a burger onto a platter and slapped another piece of raw meat on the grill. "Why, because we keep missing Perry?"

"Dumb luck."

"I'm not so sure about that. I've read up on her after Burns gave us the 'Rome is burning' lecture. Lady is good at what she does. No question. Hell, I'm surprised Burns didn't try to recruit her at some point."

Hope took a swallow of beer and watched the boys throwing the ball. "Sterilized weapons, cocked and locked. What bullshit. I'm a dad. I got a mortgage. I've been married fourteen years and I still have the hots big-time for my wife. I'm not some damn machine."

"To them we are. That's all we are. Fungible. Use up some shells, they got more where we came from. We're just rounds in a magazine."

"How many more do you figure?"

"Never really thought about it, because I could never verify my guess."

"But why meet at the Pentagon? Especially since no one else there knows what we're up to."

Reiger prodded a burger with a long fork. "DNI isn't like the spider at the center of the web. It's more like the snake slithering through the backyard. A mandate to go everywhere, see everything. Pentagon is as big an intelligence player as they come. Used to going its own way, sucking down dollars and data. We saw that when we were in uniform, Don."

"For sure we did."

"But even it has to kowtow to DNI. And so Burns makes the rounds, has offices everywhere, Langley, NSA, National Geospatial."

"And the Pentagon?"

"I know two- and three-star generals who hate the DNI's guts for all the good it'll do them. Sam Donnelly does the daily presidential intelligence briefings now instead of the DCI. Locked tight. You got the man's ear and trust, you can't lose. You're golden."

"Yeah, but Burns is a piece of work. Half of me wishes he'd drop from a stroke."

"And the other half?" Reiger said grinning.

"Nothing you haven't thought about."

Reiger put some cheese on top of an almost done burger. "Read up on him too when we were recruited for this. Vietnam vet. One hard-ass guy. Medals out the ying-yang. Guy was as brave as they come, did his thing, laid it all out there for the Stars and Stripes. Flipped to the intelligence side soon as Saigon fell. Wounds made him unfit for active duty."

"The leg."

"Right. He's in his sixties. Could have got out before now, but apparently he's got nothing else in his life."

"Wife? Kids?"

"Wife left him, apparently his two kids did too."

Hope looked impressed. "Where'd you get that scuttlebutt?"

Reiger cracked a smile. "Your security clearance isn't high enough."

Hope finished his beer. "The hell you say."

"A hardass," Reiger said again. "Loves his country, though. Do anything to protect it. And he expects us to do anything to protect it too. And anything covers a lot."

"Piece of paper, Karl. That's what we need. Our get-out-of-jail-free card."

The ball flew toward them, landing a couple feet from the grill. Reiger snagged it and threw it back to his oldest son.

"Thanks, Pop."

Reiger pointed at the black sedan that had just pulled into the driveway next to the minivan. The man who got out wore a plain suit that did not stand out in any way. It was the sort that Reiger and Hope wore while on duty, allowing them to just blend in. In the man's hand was an equally plain white envelope.

"Well, here it comes right now, Don. I guess we're back to killing Americans."

"I don't like this any better than you, but don't get cold on me now, Karl."

"I've been cold ever since I put a round in Jamie Meldon's brain."

He slapped another piece of raw meat on the grill and watched it sizzle.

AFTER PHONING her sister that morning, Mace picked up Roy and drove him in to work. When they arrived she told Roy about the call.

"So you didn't tell her about Meldon having dinner with Diane, but just about the DNA testing?" he said as he climbed off the bike.

"That's right."

"Mind telling me why?"

"It could be the key to breaking this case. If I'm going to use this sucker to get back on the force *I* have to solve it. And I don't want Beth to get in trouble for pulling strings for me."

"I can understand that. You really do care about her."

"She's pretty much all I have left."

"Hey, haven't I gotten a little bit in the loop?"

She smiled. "You're sweet, Roy. And yes you have." Her expression hardened. "So what's the connection between Meldon and Tolliver?"

"It has to predate her coming to Shilling & Murdoch. She never once mentioned him, and I never saw him come to the firm."

"Wouldn't have been some legal dealings?"

"We don't do criminal work. What other legal dealings would they have?"

"Okay, like you said, it must predate her time at Shilling. Where was she before?"

Roy thought for a moment. "She mentioned New Jersey."

"I read that Meldon used to practice law in Manhattan. If she was in Newark or thereabouts, that's practically the same place.

They could have had dealings then. She was in private practice up there too?"

"I think so."

"It's funny."

"What?"

"The D.C. cops got pulled off Meldon's murder."

"You mentioned that but didn't tell me why."

"Beth didn't know why but she was pissed about it. She and Mona Danforth had *words* about it while we were at Café Milano. But the thing is, whoever's investigating Meldon's death should have retraced his steps too. They could've found something or knew that he was meeting with Tolliver. And let me tell you, if their deaths aren't connected it's like the mother of all coincidences. And I don't believe in coincidences anyway."

"So we find Diane's killer, we get Meldon's murderer too."

"That's sort of the plan."

"Any way to find out who *is* investigating Meldon's homicide?"

"If I ask Beth she'll want to know why. I can try a couple other sources. Meantime we need to follow up our own leads."

"But that waiter could call the cops and tell them what he just told us."

"He could but I doubt he will."

"Why?"

"He's probably forgotten about it. It just comes with the chronic ADD mentality of that generation that believes that twittering actually constitutes personal interaction."

"Hey, that waiter was about the same age as me."

"Sorry. So can you find out where Diane worked before Shilling?"

"Yeah. But let me write it down. Otherwise I'll probably forget we even had this conversation because of my generational ADD."

"Oh, Roy, at least you make me laugh."

"Well, while you're laughing I also just remembered where I saw the initials DLT."

"DLT?"

"It was at the bottom of the last e-mail Diane sent me."

"I saw that. Just figured it was her initials."

"That's what I thought too, but she never signed any other e-mails that way."

"Okay. So what else could it mean?"

"I'm betting DLT stands for Daniels, Langford and Taylor."

"And they are?"

"The escrow agent that Shilling & Murdoch uses for all of its closing transactions. Their offices are up on K Street, right in the middle of Lobbyist Alley."

"And they're significant why?"

"They do the money wire transfers for our deals. Billions of dollars go through their office, at least electronically. Billions."

"Okay, billions of anything always gets my attention. What do you think you can find out?"

"I can check the firm archives for a start. I can look through closing docs for the deals that Diane and I worked on, check escrow letters, electronic funds transfer confirmations, that sort of thing."

Before he walked inside she said, "Call me with whatever info you can get on Diane. I'll follow it up from there. But you need to focus on repping the Captain. With Mona on the other side waiting with fangs bared, you're going to really need to bring your A-game."

She roared off, leaving Roy to trudge into the building, his briefcase smacking against his leg.

Ned nodded to him from the security desk.

"You okay, Mr. Kingman?" he asked.

"Never better."

86

MACE DROVE BACK to Abe Altman's place and checked on Alisha and Tyler. She found the pair in Altman's study going over specifics of the program Altman had designed. They looked up when she poked her head in. Ty still had the basketball and was bouncing it in a corner.

"Where's Darren?" Mace asked.

"He left," said Alisha. "Didn't say where he was going and didn't say when he be back. I'm worried about him."

"Hey, Razor can take care of himself." This was a lie, Mace knew. When it came to people like Psycho you'd need an Army battalion to take care of yourself. She walked back to the guesthouse, went up to her bedroom, and pulled something out of her closet. It was the baggie of shell casings the honor guard had given her at her father's funeral. She sat back on the bed and held the bag on her chest, staring at the ceiling. It was so stupid of her to have opened the coffin. Every time she thought of her father, it began with that horrifying image before she could manage to push it aside.

She rattled the metal in the bag.

Okay, Dad, what do you think I should do? Let Beth run with this or keep chugging on? I want to be a blue again, Dad. I have to be a blue again.

She rattled the casings some more, as though trying to get better reception. There was no answer. There would never be an answer. She wasn't a little girl anymore who could run to Daddy for help. These were her problems to solve. Only there was no right or wrong answer. There were only choices. Her choices.

She put the precious bag of used ordnance away, slipped over to the window, and looked over the grounds. Her gaze, by habit, sought out all places of potential danger. Entry points, the shadowy spaces under trees, a secluded corner. She thought for a second that she had seen Rick Cassidy flit by, but it happened so fast she couldn't be sure.

Feeling suddenly lethargic, she scooted down to the kitchen and made some coffee. She brought it back up to the bedroom with a peanut butter and jelly sandwich with sliced bananas on toasted wheat that she'd made with her own two hands. It undoubtedly would not have met Herbert's high culinary standards, but it tasted damn good. Finished, she lay back on the bed with the thought of just resting her eyes. She hadn't really slept in a long time. It was finally catching up to her. Just a few minutes . . .

The vibration woke her. She sat up groggily and looked around for a moment, disoriented. A moment later she snatched her phone from her pocket. As she hit the answer button she noted the time.

Damn, I've been asleep for hours.

"Hello?" She glanced out the window where a gentle rain was starting to fall.

"It's Roy."

"I didn't recognize the number. Where are you calling from?"

"My health club. Just call me paranoid. If they can tap computer cameras, you know?"

"I know. So what's up?"

"Got something to write with?"

She grabbed paper and pen off the nightstand. "Shoot."

"Okay, just so you know, everyone in the firm hates my guts."

"And how magnanimous you'll be when you turn out to be right."

"No, I won't. I'll tell them to eat shit and die. Anyway, I checked out some stuff and talked to some people. I've got Diane's ex-husband's name and number. He lives in Hawaii so you can call him today if you want. It's morning there now."

"Okay. What else?"

"Apparently the divorce was not all that amicable. I'm hoping that the ex can give you some more info on that. Maybe the name of the lawyer who represented Diane."

"And the connection to Meldon?"

"No clue at this point, but at least it's a start."

"What about DLT?"

"I'm planning to sneak down to the archives tonight and poke around."

"Listen, Roy, you staying there after hours alone is not a good thing."

"I'm not sure if anyone here is involved, so I can't exactly waltz down to archives and start going through boxes. I'll find what I can and take the stuff home."

"Why not come to Abe's instead? We've got real security here."

"You think he'll mind?"

"I think the place is so big you could roll in with a tank brigade and he'd have no clue you were even here."

"Okay, maybe that's smarter."

"And that way we can both go over the docs you found. It'll be faster. Are you going back to see the Captain?"

"As soon as I'm done here. They just notified me that the presentment is tomorrow morning at Superior Court. I need to go over some details with him to the extent he can remember any."

"The presentment's pretty perfunctory, right?"

"Nothing's perfunctory when Mona Danforth is in the picture. They'll have to get a grand jury to issue an indictment since it's a first-degree felony."

"Or they can just return a No Bill."

"What, did you enroll in law school this afternoon?"

Mace said, "I was a cop. I've been in court more than most lawyers."

"But there's no way she's not going to get an indictment returned on these facts. They might as well just dispense with the preliminary hearing. They've got more than enough to show cause for the prosecution to go forward. The Captain will be arraigned on murder in the first and a trial date set. Any word from your sister on the semen sample?"

"Uh, hold on a sec."

Mace quickly checked to see if she had any phone messages on the off chance that she had slept through a call from Beth. "No, nothing yet."

"Well, let me know the minute you do. I don't want to be blind-sided by that when I walk into court tomorrow."

"And when you do your firm will know for sure where you stand."

"I know. And they'll fire me. That's why I'm going through the archives today. I probably won't get another chance."

"Good luck."

"You too."

Mace clicked off and punched in the number for Joe Cushman, Diane Tolliver's ex-husband who was now living in the Hawaiian paradise.

Must be nice.

CHAPTER

87

THE COOKOUT was over, the sunshine was long gone, replaced with light rain, and Reiger and Hope were back in their plain suits and riding in their new Town Car.

"Orders all in order?" joked Hope.

"Yep, and locked away in my safety deposit box. I dropped by the bank as soon as you and your family left."

"Getting paranoid on me? Good." Hope rolled down the window and breathed in the moist air. "So who signed?"

"Everybody we need. Including Burns *and* Donnelly."

"Guess the guy finally took us seriously." Hope nodded at his partner. "Cookout was nice, Karl. Good idea."

"Yeah, I'd rather be flipping dogs and burgers right now instead of driving to this place."

Hope looked at the address that had come with the signed orders. "Warehouse in Arlington?"

"A front. They're all fronts. We'll see a 'For Sale' or 'For Lease' sign on the wall. A couple cars parked out of sight. A guy with a face you'll never remember will answer our knock, we'll flash our IDs, and the meeting will begin."

"What are we hoping to get out of this tonight?"

"What I want are some recruits to do the trigger pulls while we coordinate from the sidelines. At least that way I can hate myself a little less."

"But that's another set of testimonies in court if this goes wrong. Geez, I can't believe I'm saying this stuff."

"We need to think about it, Don. But I'm not worried about

these guys. I'm guessing Burns made sure they are not from this hemisphere. So we get the executioners in place and then the plan gets knocked together."

"I know Perry has to go down. What about the punk lawyer?"

"If he hadn't gotten in the way that night Perry would already have ceased to be a pain in our ass. But I'm not holding grudges. The order says Perry and anybody else deemed necessary. If we deem him not necessary he can go on being a lawyer after mourning the loss of his friend. I'm not looking to add to my bag of kills here. I've smoked my share of dirtbags, but none of them looked like me."

Reiger looked up ahead. "There it is. What did I tell you?"

As they drove into the parking lot the "For Sale" sign was prominently mounted on one wall of the place that was actually three separate buildings on an acre of land in a section of Arlington that had seen far better days.

"Looks to be 1950s construction," said Hope. "Surprised they haven't knocked it down and put up condos. Land in Arlington is damn hard to come by."

"Yeah, but if it's secretly owned by an intelligence agency that doesn't give a crap about cash flow, that is not your definition of a motivated seller."

Reiger drove through a narrow opening between two of the brick buildings and stopped in the middle of the small interior courtyard.

"Like I said, couple of cars parked here. Now all we need is the faceless guy answering the door and I'm a perfect three for three."

Reiger did not go three for three.

The woman who answered the door was petite with short brown hair angled around an oval face, and dressed in dark slacks, a tan windbreaker, and a pair of black-rimmed glasses. She flicked her badge and ID card at them. They did the same.

"Follow me," she said.

They fell into line behind her as she led them through the darkened hall.

"Didn't catch the name on the ID card," said Reiger.

"Mary Bard."

"Okay, Agent Bard. Karl Reiger and Don Hope."

"Call me Mary. And I know who you are. I've been tasked to help with this assignment," she said over her shoulder.

"Well, we can use the help," said Reiger. "I assume you've been read in?"

"Yes. I can see why you two are frustrated. It seems to me they've been running you around like bulls in a china shop and expecting the impossible."

"Exactly. We need to set the hit up our way instead of chasing them."

She said, "Burns told me we're to go over the logistics, call in resources as needed, and then lay the trap."

"Now that sounds like a strategy."

"Watch your step. I'll turn the lights on once we get to the interior room. Cops sometimes patrol by here."

"Understood. So where are you really from?"

"You saw my creds."

"Right, I've got several sets myself and they all say something different."

"Okay. Justice Department. That do it for you?"

Reiger grinned. "That's what they all say."

Bard smiled too. "I know."

Don Hope was looking down. He lifted up one of his feet. "Plastic on the floors?"

Reiger reached out and touched one of the walls. "And on the walls?"

Mary Bard moved with the grace of a ballerina, but also with the speed of a tiger. The kick caught Reiger in the sternum, driving him back into the wall with such force that it threw his heart out of sinus rhythm. Since there was no light, the shine of the twin six-inch blades was never seen by either man as she whirled them in a blur of synchronized motion. One knife ripped across Reiger's throat first. He didn't even have time to scream. He fell to the floor clutching his severed jugular.

Don Hope managed to pull his weapon. Before his finger could close on the trigger, she drove her foot into his knee, ripping it backwards; supporting bones snapped and tendons tore away like sprung rubber bands. He screamed in agony, at least until she gave a backhanded slash with the second knife. The jagged blade ripped his throat apart; arterial blood erupted from the wounds, spraying the narrow hall.

Hope sank next to his dead partner, his last few breaths jerky, gurgling, and then his chest ceased to heave. As if on cue the lights came on and several people moved forward. As Bard stepped out of the way, hands rolled up the plastic with the men inside it. A truck was parked in the rear of the building. Reiger and Hope were placed inside and the truck sped off.

Bard had the blood of each man on her clothes. She stepped out of them and stood there in her bra and panties until she was handed a jumpsuit by one of her colleagues. Her physique was lean, with ropy muscles in her arms, shoulders, and thighs. The heightened definition of her body and absence of fat threw the scars on her torso into sharpened relief. She zipped up the jumpsuit, turned, and entered a bathroom where she scrubbed the evidence of the twin kills off her face, hands, and hair. She took off the eyeglasses and slid them into her pocket. They were actually night optics, allowing her to see her victims in the dark far better than they could see her. A few minutes later she left by another rear door. Her Smart car started up and she drove out of the parking lot, headed west, and entered Interstate 66. She placed the call.

"Done," she said and then clicked off.

Jarvis Burns put his phone down and allowed himself a rare smile. "Now *that*, Agent Reiger, is chain of command."

As he turned back to his work, he glanced at his watch. Two minutes later, in the safety deposit box where Reiger had placed his precious orders that would enable him and Hope to walk free after the job was done, the time-released chemicals built into the document's threads did their work. In ten seconds there was nothing left except vapor.

88

I̅NCREDIBLY ENOUGH, Joe Cushman, Diane Tolliver's ex-husband, had just found out that his former wife had been murdered. It seemed news took a while to travel that far west. But then again, Mace thought, it wasn't like the death of an ordinary citizen would make the national news other than as a one-time blip, and only then because of the rather bizarre circumstances. Joe Cushman did not sound all that upset and was not planning to attend the funeral. Yet that was understandable, Mace concluded. His divorce had been final over a decade ago and he told her that he'd remarried. And as Roy had informed her, it had not been an amicable separation. Cushman had bellowed out the reason for that early on in their long-distance conversation.

"She cheated on me!"

"Who with?"

"Don't know. I never was able to find out, and then I just stopped caring."

Every few seconds he would pause and Mace could hear him dragging on a cigarette. He had the smoker's gravelly voice too, his throat and lungs probably already full of nicotine-induced lumps.

"So how do you know she was having an affair?" Mace had asked.

"All the telltale signs. She bought fancy lingerie that she sure as hell never wore for me. She started working out, lost weight, new cosmetics, weekend 'business' trips, the whole shebang. We had no kids so it was basically split up the property and go our separate ways. Still, her law firm played hardball. Hell, I even had to fork up some cash for her attorney's fees, if you can believe that."

"Why?"

"She made good money, but I made a lot more. Commercial real estate developer in New Jersey when you could print money doing it."

"Good for you."

"Yeah? Well, I don't have as much money now, but I like the beaches and the trade winds a lot better than the ice and muck in Jersey."

"You don't by chance remember the name of the firm that represented her?"

"Are you kidding? I sure as hell wrote them enough checks. Hamilton, Petrocelli & Sprissler. In Newark. Three ladies. Three hellcats more like it. Even my lawyer was afraid of them. They were so good I used them later in some of my deals."

"Thanks a lot. I appreciate the info."

"Hope it helps with whatever you're doing. Diane and I didn't get along, obviously, but nobody deserves to die like that. I'm thinking of sending some flowers."

"I'm sure that would be very nice."

Mace clicked off and looked down at her notes. She called information and got the number for Hamilton, Petrocelli & Sprissler, LLP, in Newark.

She got the receptionist and then the call was put through to Julie Hamilton.

"Yes?"

Mace briefly explained why she was calling.

"Diane Tolliver?"

"You probably would have known her as Diane Cushman. She took her maiden name back after the divorce. I spoke with her ex, Joe Cushman. He gave me your name."

"I do remember hearing something about the killing. The refrigerator, right?"

"Yes, the refrigerator."

"But I never associated Tolliver with Cushman. I mean, I knew her maiden name was Tolliver, but it just never occurred to me it was her. It's been over a decade. Murdered. My God!"

"Yes. That's why I'm calling."

"And who are you with?" This was the cautious lawyer's voice now that Mace knew so well.

"I'm in D.C. I'm helping to investigate the matter on behalf of a man charged with the murder."

"Like I said, it's been at least ten years. I can't think of any way I would have relevant information for you."

"Do you know a man named Jamie Meldon?"

"Why do you ask?"

"Because he was murdered too, right after he met with Diane."

Caution had just transformed to ice. "I'm afraid I can't help you."

"I just need to ask some questions about—"

The next sound Mace heard was the line going dead.

She immediately called back.

This time the receptionist would not put the call through.

"Please, it will only take two minutes and it's—"

The receptionist hung up on her.

Mace slowly put the phone down.

89

AFTER TALKING to Mace, Roy decided to speed up his search of the firm's records. He took the stairs down to the fifth floor. However, the archives room was locked and he didn't have a key. He trudged back to the sixth floor and headed to the mail room. Dave was there sorting letters and packages for the last delivery of the day. "Where's Gene?" Roy asked about the person who manned the archives room.

"Left early. Doctor's appointment. You need anything from down there?"

"It can keep. I'll let you get on with your deliveries."

"Is it true you're going to be the lawyer for that guy they arrested?'

"Why? You want to bust my chops too?"

"No, I thought that's what lawyers were supposed to do. I mean, you can't not represent somebody just because he's not popular, right?"

"Dave, that's the first intelligent thing I've heard today."

Dave headed out with his cart while Roy pretended to follow him out, then he circled back and closed the door to the mail room. He jogged to the very back, lifted the door to the dumbwaiter, climbed in, hit the green button, and pulled his arm back. The door closed, the machine gave a little jolt, and Roy was on his way.

On the brief ride down he thought about the other time he'd been inside here. Wrapped around Mace's body. It *had* been a flashlight in his pocket, though he couldn't say he hadn't been a little aroused, what with her proximity to him and the adrenaline rush that came with knowing your life might soon end violently.

Maybe they should try that technique at the sperm bank.

The dumbwaiter stopped and the doors slid open.

Roy climbed out and looked around. The room was dark but he had to make sure. He did a slow circuit of the large room with its rows of shelves and stacked boxes. He slipped his small flashlight out and shone the beam around. He knew generally how the filing system was set up here and made a beeline to one section. This was where most of his and Diane's client files were kept. He started opening boxes. Securely attached to the inside top of each box was a small hard plastic case. Inside the case was a flash drive containing an electronic record of everything in that box.

The firm had been in the process of scanning all these documents onto their computer system, but it had gotten complicated, because not all lawyers at the firm were authorized to see everything. And certain clients only wanted the attorneys who worked on their matters to be able to access the documents. The problem could be partially solved by requiring passwords to access certain files, but lawyers were notorious for losing such information or even letting colleagues who were not authorized use the passwords. The firm's solution had been to keep the paper archives along with the flash drive in this room. An attorney had to be authorized to look through or take boxes out, and the flash drive was password-protected.

Even though Roy was authorized to look at the boxes he needed, he felt sure that Ackerman would put the kibosh on him looking at anything. He quickly went through a dozen boxes and pulled the flash drives from each and pocketed them. This, he told himself, was only a minor crime compared to the felonies he and Mace had been committing lately. He decided against climbing back in the dumbwaiter and riding it back up just in case someone was in the mail room.

He edged open the door to the archives and looked around. No one was within view. He slipped out and walked quickly through the suite, out the door, and up the stairs back to the sixth floor. He was about to put the first flash drive in his computer when he noted the Post-it he'd stuck over the camera port.

What if they've hacked into my computer? I put the flash in and they'll know what I'm looking at.

He slipped the device back in his pocket, grabbed his briefcase and jacket, and headed to the door. When he opened it he came face-to-face with Chester Ackerman and two security guards.

Ackerman held out his hand. "I would like your key card right now."

"What's going on, Chester?" Roy looked at the two beefy uniforms. "Who are these guys? Did you finally replace Ned like I suggested?"

"They're here to ensure that everything goes smoothly."

"Smoothly? I told you I'd let you know about my representing Dockery."

"And I just called the courthouse and found out that you are his attorney of record and will be representing the killer at a present-ment hearing tomorrow morning."

"Why'd you call the clerk's office?"

"Because I don't trust you. And it seems my instincts were spot-on. Your card?"

Roy handed it over. "Can I at least get my personal things?"

"We'll send them to you. And I think a search of your person is in order."

Roy drew closer to Ackerman. "You lay one hand on me I own your houses, your cars, your retirement plan, and this firm." He glanced at both guards. "You rentals want a piece of that?"

Each guard looked nervously at the other and took small steps back.

Ackerman snapped, "Fine, just leave the premises now, before I have you charged with trespass."

"And you have a great day too."

Roy walked out of the firm while lawyers and staff watched from every nook and cranny. He half expected them to start cheering when the door closed behind him. He passed Ned in the lobby. The man was slurping down a giant Coke.

"Hey, Mr. Kingman, did you see those two security guards who came in?"

"Oh yeah."

"Everything okay?"

Roy jingled the flash drives in his pocket. "Oh yeah."

90

Roy stopped at his condo, grabbed some things, and called Mace on the way over to Altman's. He filled her in on what had happened, and she did the same on her conversation with Joe Cushman.

"Herbert is making like a seven-course meal," she said. "But to tell the truth, I'm dying for a greasy burger and fries."

"I'll pick up some on the way. We'll probably have to work through dinner anyway."

He got there an hour later. They ate in the guesthouse in case Herbert happened by and saw them with charbroiled meat and salty fries dangling from their mouths. Mace finished off the last bite, took a long slurp of her Dr. Pepper, and sat back.

"Where are Alisha and Tyler?" Roy asked.

"Up at the main house being fed, among other things, couscous, pork tenderloin with a reduction sauce, and tempura green beans with a nice crème brûlée done in the classic style for dessert."

"Did Herbert tell you that?"

"No, he actually prints menus every day. He dropped one off at the guesthouse. He was not happy to hear we were going to be missing his latest masterpiece."

"I'm not sure a three-year-old is going to be into couscous and classic crème brûlée."

"Oh, for Tyler he prepared his extra-special spaghetti with hand-formed meatballs and Rocky Road for dessert. I think Herbert likes having kids around."

Mace had borrowed a laptop computer from Altman and during

dinner Roy had been scrolling page after page of the content on the flash drives.

"Got anything yet?" asked Mace as she settled next to him.

"Nothing pops out."

"Coffee?"

"Yeah, by the gallon, please."

She made the coffee and carried a tray back in with the pot and two cups along with cream and sugar containers, and set it down on the coffee table. She poured out the beverages.

"Cream and sugar?"

"Yeah, thanks."

She made it up and passed it to him.

Roy took a sip. "Good coffee." He glanced up at her and smiled.

"What?" said Mace suspiciously as she held her cup.

"I don't know, I guess I never pegged you as the domestic type."

"I'm not, so don't hold your breath waiting for the apron and string of pearls."

"Still nice."

Mace was about to shoot off another stinger but paused. "Yeah, maybe it is."

"So you really think you need to go to Newark?"

"The lady lawyer freaked on me when I mentioned that Jamie Meldon had been murdered too after meeting with Diane. She knew him; that was clear."

"But if you go there's no guarantee they'll see you."

"And if I don't go it's a hundred percent that they won't see me. At least if I make the trip I'll have a shot."

"Do you want me to go too?"

"No, you've got your hands full."

"What about your work for Altman?"

"He has no problem with me chilling for a bit. He feels really guilty about Psycho. And he's been spending a lot of time with Alisha. At least he can get his project off the ground with her."

"What about the brother?"

"He was here and now he's not."

Roy was looking at the screen as he was talking to her. "Wait a minute." He clicked a function key and split the screen with one document residing in each half.

Mace leaned forward next to him. "What is it?"

"On the left is a set of wire transfer instructions that Diane and I did for a deal in the Middle East. Well, the buyer was in the Middle East, but the seller was in Ohio."

"What were they selling?"

"Manufacturing facilities tied to the automotive industry. They made things like windshield wipers, radiators, and stuff. It was part of a string of plants that were bought in five different states in a cluster sale. Happened after all the turmoil in Detroit. Total price was nearly a billion dollars."

"There's that billion number again. So what's the problem?"

"Well, the closing instructions we wrote out show where, when, and how the money was supposed to be paid. There were lots of contingencies, recording of deeds for the land, requisite corporate filings with the various state commissions, that sort of thing. It also includes the ABA routing number, bank account, and other required money transfer information."

"Roy, you're putting me to sleep."

"Okay, our instruction letter is on this side of the screen. Now, over here is the confirmation we got back from DLT."

Mace scanned the page. "I'm no math whiz, but the numbers seem to add up."

"Yeah, the dollar figures do, but look at that." He pointed near the bottom of the page at a long number comprised of many digits.

"But isn't that the ABA routing number you mentioned?"

"It is a routing number, but it's different than the one on our instruction sheet, and I don't know what it's doing here. Now, I know the money for this deal was received by the seller, or else I can assure you we would have heard about it."

"So what is that number? A mistake?"

"I guess it could be."

"Okay, how does that help us?"

"I don't know, I'm just sort of guessing here. It would be helpful to see the corresponding file or other supporting docs that DLT has."

"So do we just go in and ask them for it?" Mace said sarcastically.

"Maybe there's another way."

"I'm listening."

"It's possible they don't know I've been canned from Shilling. I just talked to someone from DLT yesterday to go over some details of a deal Diane and I were working on. If I call them and set up an appointment to go over there and meet, I might be able to sneak a peek at their records."

"But if they are involved in something that got your partner killed, you could be in danger."

"I've been shot at, chased, threatened, done the two-step with a guy named Psycho, and gotten thrown in jail. All since meeting you," he added.

Mace looked uncomfortable.

"What's the matter?" he asked.

"But I was with you when all that happened. You'd be going into DLT solo."

"I'm a lawyer, which means I can talk my way out of just about anything."

"The thing is, Roy, these people don't talk. They kill."

Thank you for seeing me at such a late hour, Beth."

Jarvis Burns was seated opposite the chief in her office. He glanced around the room. "May you spend many productive years here."

"I'm trying, Jarvis, I'm trying. What's up? Your call was . . . "

"Uninformative?" Burns said. "I don't like communicating over the phone."

"NSA isn't supposed to spy on Americans' phone calls, and certainly not on American intelligence agents."

"But still, one can never be too safe." He sat back, lifted his bad leg up, and crossed it over the other. "I won't waste your time, but I believe I owed you a heads-up." He paused and then added quietly, "Agents Reiger and Hope are dead."

Beth sat forward, her stare piercing. "What the hell happened?"

"Ambush, apparently. They were beaten—looks like torture, actually—and then their throats were slashed."

"Where did it happen?"

"We're not sure. The preliminary indicates they were not killed where they were found. Lack of blood and such." He tapped her desk with his index finger. "They were found in a Dumpster in South Alexandria."

"A Dumpster? Same as Jamie Meldon."

"Precisely, but not the same method of murder. Knife versus bullet."

"You said torture?"

"Bones broken, sternum cracked. Yes, torture."

"It could be Naylor's cronies. His butt is sitting in jail waiting for trial on domestic terrorism charges."

"I'm fully aware of Roman Naylor's atrocities."

"The point is, I told Reiger and Hope that we should have been in on this. We could have worked with them and maybe nailed those assholes."

"It wasn't my call, Beth. Hell, it's not even my case. I was sent here because we'd previously arranged for Reiger and Hope to fill you in, at least in a limited way. In fact, Director Donnelly insisted on my coming to tell you. I guess he felt obligated in a way. I didn't really know the two men, but they were still agents of this government. And we're going to do everything in our power to get the bastards who did this."

"Is there anything I can do?"

"We're working with the FBI, but I'm going to see if there's a role you can play."

"I'll be ready and willing to do whatever I can, Jarvis."

"I know, and believe me, I won't forget it."

He rose to leave. "Beth, a personal question?"

"Yes?"

"Is it true that your sister was arrested?"

She eyed him impassively. "How did you hear about that?"

"Beth, please. If we can't keep track of what's going on in our own backyard what chance do we have with the Iranians and North Koreans?"

"It was a misunderstanding. She was never charged. She said that some people in a car were, uh, shooting at her."

"Shooting at her. Where was she?"

"In D.C. Trinidad."

"Trinidad? When?"

"Middle of the night."

"Okay," Burns said slowly, shaking his head in amazement. "People shoot at each other with some frequency there, particularly at that time of night."

"She should've known better."

"But what in the world was she down there for?"

"She went back to the place where she was kidnapped. She said she just wanted to see it."

"Why would she want to do that?"

Beth sighed. "I think she has it in her head that if she finds who set her up, she can have her record expunged and can rejoin the force. That's all she wants, Jarvis. To be a cop again."

"Well, I wish her every success with that of course, but it is, well, it is—"

"A long shot? Yeah, she knows."

"And the Tolliver case?"

"What about it?"

"There was a false fire alarm there the other night. At the law firm."

Beth looked puzzled. "I didn't think you worried about things like that."

"Normally, I wouldn't. But we have data triggers, Beth. For example, a surge in hospital admissions with folks complaining of symptoms that resemble anthrax exposure coupled with suspicious air quality feed from our sensors in the Metro. So a murder in a Georgetown law firm followed by a false alarm at the same building soon thereafter that wasted a great deal of emergency resources gives me some concern. Flight lessons in Florida where beginner pilots didn't want to learn how to take off and land? In hindsight perfectly clear, but before 9/11 it seemed trivial, insignificant. Thus I can't afford to take anything, no matter how small, for granted. So the law firm activity could have been a diversion of some kind."

"A diversion for what purpose?"

"We may not know until it's too late. I get paid to worry about the entire jigsaw puzzle, Beth. That's why my gut is full of holes and I'm losing my hair at a rapid pace. Any clue on who pulled the alarm?"

Beth's face was unreadable. "Not yet. We're working on it."

"Well, let me know if you have anything."

"Will do."

"Oh, and tell your sister to just chill, Beth. You lost her for a couple of years already. You don't want to lose her permanently."

As Burns left the building he felt good about himself. He had just given Mace Perry an out. If Mace stood down on this, she got to live. It was her choice. And if she didn't stand down, it became *his* choice.

Using a credit card Altman had provided, Mace bought an on-line train ticket to Newark for the next morning. Then she drove over with Roy to interview the Captain. When they got to the jail, the two received a shock. Mona Danforth and two homicide detectives were talking to the Captain in a small interrogation room. Mona had her legal pad out and was scribbling notes fast.

Roy nearly kicked the door open after he'd spotted them through the glass and chicken wire window cut in the door.

"What in the hell are you doing?" he yelled.

Mona and the cops looked up while the Captain stuffed a whole Twinkie in his mouth.

"Hey, Roy," he said between gooey bites.

"You just blew your whole case!" Roy said to Mona, who just sat there smiling.

"And you are?" she said smoothly.

"His lawyer, lady! That's who I am."

Mona's smile faded. "The name is Mona Danforth, not 'lady.' I'm the United States attorney for the District of Columbia. So show some respect."

Mace stepped in behind Roy. "*Interim* attorney, Mona," she pointed out. "Don't get ahead of yourself."

"What the hell are you doing here?" Mona exclaimed.

"She's here with me, meaning she's allowed. But you are not. And like I said, you just blew up your whole damn case."

"Really? And how exactly did I do that, Mr. . . . ?"

"Kingman. My client has been charged. He has counsel of record.

His Sixth Amendment rights have attached. You are not allowed to have any contact with him unless I am present."

"Well, you must be a little rusty, Mr. Kingman."

"Excuse me?"

"That *was* the law. But it's not anymore. The Supreme Court overturned that requirement. Now if the defendant asks to meet with the police he can do so without his attorney present and no prejudice attaches unless you can prove coercion. I can get you a copy of the opinion if you'd like so you can come up to speed on *basic* criminal law."

"And you're trying to tell me that he just *asked* to talk with you?"

"Why don't you *ask* him yourself?" Mona turned to the Captain and patted his hand gently. "Go on, Lou, you can talk to them."

"Lou? He's my client!" shouted Roy. "Not yours!"

Mace noticed that the poor Captain's gaze was locked on the lovely prosecutor's body. Mona's skirt was short and her blouse open just enough to show some cleavage.

"Now don't be mean to hon, Roy," said the Captain. He gave Mona's hand a squeeze before she quickly removed it from his reach.

"She's not *hon*," explained Roy. "She's the lady who's trying to put you in prison for the rest of your life, Lou."

"She brought me Twinkies."

"He asked for them," Mona said quickly. "And then told my people that he wanted to talk to us."

"Did you, Captain?" Mace asked him.

"I think so, yeah. Twinkie's damn good. These ain't stale, Roy, not like them others."

Mona stood, as did the two detectives. She said, "Well, I think that wraps it up for now. I'll give you some alone time with him."

"I'm entitled to it by the law, so don't pretend you're doing me any favors." He eyed her full legal pad. "And I'm still filing a motion to suppress anything he might've told you. And I'm going to demand a full investigation on this whole damn thing 'cause it stinks, Supreme Court decision or not."

"I am curious about one thing," Mona said imperturbably.

"What's that?"

"Since I'm listing you as a material witness in this case—you did find the body after all and may still be considered a person of interest—how is it that you're going to represent Mr. Dockery in this matter with such a blatant conflict?"

Roy looked like someone had just gutted him with a hatchet.

Mona's smile deepened. "I can see from your *poker face* that you really hadn't thought about that. I tell you what, *Roy*, I'll waive any objection I might have to this little point of legal ethics, and if the judge agrees, you can be Mr. Dockery's lawyer."

"And why would you do that?" said Roy cautiously.

"Oh, you mean the quid pro quo? Well, let's put it this way, I hate defense counsel's motions to suppress. And I also hate demands for investigations. I think what we need here is a blank slate." She stared up at him expectantly, her look about as condescending and triumphant as one face could achieve.

"So in other words I forget the stunt you just pulled and you'll let me represent my client?"

"I didn't pull any stunt. I'm perfectly within my rights."

"I can seek a waiver from the court."

"Not over my objections you can't."

"So let me try to understand this. If you're maintaining you did nothing wrong here, why offer me a deal that lets me rep my client?"

"Because I want you to stay on as Lou's attorney."

"Why?"

Mona leaned forward and spoke in a low voice so that only Roy and Mace could hear her. "Because if you get disqualified, then they might appoint a *real* attorney, and that just makes my job harder. There're a ton of highly qualified public defenders just salivating to take this case, and they all know what they're doing. Why play against the varsity when the j.v. is available?" She picked up her briefcase and stuffed her legal pad in it. "See you in court tomorrow." She turned to the Captain. "Oh, Lou, before I forget." She pulled another Twinkie out of her jacket pocket and tossed it to him, like throwing a bone to a dog. The next moment she and the detectives were gone, leaving the Captain to eagerly devour the fresh offering of creamy cake.

93

Roy huddled in a corner of the room with Mace while the Captain sat staring vacantly at the wall and wiping goo off his mouth.

Roy said, "Maybe she's right. Maybe I am j.v."

Mace punched him in the arm. "Let's get one rule down, Mona is never right."

"The Captain deserves the best representation, Mace. I didn't even focus on the material witness issue. And it was big enough to drive a truck through. I would've gone in tomorrow and gotten my head handed to me. By Mona *and* the judge."

"The Captain wants *you*."

"Come on, he doesn't know what he wants. Other than Twinkies."

"You can do this, Roy. You might be a little rusty on some of the case law, and you didn't focus on the material witness angle because you knew you were innocent and you wanted to help the Captain."

"You can't rep a defendant charged with murder in the first with any rust, Mace. There's no room for error. Especially against Mona. I know you hate the woman and I do too, but she's sharp."

"And she's totally unethical. She basically bribed the Captain with junk food and cleavage."

"But that makes her even more dangerous."

"The point is, Roy, you made the decision to rep him. Your firm canned your ass over it. So do you want to go crawling to them begging for your big-dollar job back? And let a homeless vet be assigned some Perry Mason wannabe who could give a shit if the guy spends the rest of his life in the can? Is that what you want?"

"Of course not," Roy said hotly.

"Then what's the problem? Mona just laid down the challenge. She's gonna kick your ass. Okay, fine. But I don't see a guy who's so competitive that he has as his computer password the last score of his college basketball career just turning the other cheek on this. But this time it's not just a game. And the Captain needs you. He needs *you*, Roy."

Roy looked at Mace, then at the Captain, then back at Mace. "Okay, but I'll need help to dig up some useful stuff."

"Consider it done."

"You? But you're going to Newark tomorrow to run down this Meldon lead."

"This Meldon lead may point us to whoever killed Diane."

"Do you really believe that?"

"I don't know what to believe right now. But I can't afford to cut corners on this."

"Fair enough."

"So you're good to go on this?"

"I am."

"Then I guess I can tell you."

"Tell me what?"

"Beth had Lowell Cassell call me on my way over here."

"And?"

"And there was no yolk buffer in the sperm found in Diane. It didn't come from Potomac Cryobank."

He glanced over at the Captain, who was picking something out of his teeth.

"Okay, gut check time. Do you think he did it?"

Mace looked over at the old soldier too. "I talked to Beth about that. She said she agreed there was some strange stuff going on with Diane and your law firm. But she also said her murder could be entirely unrelated to all of it. That it could have just been a crime of opportunity."

"So you think he did it?"

"No, Roy, I don't."

"Then how the hell does all this make sense?"

"It makes perfect sense. We just have to figure out how."

THEY SPENT another hour trying get some answers from the Captain. The conversation was often one-sided, however, as the vet lost interest, snoozed, went off on multiple and irrelevant tangents, or asked for more Twinkies. He couldn't adequately describe the man who'd met him on the street and asked if he wanted to make a quick two hundred bucks. He was variously big, short, fat, thin, bald but with hair. He hadn't gone in the front door of the place; he didn't recall the sign. He did say that he'd rummaged in big green trash cans while the man got things ready. Mace made a note to check the back of Potomac Cryobank for those types of receptacles. He did remember going inside a dark, small room. He'd been given a cup, and a "girlie" magazine. It had taken him a long while, but he'd delivered the requested sample and then gotten his money.

"Anything you can remember about the place, Lou, anything?" Roy asked.

"The smell."

"What did it smell like?" said Roy.

"Hard to say." He stroked the wattles on his neck. "Not like me. Real clean."

Roy looked at Mace. "It did smell really antiseptic in there. Like a hospital."

"Well, it is like a clinic."

"Yeah, but that's hardly concrete evidence for a court."

"Like you were expecting that from him?" Mace said in a low voice.

They left the Captain and returned to Altman's guesthouse,

where Roy began formulating his strategy for the next morning's hearing.

"It'll be quick and perfunctory," he said. "I'll plead him not guilty. Mona will ask for detainment and then get an indictment probably pretty fast. Then the real work begins. When do you leave for Newark?"

"Seven o'clock Acela train. Gets into Newark around 9:30. The law office is about twenty minutes by cab from the station. I can talk to them, hopefully get somewhere, grab the train back, and be here tomorrow afternoon."

"I can call you with the details of the hearing."

"You going to ask for him to be released on personal recog?"

"No. He has a roof and three squares a day in jail."

"And if somebody is setting him up, he's safer in there."

"Yeah, maybe we should get arrested too."

They both looked up when a ball bounced down the stairs and rolled to a stop next to Roy's foot. He palmed it. The next moment Tyler came running down the stairs looking frantically around. When he saw the ball in Roy's hand he darted over, his arms spread wide.

"Ty, what you doing up this late?"

Alisha had appeared at the top of the stairs as soon as Roy handed the ball to her son. She said, "I'm sorry 'bout that. The boy just won't go to sleep. He was bouncing the ball and it got away from him."

Mace tapped Roy on the thigh. "This kid was making layups and dribbling the ball like a real pro, weren't you, Ty?"

The little boy looked at her and his mouth opened, his eyes blinking rapidly.

Mace patted Roy on the shoulder. "This guy here played college basketball. He could've played in the NBA if he could've jumped a little higher."

"Among other things," Roy added.

"You know, you've been doing the legal thing all day, how about taking this big guy over to the gym and let him show you what he can do. Give you a chance to clear your head." She added, "Ty, you want to show Mr. Roy here some of your moves?"

Roy said, "I really should finish—"

But when Ty reached out and gripped Roy's hand tightly, his little mouth still wide open, Roy quickly stood. "Okay, Ty, I'm a little rusty, so take it easy on me, all right?"

"Can I watch?" asked Alisha.

"I was going to suggest it," said Mace.

Roy glanced back at her. "You want to come? Maybe we can do our HORSE tricks for him."

"You go on. I'm gonna hit the sack. I'll have to leave here early to get the train."

When the three of them disappeared out the door, Mace gave them a couple of minutes to get to the gym and then she punched 411, got the number, and made the call.

"Doc, it's Mace Perry. I know it's late, but you got time to meet?"

Lowell Cassell was at his row house in southeast D.C., but he agreed to meet Mace at a coffee shop near Union Station. Mace thanked him, clicked off, grabbed her leather jacket, and ran for the Ducati.

CHAPTER

95

"IT REALLY IS CRAZY for me to be meeting you like this, Mace," said Lowell Cassell.

"Why? I'm just an ordinary citizen."

"An ordinary citizen who I believe is assisting in the defense of an alleged murderer who is right now cooling his heels in a D.C. lockup." When she looked surprised that he knew this, Cassell added, "The water-cooler gossip does reach the morgue, you know."

"Well, I wouldn't really call what I'm doing assisting. And I really did want a nice cup of coffee. I used to come here a lot when I was a cop. Open twenty-four hours. We'd pop in here after hoodling for a bit if the radio was quiet."

Cassell leaned forward and spoke in a low voice even though there wasn't another customer in the place. "I really went out on a limb by allowing you access to my files. In fact, if that comes out, my career is over."

"It will never come out, Lowell. I will die before that comes out."

He sat back, apparently satisfied. "I think you would."

"So why did you do it then?"

"The files?" He spooned more sugar into his cup. "Because I like you."

"Not a good enough answer for a possible career-ender."

"Blunt, just like your sister."

"I like to think I'm more diplomatic."

"I understand that Mona Danforth is personally trying this case?"

"That's right. I'm sure it's only for altruistic reasons."

Cassell took a sip of his coffee and picked at a pastry on his plate.

"Come on, Doc. I know the sperm was pure, no yolk stuff."

"That's right. I assumed you were the reason Beth had me check that."

"The guy said someone paid him two hundred bucks to do it in a cup."

"The homeless vet?"

"Yep," answered Mace.

"You think he just made that up? I mean, sperm in a dead woman is pretty convincing evidence."

"I agree, and no, I don't think he made it up. The guy spends most of his time thinking about Twinkies."

"Circumstantial is also pretty strong."

"Right again. Our work is cut out for us."

"So you *are* working this one?" said Cassell.

"If I can't be a cop, you know."

"I know. Solve a big one."

"Only thing keeping me going."

"What happened to you was an injustice, Mace."

"Thirty percent."

"What?"

"That's roughly the percentage of cops at MPD who think I was bad."

"That means seventy percent think you were railroaded. A politician would love to have those approval ratings."

"Well, for me anything less than a hundred sucks."

"You can't live your life trying to make people understand something they don't want to understand."

"I'm not doing it for them. I'm doing it for me."

"I guess I can see that."

She tapped his hand with her finger. "So why did you agree to meet with me tonight?"

"To tell the truth, I'm not sure."

"Something's bugging you, isn't it?"

"The sperm."

"But it wasn't yolked."

"Planted sperm."

"Okay."

"It's happened before, but not very often. In fact, it's about as rare a forensic misdirection as there is, but not impossible. But the thing is, if you do it and do it well, a conviction is almost inevitable."

"So you think it *was* planted?"

"The cervix."

"Come again?"

"The semen was high up on the cervix. I mean really high. I've read Dockery's arrest file. Nearly sixty. Living on the streets for years. I actually saw him in the jail. I haven't examined him, of course, but to my doctor's eye he has many serious health problems. Arteriosclerosis almost certainly, high blood pressure, probable diabetes, basal cell carcinomas on his face. He's at high risk for stroke, aneurysm, and various cancers. And I would bet a thousand dollars that he has an enlarged prostate and possibly even cancer there."

"Meaning?"

"Meaning that for him to be able to even get it up is a miracle, much less rape the woman and shoot his semen that far up in her cervix."

"Well, he said he did it in a cup."

"A cup is not a woman's vagina. Did he say how long it took him to do it in the cup?"

"He said it took some time. He also told us they gave him a girlie magazine."

"I would bet it took him a long time even with the girlie magazine."

"That could be important, because Tolliver wasn't at the office more than two hours before she was killed. And chances are it was a lot less than that. Maybe thirty minutes to an hour."

"No problem for an eighteen-year-old. But if a guy in Dockery's condition can get an erection in less than four hours, if at all, you can give me what he's taking. Do you know why the pharmaceutical companies make billions of dollars off stuff like Viagra and Cialis?"

"Because older guys can't get it up without help?"

"Exactly, especially for guys Dockery's age. And keep in mind this is just between you and me. I won't repeat this on the witness stand. You can get your own expert. Under the law my findings are an open book for the defendant's counsel to use. But he has to draw his own conclusions and what I've said is just speculation. I really can't form an opinion about it."

"Understood. But speculate on one more thing. Do you think they might have given Dockery a pill to help him do it in the cup?"

"I wouldn't bet against it."

"Hopefully, he'll remember when we ask him. He's not that stellar on details. And they could've stuck it in a Twinkie. But how long would the sperm last in her? If Dockery is telling the truth, they had to get it from him, store it, transport it to the crime scene, and shoot it into her. Someone I talked to said the stuff breaks down after a while. That's why they have to yolk it."

"It does. The motility and other elements do degrade. The sample I examined hadn't been there longer than seventy-two hours."

Mace sat back. "How about less than twenty-four? Say he gave the sample on Sunday and she was killed on Monday?"

"No. Longer than that. At least three days."

"You're sure?"

"I'd stake my reputation on it."

"That's good enough for me." She stood. "Thanks, Doc."

"For what? I'm not sure I was very helpful."

"No, I think you cleared up a lot. The only problem is, if what I'm thinking is right, I've got a ton of new questions that need answers."

"I hope you get them."

"Me too."

A few minutes later Mace burned down the road. She wasn't heading back to Abe Altman's manse. She was heading to Georgetown. If she was right then there was a force behind all of this that scared her. In fact, it might just scare her right to death.

CHAPTER

96

JARVIS BURNS LEFT his office building late and hailed a cab. When he was with Sam Donnelly he traveled by motorcade. On his own, public transportation was deemed good enough. He didn't mind. In fact, it was the perfect opportunity to take in another meeting.

He settled back against his seat in the taxi. The cabbie eyed him in the mirror. He wore a white loose-fitting cotton shirt, and in his own country would have also had a black-and-white kaffiyeh on his head, which symbolized the man's Palestinian heritage. This man, Burns knew, had just flown in from the Middle East. He typically lived at thirty-five thousand feet for extended periods of time, passing over oceans and also arid geography where men killed each other with great frequency over issues of religion, land, natural resources, and simple, intractable hate.

"Mahmud," Burns began. "How are you, my friend?"

Mahmud studied Burns closely and then pulled the cab from the curb. He had spent most of his life in constant conflict with others, had lost both parents and two siblings to violent deaths. His parents had been betrayed by those they thought were friends. Therefore their son trusted no one. He had known desperate poverty and didn't care for it. He had known what it was like to be powerless and cared for that even less. He carried bullet holes and bomb shrapnel in his body. He had been a fierce warrior for his cause. Yet he had come to realize that there were other ways to play the game that did not involve the risk of imminent death. And that there were other rewards to be had while one was still living.

In crisp English he said, "I am here. I never take that for granted."

"I share that philosophy."

"Keep your friends close but your enemies closer, Jarvis," he said. "I think your country is finally learning the value of this. Isolation emboldens those who hate you. It allows them to paint a picture of your country to their fellow citizens, and it is never a pretty picture when they do."

"Agreed, agreed," Burns said hastily.

"But that is not what we need to discuss?"

"I wanted to make clear that the situation that has arisen is truly under control."

Mahmud gave him a piercing look in the mirror. "That is good to hear. It was unfortunate, very unfortunate. How exactly did it happen?"

"We believe we've pieced together the sequence of events. It was a chain that should have been broken at numerous points along the line, but unfortunately was not. An inadvertent glimpse at a laptop screen on a flight back from Dubai started Diane Tolliver down the road that would eventually lead to her termination. From there she became ever more curious, comparing documents, making inquiries, and gathering information. Fortunately, she made the mistake of trusting someone. That's how we became aware of the issue."

"A close call, then."

"The blame lies entirely on our side. But I didn't want you to think that it would linger. Or that it will disrupt what we are trying to do. It will not. I give you my word."

"Your word means a great deal. You too have sacrificed much for your country."

"It was my honor and privilege."

"I have stopped thinking about such things."

"That saddens me."

"It is actually uplifting to *me*."

"The money, yes. I can see that. But we are doing the right thing too. It's what we all want. My country in particular."

"If it was what your leaders wanted, my friend, you and the director would not be doing all of this on your own."

"We're not alone, I can assure you. However, sometimes the leadership is unwilling on the record to take the steps necessary to achieve essential goals. But they would not begrudge us the opportunity to employ sufficient if unpopular methods."

"Right. The less they know the better."

"I would not put it exactly that way."

"You talk of course about violent death; the execution of your own people if it jeopardizes those goals. Americans have always been reluctant in that regard. Frankly, I have always seen that as a weakness."

"We are a civilized people, Mahmud."

"Well, perhaps one day my people will be as unfamiliar with violent death as your people are, Jarvis. What a great thing that will be."

"I hope to live to see that day."

"I would have to say that your chances of doing so are far better than mine."

"I hope you are wrong there."

"Even if I'm not, so what? There will be others to take my place. For a people so certain that there will be an afterlife of paradise, you Americans value life too much. None of us are irreplaceable. Even if bin Laden dies, there will be others. That is the way the world works. That is what keeps you gainfully employed, correct?"

"I would happily retire if there would be no more bin Ladens, Mahmud."

"Then you will never retire, my friend. If you require us to assist in 'cleaning up' this problem you will let me know?"

"I think I have the right people for the job."

"So many have said and yet been wrong." There was an edge to the Palestinian's words that caused Burns to draw his gaze from the mirror where he'd been watching the man's eyes and instead look out the window.

"I understand that your people have to survive. By any means possible."

"They have nothing. This way they have something. The money cannot stop now. They have grown used to it. If you don't pay, others will. Your leaders are very shortsighted in that regard. That is why we've had to go this route. Cash trumps all."

"It won't stop. I guarantee it."

"That is good, because they do not love your country. But they can be bought. Anyone can be bought, it seems." He paused and added bluntly, "Even me."

"Enemies closer."

"Allow no one to ever convince you otherwise."

A few minutes later Burns left the cab and climbed into the backseat of a waiting Town Car and turned to the woman sitting next to him. Mary Bard had discarded the jumpsuit and was dressed in much the same way as she had been when disposing of Karl Reiger and Don Hope.

"I appreciate your professionalism," Burns said. "In a difficult assignment."

Bard shrugged. "One assignment is much like another assignment. They vary only in degrees of complexity."

"Moral as well as logistical?"

"I leave the moral debate to others. The logistical side is quite enough for me."

"I can provide fresh orders for you if you require them," Burns said, testing her.

"I have my orders. Your director has told me to assist you and only you in any way you require."

"I must make a note to ask to have more people like you sent my way."

"For that you will have to talk to my superiors in Moscow," she said.

"I will."

"So what do you wish me to do?"

"I need you to be on the watch for two people." He showed her pictures of Roy Kingman and Mace Perry. She stared at them for a full minute.

"You can keep the photos," he said.

"I don't need them. They are now in my mind."

"All right. We're setting up perimeter defensive positions. But together with that I need to locate some bait, just in case."

"I'm very good at finding bait."

"I know that you are."

CHAPTER

97

Mace parked her bike behind the building and got off. Her gaze scanned the rear parking area, which had space for ten slots. As she stepped forward she could see the names of two doctors stenciled in yellow on the asphalt in side-by-side parking slots. The big shots always got their own space, she thought. A short stack of steps led up to the back door, which was solid wood. There were two windows in the back, both barred and curtained.

And there were the green trash cans that the Captain had mentioned. Not that that helped very much since there were only a million of them in the area and they all looked the same. She heard the clink of boots against the pavement before she heard the voice.

"Can I help you?"

She turned to see the rental cop walking toward her, his hand resting lightly on the top of his sidearm. He looked to be in his fifties and was probably a retired cop making some extra money. To her, he had the ease but also the awareness of a guy who'd walked a beat and talked the talk for a lot of years.

"Just checking the place out."

He looked at the rear of Potomac Cryobank. "Just checking it out? Or casing it?"

"I'm not really in the market for sperm right now."

"Lot of people are. It's a hot commodity."

"I bet. You guarding the place?"

"Not out for my health."

"You former MPD?"

"You a cop?"

"Used to be."

"I'm retired now. Do security full-time. What was your beat?"

"Mostly Six and Seven Ds."

"Okay, you earned your stripes."

"I'm doing some PI work now."

"Involving this place?"

"I was hired by a lawyer to check out an alibi that has to do with the sperm bank. Don't think it's going to fly, but you have to go through the motions."

"What sort of alibi?"

"Guy says he was around here going through trash cans when something else was happening at another place."

"And at this other place the something happening was a crime and your guy was arrested for it?"

"You're a fast learner."

"Not really. Story's always the same."

"I've actually been in the sperm bank. I thought it had a security system."

"It does."

"So why you too? Is sperm really *that* hot a commodity?"

"I asked that very same question myself. I'm not some college kid wanting to make some extra bucks or some cop wannabe who doesn't give a crap. I go into a situation I want to know what's what. They told me that the security system had been acting screwy here and so they needed feet on the pavement."

"Acting screwy?"

"Yeah. Energy spikes maybe, or a freak wire or software glitch. But they came in one day and found the alarm not even on. And the nurse said she remembered setting it. She was the last to leave."

"Did you talk to the nurse?" He nodded. Mace described the woman that she and Roy had spoken with.

"Yeah, that's the gal."

"She's pretty efficient. If she said she set it, I bet she did."

"Anyway, they had the alarm company come over but they couldn't figure out what had happened. And there was no record of any break-in or anything, or the alarm going off or any sensors being tripped. It was like the system just went to sleep for no reason. I don't think anything turned up missing and there was no evidence that anyone actually broke in. But the folks still got worried and they're in the process of changing the whole system over. Until they get it done, I'm here."

"Do you remember when all this went down?"

"Why are you interested? Think it has to do with your alibi?"

"Never know. And I'm just naturally curious."

"Most cops are." He stroked his chin. "I got the call to come here on Thursday. So I guess Wednesday of last week."

"I thought you might say that."

He looked surprised. "Why?"

She fired up her bike. "It's a real long story. You might read about it in the papers one day."

CHAPTER

98

MACE HAD LEARNED from her sister that as soon as the Captain had been arrested, the office elevators had been reprogrammed so they would not stop at the fourth floor. The construction workers had not been happy about having to haul their stuff up the stairs, but that was just the way it was. Public safety trumped aching backs.

Mace slowed her Ducati as she drew close to the area. She figured that no one had worked late in the building or come in too early ever since Roy had discovered Diane Tolliver's body in a refrigerator. But still she scanned the building façade looking for signs of anyone being on-site. Her other concern was the possibility of a cop car posted somewhere close by.

Satisfied that the area was clean of surveillance, she parked her bike a block over from the building and made it the rest of the way on foot. She entered the garage. There were no cars parked there. The garage elevators were dead ahead.

Seconds later she entered the lobby, scooted behind the security console, and reached the entrance to the stairs. She paused for a moment, studying the door to the broom closet. She reached for the knob, her other hand in her pocket, and then ripped it open. The only thing that flopped out was a mop.

She made her way up the stairs and reached the fourth floor. Mace crab-walked across the room so as to keep below the window line and reached the small cubby area where the toilet and refrigerator were located. The length of chain was right where she had dropped it when she and Roy had been chased through the building.

She picked it up and eased over to the refrigerator. It was a big, older Amana model with the refrigerator part up top and a smaller freezer unit with its own little door down below. Using her penlight she could see several small rust stains on the white enamel skin of the appliance. She looped the chain around the fridge and held it tight. The stains were right where the chain touched it. She opened the fridge door. There were some plastic containers of food, a few cans of soda, and a battered gray lunch pail.

Roy had told her what the Captain had said about the chain. Roy had dismissed it as the construction guys protecting their food. Mace had initially thought that too. But not now. Now the chain made sense for a far different reason. They couldn't have the Captain stumble on the body over the weekend while he was looking for some chow. So they'd locked him out and Diane Tolliver's body in.

She hadn't been murdered on Monday morning. She'd been killed on Friday night, probably right after she sent Roy that e-mail when she returned from her dinner with Meldon. And the fridge wasn't the only reason Mace thought this. Now the autopsy results started to make sense. She gazed at the microwave next to the fridge. The microwave. She remembered Roy telling her . . .

She slipped back down to the lobby and from there into the little room behind the security console. She saw the microwave perched on one shelf. She tried to turn it on. Nothing happened. It was broken. She hurried back up to the fourth floor, pulled out her phone, and called Roy.

"Hey," he said. "That Tyler is something else. We've been playing ball all this time and the kid is still running circles around me." He paused. "Wait a minute, I thought you went to bed? Where are you calling from?"

"Diane wasn't killed on Monday morning. She was killed on Friday night."

All she got after that was silence.

"Roy, did you hear me?"

"Mace, where are you!"

"On the fourth floor of your office building."

"What! Are you crazy?"

"Did you hear what I said?"

"Yes, I did, and I feel like somebody just hit me with a two-by-four. Why do you think she was killed on Friday night?"

"Think about what was in her stomach."

"The autopsy report said steak, veggies, potatoes, stuff like that."

"Exactly."

"But you found all that food in her town house garbage can."

"It's also the exact food she had on Friday night at Simpsons when she had dinner with Meldon. And Lowell Cassell's report said that there was a strong smell of garlic in the gastric contents. I knew something was bugging me about that. I searched her kitchen and found not a trace of garlic anywhere, not even in the trash. But I recalled from looking at the menu at Simpsons that they serve garlic mashed potatoes. I think whoever killed her knew what she'd eaten at the restaurant and planted all that stuff at her house to make it look like her last meal had been *there*, on Sunday night instead of on Friday night at Simpsons. Only they either didn't know about the garlic or screwed up. And according to the autopsy report her stomach lining was really green from the spinach. I don't think it got that way from it sitting in her gut overnight. More like over two days."

"Then the body?"

"They killed her in your office on Friday night. Then she was put in the fridge on the fourth floor, probably while the Captain was asleep in another part of the construction space. You told me that he said he went to sleep when he got there and didn't know if the chain was on there when he arrived. I'm sure it wasn't because Diane didn't get back to the office until after ten and the Captain was already on the fourth floor by then. So they threw her in and chained the fridge shut. The nail and hammer crew doesn't work weekends. And the Captain left on Sunday like he said, because he probably ate what was lying around the fourth floor on Saturday, found he couldn't open the fridge, and decided to bag it. They moved her body to the fridge in your office early on Monday morning. Then you found her."

"Why not just leave her in our fridge for the weekend?"

"They couldn't be sure some lawyer might not come in to work and pop open the fridge. And they couldn't wrap a chain around *your* refrigerator. And most importantly, I think they did all this to set up the Captain for the fall."

"I guess they could have found out he was sneaking in the building."

"I've got a theory about that too. And I discovered that the sperm bank had an alarm system failure on Wednesday of last week."

"You think that's when they got the sample from the Captain?"

"The place is closed on Wednesdays and Sundays. Sperm only lasts so long. Cassell told me that the sperm in Tolliver clearly had been there longer than a day but not longer than three days. They probably put it in a freezer after they got it from the Captain on Wednesday to preserve it temporarily. Then after they killed Toll-iver, they injected it into her vagina on Friday night. Cassell told me that a guy with the probable health problems of the Captain couldn't have had an erection in just an hour or so on Monday morning. And he couldn't have ejaculated to the degree required to place the sperm that high up in her cervix. But I bet a syringe would've done the trick."

"This is incredible, Mace."

"But it fits. The temp in the fridge keeps the body from decom-posing. Two hours or two days in an icebox, it's almost impossible to tell the difference, particularly when she was lying on the floor for all that time while the police were investigating. And then the body was taken to the morgue and stuck in a chiller bed. All the normal forensic indicators got messed up big-time."

"But I thought she sent e-mails and made phone calls over the weekend from her house."

"E-mails prove nothing. Anyone could have sent those. And it seems all the calls she made over the weekend were to people she didn't know. So they couldn't recognize her voice. I learned there was one neighbor who saw her but only really observed her drive off. He couldn't make a positive ID. And the lady apparently didn't have many social friends; she used an escort, after all. The imposter probably stayed at her house all weekend playing the role of Diane. She drives her car to the office early Monday morning so no one else would be around to see, goes up in the elevator, and enters the office suite, which leaves an electronic trail of her movements. Then she turns around and walks back out."

"But Ned swears he heard her come in on Monday morning."

"Yeah, Ned. Remember he was in the back microwaving his breakfast?"

"Yeah, that's why he said he heard her but didn't see her."

"But you told me the day porter was on the fourth floor heating up his soup in a microwave. Why not use the one in the room behind the security console? The one Ned said he was using that morning?"

"I don't know."

"Then I'll tell you. Because the microwave in the lobby is broken. I bet if we ask the day porter he'll tell us the same thing. That it's been broken for a while."

"So are you saying fat, stupid Ned planned all this and killed Diane?"

"He's fat, but I'm not sure how stupid he is. And I don't think he did any of this alone. I think he looked the other way when the Captain sneaked in the building, because he was told to."

"Mace, we need to go to your sister and tell her all of this. I'll meet you there."

"And tell her what? A bunch of speculation? Because that's all it is. We don't have solid proof of anything."

"So what do we do?"

"You prepare for your hearing tomorrow. I'm going to Newark. We say nothing. But we keep an eye on old Ned and he might just lead us to where we need to go."

"I don't want you getting your neck crushed by that guy."

"I'd hear him coming from a mile away just by the fat sloshing."

"Okay, but will you get back here please? At least then I'll know you're safe."

"Oh, Roy, you really do care," she said sarcastically.

"If anything happens to you, your sister will blame me. And I'd rather be dead."

She clicked off and walked quickly over to the exit door. She closed it behind her and was turning to walk down the stairs when something hard slammed into her head.

As she hit the floor already unconscious, Ned stood over her. While he was still heavyset, he didn't appear to be as fat as before. He was dressed all in black, was wearing gloves, and moved nimbly as he picked the woman up and slung her over his shoulder. He reentered the construction site and punched in a number on his cell phone.

The voice answered.

Ned said, "Got the bird. On the fourth."

Jarvis Burns sat back in his armchair and put aside the file he was reading.

"Acknowledged," he said.

"Orders?"

"Unchanged. Proceed. Copycat."

"Roger that."

Ned clicked off and carried Mace over to the refrigerator. He searched her and found her phone, which he tossed to the side. He cleared out all the food and shelves, wedged her inside, closed the door, and wrapped the chain around it. Then he inserted a padlock in the chain links and smacked it closed. He tried to pull the door open, but it barely budged a centimeter. A moment later he was hustling down the stairs to the lobby.

In his home on Capitol Hill, Burns picked up the file once more. "I gave you another chance, Mace. Too bad you didn't take it."

As he turned the pages he put Mace Perry completely out of his mind.

CHAPTER

99

When Mace came to she felt like she was going to throw up. As she fought the nausea she wondered why she was having trouble breathing. She reached a hand up and touched the large knot on her head. She could feel the clotted blood there. Someone had really whacked her. She started to shiver. It was cold.

Where the hell am I?

She started to get up and then quickly realized she was in a confined space. A very cold confined space.

"Oh shit!"

She felt around in the total darkness, her hands bumping into the smooth frigid surfaces. She scrambled in her pocket, found her penlight, and turned it on. As soon as the illumination confirmed where she was, Mace groaned. She pushed hard against the door with her shoulder. It barely budged. She knew why. The chain. Just like Diane. Only she was already dead.

And I will be very soon unless I get the hell out of here.

She reached down and unbuckled the belt that she'd gotten from Binder's weapons shop. It had a very special clasp to it. A few seconds later she'd pulled the four-inch knife free from its holder hidden in the elongated metal buckle. She angled her body around and slipped the blade in the slit where the door met the frame of the appliance. There was a molded plastic shelf unit built into the door and the supporting frame for this was right in her way. Yet she managed to work around it and finally reached the flex strip that created a vacuum seal when the door was closed. She inserted the blade in the slit between the two strips and maneuvered it around. If she levered hard enough, she could feel a trace of air. She pushed very hard once and with a sucking sound the vacuum seal broke slightly. Now she could see a sliver of semidarkness, which represented the more illuminated space outside of the death trap she was in.

But a sliver wouldn't cut it. It didn't let in nearly enough air. She was already shaking with the effort of maintaining the break in the seal. A second later her strength failed and the opening resealed itself. Okay, if she didn't suffocate to death the cold would do her in. Would Roy come looking for her when she didn't show? He knew where she was. But it would take time. Perhaps hours, when she had air maybe for another few minutes. Her chest started heaving as her lungs sought out every precious molecule of oxygen. Her mind started to fog up, signaling the lungs that these molecules were far from enough to keep everything going.

The insulation strip!

Holding the penlight between her teeth, she began hacking at it with her knife. The blade struck through it easily and it came away in long strips. Very soon she could feel the air start to flow in more steadily. And if she wedged her head against the door, she could actually see outside. She poked the blade through this new opening and lifted it up and down. On the downward stroke it hit the chain. There was no way she could saw through the chain with the knife in less than a day if at all. But at least she could breathe. Now the issue was the cold; she was still freezing to death. She looked up and saw it built into the top of the fridge's interior: the temperature dial. It was set on four. Seven was the coldest, she quickly discovered. She reached up and dialed it back to one, the warmest. She had no idea in refrigerator technology how "warm" the number one setting would be, but she didn't want to find out it was still in hypothermia range.

Mace started rocking her body front to back. The Amana was a tall appliance, and she was betting there wasn't much in the lower freezer section to anchor it. As much as the confined space would allow her, she kept rocking. She'd hit one side with her legs and then slam against the other side with her back. Very quickly her entire body felt like she'd been hit by a car, but she kept going. She could feel the Amana start to lean a bit, to the right and then to the left. As it kept going, the appliance started to walk, like a washing machine out of control. Encouraged by this, she started flinging herself back and forth with renewed energy.

One last smash against the molded plastic with her combat boots and the Amana finally toppled over sideways. Mace braced herself for the impact, which was easy enough to do since she was wedged in. Still, when the fridge hit the concrete floor, her head banged against the hard interior wall right where the bump on her noggin was and she felt herself black out for an instant.

But she'd accomplished her goal. She could no longer hear the slight hum of the Amana's motor. The power cord had come out of the socket. Now she had air. And she would soon have warmth. But she was still trapped. She had hoped that the collision with the floor might have caused the chain to slip off, but no such luck. One push against the door told her that. She looked down at the molded plastic floor. Below that was the freezer compartment. The chain couldn't be around that door too. She started stomping her feet. The floor was hard, but she could feel it give just a bit.

She worked her body around so that she was nearly upside down. Taking the knife, she started hacking at the plastic but couldn't find traction as the blade just skidded off the smooth surface. She turned back around so that she was sitting up in the box and looked around. She grabbed a portable shelf off the doorframe and pointed the knife into the floor, then put her foot on top of the handle and pushed down with as much force as she could, lifting her butt off the interior floor and pressing her back against the top of the box to provide more leverage. Twice the knife slipped out, but the third time she felt it bite into the plastic and stick there. She took the shelf and started whacking the butt of the knife with it. She didn't have much room to operate, so the swings were shortened, but after a few minutes she could see that the blade was now two inches deep in the plastic floor. She raised herself up, put her foot on top of the handle, and steadily pushed down, her back flat against the ceiling of the fridge to give her additional downward force. The knife slowly pushed through the floor. When it hit the hilt of the blade it stopped.

Mace moved her foot away and with much effort she flipped over and started to saw away at the floor, the blade moving centimeters as it cut into the hard plastic. She withdrew the blade and, using the same stick and pound method, made similar cuts in four other spots. When that was done she slipped the knife back in the belt clasp, rose up again, and started stomping in the middle of all the cuts, her back so tight against the ceiling of the fridge that she felt her spine would snap.

She wasn't sure how long it took, but she felt the floor finally give. A few seconds later the plastic cracked in one spot and then another. A minute later a whole section of it tilted upward. She threw her weight at the spot opposite this and the entire floor broke away and heaved up like a sheet of ice. She fell through this opening and gasped as a jagged edge of hard plastic ripped into her thigh; now warm blood flowed into the cool interior.

She carefully worked her body downward, keeping as far away from the torn edges of the plastic as she could. Her feet hit the freezer door and she kicked it open. She kept sliding downward until she cleared the floor of the fridge unit and her head and torso were in the freezer compartment. Then her feet were out on the concrete floor and soon the rest of her was too.

She sat there for a minute, her head and lungs pounding and her stomach churning. Then she rose on shaky legs and looked around. She slipped out her precious knife and held it in a defensive position. She doubted whoever had stuck her in the death box was waiting around for the finale, because she'd made so much noise he would've come running to finish her off. Yet after her narrow escape she was leaving nothing to chance. After she saw the blood pooling on the floor she found a rag and made a crude bandage for her leg wound. Then she found her phone where it had been tossed, and called Roy. He was already on his way downtown because she'd never shown up at Altman's.

"I'll be there in ten minutes," he said after listening to her woozy account. "Call the cops right now."

This time Mace did exactly what he told her to. Within three minutes two patrol officers had kicked open the door to the fourth floor calling out her name. Three more cops joined them a few seconds later. Two minutes after that Beth Perry came flying up the stairs. She walked directly over to her sister and wrapped her arms around her.

Mace felt the tears slide down her cheeks as she hugged her sister back, as hard as she could. It was like she was twelve years old again. She had been wrong. She still needed to be held sometimes. Not often, but sometimes. Just like everybody else.

Beth called out to her officers, "Is this floor secure?"

"Yes, Chief."

"Then search the rest of the building. Leave a man posted to this door. I'll stay with her. And call an ambulance."

The men headed out.

Mace felt her legs start to give out. Beth seemed to sense this too and half carried her over to a plastic crate turned upside down and sat her down. She knelt in front of her, her gaze switching to the remains of the fridge and then back at Mace. The tears started trickling down Beth's face as she gripped her sister's hand.

"Damn it, Mace," she said, her voice cracking.

"I know. I know. I'm sorry."

"You didn't see who did it?"

She shook her head. "Happened too fast."

"We need to get you to a hospital."

"I'm okay, Beth."

"You're *getting* checked out. You've got a knot the size of a golf ball on your head. And your right leg is covered in blood."

"Okay, okay. I'll go."

"And on the ride over you're going to tell me exactly what is going on."

Moments later Roy came bursting through the door, the officer posted at the door tightly gripping his shoulder.

"Mace!" yelled Roy. He tried to rush to her but the cop held him back.

"It's okay," said Beth. "I know him."

The man let Roy go and he sprinted across the room and put his arm around Mace. "Are you okay? Tell me you're okay."

Beth rose and took a step back.

"I'm all right, Roy," said Mace.

"But we're still taking her to the hospital," said Beth. "And you can ride with us, Kingman. I know you're up to your wingtips in this too. And I want to hear everything."

She grabbed his shoulder and spun him around to stare at the trashed Amana.

"Too close, Kingman. Way too damn close."

100

An hour later it was determined that Mace did not have a cracked skull.

"Your head must be extremely hard," said the emergency room doctor.

"It is," Beth and Roy said simultaneously.

Her leg stitched up, a bandage on her head, and a prescription for pain meds written, they left the hospital in the early morning hours. Roy and Mace had told Beth some of what had been going on during the ride over, but now she insisted on driving them back to Abe Altman's so they could tell her the rest. Mace's Ducati had been picked up by a police flatbed and also driven over to Altman's.

In the guesthouse, they spent another hour bringing the police chief up to speed on their findings.

"We'll get a BOLO out on Ned Armstrong right now," said Beth, and she took a moment to make this call. After she'd relayed the order, she said, "He may have been the one who attacked you."

"If so, I look forward to returning the favor," said Mace as she lay on couch with a baggie of ice on her head.

Roy said, "He's probably long gone by now."

"How do you figure?" asked Beth.

"If he did put Mace in that fridge he probably hung around for a while to watch the building. He would have seen the police and Mace walking out alive."

Beth shook her head. "We can't take that chance. Ned is obviously not working this alone. So you two are getting round-the-clock protection."

"I've got a case to try," said Roy.

Mace sat up. "And I've got a fat asshole to catch, among lots of others."

"You can leave that to the police now. You should've left it to us from the get-go."

"Hey, I've done a lot of the heavy lifting already," objected Mace.

"And what, you think I'm going to do an end run and take all the credit if we do break this thing?"

"Damn it, Beth, we had this talk. I'm going to keep working this."

"Why don't you start learning that the rules *do* apply to you?"

"I would, except they always seem to be stacked against me!"

"That's just a pitiful excuse."

"I need to do this, Beth," Mace yelled, jumping off the couch. The baggie of ice slid to the floor. For a moment it looked like blows might be launched.

Roy stepped in between them, one hand on each of their shoulders.

At the same time both women cried out, "Stay out of this!"

"No!" he shouted and pushed each of them back. Mace landed on the couch and Beth in a chair. Both sisters stared up at him in shock.

"You just assaulted a police officer, Kingman," snapped Beth.

"Oh, right, throw that in his face!" retorted Mace.

Roy barked, "Will both of you just shut up and listen for one damn minute!"

The women glanced at each other and then back at him.

"Okay," said Roy. "Okay. These people have done things that take enormous resources and manpower."

"And your point?" said Beth.

"That we work together," Roy answered simply. "Like Mace said, she's done a lot of the heavy lifting. I've got a way into DLT to see what that brings. Chief, you've got resources that neither of us have. All I'm saying is that it makes a lot more sense for us to work together. I think we all want the same thing here, even if it is for different reasons."

Beth pulled her gaze from Roy and looked down. "Maybe we can work together."

"Then we need to tell you one more thing," said Roy. He looked nervously at Mace.

She said, "The guy Tolliver was having dinner with Friday was Jamie Meldon."

"How the hell do you know that?"

"Waiter at the restaurant recognized him," said Roy.

Beth looked puzzled. "I've got a contact who thinks Meldon was killed by domestic terrorists."

Roy shook his head. "We think he was killed because someone saw him having dinner with Diane. The lady knew something and they were afraid she'd told Meldon. The guy was a federal prosecutor after all."

Mace added, "And they didn't wait long. Dinner on Friday night and Diane killed right after. Meldon never made it past the weekend. Watkins is probably dead too. That's why I need to clean myself up and head to Newark in a few hours."

"What's in Newark?"

Mace explained about the law firm that had represented Tolliver in her divorce.

"And I've got the presentment this morning," added Roy. "But after that I'm going over to DLT and see what I can find out."

"And what would you have me do?" asked Beth.

Mace said, "Hopefully, you'll find Ned."

"His prints are probably all over the front lobby. We can run them through the databases." She stood. "If I let you do this," she began, staring dead at her sister, "you are to report in regularly and you are not to go into any dangerous situation without backup. No more fourth floors, you got that?"

"Loud and clear. I don't think I can ever even own a refrigerator again."

Roy said anxiously, "So are we good to go?"

Beth glared at him. "Yes, but we go by *my* playbook, not yours."

CHAPTER

101

JARVIS BURNS sat in his cluttered row house in southeast Washington near the Capitol rubbing his forehead. Three Advils had not done the trick, but he had a bottle of Dewar's in his drawer that might. He looked up at the man who sat across from him. Ned Armstrong. Real name Daniel Tyson. He'd worked for Burns for ten years and had never failed him. And yet the only reason he had not sent Mary Bard for a final meeting with Tyson was the fact that the man had followed Burns's order to the letter.

Put her in the fridge alive.

"A bullet to the head would be better," Tyson had told him at the time.

And he'd been right, of course. But Burns wanted the woman to suffer. He wanted her to wake up and see the hopelessness of her situation with warmth and air only a few inches away. It had been a mistake, a rare occurrence for him, but still a mistake.

"You said she went to the microwave and saw that it was broken?" Burns asked.

"She never said anything, but that seemed to be what she was thinking. So she might know I was lying about that. And if they know Tolliver was dead on Friday, they'd know I lied about that too."

"And you didn't hear who Perry was talking to or what she said while on the fourth floor?"

"I was waiting on the other side of the door. I just heard mumbles."

"We can check her cell phone records. Probably either her sister or Roy Kingman. If the former, the concern is vast. If the latter, it might be manageable."

"But they took her to the hospital, sir. And Beth Perry was there. She might've talked about what she knows."

"She may know about the subterfuge regarding Tolliver's death. And the fact that you might be involved somehow. If you disappear then they might think you did it acting alone, and then tried to cover it up."

"Perhaps," said Tyson, as he shifted his bulk in the chair. "But they went to the restaurant where Tolliver ate on Friday. If they put two and two together?"

"I am fully aware of the ramifications of that potential development, Tyson. No solution is perfect. We are clearly in damage control territory. We knew something like this might happen. That was why we had you stationed there as the security guard. Gave us eyes and ears on the ground and complete access to the building. It also allowed us the intelligence about the old soldier sneaking in."

"He makes the perfect patsy."

"Maybe not so perfect now. They must've figured out that the sperm was planted, and that he is not nearly smart enough to pull this off. That was always a risk."

"But unfortunately my own cover is probably blown."

"You're on the next agency flight to Riyadh. You'll spend two years there to let things quiet down before reassignment. I strongly suggest you lose about eighty pounds and have facial reconstructive surgery by approved agency surgical personnel. I'll provide full paper coverage for you. We may be able to convince them that you are indeed one of the great serial killers of all time."

"I'm sorry the mission wasn't successful, sir."

"It was my call, my fault. You were following orders. That is what you're supposed to do. I will never blame you for that."

"Will you require a close-out report?"

"No. Enjoy Saudi Arabia." Burns nodded at the door. A few seconds later he was alone once more.

He spent most of his time alone, thinking through the next doomsday scenario. He was tasked to keep America safe by any means possible. He thought about nothing else 24/7. He had used his muscle, training, and wits in uniform for his country. And now in a suit and tie he used what he had left to serve America.

He spent twenty minutes on three different calls. As he set the phone down for the last time, his mind went back to Mace Perry.

He didn't like losing. Never had since he was a small boy running through the cornfields of Kansas chasing dreams. She was good, but she was still just a street cop.

He picked up his phone and made another call. "It's time for the contingency plan," he said into the receiver.

It was very late but Chester Ackerman was awake and sitting in the living room of his lavish apartment in the Watergate Building. The managing partner of Shilling & Murdoch had traded his suit, wingtips, and braces for khaki pants, an orange cashmere sweater, and Docksiders. As soon as he heard Burns's voice his thoughts about taking a ride the next day in his forty-foot cabin cruiser vanished.

Ackerman put his tumbler of scotch and soda down, sat up straight, and gathered his courage to say it. "I really think I should maintain a low profile with all this. I already told you about Diane when she came to me asking questions. I fired Kingman. I've kept the money flowing. I think I've done enough."

Burns's retort was like a cannonball fired right into his belly. "You've also made a bloody fortune for basically sitting on your fat ass because of business deals that I got for you! Now here's where you repay the kindness of your beneficent government. So just shut up and listen. You should already have the legal documents prepared like I told you to do."

"I do," he said in a shaky voice, his meager courage gone.

"Now you will act exactly in accordance with my instructions. And if you don't . . ."

Burns spoke uninterrupted for nearly ten minutes. When he'd finished he hung up and leaned back in his chair.

That sonofabitch has made more in one year than I've made in my entire life. A draft dodger who pays his first-year know-nothings more than I'll ever make. And he wants to lay low. He wants to take a time-out after making millions! He's done enough!

Part of Burns wished that Ackerman would fail to follow his orders just so he could order the man's execution. Mary Bard could probably kill him with simply a stare.

Don't tempt me, you parasite. Don't you dare tempt me.

102

Early in the morning the Ducati roared through the gates at Altman's estate. The female police officer driving it would take any followers on a two-hour ride around the Virginia countryside. A few minutes later the Bentley pulled past the gates, Herbert at the wheel. He was on his way to the market. But he had one delivery to make before then and it would take him into the heart of D.C.

Mace Perry lay in the backseat of the car.

Thirty-five minutes later she was walking through the cavernous Union Station. She got her ticket from the self-serve machine and boarded the Acela train a few minutes before it was to leave. She snagged a window seat and for the next two hours or so watched the scenery of the Northeast go by as she thought about her upcoming encounter with the law firm of Hamilton, Petrocelli & Sprissler. She grabbed a cab at the station and walked into the law firm's suite in a twenty-story building in downtown Newark fifteen minutes later.

The place was all polished wood and marble with tasteful paintings on the wall. It looked very old money, yet Roy had looked up the law firm on an online legal directory for her and told her that it had only been in existence for fifteen years. The firm specialized in divorce and other civil litigation, and had three female partners, Julie Hamilton, Mandy Petrocelli, and Kelly Sprissler. They were all from New Jersey, had graduated from the same law school in the same year, and had returned to their roots to open the firm. From what Roy had been able to find, the practice had been a success from nearly day one and each of the name partners had stellar reputations

in the Newark legal community. The firm currently employed a total of fourteen attorneys, and they were known in the area as a
go-to legal shop for high-profile divorces, many of which came from
nearby Manhattan.

The receptionist, a polished-looking woman in her early thirties,
made a face when Mace told her who she was and why she was
there.

"They don't want to talk to you," she said bluntly.

"I know. That's why I came all this way. It's really very important. Can you at least let them know I'm here?"

She made the call, spoke briefly with someone, and then put the
receiver down.

"That was Ms. Hamilton."

"And?" said Mace hopefully.

"She wishes you a safe trip back home."

"Can I talk to her on the phone?'

"That would not be possible."

"I can wait here until they come out."

"Ms. Hamilton anticipated you might say that, so she told me to
tell you that the building has excellent security and that spending
several months in jail for trespass was probably not a good use of
your time."

"Wow, I haven't even met this woman and already I like her.
Okay, I'll just have to turn it over to the FBI. I know some of the
agents in the field office up here. They're good people, and very
thorough. Since this is a murder investigation with possible national
security implications, I hope the firm can do without its computers
for a while."

"What do you mean?" the receptionist said in a stunned tone.

"Well, it's standard operating procedure for the Feds to confis-
cate all computers during an investigation like this."

"You said national security?"

"Jamie Meldon was a U.S. attorney. His murder may be tied to a
terrorist organization."

"Oh my God. We don't know anything about that."

"Well, the FBI likes to find that out for itself." Mace pulled out her phone, hit a speed dial button, and said, "FBI Special Agent Morelli, please. It's Mace Perry."

"Wait a minute!"

Mace eyed the woman standing in the doorway. She was about forty, Mace's height, a little heavier, and dressed in a jacket and skirt with black hose and heels. Her brown hair was cut short and precisely traced the outline of her head. Mace clicked off the phone. She'd only dialed 411 after all. "Are you Julie Hamilton? I recognize your voice from the phone call."

"I can give you five minutes."

"Great."

She walked down the hall with Mace scurrying after her. On the way Hamilton leaned into two other offices and gave the people inside a nod of the head. When Mace and Hamilton entered a small conference room, two other women joined them.

Hamilton indicated with her hand, "My partners, Mandy Petrocelli and Kelly Sprissler."

Petrocelli was tall and big-boned with dyed blond hair, while Sprissler was short and wiry and her reddish hair was clipped back in a tight braid. All three women looked tough, professional, and were probably excellent at their work, Mace assumed. If she ever did manage to marry someone and things turned ugly, she'd probably call one of these women to rep her.

"I'm Mace Perry, a private investigator from Washington."

"Get to the point," interjected Sprissler in a harsh tone.

"The point is Diane Tolliver was brutally murdered at her law office on Friday of last week and her body stuffed in a fridge. A few days later Jamie Meldon was found inside a Dumpster. On the night Diane was killed, she and Meldon had dinner together. We think she knew of some illegal activity and might have been trying to get Meldon's help. What we don't know is why she picked him. From what we've been able to determine so far, they never had any connection."

The three lawyers glanced at one another. Hamilton said, "You mentioned out in the lobby that this case had national security implications?"

Mace nodded. "Terrorism potential."

Petrocelli said in a booming voice, "If so, why are you here and not the FBI?"

"I wish I had a good answer to that, but I don't. All I want to know is how Meldon and Tolliver knew each other."

"How did you even find out about us?" Sprissler interjected.

"Joe Cushman. Diane's ex. He spoke highly of your firm."

"That's because we took him to the cleaners during the divorce," said Petrocelli.

"Now we're on retainer to his company," added Sprissler. "That's the mark of good legal work, turning adversaries into clients."

"But getting back to why you're here," said Hamilton.

"Right. How did Meldon and Tolliver know each other?"

"I guess it's all right to tell you. It's public record anyway. Before we were retained to represent her, Jamie was Diane's counsel of record in her divorce proceedings from Joe."

"While he was in private practice in New York?"

"That's right."

"But I was told he was primarily a mob lawyer."

Hamilton said sternly, "Jamie represented many companies and individuals that were involved in myriad civil and criminal matters. I would not describe him as a mob lawyer."

"Okay, but did he also handle divorce cases in New Jersey?"

"Diane lived in New Jersey, although she practiced law in Manhattan," said Sprissler.

"A very common occurrence," added Petrocelli.

"But did Meldon handle divorce cases as a 'very common occurrence'?"

Hamilton cleared her throat. "No, he didn't."

"Is that why he passed the baton to you?"

"We'd worked with Jamie before. He knew we specialized in marital law cases."

"So why not just get you on board from the get-go?"

"There was a matter of timing," explained Hamilton.

"Timing? I know divorce cases can last years. What was the hurry?"

"Jamie got a restraining order against Joe Cushman. He was making threats apparently against Diane. The order had to be obtained quickly for obvious reasons, although having gotten to know Joe over the years I don't believe he meant any of it."

"But that still doesn't explain why Meldon was involved in the first place. *How* did he know Tolliver?"

"I'm not sure that is relevant to anything," barked Sprissler, who looked like she wanted to leap over the table and take a bite out of Mace's leg.

"Well, I think it's relevant. And I damn sure know the FBI would think it was."

"They were friends," said Hamilton after a few tense moments of silence.

Mace arched her eyebrows.

"*Very* good friends," amended Hamilton.

"I see. Did Joe Cushman know they were having an affair?"

"While neither confirming nor denying the accuracy of your words, from a purely hypothetical basis, I would assume not."

"But they didn't end up together," said Mace.

"Jamie's wife developed breast cancer," said Petrocelli. "Let's just say he did the right thing by her."

"We were surprised when he moved to D.C. and became a U.S. attorney," added Hamilton. "But in a way we understood. He wanted to make a clean break of it."

"We were stunned to hear about his death," said Sprissler.

"So were a lot of people," said Mace.

She asked a few more questions, got nothing else helpful, and headed back to the train station. It was good to finally know of the connection between Tolliver and Meldon, but it didn't really advance the investigation as far as Mace could see. As she sat down to wait for her train, it seemed like they were right back at square one and running out of time.

CHAPTER

103

Roy stepped into C-10 for the first time in two years. C-10 was the courtroom where presentments were held in D.C. Superior Court, which was where the Captain was being tried for murder. The place was crammed because C-10 heard all presentments, from relatively minor crimes all the way to the most serious felonies. The defendants who were not in custody sat with their attorneys in the courtroom waiting for their case to be called. Those defendants who were already in jail were held in another room until it was their turn before the judge.

Roy took a seat on one of the crowded benches. As he looked around he could see various defendants gabbing while they were waiting. C-10 was a good place for the criminal classes to catch up with each other, he'd found. When he'd been a CJA he'd more than once had to pull his guy away from another street punk because they were plotting out some future crime right in front of the judge.

Roy suspected that his presentment would be called first, for one reason only. And that reason walked in at one minute to ten, sixty seconds ahead of the opening bell for this C-10 cattle call. Mona Danforth was dressed for battle in navy blue Chanel with a white pocket kerchief, three-inch heels, and lips set in a perfectly horizontal line. Her golden tresses oozed the scent of hairspray like blood from a finger cut.

One minute later the judge entered, everyone rose, and the bailiff called the case. The Captain appeared from behind a door with a police officer on either side of him. He joined Roy at the defense counsel table while Mona stood ready at the prosecutor's table. The judge smiled down at Mona and rested his glasses near the end of his nose as he read over the papers. At this juncture, no evidence was presented by the two lawyers. It was strictly done on the record thus far. And that record completely favored Mona.

The judge said, "Ms. Danforth, I haven't seen you in C-10 in a while."

"Good to be back, Your Honor."

The judge riffled through some notes and then glanced over at Roy. "Plea?"

"Not guilty, Your Honor," said Roy while the Captain stood beside him idly gazing around the room.

"Duly noted. Ms. Danforth?"

"The people request a 1325-A hold. The defendant has no job, no home, and no family locally. We consider him to be a flight risk, and that, coupled with the serious nature of the charges, warrants continued confinement."

"Defense objections?" the judge asked, peering at Roy.

"No, Your Honor."

"I understand that we might have a conflict with defense counsel?"

"It's been resolved, Your Honor," said Mona quickly.

The judge looked from her to Roy. "Is that correct?"

Roy glanced once at Mona and then said, "That's correct."

"Mr. Kingman, the record says your client is homeless and presumably not in a position to hire an attorney. And yet you're not a public defender."

"I'm doing the case pro bono."

"How generous of you."

"I used to be CJA."

"Used to be?"

"I left to go into corporate private practice."

"How long did you practice criminal law in this court?"

"Two years."

The judge laid his glasses down on the bench. "This is a rape and murder-one charge. It doesn't get more serious than that."

"I understand that, Your Honor. I've handled murder cases before."

"How many?"

"At least ten."

"How many of those went to trial?"

Roy licked his lips. "Three."

"And your record in those trials?"

"Unfortunately, I lost all of them."

"I see." He turned his attention to the Captain. "Mr. Dockery, do you want to have Mr. Kingman as your counsel? If not, there are many experienced public defenders that will represent you at no cost."

Roy held his breath, praying that the Captain didn't start asking for Twinkies.

The Captain merely said, "Yes sir. Roy's my lawyer."

"Ms. Danforth?"

She smiled and said coolly, "The people feel that Mr. Kingman is up to the task of *adequately* defending Mr. Dockery's interests in this case. We have no objection to his continued representation."

The judge looked skeptical of this but said, "Okay. The court finds the people have met its burden and the defendant will be detained until further notice." The judge rapped his gavel and the next case was called.

Roy turned to the Captain. "You doing all right?"

"You think I can keep staying there? Three squares and a bed."

"I think I can pretty much guarantee that for the foreseeable future. But look, Captain, we're going to get you out of this, okay? You're not going to prison over this."

"If you say so, Roy. I just want to get back in time for lunch."

He was led off by the police officers and Roy headed out of the courtroom.

"I'm impressed, Kingman. I would've bet your pants would be wet by now."

He turned to see Mona behind him.

"I hope your legal work is as bad as your quips."

"I guess you'll find out sooner rather than later."

"What's that supposed to mean?"

Mona pushed open the courtroom door and motioned Roy out.

She followed. Halfway down the hall Roy flinched as a column of media folks charged toward them. They started shoving mikes, recorders, and notepads in Roy's face while firing off questions at him. "What the hell—" He darted a glance at Mona, who didn't seem surprised by all this attention.

She said, "If you want to play in the big leagues this comes with the territory."

Roy shoved through the crowd as Mona started making prepared remarks. Even as he pushed through the wall he was at risk of being hurled right back into the pit by the sheer weight of the media. That is, until a long arm came out of nowhere and snagged him, pulling him through a side door that slammed shut in the faces of the trailing reporters.

Beth let go of his arm and stepped back.

"Thanks, Chief."

"I figured Mona would pull her usual crap. How'd it go in there?"

"No surprises."

"You can leave through that hallway," she said, pointing to her left.

"I know this is awkward for you, Chief."

"What is?"

"I mean, technically you're on Mona's side. If we prove our case, she loses. In fact, she might look like an idiot in the process."

Beth punched him lightly on the side of the arm. "Keep talking like that, Kingman, I might just grow to tolerate you."

Roy thought he caught a glimpse of a smile as she strode off down the hall. Outside he was heading for his car when a lanky young man in a tweed blazer approached.

"Roy Kingman?'

"Yeah?"

The man thrust a set of rolled documents into Roy's hands. "Consider yourself served." As the guy hurried off, Roy examined the papers.

Shilling & Murdoch was suing him.

CHAPTER

104

SAM DONNELLY did not look particularly pleased as he left the White House in a small motorcade. He was a former Army two-star turned congressman who'd been elevated to the top spy slot based on political payback and his years of military duty, and also because of his membership on the House Intelligence Committee. He'd grown gray in service to his country and had a reputation as a no-nonsense administrator with a hands-on approach.

Jarvis Burns sat across from him in the limo, which had a sound-proof wall separating the driver and a bodyguard from the rear seats. Burns had fought with Donnelly in the swamps of Vietnam before each had gone his own way in life after the military. Once they hooked back up, Donnelly's faith in Burns had allowed him pretty much free rein to run one of the most important top-secret programs in America's counterterrorism operations.

"Tough meeting?" Burns said.

"You can say that."

"Wish I could have been there."

"The DCI gets a burr up his butt from time to time. Just wants what he calls the big boys in the room. I'll throw him the bone. It's not like I can risk making him into an enemy. The DNI is only first among equals."

"It's an unwieldy structure we have. Most countries are far more streamlined on the intelligence side."

"With so many 'intelligence' agencies all jockeying for turf and budget dollars it is pretty much guaranteed that nothing will ever be streamlined on this side of the Atlantic."

"But the results speak for themselves."

"Absolutely they do. There hasn't been a terrorist attack on American soil since 9/11. That is not by happenstance. What we're doing is working. The president understands that. That is the most important thing."

"And so does the public."

"Well, if they knew some of the folks we were bankrolling it would not go over well."

Burns nodded. "But a bag full of rials or dinars doesn't cut it anymore. It's a big business keeping this country safe. We have money and/or financial distribution channels and they don't. They have things we need. It's a simple business transaction."

"It's a deal with the devil, plain and simple."

"But less of a devil than the ones we're fighting."

"How do you keep them straight, Jarv? They keep changing on us. We're paying off the same bastards that just last year were shooting at us and blowing us up."

"We're fighting the good fight with the tools we have, sir. What's the alternative?"

Donnelly gazed out the window as the famous monuments whirled by outside. "There's no alternative, at least for now," he groused.

"We all do what we have to do, sir. You're a political appointee. I'm just a working man."

Donnelly didn't look pleased by this statement. "They can subpoena *anybody*, Jarv. Including you. Don't ever forget that."

"I'm sorry if I conveyed a different impression."

"And everyone is expendable, including you."

"I never thought otherwise," said Burns in a deferential tone.

"We did what we needed to do to survive in Southeast Asia. I'm not proud of all of it, and maybe I'd do things differently today, but I'm not second-guessing anything with my country's security at risk."

"We'll get through this, Director."

"Will we? Well, just remember this, in my agency sacrifice starts from the bottom and works up. Don't ever lose sight of that, Jarv. Don't ever." Donnelly gave the other man a prolonged stare and then looked away. "Money is as tight as I've ever seen it. And if we don't keep paying the sons of bitches, we're going to have a suitcase nuke go off somewhere where we don't want it to. The ends do justify the means. When I was in Congress I would've launched an investigation of any agency head who uttered those words. Now that I'm in the hot seat I can definitely relate."

"The money will continue. The stakes are too high."

"What's being done with Reiger's and Hope's families?"

"As far as they're concerned the two died while serving their country. They'll be taken care of financially, of course."

"I was deeply disappointed it came to this."

"As was I."

"You've got to have the stomach for this sort of thing. We had to deal with this shit in 'Nam. We worked with whoever we had to, to get the damn job done."

"The younger generation just doesn't seem to get it."

"But Mary Bard is a hell of an asset to have."

"Quite accommodating of our Russian friends."

"Even Moscow is scared of the terrorism beast. They've got money now, and an economy worth protecting. They know they're a target. So I snagged her from the FBI as soon as I heard she was in town. I've worked with her before actually. Steve Lanier, the AD, was not pleased, I can tell you that."

"I'm sure. I'm looking forward to deploying her again."

"Don't overuse her. There are enough damn bodies floating around as it is."

"Absolutely, sir."

But one or two more won't really matter, thought Burns.

105

I APPRECIATE you meeting with me, Cassie."

Roy was walking along K Street with Cassie Benoit, who worked at DLT, the escrow agent Shilling & Murdoch used for its business transactions.

"No problem. I was heading out for a sandwich anyway. What's up?"

"Just a document snafu, at least I think. You remember the Dixie Group purchase we closed two months ago?"

"A bunch of shopping malls in Alabama and Texas. Purchaser was a partnership in the U.A.E."

"Good memory. That's the one."

"What's the snafu? Money got there, I know that."

"Seven hundred and seventy-five million plus assumption of debt."

"I remember it was something like that. I can't keep all the figures straight after a while. Too many deals."

"Tell me about it."

"But anyway, we only dealt with the cash, not the debt assumption, of course," she said, biting into her tuna fish sandwich as they walked along.

"The cash got there, but two of the contingencies may not have been met."

"Which ones?'

"One deed recordation might've had a problem. And there's an outstanding issue with the anchor tenant in the Dallas–Fort Worth mall that was supposed to be resolved prior to the funds going out. There was supposed to be a release in the file but there's not."

"Shit, did we screw up?"

"I don't know. I'm not sure if we screwed up either. I wanted to come by your office and take a look at the records you have."

"I'm swamped today, Roy. That's why I'm eating my sandwich on the run."

"How about after office hours?"

Cassie looked doubtful. "I had concert tickets at Constitution Hall."

"I haven't mentioned anything to the client. I was hoping to clean up the issue before anyone had to make those calls. And you know the U.A.E. guys. If there was a foul-up you and I might have to jump on a jet and go and apologize to the sheiks."

The blood drained from Cassie's face. "But I hate to fly."

"Better we get it resolved on this side of the world, then."

Cassie sighed and threw the rest of her sandwich into a trash bin. "How about seven tonight? Everybody will be gone but I can let you in."

"That sounds perfect, Cassie, I really appreciate it."

Roy left her, checked his watch, and called Mace. She filled him in on her meeting in Newark. She also told him she'd tried to catch an earlier train, but it was full. And the train she had just gotten on was delayed because a piece of equipment on a train in front of them had fallen off, been run over by the engine, and part of the power grid for the Northeast corridor might have been damaged.

"It's going to be a while," she'd said glumly. "Maybe tonight. Hell, I could probably walk there faster."

"Let me know when you get in. By the way, I'm being sued by my old firm."

"What? Why?"

"I looked at the complaint. It's all bullshit."

"Well, if I hear of a good lawyer I'll let you know."

A minute before seven, Roy appeared at the office of DLT. The firm shut down at six-thirty, which seemed early but DLT opened at six a.m. because of all its international work. After long days of crunching numbers, meeting strict deadlines, and authorizing the catapulting of electronic currency around the globe, most of the firm's employees stampeded to the door right at closing.

Cassie answered his knock and let him in. She had taken her hair out of its usual bun and it swept around her shoulders. Her heels had been replaced with socks and tennis shoes.

"I pulled the docs that we have," she said. "Come on back."

"Great. Thanks."

"I went through everything but I couldn't find what you were talking about. But then I'm not a lawyer."

"That's okay, I'm sure I'll be able to figure it out."

He went over the records slowly, looking for an opening while Cassie hovered behind him in her small office. He noted the pack of cigarettes sticking out of her purse where it lay on her desk. He looked up and smiled. "This may take a while. You want to smoke 'em while you got 'em?" He tapped the protruding pack of cigarettes.

"I've been dying for one since lunch. But it's a no-smoking building and I've had no time to sneak out."

"The sidewalk is an option right now."

Cassie's fingers curled and uncurled slowly as she eyed her pack of Winstons. "Okay, I give. I won't be gone that long. I might actually need two cigs."

"And isn't there an Au Bon Pain across the street?"

"Yeah, I love their stuff. Our coffee sucks."

"Then go smoke and when you're done go get us some java." He gave her some money. "Take your time. Looks like we're going to be here a while. No room for error with the Middle East guys," he added ominously.

As soon as she was gone, Roy started clicking keys on her computer. Luckily he didn't need her password as he was already in the database. He wasn't familiar with their electronic filing system, but he figured searching the names of clients would be sufficient. And he was right. He quickly skimmed half a dozen transactions that he and Diane had worked on over the last eighteen months. Now he understood why Cassie had been confused about the dollar amount earlier.

The escrow instruction letters that Diane and Roy had prepared for these deals, which basically told DLT how much money would be sent and on what conditions it could released, did not match up with the DLT records in one critical respect.

The cash.

From his own records Roy had jotted down various facts for each of the six transactions he wanted to compare with DLT's records. The Dixie Group shopping center deal had been for $775 million plus debt assumption. That's what Roy had written down from the Shilling & Murdoch instruction letter they'd sent DLT. DLT had scanned all the instruction letters into their computer system. But the instruction letter Roy was looking at, which appeared to be on Shilling letterhead, had the cash purchase price at $795 million, a $20 million discrepancy. At her level, Cassie would not have caught this because she just followed the instruction letter. And if the funds coming in matched the amount stated in the letter, there would be no red flag. And apparently the incoming funds *had* matched.

Roy sat back. Why would his client in the U.A.E. have sent extra money? No purchaser paid more than the contract price. Or had the client even sent the extra money? He clicked a few computer keys and looked at the confirmation slips on the wire transfers for some of the deals. Money wires coming in from overseas were dealt with a bit differently from wires between U.S. banks, particularly after 9/11. Roy knew there was a list of sensitive countries and American authorities kept a close watch on monies flowing from these places into the United States in case they were being used to fund terrorist activities.

All bank wires, whether domestic or foreign, still ended up moving through the Federal Reserve System in some fashion and with varying levels of scrutiny. But it was still an arena that was fraught with the potential for abuse. Roy glanced at the date of the instruction letter he was looking at on the screen and then looked at the cheat sheet he'd prepared from his own records. The date on the screen was two days after the one from Roy's records. He knew that instruction letters were updated all the time as conditions changed. But conditions hadn't changed in this instance. Roy's date was for the absolute final instruction letter. Someone else had later changed it, and had added $20 million in the process.

He remembered the string of extra numbers that he'd seen on the computerized records he and Mace had looked at over dinner at Altman's guest house. He inputted the name of that client and looked at the instruction letter for that deal. Roy knew that the purchase amount had been $990 million for the manufacturing facilities. But on the instruction sheet another $25 million had been tacked on and the date on the letter again was after the latest date Roy had. And on a confirmation sheet it showed the $990 million going to the seller's bank in New York. But where did the other monies go? To another bank? And who'd sent it? Again, Roy didn't think his client had thrown in an extra $25 million out of the goodness of their heart.

Roy sat straight up as the answer hit him.

This was a classic piggyback scheme.

You open the financial tunnel with a legitimate transaction coming from a country in the Middle East *not* on the sensitive list. The purchase price goes out, but added to it are funds from another source. The legit dollars run interference for the illegitimate dollars and, when they reach the U.S. pipeline, the purchase-price dollars go to where they're supposed to, and the other dollars go somewhere else. But if the instruction letter has the overall correct amount and delivery accounts for the monies, no one would be the wiser. And if an audit was done later the facts might be so muddled that no one could figure it out. There was so much electronic money flying around the world that it was like trying to track down a particular molecule of air.

Roy knew what this was. This was a way around the Patriot Act, which obviously was very concerned about suspicious transfers of money. The extra funds could have come from anywhere, including enemies of the United States.

These could be drug dealers laundering money. Or operating funds for terrorists. Or spies.

And they might have someone at DLT on the inside. And then it struck Roy. DLT was just following instructions. It was far more likely they had someone at *Shilling* in their pocket. He looked at the revised instruction letter. It had Diane's electronic signature on it. But that was easy to get. Especially for someone in management at the firm.

Chester Ackerman. The biggest rainmaker at the firm.

He doubted Ackerman was the driving force behind this. But he felt sure the man knew who was. Roy inserted a flash drive in the USB slot and made copies of as many pages as he could and slipped it in his briefcase. He was walking to the office foyer when he heard Cassie open the door.

"I'm all done, Cassie," he called out. "Found the problem."

The door closed and he stopped.

It wasn't Cassie. It was a petite woman with brown hair, but her gun looked awfully big.

CHAPTER

106

MACE NEARLY LEAPT off the train when it finally pulled to a stop in Union Station. A short trip had turned into an all-day affair. It was already dark outside. She would wait until she got outside to call Roy. Hopefully he had struck pay dirt at the escrow firm.

So intent was she on her thoughts that she never saw the man visibly react as she walked by him in the station and headed for the cab stands. She never saw him pull his cell phone and make a quick call. Never saw him walk up behind her. She did notice when the pistol was wedged against the small of her back.

"Keep your mouth shut or you're dead."

She tried to look back but he pushed the gun deeper. "Eyes straight ahead."

"This place is packed with cops," she said. "How about I start screaming instead?"

"See them kids over there?"

Mace's gaze darted to the left where a group of kids in school uniforms were standing with two older women.

"I see 'em."

"Then you see the dude right behind 'em?"

Mace saw the dude. Big and angry-looking. "Yeah."

"Well he's got a grenade in his pocket. You give me any shit, he's gonna pull the pin, drop it in that trash can, and walk away. Then the kiddies go boom."

"Why the hell are you doing this?"

"Shut up and walk!"

He maneuvered her up the escalators, out to the parking garage, and then far down to a remote corner of the place where no else was around and only one vehicle was parked, a black Escalade. Four men got out as they approached.

Mace flinched when she saw him.

Psycho was not smiling this time. No sparkle in the eye, no levity at all in his features. The man looked all business.

"Dead bitch walking," he said grimly.

"I thought we had a deal," said Mace. "No harm, no foul."

All that got was a backhanded punch from Psycho that dropped Mace on her butt. She sat there wiping the blood off her cheek before one of the boys ripped her back to a standing position just in time for Psycho to knock her on her ass again with an uppercut to her gut.

Mace was tough, but one more hit like that and she wasn't going to be doing much else other than lie in a nursing home bed and dribble into a cup. She turned to the side and threw up right before she was jerked back to her feet. She stood there tottering.

Blood flowing from her nose and cracked mouth she managed to say, "One request."

"Do you understand that I'm about to kill you?"

"That's why I figure I better ask now."

"What?"

"You're a big tough guy. You just knocked me on my ass twice. You're gonna kill me."

"So?"

"So, let me have one punch. Right to *your* gut. You can even harden up the six-pack before I do it."

"What are you, one-ten?"

"About. And you're over two, I know."

"So where's that gonna get you?"

"Satisfaction before I die."

"How do I know you're not some kind of kung fu princess?"

"If I were, you think I'd be letting you kick my ass?" She spit blood out of her mouth and ran her tongue over a loosened tooth. "Hey, but if you're afraid of a girl."

Psycho reared back his fist to hit her again, but stopped when she flinched. He grinned. "You ain't no kung fu nothing. I know, because I am. Double black belt."

"Figures," said Mace wearily, wiping blood off her chin with her jacket sleeve. "So it's a yes?"

Psycho looked around at his guys, who all looked back at him with amused expressions. Mace also glanced around. There wasn't anyone to help her. They were in a dark, deserted corner in the pits of the parking garage. She could scream her lungs out and it wouldn't matter. But she suddenly did see one thing that might help matters. If she lived long enough.

"Okay. But soon as your little love tap connects, we're putting your butt in that SUV, taking you to a favorite place of mine, putting a bullet in your brain, and dropping you in Rock Creek Park."

"Tense the six-pack, Psych. I'm gonna give it all I got."

Psycho zipped open his jacket and exposed a flat belly that Mace knew was probably hard as iron. She was actually surprised no one had noticed, but it was dark out here and so they apparently hadn't seen what she'd done. Her blow was efficiently delivered, driven right into the man's diaphragm. Mace had been right, it was hard as rock. But it didn't matter. The 900,000 volts in her zap knuckles didn't really care how hard someone's gut was. Psycho dropped to the concrete shaking like he was holding a live wire, his mouth making little burps of sound, his eyes popping and fluttering.

His stunned crew just stood there watching him.

Mace sprinted off.

The guy who'd originally grabbed her in the station shouted, "Hey!"

Mace knew she'd never make it. Even as she ran she tensed for the shots that would be hitting her any moment now. The squeal of wheels made her look to her left. The Nissan was coming right at her. She threw herself to the side, only to watch it miss her by design and whip around and come to a stop between her and Psycho's guys.

"Get in!"

Mace jumped to her feet.

"Get in!"

"Darren?"

Alisha's brother had his gun out and pointed it at Psycho's on-rushing crew. He placed two shots right over their heads, and the two lead guys hit the concrete, making draw pulls of their own on the way down.

Mace ripped open the Nissan's passenger door and threw herself in. There was another squeal of wheels and the Nissan shot forward. Mace ducked as bullets pinged off the metal and one round cracked the rear window glass. They rounded a corner and Darren floored it. Two more curves and they zipped out of the garage. Five minutes later they were two miles away and Mace finally sat up in her seat.

"Where the hell did you come from?" she exclaimed. "How'd you know I was even there?"

"Didn't. I was tailing Psycho. Saw what was going down. Figured you needed a little help."

Mace strapped on her seat belt. "Now I know why they call you Razor."

"Got some napkins in the glove box. Don't want you bleeding all over my seat," he added in a surly tone.

"Thanks." She pulled some out and wiped off her face. "Why were you tailing that guy?"

"Why you think?"

"There are several endings to that sort of plan, and none of them are good."

"What you want me to do, let him walk?"

"He's not going to walk."

"That's right, you gonna handle him. That's what you said. Well, you handling him all right. But for me, your ass is dead tonight."

"Hey, don't forget my zap knuckles."

Darren grinned, probably in spite of himself. "That was cool seeing him on his ass like that shaking like a dude coming off meth."

Mace palmed her phone. "Okay, we have kidnapping, assault—"

He glanced at her. "What you talking 'bout?"

"The crimes Psycho and his guys committed tonight."

"Right. He'll have ten people say he was twenty miles away."

"You didn't see it, then?"

"See what?"

"The security camera in the corner of the garage." She punched in a number. "Beth, Mace. Yeah, I'm cool. Just got into D.C. I brought you a present. A guy named Psycho, tied up in a nice little bow."

107

It was amazing to Roy how quickly and efficiently he was bundled out of the building. The truck had driven for an indeterminate amount of time. He was tied up, gagged and blindfolded, and they'd put something in his ear that buzzed constantly so he couldn't even listen for helpful sounds that might aid in telling him where they were headed. Now he was seated at a table in a room that he sensed was part of a bigger facility. He tensed when the door opened and the woman walked in.

Mary Bard sat down across from him, her hands clasped in front of her and resting on the table. Roy was no longer tied up and the gag and blindfold had been removed. They obviously didn't care if he could identify any of them. They clearly didn't anticipate him sitting in a witness box.

"Who are you? What do you want?"

"You watch too much TV," said Bard with a bemused expression.

"And what exactly did you expect me to ask?"

"Do you want to live?" she said simply.

"Yes. But why do I think it highly unlikely?"

"It is *very* unlikely," she conceded. "But not impossible. And in your situation, it is the impossible you must strive for."

"Like this?" He leapt across the table and attempted to grab her. He outweighed her by at least a hundred pounds and was nearly a foot taller. When he woke, he was lying on the cold floor on his stomach. His right shoulder felt like it was out of its socket. He slowly sat up, holding his damaged wing.

Mary Bard was once more seated at the table and staring at him with the same inscrutable expression. "Are you finished playing John Wayne?"

John Wayne? She either doesn't watch much current TV or isn't from America and subsists on a steady diet of decades-old movies.

"How did you do that?" he asked, grimacing with pain.

"I could tell you, but you wouldn't understand, so what would be the point?"

He got to his feet and slumped down in the chair, holding his injured shoulder. "I think it's popped out of joint," he said. He felt sick to his stomach.

"It is. Would you like me to put it back for you?"

"How about some morphine instead?"

"No. You need to be completely focused for what is coming."

She walked around the table and stood next to him. "Turn toward me."

"I swear if this is some kind of trick, ninja chick or not, I will—"

She moved so fast he had no time to react. There was a pop, an instant of gut-wrenching pain, and then his shoulder was back in place.

She sat back down while he gingerly moved his arm around, testing her work. "Thank you."

"Pleasure," she said as she stared at him.

"You're not American, are you?"

She shrugged. "What does it matter what I am?"

"Okay, I'm focused. What do you want?"

"We want you to text Mace Perry. We want to meet with her too."

Roy sat back. "I don't think so. You've got me, you're not getting her too."

"Mr. Kingman, you really should reconsider."

"Okay, I will. You want me to text Mace. Ask her to meet me in some out-of-the-way place so when you grab and kill her no one will even know. And then you'll just kill me too. I'm thinking about it, thinking about it." He paused and said, "Go to hell, lady."

"We can of course text her ourselves using your phone."

"Then why even ask me?"

"As a test, of course."

"Did I pass or fail?"

"I don't know yet."

"So where does that leave us? If you let me call her, I'll warn her it's a trap. And since I've never sent her a text before, she'll be instantly suspicious if she gets one. She's sort of paranoid by nature. And she'll call me. And when I don't answer. . . ."

"Yes, we thought the same thing."

"I figured it out, you know. The money thing. The piggyback ride. Dialing for terrorists? Is that what you are? You don't look Middle Eastern but are you one of bin Laden's babes?"

"I am not anyone's babe," she said, her voice rising slightly.

"Okay, but maybe you should consider this. Mace doesn't know any of what I found out. And neither does anyone else. I never had a chance to tell anybody."

"Your point?"

"You don't need Mace. You've got me. You kill me, it's over."

"I doubt it would be over."

"What do you mean?"

"My briefing on Mace Perry leads me to conclude that if you are in danger she will stop at nothing to try and help you."

"Your *briefing*? Okay, what government do you work for?"

For the first time Mary Bard exhibited a touch of chagrin. Her lips compressed slightly and there was a certain irritated look to her eyes.

When she didn't answer him, he said, "I'd say the impossible just got *wildly* impossible. I'm never walking out of here, so what incentive do I have to help you?"

There was a buzzing sound. Roy looked around for a moment until he realized it was the woman's phone vibrating. She rose, went to a far corner, and answered. She barely spoke, mostly listened. It dawned on Roy that the room was probably wired for both sound and video. Who was out there?

Bard put the phone back in her pocket and retook her seat. "No incentive at all. But the fact is she will come to try and save you once we tell her we have you. You see, you're the bait."

"Her sister is the D.C. police chief. If she comes it will be with an army."

"No she won't. Because we will tell her that will ensure your death."

"But her coming alone she knows will ensure *both* our deaths."

"And yet she will do so."

"How the hell are you so sure?"

"Because if it were me, I would do the same thing."

108

Mace was sitting in the living room of the guesthouse with a bag of ice on her swollen cheek. She'd tried to call Roy numerous times and hadn't received an answer. The phone call she'd just gotten, however, had stripped the mystery out of this. They had Roy. They wanted her too. If she didn't come, he was dead. The deadline was twenty-four hours from now.

She just sat there, icy water dripping down her face. For one of the few times in her life she didn't know what to do. Then, as if her hand were being guided by some invisible force, she picked up the phone and made the call. Beth arrived in twenty-seven minutes, the roof lights of Cruiser One still whirling as she leapt from the ride and sprinted to the guesthouse. A quick discussion with Mace filled her in.

"Where do they want you to meet them?" Beth asked.

"They will kill him if I don't go alone."

"And if you do they'll kill both of you. Kingman may already be dead, Mace."

"No, he's not dead."

"How do you know?"

"I just know, okay?"

The two stared at each other. Finally, Beth said, "You know, Kingman made some sense when he said you and I should be working together instead of against each other."

"We used to make a pretty good team."

"We've been reactive this whole time. Chasing phantoms down alleys."

"Or getting shot at by them."

"What do we know? I mean, what do we really know about all this?"

"Beth, we don't have time to sit and noodle this."

"If we don't sit and figure this out, Kingman *will* be dead. We've got nearly twenty-three hours. If we use it properly that's a lifetime."

Mace drew a deep breath and calmed. "Okay, I'll start. Diane Tolliver had dinner with Jamie Meldon and then was murdered. Soon thereafter Meldon was killed too."

Beth said, "Meldon's investigation was taken over by people I don't know, and even the FBI was called off the case. I've made inquiries and it seems Meldon might have been the target of a group of domestic terrorists."

"But that would mean that Tolliver was killed because of her connection to Meldon and not the other way around."

Beth looked puzzled. "But according to what we've found out about the two refrigerators, Tolliver was killed on Friday night, before Meldon, and Dockery was supposed to take the fall."

Mace picked it up. "I found out in Newark that Meldon and Tolliver had an affair years ago. If Tolliver had found out something and needed help, she might've gone to him, especially since he was a U.S. attorney."

"But that suggests *Meldon* was killed because of his ties to Tolliver, not the other way around."

"Roy and I were chased through the law firm. And I'm convinced there was spyware on Tolliver's computer. That again supports the theory that she was the key, not Meldon."

"And you ran into an impersonator tossing Andre Watkins's apartment." She glanced sharply at Mace. "The imposter, he strike you as being one of Roman Naylor's cohorts?"

"No, way too slick and sophisticated for that. And Meldon had no connection to Watkins. Only Tolliver. And they manipulated the time of her death to throw us off. I don't see Naylor's 'bubbas' running around putting steak and veggie residue in the lady's trash, planting sperm in her, and installing spyware on the woman's computer."

"And the movement of money at this DLT escrow agency?"

"Tolliver again. And Roy said billions passed through that agency in connection with Shilling & Murdoch clients. And he said the managing partner, Chester Ackerman, was sweating bullets."

"Kingman mentioned he has clients in Dubai."

"I gather a lot of their clients are based in that region."

"So presumably some of these billions were coming from the Middle East?"

"Guess so." Mace grew rigid. "Are you thinking what I'm thinking?"

Beth pulled out her phone.

"Who you calling? Your buddy the DNI?"

"Sam Donnelly? Not yet."

She spoke into the phone. "Steve Lanier please, it's Chief Perry."

"Steve Lanier? Isn't he—"

"FBI AD, yeah."

"Hey, Steve, Beth. I really need to talk to you. Yeah, it's very important."

Two hours later they were seated across from Lanier at the FBI's Washington Field Office and had just finished, in alternating bursts, telling the man their findings.

Lanier leaned back in his chair. "Beth, I've seen some serious crap in my time, but this just blows my mind."

A man entered the room and handed him a file before leaving.

He opened it and scanned the contents. "We got nothing back on the Meldon investigation. Hell, I don't even think there was one. That should've been a red flag. But we did manage, with a lot of finagling, to get autopsy reports back on Agents Hope and Reiger."

"Jarvis Burns told me about that."

"I'm sure. Their throats were surgically sliced. A real professional job."

"Okay, what does that tell us?" asked Beth.

Lanier closed the file. "That tells us we've got a major problem."

"We knew that already," said Mace.

"Not what I meant." He spent the next five minutes filling the sisters in on what he did mean.

"Then it seems pretty clear," said Beth. "What we have to do."

Mace nodded. "I'm with you."

Lanier looked between them. "Did I miss something?"

"It's a sisterly thing," explained Beth as she leaned forward and started talking fast. When she stopped, Mace jumped in and took up the line of thought.

"We'll need Sam Donnelly for this," said Lanier.

"Absolutely," said Beth.

Thirty minutes later, all three rose to implement the plan they'd just hatched.

CHAPTER

109

It was the next night and Mace was in western Maryland pushing the Ducati as hard as it would go. The deep rows of trees on either side of the road flicked by, like the black-and-white frames from an old film projector. She reached the crossroads and turned left, traveled another mile, and hung a right. Five hundred yards later she saw the old farm up ahead. She slowed the Ducati and then came to a stop, her boots hitting the dirt. Her eyes were tearing up a bit. Not from emotion. She was wearing a very special pair of contact lenses.

The falling-down house was to her right, listing like a ship in high rolling swells. To her left was an old silo rising into the sky. She could see that farther down a dirt road was the place she'd been told to go to: the barn. She saw no lights on, which didn't surprise her. She twisted the bike's throttle and headed toward it. Five feet from the barn she cut the engine, slipped off her helmet, and moved forward. Car lights immediately shot on to her left. She held up her hand to shield her eyes. The three men came forward. When they reached her she stumbled and grabbed one of the men for support. The tiny device in her hand with a special adhesive backing was transferred to the inner side of the man's sleeve.

"Stand still," one of them barked.

Mace stood rigidly as another man gave her an expert patdown and then ran a scanner up and down her body. He took his time and ran it several times over her head.

"No follicle implants with tracking devices," she volunteered helpfully.

"Shut up," said the first man.

They herded her to the waiting Range Rover and pushed her in. On the ride they chattered away in a language she'd never heard before. They looked hard and tough; their gaunt faces and lean, athletic physiques evidenced an existence far removed from the typical comforts enjoyed by folks in the West. The Range Rover slowed after driving for what Mace had calculated was eight miles, all on back roads. The silhouette of a large structure suddenly appeared out of the darkness. As the vehicle approached, a stark break in the darkness suddenly appeared as two large double doors were opened. The Rover drove through this gap and stopped. The wide doors closed and the men climbed out of the Rover, pulling Mace with them.

She stood there and looked around. They were in what seemed to be an old manufacturing facility. There was a large open area where rusted tables were situated along with a wrecked conveyor belt. Piles of junked tools lay around the littered floor. A catwalk ran around the perimeter of the second level and a lift chain was suspended from the center of the A-frame ceiling and descended straight down until it stopped about eight feet from the floor. A row of metal support posts ran down the middle of the building, bisecting it. The only light came from a single bank of fluorescents hung overhead controlled by a power box on the wall next to the double doors.

"Roy!"

Roy was sitting on his butt and tied to one of the support poles. He called out furiously, "Why the hell did you come?"

"I told you it was what I would do," said a voice.

Mace turned to see Mary Bard walking toward her from the other end of the building. She was dressed in tight black pants, a short-waisted jean jacket, and thick-soled boots.

"I'm here," said Mace. "So why don't we get this done."

"You are too impatient," said Bard.

Mace glanced over at Roy. "What do I need to do so he goes free?"

"I'm not going anywhere," shouted Roy as he struggled to stand.

"What do I need to do?" Mace said again.

"I'm afraid there is nothing you can do."

"So you just kill us both? Others know about this. They won't let it drop."

"But we won't have to worry about the two of you anymore."

Bard slipped the pair of knives that she had used to kill Reiger and Hope from a holder riding on the back of her belt.

Roy looked helplessly at Mace as Bard advanced. "Mace, she's some kind of hand-to-hand combat freak. She laid me out in like a second."

"Well, Roy, and don't take this the hard way, but you're just not that tough."

Bard stopped her advance and eyed Mace, the dual knives motionless in her hands. "And you think you are?"

"I'm still here, aren't I? I mean, Reiger and Hope tried to kill me but didn't get the job done."

"They were incompetent."

"And that's why you were ordered to kill them, right?"

Bard's eyes glittered at this comment. "It doesn't matter, does it?"

"You're from Russia. Federal Security Service."

"I am impressed. I thought my accent was gone."

"It wasn't a guess on my part. I hear you guys are like the best assassins out there, except for maybe the Israelis."

"I will try not to disappoint you tonight."

"I've got a knife in my belt clasp. How about you let me use it to defend myself? It's still two blades against one, but it'll be a little fairer. I'm clearly not in your league, but I've got a few moves. Let you practice your stuff for the next time."

Bard looked around at the heavily armed men surrounding Mace. "All right."

"But—" began one of the men.

She barked something in the man's tongue and he fell silent.

While the other men pointed their guns at Mace, she undid her clasp and slid out the knife. She examined the slightly dulled blade. "This baby got me out of a very tough situation."

"I don't think it will work again."

Bard started moving in a circle, the blades twirling in front of her.

Mace stood flat-footed, studying the other woman's tactics.

Bard said, "No tears? No begging for mercy?"

"Everybody has to die one day."

"And this is your day."

"Or yours," said Mace.

CHAPTER

110

"WHAT THE HELL happened, Jarvis?"

Beth was standing in her office in front of a large-screen TV with a remote feed that Jarvis Burns's techs had set up. After leaving the WFO the previous night, Beth had immediately called Sam Donnelly and told him what had happened with Roy Kingman. Donnelly had sent Jarvis Burns to help oversee a rescue operation. Things had been going well until they'd lost track of Mace. A guy in a suit and wearing a headset was frantically typing on a portable keyboard while barking instructions into his headset.

Burns remained focused on the screen where they could see the live feed from the camera mounted on the chopper's skids. The countryside below looked dark and vast. "The plan was the best we had under the circumstances, Beth. We had two stealth units on the ground following her. The tracker was on her Ducati. They will have moved her in another vehicle, but our units should have been able to follow."

He turned to the tech. "Get the ground commander on the horn ASAP."

Seconds later the tech handed the headset to Burns, who listened for a bit and then tossed the headset back to the man before turning to Beth. "They were ambushed. Took heavy fire and casualties. They're out of the hunt. We've got a mole somewhere, Beth. That's the only way they could have found out."

Beth slapped her desktop. "Now we have no idea where she is."

"We have *some* idea," replied Burns calmly. "We had a clear signal out to the abandoned farmhouse and we've got two stealth choppers as backup in the vicinity." He tapped his tech on the shoulder. "Phillips, tell the air support commander to perform a ten-mile grid perimeter sweep. We need to all watch the feed and see if anything pops."

"That will take too long!" snapped an exasperated Beth.

"Not in the choppers it won't. It makes sense that they didn't transport her too far for a number of tactical reasons. With a little bit of luck we'll pick up the trail again."

"And if we're not lucky?"

"I'm doing the best I can, Beth. Remember, you called Director Donnelly in at the last minute. I'm good, but I'm *not* a magician."

Beth calmed. "I know. I'm sorry. It's just that—"

"She's your sister." He laid a hand on Beth's shoulder. "I know, Beth. I swear we'll do everything in our power to bring her back safe."

"Thank you, Jarvis."

"In the spirit of fair play, I propose to allow you the first move," said Bard, who had edged closer to Mace with each move.

"And in the spirit of fair play, I propose to kill you any way I can."

"So you don't want the first move?"

"No, actually I do. But I want them out of the way." Mace pointed to the gunmen arrayed around her. "No bullets in the back if I get the upper hand with you."

Bard hesitated and then motioned to the armed men to clear the area. Mace backed away until she reached the far wall, her knife held in front of her.

"I'm waiting," said Bard. "For the first move."

"And I'm still thinking of what that first move should be."

"This is ridiculous. If you—"

Mace lunged and her hand slammed down on the lever connected to the power box on the wall. The building instantly went dark. With a flick of her wrist, Mace tossed her knife. It flashed across the space and lodged in the chest of the gunman closest to her. He collapsed to the floor, the blade tip resting in the left chamber of his heart.

Mace had no trouble seeing in the pitch dark because she was wearing a pair of latest-generation contact lenses that were actually advanced optics that instantly adapted to all levels of light or darkness. They'd been a gift from the FBI for a situation just like this. From her earlier observations she knew there were four gunmen on this level and three more on the catwalk. They had Heckler and Koch UMPs and MP5s. And she desperately needed some firepower before the bandits figured out a way to light up the place again. She slid across the floor to the dead man and snagged his submachine gun and two extra mags.

Mace opened fire. One of the guys shooting in her vicinity jerked around as two of her rounds impacted his neck and torso. He managed to squeeze off a few more wild rounds before he went down and stayed there. Mace immediately rolled six feet to her left as bullets pounded her last firing position, the bandits taking aim at her previous muzzle flashes. She caught another guy in both knees with another burst. He dropped screaming, but kept firing. Her next round slammed into his face and his UMP went silent.

Lines of fire started coming from the catwalk. Forty-caliber rounds ricocheted off the concrete floor as Mace threw herself behind the guts of a retooling machine and fired off the rest of her mag, dropped it, and slapped in a new one as return fire pinged all around her. A chunk of wood got blown off the end of the table she was behind and she felt the tailing rip into her shoulder and slice across her cheek. Warm blood flowed down her face. Another round cut a groove across her left thigh, searing through her pants and tattooing her skin black.

She sprayed rounds at the catwalk, but even through her optics she couldn't see much because of the smoke from all the weapons discharge. The remaining shooters had taken cover as well. And they had the high ground and superior firepower. Mace was pinned down. The logistics were depressingly simple. Without help it was only a matter of time before they were dead.

"Mace!'

She looked behind her to see Roy slumped over, his face twisted in pain. Even from this distance and with her field of vision a ghostly green Mace could see what she knew was his blood seeping across his shirt. Mary Bard was stooping over him, her knife pulling back for the final stroke while he frantically kicked at her.

"Roy!"

The explosion catapulted both front sliding doors a good ten feet across the floor. Out of the smoke came a sight Mace would never forget.

Twenty FBI Hostage Rescue Team armored assaulters loaded for war emerged from the smoke. Just the sight of these guys was enough to scare the hell out of anyone no matter how battle-tested. Knowing what was coming, Mace instantly dropped down and pulled the plugs from out of her boots and stuffed them in her ears. A second later an array of flash-bangs detonated.

As the HRT laid down precise walls of fire at the enemy positions exposed to their night optics, Mace turned and raced toward Roy. Mary Bard was on her side, dazed by the flash-bangs, blood trickling out of one ear. When she tried to rise up and finish off Roy, Mace leapt, the butt of her UMP catching the woman flush on the temple. She crumpled to the floor.

The all-clear sounded a minute later. Someone hit the wall lever and the interior of the building exploded with light.

"Man down," screamed Mace. In the darkness she'd ripped open Roy's shirt and used the cloth to stop the bleeding. As the medical support personnel that came on every HRT operation rushed forward, Mace told Roy, "You're going to be okay."

"I don't feel like I'm going to be okay."

"You can't die, Roy."

"Why?"

"I've got a pretty good feeling I'm going to need one kick-ass lawyer, and you're the only one I know."

He managed a weak smile before the medics took over. A few minutes later the chopper lifted off with them on their way to the nearest hospital.

CHAPTER

111

FORTY MINUTES later the tech with the headset jerked upright in his seat. On the screen an explosion had just rocked the camera. Beth put down the call she was on and joined them. They all stared dumbfounded at the sight on the screen as a fireball lit the sky.

"My God," said an obviously shaken Burns. "They detonated a bomb." He turned to the tech. "Get that chopper on the ground ASAP."

The tech relayed these instructions and they watched as the chopper headed downward. A moment later the camera feed went dead. A tense minute went by and then the tech jerked again as a stream of words came over his headset. He nodded blankly, his face pale. He turned to the others. "The building was destroyed. There does not appear to be any survivors."

"Are they sure it's the right spot?" said Beth.

"They just pulled a body from the site," said the tech as he glanced nervously at Beth. "A female body with a positive ID."

"My God, Beth," said Burns. "I'm so sorry."

"I am too, Jarvis. I am too. Very sorry."

Something in her tone made him look sharply at her.

"Beth? Are you all right?"

"Okay," Beth called out loudly in the direction of the door.

It opened and in walked Sam Donnelly, along with a half dozen security officers. Behind him came Steve Lanier, the FBI AD, who was wearing a broad smile.

Burns looked from his boss to Beth and then back to his boss. "Sir, what the hell is going on here?"

"I'm sorry, Jarv. It's all over," said Donnelly sadly.

"What is all over?"

"Your secret op. With the FBI's help we set this trap for you. I'd long suspected that something was going on I wasn't aware of. I'm sorry it turned out to be you."

"But—" began Burns.

"Sacrifices, Jarvis. We talked about this before. The national security of this country comes before all."

Burns and Donnelly shared a pronounced stare.

"You will of course have the full support of the DNI if it turns out we were wrong," added Donnelly.

"I see. Thank you, sir. I'm sure everything will be worked out."

Donnelly turned to Lanier. "I think we can handle it from here, Steve. The FBI isn't cleared for this. But I appreciate the assist. I'll have my people—"

Beth approached Burns. "Were you really going to do it, Jarv?'

"Do what?'

"Fall on the sword for Sam?"

"What?" said Donnelly sharply.

She turned to him. "Sacrifices? The full support of the DNI? We'll take over now? We'll never see Jarv again. You'll just move him to Jordan or Iraq to continue doing what he's doing."

"Which is of course what you ordered him to do," added Lanier.

"I have no idea what you people are talking about," said Donnelly furiously.

"If I were you," Lanier said to Donnelly, "I'd save any comments for your defense." He motioned to his men. They moved forward and cuffed Donnelly, Burns, and his tech.

"How dare you!" said Donnelly angrily.

Lanier sat down in a leather chair across from Beth's desk. "Chief, would you like to do the honors?" he said. "I'm a little sick to my stomach, personally."

Beth leaned against the edge of her desk. "Jarvis, do you know when you told me that you were aware of the death of Diane Tolliver, the fire alarm pull, and the rest?"

"What of it?" said Burns with a wary expression.

"When I seemed amazed that you knew this, you remarked that if you couldn't keep track of things going on in your own city how could you be expected to know what was going on in the rest of the world."

"I'm afraid I'm not seeing your—"

"I took you at your word, Jarvis. I accepted that if anything big were going on in D.C., you and Sam would know about it. And if you two weren't doing anything to stop it, it occurred to me that that might be because you were *behind* it. I also tracked Hope and Reiger to the Pentagon one night. I knew they had no military connection, but I was aware that DNI had a satellite office there. And when we learned of the connection between Diane Tolliver and Jamie Meldon, and the fact that she'd been killed on Friday instead of Monday, I knew there was something more here than an old vet raping and killing. We had no proof of anything, so I went to Steve and we hatched a plan to see if we could get that evidence."

"A plan?"

Beth pointed to the screen. "This plan."

Donnelly said, "My God, Beth, I have no idea what you're talking about. But am I to believe that you sacrificed your sister to see if some nonsensical idea was valid or not?"

Lanier said, "Mace is fine. We sent in HRT. We were able to track them when Mace slipped a bug on one of the bandits before they scanned her. The chopper took her and Kingman to the nearest hospital."

Burns glanced nervously at the screen. "Well, apparently the report we received was erroneous. I am very glad that she's all right."

Beth said coldly, "The hell you are, Jarv. You and Sam did your best to kill her. This whole thing tonight was an elaborate charade by you. The camera feed was bogus. You didn't have any choppers out there. No stealth units. All smoke and mirrors."

"You are utterly mistaken," said Burns.

"Don't say anything else, Jarvis," cautioned Donnelly. "We'll get this all straightened out."

"The hell you will," exclaimed Beth.

"You have nothing!" retorted Donnelly. "No proof. And once I speak to the president, heads will roll."

"Oh, the proof's not a problem," she said. "The evidence is overwhelming."

Lanier said, "HRT has several of your goons that you imported to do your dirty work."

"You'll accept the word of 'goons' over ours?" Donnelly said. "Do you realize how ridiculous that will look in court? I strongly suggest that you save yourself the embarrassment, release us immediately, and we'll just drop it here and now."

She said, "What really bugged me was the fact that you disrespected me."

"How exactly did I do that?"

"By assuming I wouldn't be smart enough to figure it all out."

"You still have nothing."

Lanier looked at Beth and then nodded at one of his men. "Bring her in."

A cuffed Mary Bard, her head bandaged, walked in with an armed escort.

"Mary Bard," said Lanier. "Recruited to this country to work with the FBI until you stole her from us, Sam. When I learned how Reiger and Hope died, the surgically precise cuts in the throat, it got me remembering about a little joint op she did with CIA last year."

Bard said bitterly, "The director told me the people tonight were traitors and had killed innocent people. That their terminations had been authorized by your government."

"Shut the hell up!" screamed Donnelly.

"She killed them. *She* killed them," cried Burns. "Not us."

Beth glanced at Lanier. "Can you please get them out of my sight before I shoot all three of them?"

Later that night Beth Perry strode into the hospital and saw her sister standing at the end of the hall. When Mace looked up and spied Beth she walked toward her. The two sisters met in the middle, flinging their arms around each other.

"God, you were great tonight, Mace."

"We both came up with the plan, sis."

"Yeah, but you were in the line of fire executing it, not me. You could have died."

"You're the chief. I'm expendable."

The two women stepped apart and Beth looked at the bandage on Mace's face and the bulge under her thigh. "Are you okay?"

"I got hurt worse than this falling out of bed."

"Liar. How's Kingman?"

"Out of surgery. They said I could see him for a couple of minutes. Do you want to come?"

Roy was still heavily sedated but his eyes opened when he heard Mace's voice. She wrapped her hand around his.

He said weakly, "Everything okay?"

"Everything is great," said Mace. "Beth is here."

Roy slowly turned his head to look at the chief. She reached down and touched his face gently.

"Hey, Roy, I need to tell you something."

"What's that?" he mouthed.

Beth glanced over at Mace before answering. "If you want to keep hanging around Mace, it's okay with me." She leaned down and kissed him on the cheek.

As the sisters walked down the hall to the waiting room Mace said, "You know, you finally called him Roy."

"Yeah. That's because he earned it."

112

So as I said, I'm thrilled to be here today to announce that all charges against my client, Louis Dockery, have been dropped. He has been released from custody and the Veterans Administration has taken it upon itself to see that such a decorated soldier will no longer be living on the streets."

This time Roy was having no problem handling the siege of reporters in front of the steps to D.C. Superior Court. His shoulder and side bandaged, he had just finished his remarks. Standing a few feet from him, a look of absolute revulsion on her face, was Mona Danforth. The only reason she was here was because the mayor and the head of the Justice Department had "requested" that she be present.

One reporter called out, "Mr. Kingman, how did you injure yourself?"

Roy smiled. "During the course of the litigation I accidentally impaled myself on one of Ms. Danforth's legendary stilettos."

The roar of laughter lasted so long that Mona finally stalked off, her face nearly as red as her lipstick. As she made her way inside the court building she bumped into someone.

"Hey, Mona," said Mace. "Isn't it a great day when justice finally triumphs?"

"Go to hell!"

"Nah, it'll be way too crowded with both of us there."

"I'm still going to press assault charges against you for attacking me in the ladies' room. You chipped one of my teeth."

"God, I'm really sorry, Mona. But there's somebody here who wants to give you something."

They turned to see Beth walking up to them with an envelope in hand.

"Here you go, Ms. Interim." She thrust the envelope in Mona's hands.

"What the hell is this?"

"Affidavits from my two detectives you coerced into working with you. They are prepared to testify that you initiated contact with Lou Dockery without benefit of his counsel being there, breaking numerous ethical canons and also the law. Since the U.S. Attorney's Office will be conflicted out over this one, the Justice Department will be prosecuting you."

Now Mona's face turned as white as the envelope she was holding. "Prosecuting me?"

"Yeah," said Mace. "You know, that whole court thing that ends in the bars being slammed behind your ass? If you want I can give you some tips on prison etiquette."

After the press conference was over, Mace, Beth, and Roy climbed into a government sedan and headed to a meeting that they really would rather have avoided. On the way over, they discussed what had happened.

"So the Captain is really going to be taken care of?" asked Mace.

Roy nodded. "The VA guy said he would take it as his personal mission to get him the care he needs. And I'm going to be checking. But I did tell them to order a truckload of Twinkies."

"God, Mona was pissed," said Mace. "You really think they'll nail her this time?"

Beth replied, "All I know is when I showed the affidavits to the DOJ lawyer he screamed out, 'Thank you, Jesus.'"

"And Psycho?" asked Roy.

"Signed, sealed, and delivered. When his gang saw the surveillance video from the security camera in the train station parking lot they rolled on him. They should be able to put him away for a long time."

"And Alisha, Tyler, and Darren?"

Mace answered. "Alisha's enrolled in a GED program. Tyler's being seen by a specialist from Johns Hopkins, and Mr. Razor is going back to school too. He apparently graduated from high school but never bothered to pick up his diploma. He's going the community college route for now. He'll probably be running the world in about ten years."

"So are you still going to be working for Altman?" Roy asked.

"Hey, I made a deal. I'm not going back on it. What about you? You could go back to Shilling."

"Haven't made up my mind yet. But they did drop the lawsuit against me."

"How's the wound?"

"Won't be playing ball anytime soon."

"I know, I'll take you on in HORSE, one-handed style."

"You're on."

The smiles faded from both their faces as the car slowed. They looked out the window as they stopped at the armed gate. The driver flashed his creds and they headed on.

"So what do you think is going to happen in there," Roy said, indicating the two-story building they were heading to. It was set on a multi-acre college-style campus.

Beth spoke up. "I always expect the worst. And today I think I'll be justified."

113

Beth's Glock had been confiscated at the door. Mace could tell that her sister was not happy about that just by the way her right fingers continued to flick at the empty space there. An armed escort led them down a long hallway where every single door was closed and also had a security lock. No open-style cubicle system here, thought Mace.

They were led into a spacious office with the typical wall of photos and shelves of awards and memorabilia that a high-rising public servant invariably collected. The Director of Central Intelligence, or DCI, was there along with a gent in uniform from the Defense Intelligence Agency, or DIA, someone from NSA, and a fourth gentleman that Mace had seen on TV recently and knew was very high up at the White House. There was no one else present.

"I thought Steve Lanier from the FBI would be here," commented Beth.

"No, he won't," said the DCI bluntly. "But I want to thank each of you for agreeing to come today," he added in a more gracious tone.

"We really didn't have a choice. And we're all here for the same reason," said Beth. "We want information."

"Well, I'm here to provide it, as much as I can."

Beth sighed and sat back, her face showing her displeasure at this disclaimer.

"Under normal circumstances your sister and Mr. Kingman would not even be allowed to know the location of this building, much less be here. Even you, as police chief, would not be allowed in."

"These are not normal circumstances," said Mace.

"Truly not," agreed the DCI while the NSA rep nodded.

"Well then, what can you tell us?" asked Beth. "What happened to Donnelly and Burns?"

"Removed from their posts, of course."

"Removed from their posts?" said Mace, half coming out of her chair. "What, do they get early retirement and a gold watch too?"

"It doesn't quite work that way in the intelligence field, Ms. Perry."

"Will they be prosecuted?" asked Roy.

"That is not possible," said the fellow from the White House.

"The hell it isn't," snapped Beth. "They masterminded the murder of at least five American citizens and did their best to make it seven."

"And in the process let a military veteran take the fall for it," added Roy heatedly.

The DCI put up his hands in mock surrender. "Their acts *were* heinous. I am in total agreement with that."

"But I sense a *but* coming," said Beth.

"But to prosecute them would mean the truth would come out."

"They were rogues, doing their own op. The higher-ups might have to officially take responsibility for that, but the blame still lies with them," argued Beth. "Hell, the FBI prosecuted Hanssen. The CIA did the same with Ames. It's not exactly new territory."

"You are not in possession of all the facts."

"Then enlighten me."

The fellow from the White House interjected. "Their actions were not authorized by anyone higher up on the chain of command; I give you my word on that."

"But other things they did *were* authorized?" said Mace.

"Illegal things?" added Roy.

The CIA director looked at him. "You ventured to the escrow firm, DLT?"

"I did. And I found a pretty slick piggyback scheme using legitimate business transactions to cover other movements of money."

"But no hard proof of same?"

"No."

"What are you getting at?" asked Beth.

"We're at war, Chief. It is not a conventional war. Most Americans realize that by now. We fight fire with fire. And we also fight dirt with dirt."

"Meaning?"

"Meaning that intelligence is king and who gets the most accurate intelligence wins. And the people who possess that intelligence are often folks that, well, that we would not ordinarily choose to associate with."

"Meaning, at least in the eyes of the American public, our enemies."

"Our usual allies are virtually powerless to help us in this fight. We combat the devil by working with the devil. And since they obviously aren't helping us out of the goodness of their hearts . . ."

"The piggyback scheme was a way of paying off people for intelligence?" said Roy.

"Again, I can't answer that."

Beth spoke up. "But if so, and Diane Tolliver found out and then told Meldon, why kill them? Couldn't you have appealed to their patriotism? Jamie certainly wouldn't have done anything to jeopardize this country's interests."

The DCI said, "The real truth is that Donnelly and Burns went way past all orthodoxy in getting the monies needed to pay off these folks. And while these sums started off relatively small, they have, over the years, become enormous."

"And Congress wouldn't appropriate the needed funds?" said Beth.

"You know the deficits we have now."

"So how did they manage the money part?"

"They have not been particularly cooperative. But we have been able, with a little digging, to gain a fairly clear picture of what happened."

"And so what does that picture tell us?" asked Beth."

Something, unfortunately, that none of you are cleared for."

"That is bullshit," barked the chief. "After all this, you're telling me that you won't read us into what happened?"

"Suffice it to say that a lot of the money coming through those piggyback pipelines Mr. Kingman mentioned was very, very dirty. And in order to launder it, Donnelly and Burns were charging a substantial fee. Those monies were used to purchase support."

"Drug dealers, weapon runners, slavery rings?" said Beth.

"Neither confirm nor deny."

"Now that you've basically told us nothing, why did you really ask us here?"

"If any of this comes out it will do this country great harm. I daresay it would destroy any hopes we have of winning the war on terror."

The White House representative added, "It would embolden our enemies. It would weaken our position around the globe. Nothing good will come out of this."

"You mean other than two bastards being punished for their *heinous* crimes?" shot back Mace.

"It's not that simple," murmured the DCI.

"Yeah, it's never that simple for people in high places. But the little guy does something like this he gets squashed like a bug."

Beth shook her head in frustration. "And what exactly do I tell Jamie Meldon's family? And Diane Tolliver's friends?"

"I don't have a good answer for you. In Meldon's case I can tell you that his family will never want for money. Uncle Sam is picking up the tab there."

"Gee, all it cost them was their husband and father," said Mace bitterly.

"If you think I like this any better than you do, you're mistaken. But that's just the way it has to be."

"And Mary Bard?" asked Beth. "Funny name for a Russian, by the way."

"Her father was an American, a defector unfortunately. She's been returned to her country. She really was only following orders. And she's an excellent field agent. We may very well use her again."

Mace looked ready to burst. "I don't believe this crap. That lady was going to kill me and Roy. She *did* kill two American agents. And I thought the Russians weren't exactly our best friends."

The DCI looked at her curiously. "Frankly, Ms. Perry, you obviously don't understand the intelligence business. Enemies and allies are often interchangeable."

"*Frankly* I consider the term 'intelligence business' not only a misnomer but a freaking oxymoron."

Beth spoke up. "Mace cracked this case. She should be reinstated to the police force."

The DCI shook his head. "I'm sorry. That won't be happening. That would entail the truth coming out."

"So she gets zip," said Beth.

The uniform from DIA cleared his throat. "Sacrifice for the greater good."

Mace glared at him. "I'll be sure to tell that to my probation officer, thanks."

The White House rep stood, signaling that the meeting was over. "We very much appreciate all your help in this matter. As does the president himself, which he wishes he could make public but of course cannot for national security reasons."

"Big shit," said Mace as she turned and walked out of the office, Beth and Roy trailing her.

CHAPTER

114

Beth drove them back to Altman's house. Before she left to return to work she told Mace, "I know you've got the job with Altman, and it doesn't take a rocket scientist to see that Roy will be taking up some of your time too. But don't forget your big sister."

"How could I? Every time I need her, she's right there."

"I can say the same about you."

"No, you really can't, Beth. I wish you could, but I've fallen down on the job."

"It's just a firstborn's fate in life," she said, attempting a smile.

"Was it my imagination or did the DCI seem really pleased about the turn of events?"

"Oh, no, he was. Now that Donnelly went down, guess who's back in charge of the intelligence world and doing the presidential daily briefing?"

"Right."

They shared a brief hug before Beth Perry turned back into Chief Perry, climbed into Cruiser One, and headed back to town to fight crime.

Roy said, "I don't have any plans today. How about going out to lunch with a former college basketball player turned one-armed paper hanger? I'm buying."

"Sounds great. I can help you cut up your food and wipe your mouth for you."

"Yeah, that'll be great practice for down the road."

"Down *what* road?" Mace said sharply as she gave him a piercing stare.

He took a step back, his face turning red. "Uh, the road where I left my mouth with my size thirteen feet in it."

"Oh, Roy, you're so cute."

"Seriously, do you want to go?"

"I'd love to."

Late that night Mace climbed on her Ducati and fired it up. Two minutes later she was ripping down the highway into D.C. She hit the Sixth District and wound her way to the spot where her life had changed forever. Now the sight made her gut clench and her cheeks flame. But there would come a day she told herself when this spot would fill her with supreme satisfaction instead of heartbreak. And when that day came—and it would—Mace Perry would really be back.

The wink of a car's lights made her turn around. She started when she saw the person climb out of the police cruiser.

Beth was still in uniform as she walked over to her and stood beside her sister.

"I thought you might come down here tonight."

"It's scary sometimes how well you know me."

"We are sisters. And . . ." Beth fell silent.

"You were going to say *and cops,* right?"

"We're not giving up on it, Mace."

"I know." After a few moments of silence, Mace said, "Why do I think Donnelly and Burns are sitting in an office somewhere doing business as usual?"

"Because they probably are."

"Some justice."

Beth stared up at the old apartment building. "It doesn't look so bad anymore."

"What are you talking about? It's a dump."

"A little elbow grease, some paint."

"What?"

"It's being turned into a rec center for the community."

"Since when?"

"Since I got the mayor to approve it yesterday."

"Why?" Mace asked.

"Why not? It's an old building that serves no useful purpose. We could leave it here until it falls down. Or we can change it into something that's useful. A way of moving forward. Applies to buildings. And people."

Mace gazed at the place for a long moment. "You and Dad were always much better with symbolism than me."

"I always thought you and Dad were a lot more alike."

"Really?" said a surprised Mace. Beth nodded.

Mace glanced over at Cruiser One where the driver sat patiently. "You done for the night, sis?"

Beth stretched out her back. "Yeah, I was thinking of actually heading home and reading a book in the bathtub."

"You want a ride?" Mace eyed her Ducati.

"What? On the bike?"

"Problem with that?"

"No, it's just that, well, the liability factor if the chief of police—"

"Oh shut up and get on. You can use Roy's helmet."

On the way home, with Beth holding on to her tightly, Mace popped a wheelie and held it as she streaked down the GW Parkway, freaking out motorists as she flew past.

Beth started to scream something in her ear but then stopped. And then the by-the-book chief of police did the unthinkable. She held out her arms straight from her sides, leaned into her sister, and started making whooping sounds.

The sisters were headed back to the safe area of D.C., where people didn't shoot each other over five-dollar crack scratches or to gain elusive respect. But they knew their hearts and their professional lives would always be on that unpredictable side of the line where you ran toward the fight and not away from it. That was where they really belonged.

The front wheel hit asphalt. Mace gunned the throttle and the Perry sisters disappeared down the road.

ACKNOWLEDGMENTS

To MICHELLE, the primary reason I write about strong, independent women.

To Mitch Hoffman, for good counsel, excellent critiques, and well-placed cheers.

To David Young, Jamie Raab, Emi Battaglia, Jennifer Romanello, Tom Maciag, Martha Otis, Anthony Goff, Kim Hoffman, and all at Grand Central Publishing, for helping me every step of the way.

To Aaron and Arlene Priest, Lucy Childs, Lisa Erbach Vance, Nicole Kenealy, Frances Jalet-Miller, and John Richmond, for being so supportive.

To Maria Rejt and Katie James at Pan Macmillan, for all your great work.

To Grace McQuade and Lynn Goldberg, for keeping my name out there.

To D.C. Police Chief Cathy Lanier, for allowing me to see a terrific slice of the job.

To Lt. Morgan Kane, for coordinating everything and being patient and professional.

To Officer Rob Calligaro, thanks for the education and the boat ride.

To Officer Raymond Hawkins, thanks for the ride and the great insight.

To United States Attorneys Jeffrey Taylor and Glenn Kirschner, for your courtroom knowledge and expertise of how the D.C. criminal system works.

To Tom and Bob, for financial brainstorming.

To Dr. Monica Smiddy, who makes my forensics look so good.

To Dr. Alli Guleria, as always, for your help.

To Bob Schule, for your advice and political expertise.

To Tanmoy Mukherjee, M.D., for your medical expertise.

To the charity auction "name" winners. Don, I "hope" I did the name justice. To Julie, Mandy, and Kelly of Hamilton, Petrocelli & Sprissler, I hope you liked your page time.

To Lynette and Deborah, for doing what you do so damn well.